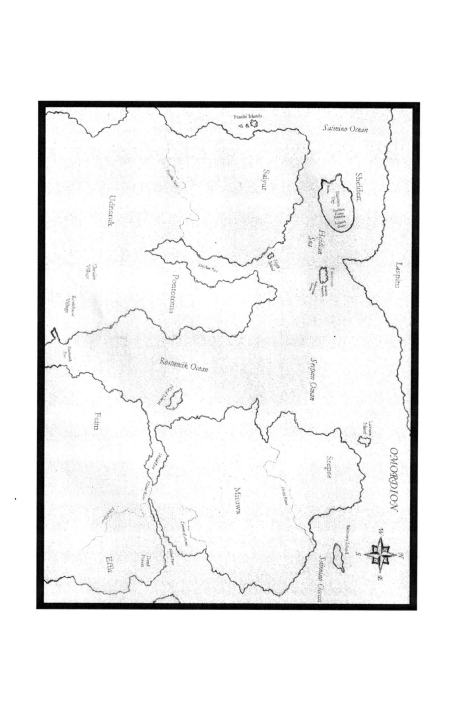

SECRET OF
OMORDION

Book One of the Omordion Trilogy

*To Helen,
I hope you enjoy
the journey!
Best Wishes,
Nande*

NANDE ORCEL
• December 2016 •

abbott press®

A DIVISION OF WRITER'S DIGEST

Abbott Press books may be ordered through booksellers or by contacting:

Abbott Press
1663 Liberty Drive
Bloomington, IN 47403
www.abbottpress.com
Phone: 1-866-697-5310

ISBN: 978-1-4582-1092-0 (sc)
ISBN: 978-1-4582-1093-7 (hc)
ISBN: 978-1-4582-1094-4 (e)

Library of Congress Control Number: 2013914512

Printed in the United States of America.

Abbott Press rev. date: 2/27/2014

*To my son, Jaden, the bright light
that shines in a dark cave.*

ACKNOWLEDGEMENTS

I would like to thank my family. Throughout all the hard times, they have stood by me and given me helping hands when I needed them the most. Without all of you, I wouldn't be where I am today. For that, I am truly grateful.

I want to thank my son Jaden, to whom I dedicate this book, and my goddaughter Leena Marsan, for listening as I read and reread the chapters of this book and falling in love with my characters. Your opinions meant so much to me!

I would like to thank my sister, Eschine Piris and her company, Special Moments 4 a Lifetime, for my website. I just love staring at it. All day.

Thank you Sarah Nesiah, for patiently reading the entire first draft and everything else that came after it, and for being *honest*. You have helped me throughout most of the agonizing revision process. I'm sorry I couldn't find a place for a chinchilla in this book…

Thank you, Andrea Broomes. Even though you are a single mother of two boys, you still managed to read the chapters I sent you and gave me a helping hand with the editing process. Your enthusiasm for my book was an incredible motivation when I felt like it would never be ready.

Last, but not least, thank you to all of my friends for giving me the confidence I needed to forge ahead all of these years, helping me feel absolutely amazing for writing a novel, and believing in me. I love you guys!

PROLOGUE

"If we get caught—"

"We won't! I promise."

A teenage boy walked quickly with his friend through their village and into the forest. The moon was shining brightly through the trees and they could hear crickets waking up all around them.

Stepping on a branch, which made a loud noise when it broke in half, the boy froze to listen for any sounds from the village.

His friend stopped and rolled his eyes. "Are you serious?" he said. "They can't *hear* us."

"You don't understand," the boy said. "If I get caught, it'll be chores every day for the next *millennium!*"

"Come on. They won't even know we did it. We'll be home before you know it."

The boy hesitated but followed his friend through the darkened forest, being careful not to follow the commonly used paths to avoid being seen. They heard the sound of the rushing water before they could make out the banks of the Hechi River, which separated their country, Mituwa from the Srepan border. The boy's father had promised to take him to visit the ancient ruins in Srepas. He was looking forward to the trip but didn't know if he would still be able to go if he and his friend were caught.

His friend suddenly laughed out loud, interrupting his thoughts. "Oh, what I wouldn't give to see the look on the old seer's face when his boat starts to sink."

The boy gave a nervous laugh. "He won't even know what's happening until it's too late."

"It'll be the first time he'd get a good wash, I bet!"

"Maybe the smell will go away for a while. We won't have to hold our noses at the village meetings."

"'The trees!'" his friend shouted, mimicking the seer in a high pitched voice. "'The animals! You must be *one* with nature!'"

"Keep it down," the boy said, laughing. "You don't want them to hear us."

The two boys found the wooden boat they were looking for, the only one tied to the dock with a makeshift bed made out of leaves, sticks, and manure. 'For warmth' on cold nights, the seer always explained.

"Did you bring it?" his friend said.

"Yes, of course." The boy reached out and handed his friend the cork screw he was holding. "Should be enough to make a small ho—" He froze, his heart doing a small flip-flop in his chest. "Do you smell that?"

His friend sniffed the air. "It smells like *smoke*."

Both boys looked up into the sky and saw it. A huge plume of smoke rising from the direction of their village. They then heard the screams, carried towards them with the wind. Without so much as glancing at each other, they ran back towards the village. In the forest, the smoke was much denser, making it hard to see, but they knew where they were going. It was their forest, they knew each tree, each and every path made by their families and the generations before them.

Nothing could have prepared them for what they saw when they came out of the forest. Their whole village was on fire. Every home. Every stable. Every wagon. The animals could be heard bellowing for someone to release them from their burning quarters. But it wasn't the fires that shocked the two boys the most.

Soldiers. King Tholenod's soldiers. They were rounding up the villagers, linking them together with chains, beating or killing anyone who resisted.

Why are they doing this? the boy thought. *What wrong have we done to upset the king?* His mind was racing. It just did not make any sense.

His worst fears were realized when he spotted his parents among the captured. His mother was screaming and crying, leaning against his father who was holding her, trying to calm her down. In that moment, his eyes locked with that of his son's and he looked frightened. His mother stopped screaming when she saw him too and she looked around fearfully. Then his parents began gesturing for him to leave, to run away.

"We have to get out of here!" the boy told his friend.

It was then that two soldiers grabbed his friend, who started screaming. The boy turned to run but was tackled by two other soldiers. Knowing he may have a chance to lose them in the forest, he struggled, hoping they would release him for a moment. Only one moment. That's all he needed. When the soldiers picked him up off the ground, he kicked one soldier hard in the groin and bit the other one's hand. As the soldiers released him, he took off running towards the forest. He hadn't realized they had already clamped a chain to his ankle when they tackled him. He fell to the ground when one of the soldiers grabbed the chain. He was then dragged back towards them. He tried to pull himself free, to prevent the soldiers from grabbing him again, but his efforts were useless. They were simply too strong for him.

Roughly, the soldier, whose hand he had bitten, stood him up and yanked his hair back hard so his neck was exposed. The other soldier pulled out his sword. "We don't need this one," he said. "We've got plenty."

PART ONE
LOCHENBY

CHAPTER 1

"Are you okay?"

Hamilda Shing snapped back into focus after opening an official letter sent to her from the Western Army. She was sitting at her kitchen table, next to her husband, Captain Jogesh Shing. He was staring at her, his brown eyes questioning. The letter told her of a mission she was offered with no option for refusal. She had read the first few sentences and could not bring herself to continue.

"They can't be serious," Hamilda said, but she knew they were. The fate of the entire planet had been dropped in her lap.

"But this is what you've been waiting for," Jogesh said. "You have an opportunity to use your abilities to help people."

"Yes, but I did not expect this to happen—at least not in my lifetime." She lowered her green eyes and refolded the letter. "I don't think I can handle it."

"You are the best person for this job. Could you see anyone else doing it better than you?"

Hamilda contemplated her husband's question for a moment before responding. "No, but—"

"Hamilda. Things will work out just fine." Jogesh squeezed her hand, giving her a comforting smile. "What else does the letter say?"

"Here. You finish it." Hamilda handed the letter to Jogesh, suddenly not in the mood to continue, and he eagerly took it from her. He was always jumping at the opportunity to be her support system when she'd been given a task to do, always staying so positive about everything. She wished she could be more like him.

"Bontihm suggested that you be the one to carry out this mission. You will meet with the chosen five children tomorrow morning. These children come from the free lands of Laspitu, Pontotoma, Saiyut, and Udnaruk." Jogesh finished reading the letter and frowned. "Also..."

Hamilda started to feel slightly nauseous. She knew by his tone that it was not going to be good. "What is it?"

Jogesh looked at her sadly, as if he wished he could take back the words he was about to say. "You are to teach them for thirteen years at ... Lochenby."

Lochenby.

Of course it had to be there. The boarding school she attended when she was little until the ... accident. Fear rose in her heart. How could she go back there? She told herself she would never return, that she would never go back to those dreadful memories. But they came flooding back to her like a bad dream. The screaming. The hallucinations. The realization that she was never going to be normal again.

An explosion of words erupted from her mouth. "What? How can Bontihm agree to this? What could he have been thinking? Do you think I could convince them to do it at another school? There's this wonderful school located not too far from here. Oh, what's the name of it ...?"

Hearing the fear in her voice, Jogesh leaned over and pulled her into a loving embrace. "You can do this, Hamilda. You are being put there for a reason. You can't run from your past. Maybe by teaching these children, you can finally put your past behind you and accomplish your dreams. You'll make an excellent teacher."

Hamilda studied him, down to his similar olive complexion and his short, curly, black hair. This mission meant she would have to leave her home and be away from his army base. She buried her head in his chest and sighed heavily. She had a strong feeling it wasn't going to be as simple as he thought.

Lochenby: School of Knowledge. It loomed in front of her. As Hamilda stepped through the tall, wrought-iron gate, she took a moment to remember the fine details of the school and how it was fifteen years prior, when she was seven years old.

The school used to be a castle, constructed over three hundred years ago. The old, gray-brick school was five stories high and U shaped with a beautiful garden in the courtyard. The grounds were extensive, with paths going to the dormitories to the left and the cafeteria and gymnasium down the paths to the right. She remembered the big lake that was beyond the gardens behind the school. And even further beyond that—*the woods*.

Hamilda inhaled sharply and squeezed her teary eyes shut. Her hands felt clammy and beads of sweat rose at her temples. She reached for her handkerchief in the right breast pocket of her navy blazer and dabbed at her green eyes. She then straightened out her navy skirt, patted down her long, curly, black hair, and cleared her throat while trying to maintain her composure.

"I have to get it together," she said, as she walked down the driveway leading up to the massive entry doors of Lochenby, dragging her suitcase behind her. "I can't let this place affect me."

"Mrs. Shing?" the man who welcomed her at the door asked. He was a tall, slightly balding man with wide eyes and a thick bushy beard and mustache.

Hamilda cleared her throat. "Yes," she said.

"I'm so happy to finally meet you." The man shook her hand. "My name is R. T. Rohjees and I am the principal at this school. Please follow me. They are waiting for you."

Oh great, I'm late. Hamilda sighed and nervously walked through the doors. After instructing her to leave her suitcase by the entryway, Rohjees directed her to an elevator and then to the fifth floor. Until the elevator came to a stop, Hamilda kept rubbing her hands together and taking deep breaths, letting them out slowly to calm her nerves.

The fifth floor was a very colorful nursery arranged with an amazing amount of vibrant playthings. Separated rooms lined the right wall where students from the ages of two to five were taught, the youngest ones being the children of the faculty.

Rohjees gestured to the second large classroom. "Right in here, madam. Room 5B."

Taking a deep breath again, Hamilda willed herself to take a few steps into the brightly colored room. She was the last to arrive. The children and their parents were there along with an army general and four adults she did not recognize. They stopped chatting when she walked in and looked her way.

Hamilda suddenly felt very self-conscious.

The general walked over to her and shook her hand. "It's good to finally meet you, Hamilda Shing. I am General Komuh of the Western Army branch located in Sheidem City."

"Nice to meet you," Hamilda said, astonished by his appearance. He was a massive man with broad shoulders, bushy eyebrows, and a mustache that extended down the sides of his mouth. The fierce and determined look in his eyes was appalling, almost frightening, causing Hamilda to hold her breath. She sensed something strange about him, but she could not pinpoint what it was.

"Please come with me." He guided her away from the children and their parents and toward the four people at the front of the room. "Gentlemen … and Lady," he began with a friendly smile, nodding at the only woman in the group of four, "I would like to introduce you to Mrs. Hamilda Shing." Turning to Hamilda, he said, "Mrs. Shing, these are the emperors of our beloved countries."

Hamilda was shocked. She had not anticipated meeting any of them. Her stomach dropped to her knees and her cheeks flushed so quickly, she was sure her face was turning beet red as she stood there. She smiled. It was all she could do besides running out of the room and not looking back.

Standing next to General Komuh was a brown-haired woman, who seemed to be in her early forties. She introduced herself as Emperor Kolhi, leader of Laspitu, the coldest country in the far North. "It's so nice to meet you!" she said, beaming.

"Likewise," Hamilda said, almost forgetting to breathe.

Next, she was introduced to the leader of Saiyut, Emperor Vermu, a short man with white hair and a beige complexion. Saiyut was south of the large island of Sheidem. An older, light-skinned, gray haired man introduced himself as Emperor Mashie, leader of Pontotoma, the country east of Saiyut. Finally, Hamilda was introduced to Emperor Trusa, a dark-haired, dark-skinned man from the southernmost country of Udnaruk.

After the introductions were made, General Komuh directed their attention to the children and their families, seated at the other end of the colorful room. "As you are well aware, ladies and gentlemen, the

Alliance of Eastern Omordion has been relentlessly attacking us and will stop at nothing to gain control of our resources and enslave us all. These children are our hope for the future. The fate of our children's children lies in their hands. We cannot predict what will happen in the next thirteen years, but we can only hope for the best. In the meantime, our army will fight as hard as it can to keep the Eastern Alliance from breaching our borders." The general placed his hand on Hamilda's shoulder. "Mrs. Shing has been given the opportunity to mold these children into great leaders and fighters and to teach them everything … well, whatever it is she knows." He cleared his throat. "I will instruct them in the art of war when the time is right. For now, it is up to you, Mrs. Shing, to raise them to be fine, outstanding individuals."

Feeling heat rising to her ears again, Hamilda nodded her head. "I'll try my best, sir."

"Good. Now let me introduce you to the children." Komuh took her by the arm, excused himself from the emperors, and led her to the other side of the room.

The children, Hamilda observed, were no more than five years old. There were five of them, like the letter had promised. Two boys, one girl, and a girl and boy pair who appeared to be twins.

Komuh turned to look at her. "As you can see, there are five of them," he said, as if reading her mind. "The *Dokeemi* Council counted the twins as one unit because they are from the same country."

Hamilda frowned at the notion that he ignorantly got the name Dokami incorrect. One would think he would take the time to get that minor detail right when dealing with such an important mission.

"The Dokeemi Council couldn't be here today, which is unfortunate," Komuh said.

Hamilda nodded. No one had actually been in the presence of the Council or knew who they were. The only person in Western Omordion who could get in contact with them was the current Dokami Wise Man, Bontihm Fhakaemeli, who was also Hamilda's mentor. Bontihm was the one who suggested giving away their secret to the leaders of the West in order to help save their planet. A secret that had been uncompromised for three hundred years. Hamilda hoped his decision was a sensible one.

As they walked over to the children and their parents, the families stood up. The first family, on their left, smiled and bowed their heads as the general and Hamilda approached. They were dressed in splendid costumes of bright colors and sparkling gold. Their complexion was the color of cream and they had straight black hair and almond shaped brown eyes. It was obvious they were very prolific by their clothes and their manner of speech. Their son, who was five years old, had shoulder length hair, tied together to resemble his father.

"This is the very prestigious Bayaht family of Saiyut." General Komuh gave a little bow to them, prompting Hamilda to do the same. "Keshi Dayaht," he gestured to the mother, "is the daughter of Emperor Vermu."

Hamilda glanced at the Emperor, who was busy having an imperative discussion with the other leaders. She had no idea that Emperor Vermu was of Dokami descent.

"Surprisingly, their son was not chosen because he was the Emperor's grandson."

Keshi offered her hand to Hamilda. "How do you do?" she said.

Feeling small and intimidated again, Hamilda shook her hand. "Very well, thank you," she replied in a small voice.

"This is our son, Fajha." Raising her voice and speaking slowly, Keshi touched the boy's shoulder. "Fajha, this is going to be your new teacher."

"Hi!" Fajha boldly stuck out his hand for Hamilda to shake.

She promptly shook it. "Hi—"

"One day, I'm going to be as big and powerful as my puppa is," he interrupted.

"Right you are," Hamilda agreed.

"He's an em, uh, emper, you know? But does that mean I have to live in his house?"

Hamilda giggled. "Probably not."

Fajha made a face and wrinkled his nose. "Good, because it doesn't *smell* right."

His mother gave him a quick tap to silence him. "That's enough Fajha," she whispered.

"Yes, mam," he said softly, looking down at his feet.

General Komuh took the opportunity to introduce her to the next family standing to the right of the Bayahts. "Mr. and Mrs. Croit of Pontotoma, I would like to introduce you to your son's teacher, Mrs. Hamilda Shing."

Hamilda couldn't help noticing how beautiful the family was. They were dressed as if they were attending a dinner party. The mother wore a short, purple cocktail dress and the father and son wore black suits with purple and black striped ties. All three had caramel-toned features. The father was tall and well built, possibly in his late twenties and the mother was of medium height with light brown, curly hair and hazel eyes. Their son was astonishingly beautiful also. He had his father's features but his eyes and hair color were taken from his mother.

Mr. Croit greeted her. "It's very nice to finally meet you," he said. "This is our son, Atakos. My ancestors were very strong Dokami. I have not inherited any of their traits but my son here has already shown remarkable strength at the age of five. He was chosen over a hundred children his age because of his amazing talent." Feeling proud, he put his hand on his son's head. "You will find him to be a very willing participant and an easy learner. I have not been able to teach him much but I'm sure you can teach him a great deal."

"I promise I will teach him all I know." Hamilda bent down and shook Atakos' hand. "Strong grip you have there, pal."

"I don't want to leave my family," Atakos abruptly told her. Tears sprung up in the eyes of his mother, who quickly looked away to wipe them, hoping he would not see her cry.

Hamilda dropped her voice down to a whisper and touched the boy's face. "You have to be brave Atakos. Everything will be alright. Before long, you'll see your parents again, ok?"

"Promise?" sniffed Atakos.

"I promise." She gave his shoulder a reassuring squeeze and stood up. Mrs. Croit mouthed the words 'thank you' after wiping her teary eyes once more.

General Komuh directed Hamilda to the next group of people standing behind the Croit family. "I would like to introduce you to the Emyu family from Udnaruk."

This was the family who had the twin boy and girl. All of them had dark, reddish-brown features, with black wavy hair and beautiful big, brown eyes. The father, who was obviously in the military, was dressed in the black Western Army uniform, hat included, and his children were in military-like uniforms, also. Their mother wore a similar uniform but it was a long dress with buttons going down the side.

Hamilda found it very odd for the entire family to be wearing uniforms because the father was the only one actually in the army, but it was rumored that Udnaruk military men preferred their houses to be run as if they were preparing for battle. It raised their morale among fellow soldiers and boosted their ego when people took notice.

The Emyu twins were very quiet and spoke only when spoken to. The boy's name was Zimi. He had a fairly short, military-styled haircut, while the girl, whose name was Zadeia, had long hair with the front cut just above her eyes, covering her small forehead. In their uniforms, they resembled little porcelain dolls, very pretty but staring quietly, as if they knew all there was to know in the world at such a young age.

"Delighted to meet all of you," Hamilda said, after introductions were made. In sync, the Emyu family smiled and bowed their heads quickly as if they were royalty dismissing a subject.

Charming, Hamilda thought sarcastically.

Finally, General Komuh introduced the last three people standing next to the Emyu family. They were the Feriau family who derived from Laspitu. The parents were dressed casually, the mother wearing a light blue sweater and black pants and the father wearing a long-sleeved, buttoned-up gray shirt tucked into his navy blue pants. Hamilda held her breath and her heart skipped a beat when she looked at their little girl. The girl's parents had brown hair, brown eyes, and tanned features while their daughter was pale with white-blonde hair and bright blue eyes. Her hair was tied together in two ponytails and she wore a white cloak over a pretty white dress and white shoes. She looked positively angelic with a little pink on her cheeks and lips. Hamilda thought for an instant that she had seen her before. It wasn't possible, considering the girl's age and the fact that she came from Laspitu, a country in the far north, which Hamilda had never visited. But still something seemed oddly familiar about her.

General Komuh explained that the Feriau family were the only ones of Dokami origin, in all of Laspitu, that came forward, and that their daughter, Cristaden, was only four years old and was going to turn five in a couple of months. Mrs. Feriau told Hamilda that from the moment Cristaden can say sentences, she spoke of having a higher purpose in life. When they heard of the secret mission, they mutually agreed that their daughter was meant for something bigger and allowed her to participate. With Cristaden having no abilities, her mother continued to explain, if she was judged against other children, the Dokami Council would not have chosen her. They were astonished when no one else wanted to participate and took it as a sign.

Strange, Hamilda frowned. *What are the odds that out of a whole country, a country full of Dokami, not one family came forward?* Cristaden was shyly looking up at her with an awkward smile. *You have a great amount of power, little girl*, Hamilda thought, *you just don't know it yet.*

General Komuh bowed to all the families and then turned to Hamilda. "Now that the introductions have been made, the families will stay together for the night at Hotel Ramoul, in the heart of Sheidem City. In the morning, your lessons with the children will begin. Lochenby is not open for the season yet, but we must get started with them right away."

He guided her away from the children and their families and dropped his voice. "Mrs. Shing, these children are our only hope for a secure future. Separating them from all they know at such a young age, for long periods of time, could be truly traumatic. I do not believe they realize what is in store for them. We understand that, in order to achieve our goals, they have to start young and be away from distractions at home. You have to be their mother and father when they are here. You are all they will have when they need love and guidance. When there is a major crisis, you will be the one to deal with it. Since this is a secret mission, there will be no one else. This is our last hope in putting an end to this war. I'm placing a tremendous responsibility in your hands. Are you sure you can handle this? Let me know if you cannot and I will postpone the mission. And find someone else."

Hamilda could feel the heat rising at the back of her neck where the hairs were standing on end. She was terrified as her heart began to beat fast again. What was wrong with her? It was such a simple question. It would be so easy to say 'no'. But then a thought occurred to her. She suddenly found herself sitting in her kitchen with her husband looking intensely into her eyes and asking her 'Could you see anyone else doing it better than you?' Hamilda knew the answer to that question. No. Those children needed her. She had more skills than any other member of the Dokami clan because she was taught and raised by the Wise Man himself, the Master of their clan. Bontihm once told her she was pure of heart, a trait that many people cannot possess for they can easily fall into the traps of greediness, temptation, and jealousy. She was not one of those people.

It's for the best, Hamilda told herself. *I have to do this. There is no turning back.*

"I can handle it, sir," she said, determination rising in her voice with every syllable. "I know I can."

"Whew, that's a relief. I didn't know how I was going to tell the leaders of Western Omordion that we needed to find someone else or that this mission was a failure," Komuh said. Looking her directly in her eyes, he said, "Good luck and take care." With that he gathered everyone else, laughing heartily as they exited the room.

Still having trouble breathing and feeling faint, Hamilda struggled to get some air back in her lungs.

A hand tapped her shoulder, causing her to jump and stifle a scream with her hand. She didn't even notice that Principal Rohjees had come back in.

"Come with me," Rohjees said, barely acknowledging that he startled her. Once they stepped outside of the school, he stopped for a moment. "The living quarters are in the buildings to the left. The first building is where you and the children will reside. Boys on the left, girls on the right, and the teachers live in the grand tower, floors six to ten." He pointed to the top of the building nearest to the school where Hamilda could see the tower.

Hamilda nodded but she knew the living quarters all too well, especially since not much had changed in fifteen years. The haunting memories of her parents came back to her, memories of them eating dinner together every night in the teachers' lounge and the laughter and love they shared.

I cannot allow myself to breakdown. I will get through this, she assured herself, fighting back tears that threatened to fall.

Hamilda and Rohjees entered the dormitory and took the elevator to the tenth floor. Hamilda's apartment was at the end of the hallway, marked 1013. It had one bedroom, a small kitchen connected to a furnished living room, and a tiny bathroom. The couch in the living room was navy and yellow striped with one brown end table and a tall lamp standing next to it. A plain, brown coffee table stood in the middle of the floor. The bedroom had one brown nightstand on the right side of the bed with a yellow lamp on it. Her suitcase had been placed on a blue armchair resting in-between two big windows with seats overlooking the roof of the fifth floor. Everything else was white. White walls, white sheets, white carpet. Relatively boring.

Whoever decorated this place had a horrible taste in furniture, Hamilda thought, sighing deeply while looking around.

"This will be your living quarters during the semester," Rohjees said. "The lounge and conference room are on the sixth floor if you would like to relax and socialize with the other faculty ..."

He went on about where everything was and how to turn things on, but Hamilda was not paying attention to him. She was looking out of the bedroom window and missing her husband very much. She smiled, recalling the way he would gaze into her eyes and how his dimples would appear whenever he smiled and told her that he loved her. Hamilda took a deep breath in and slowly released it. He was coming to visit her at the end of the week but it seemed so far away. For now, she would have to do what was asked of her. Pulling her eyes away from the window, she redirected her focus to Principal Rohjees, who was just about done with his explanations.

"... and if you have any questions, please feel free to call me. I will most likely be in my office," Rohjees said.

"Will do." Hamilda walked him out of the apartment and, after saying goodbye, shut the door and leaned up against it, thinking how dreadfully long her first week was going to be.

CHAPTER 2

Drums were pounding.

Fires raged out of control.

The putrid smell of decaying flesh enveloped the air, which was thick with smoke.

Hamilda instinctively put a blackened hand over her dry mouth to keep from vomiting. Shouts were heard all around her as people ran to and fro, trying to tend to the wounded and move the dead. Her heart wrenched as she looked around at the devastation and the desperation of the horrified population. Many people were screaming and crying. The screams were deafening, making Hamilda want to curl up in a ball and press her hands against her ears. But she knew she couldn't stay there. She was in danger. Whoever did this was coming back.

She could sense it.

Fear gripped her, seizing her and refusing to let go. She had to fight against her frozen body and will it to move. It was coming closer. With every ounce of energy, she stood up and took a few steps towards the forest.

And stopped.

It was behind her now. She didn't have to turn around to know. It was too late. She could sense the presence of pure evil. Looking towards the forest she thought maybe she could make it. Maybe she would have enough time to escape.

With an act of sheer courage, she tried to run away from the carnage but tripped over something on the ground. Falling into the mud mingled with blood, she braced herself for the attack. But it never came. Could it possibly be letting her escape? No. It wanted her to see something. She knew that now.

Raising herself to her knees, she hesitantly turned to see what tripped her.

It was a man. He was lying on his back, his face twisted in fear. He was long dead. Already decomposing. It was not as if she could save him. But something drew her to him. Ignoring the horrible stench coming off his body, Hamilda focused hard on his face. Why did he look so familiar?

The overwhelming sadness came as a shock when she realized who it was. Tears sprang up in her eyes and she leaned to the side to vomit on the muddy ground. Reluctantly, she looked back at the dead body. Perhaps hoping it was not true. She wanted to break away and scream but, before any sound could come out, she felt the evil presence coming towards her. Daring herself to look, she slowly lifted her eyes. The paralyzing fear suddenly came back. Looking up at an evil and twisted face, she immediately noticed the eyes that sparkled red in the light of the raging fires. It was those eyes that caused her body to completely freeze when the evil being suddenly lunged at her with a shriek so loud and terrifying, she felt her eardrums burst and the blood pour out of them onto the muddy ground.

Hamilda opened her eyes and realized she had been screaming. When had she fallen asleep? Sweat was pouring down her face as she inhaled sharply to bring some air back into her lungs. "It was just a dream," she said, trying to steady her shaking hands and checking her ears for any sign of blood. "But it seemed so real."

Hamilda had visions before but this one was unlike anything she had experienced in a really long time. She reviewed it in her mind over and over again, trying to interpret it, but it did not make any sense.

It's this place.

Shaking her head and sitting up, Hamilda looked around the small bedroom. "I can't let this school get to me. So many awful memories." She didn't know how she was going to get used to Lochenby. It was unfathomable.

Remembering her mission, she forced herself to get up. There was nothing she could do about it now. She had no choice but to stay. After washing her face in the bathroom, she brushed aside the ghastly dream and finished unpacking, thinking it was going to be a *long* thirteen years.

CHAPTER 3

It was a brisk autumn morning, ten years after the children were taken to Lochenby. The school remained the same over the years, still looming dark and mysterious over the students that came through her doors, fresh from summer vacation each year. Laughing as they climbed up the stairs, the students of Lochenby did not realize that for ten years their school held extraordinary beings that have become much stronger over the years since they first entered the school at the ages of four and five. Those beings were called *Omordion's Hope* but, over the years, began to be known more as *Omordion's Doubt* to the leaders of Western Omordion who did not believe that the plan was, in fact, going to work. Only time would tell and a lot of time was not what the innocent people of Omordion had.

Many battles were fought along the borders of Western Omordion. The Eastern Alliance was growing more and more impatient with the outcomes of the battles, but they knew the Western Alliance was growing weaker each passing year, so they continued their relentless attacks. Young men and women, when they became of age, were taught to fight to protect their countries. Those who had not fought a battle in years were being asked to fight again and the cries of orphaned children and widowed spouses were heard throughout all of Western Omordion. The great island of Sheidem and other nearby islands remained unscathed by the attacks on the major countries. The Western Army even took the liberty of moving their headquarters to the island to compensate for the lack of stability and security elsewhere.

Hope, for all, was slowly fading away.

"I'm so happy to be back here," said Rhokh Grouseli, "away from the chaos of my aunts, uncles, and cousins in the city. I don't know how my parents deal with them in that big house when I'm gone. I'm glad I don't have to be in that mess all the time." Rhokh was walking into Lochenby with a very good friend of his. "How was your vacation, Atakos?"

Atakos Croit glanced at his friend and realized how much he had changed over the past few months. Rhokh was slightly taller than he remembered and his hair, which was usually a sandy blonde color, had become lighter, clearly bleached from the long days spent out in the sun. He was not as scrawny in his school uniform as he had been a few months before.

"My vacation was … relatively boring." Atakos couldn't tell his friend what he really did all summer so he usually made up an excuse or avoided answering the question. "I'm just glad to be back."

"Are you going to participate in the sword fight competition between Lochenby and the Holawal School of Arts this year?"

"Oh, yeah, Hole-in-a-wall? Wouldn't miss it for the world. We're going to rip them to *shreds* this time."

The boys looked at each other and burst out laughing.

"Yeah, last year was embarrassing," Rhokh said. "Have you been practicing?"

"Every day. How about you?"

Rhokh flexed a muscle. "Why, can't you tell?"

Atakos shot him a look and shook his head. "Try not to embarrass yourself this year."

The two friends laughed as they walked up the front steps and entered the school. They then noticed a couple of Lochenby's star athletes walking down the hall ahead of them. Bho and Len were a couple of years older and the most popular boys at Lochenby. Bho was tall and very muscular and Len was only slightly smaller than him. They both had the same olive skin and black hair. If you did not know them, you would assume they were brothers, but they were not even related. Groups of students standing at their lockers turned to greet them as they walked by.

The two boys passed a couple of pretty girls who turned and smiled. "Hi, Bho and Len," they said in unison, practically drooling.

"Hi, ladies," they replied, flashing them award-winning smiles. The girls quickly walked away, giggling.

Rhokh turned to Atakos. "Why can't we ever get that kind of attention?"

"First of all, we have to grow a few more inches and be the best at all the sports," Atakos said.

"You mean to tell me that my charming good looks and great sense of humor won't do the trick?"

"That's definitely not enough. These girls don't even know we exist."

"They will one day," Rhokh said, defiantly.

"Only in your dreams, my friend. Only in your dreams."

Fajha, Zimi, and Zadeia met each other at the twins' lockers on the second floor of the school, wearing their school uniforms. Their pleated pants and skirt were green with black lining, while their shirts were white with the school emblem on the left breast pocket. The Lochenby emblem was that of a green phoenix inside a circle with two black swords crossed behind it, the swords representing a battle once fought on Sheidem Island over a century ago, and the phoenix representing the peace since that fateful battle.

Fajha, against his mother's wishes, cut his straight, black hair to shoulder length and liked to leave it wild most of the time. He wore glasses, a trait he detested getting from his mother's side of the family. Zimi still had a military-styled haircut he received every time he went home for the summer. Throughout the year, he liked to grow it out as his way of rebelling against his father's rules and regulations, which, according to his father, was dishonorable. Zadeia was slightly shorter than her brother and had big brown eyes that set her apart from him. She still wore her black hair the same way, thick and long but cut short just above her eyes.

"We have to plan what we're doing for Cristaden's party," Zadeia said. "It's only four weeks away."

Zimi crossed his arms and leaned against his locker. "What are we going to do this year?"

"It can't be a surprise anymore," Fajha said. "No one can ever fool Cristaden. We'll talk about it when she's nowhere in the vicinity."

"Right—" Zadeia began but was interrupted by a group of teenagers walking pass them.

"Why, if it isn't the Nerd-Squad," one of them, a redheaded boy, said, laughing hysterically.

Another boy, with black and green hair saw the two approaching boys, Atakos and Rhokh. "Look. Here come the rest of the *losers*."

The students kept walking, laughing down the hall. Others noticed them laughing and joined in, whispering to each other as they rudely stared at the five teens.

"Hey guys," Rhokh greeted his friends. "I'm glad to see we're still 'popular'."

Seeing his friends' hurt expressions, Atakos tried to cheer them up. "Ignore them," he said. "They're the losers. They just don't know it yet." He smiled, trying to push the taunting out of his mind and playfully punched Fajha's arm. "Hey, what happened to you last night? Did you fly in on your private airship or something this morning?"

"Well," Fajha said, adjusting his glasses. "Actually I did. Just flew in an hour ago."

Atakos laughed and then noticed that someone was missing. "Has anyone seen Cristaden?"

Zadeia shrugged. "The last time I saw her was when we left our room this morning," she said. "She said something about speaking to an old teacher of hers in regards to some plants she brought from Laspitu."

Looking past Fajha's head, Atakos spotted Cristaden walking towards them from the end of the hall. Wearing the same uniform as Zadeia, she had knee-high white stockings and white shoes. She carried her favorite white cloak over her arm and her long, blonde hair cascaded down her back as usual. Cristaden always seemed to be glowing, well, according to Atakos. There was a change in her since summer vacation began though. Something different that made Atakos' heart actually *flutter*. Before he knew what was happening, his face grew warm. He turned away quickly so no one would notice. What was wrong with him? This was Cristaden for goodness sakes! Taking a few deep breaths, he tried not to look at her and moved his focus onto something else. Anything else. Fajha's glasses. He was sure they were brand new.

Cristaden was so happy to see her friends, the only real friends she had ever known. The only people who truly understood her and knew who she really was. It was a long summer in Laspitu without much to do and she longed to return to Lochenby each excruciating day. As

Cristaden approached her friends, she noticed that Atakos was looking very uncomfortable. His hair was tousled in little light-brown curls and his sun-kissed, caramel complexion made his hazel eyes appear greener. She instantly felt bad for him. Those teenagers must have made him feel really embarrassed. No worries. She will try her best to cheer him up.

"Hey guys, I've missed you," Cristaden said, giving each of them a warm hug. "The summer seemed so long without you." She gave Atakos an even tighter, longer hug and frowned when his body tensed and he took a step back after she pulled away.

Rhokh came up behind her then, interrupting her momentary confusion. "Hey, uh, Cristaden, what about that date? Maybe this year you might …?"

Cristaden blushed and shook her head. "I don't think so."

Atakos cleared his throat and nudged Rhokh, reminding him that he had a class to go to.

"Oh, yeah," Rhokh said, sighing. While walking away he turned to Cristaden. "Byyyye."

Cristaden rolled her eyes.

"Ok, now that he's gone, let's go," Zimi said and led the group down the hall.

Zadeia turned to Cristaden. "You should give that poor boy a chance."

Cristaden laughed and flatly said, "No."

As they were walking down to the first floor of the school, the other students turned to stare or stole quick glances at them. They were a sight to behold. Because the majority of the student body was from Sheidem Island, the fact that they were all from different countries brought unwanted attention to them. They were all smart and very friendly, unless when defending each other. They appeared flawless and graciously attractive. Unfortunately, they were constantly being teased because of those very reasons. A few snickers were heard as they glided past the gawking students, which they pleasantly ignored.

"Where does she want us to meet her?" Zimi asked, glancing at Fajha.

Fajha frowned and appeared to be concentrating hard. Then his expression softened and he said, "The lake. I think."

"Well, let's hope you're right this time," Atakos mumbled as he put on his black cloak.

As the rest of them put on their green, black, and white cloaks, they smiled, remembering the wild goose chase Fajha put them through when he tried to locate Hamilda before summer break. It was an ability he had just discovered the year before. Hamilda made him promise to keep working on it. Unfortunately, it was nothing like reading someone's mind, which would have been much simpler. It was more like trying to locate a presence and the area surrounding their aura.

"I had lots of practice at one of my grandfather's estates this summer," Fajha said.

"Which one did you go to this time?" Cristaden said.

"We went to the one in Northern Saiyut, right off the coast of the Saimino Ocean. It was glorious there, with the mountains, the trees, and the beaches. One could feel as free as a bird at any given time. I wish that I had the ability to fly. It would have made it that much better. "

Zadeia released a despairing sigh. "Sounds wonderful," she said. "I wish our summers were like that." She glanced at Zimi who sadly shook his head. Their summers were spent at a military base in Udnaruk and they were not allowed to leave the compound because of the war unless told to do so otherwise. Of course, there were people their age to spend time with but it was nothing like going to the beach or feeling 'as free as a bird'. At times, it was torturous.

So as not to be followed, the five friends waited until the halls were emptied. Then they went into a small, vacant classroom, which was used as a storage area for books and science experiments. After locking the door behind them, they exited the school through a small, hidden door in the closet at the back of the room. A dense forest of trees bordered the path on the hill that led up to the school's lake. The only person there was a woman standing at the edge, overlooking the water. She was wearing a green shirt tucked into a black pencil skirt and her curly hair was glistening black against the sun's rays. When she turned around, the green shirt seemed to bring out her bright green eyes and olive skin. She smiled as they approached her.

Hamilda was beaming with joy when she saw her students. Because of her duty to them, she was not able to have any children of her own until the thirteen years had passed. She did not feel angry about that stipulation because, in a way, they were her children. She was always sad when the summer months came and they had to part for so long, but each year her students sent her letters and she would write back, which eased the sadness.

Since Captain Jogesh Shing was relieved of his duties from the army, the school allowed him to move in with Hamilda during the school year. Having him with her helped her feel more at home within Lochenby's suffocating walls. Thinking of her husband brought her back to the five years he was fighting in the war. It was the roughest five years of her life and it was a time when the children needed her the most. They relied on her for emotional support so she always had to be strong for them. In their eyes, she was a monument of strength and dignity but, deep down inside, she was far from it.

"Hello, my pupils!" Hamilda said. She gave each of them a tight embrace and then invited them to follow her down a hidden path through the trees away from Lochenby. "Fajha. I see you've been practicing your location ability. It has finally become clearer to you."

Fajha beamed. "Yes. During my free time, I would try to locate my little sister, who hid within the grounds of my grandfather's estate. Once I learned how to focus my thoughts, I was able to find her more accurately but there were still moments when I was way off."

"Don't worry about it. Nothing is learned overnight. It will take some time but you'll eventually get it perfectly." She turned to offer him an encouraging smile and then focused her attention on Cristaden. "Cristaden, did you bring those flower seeds you had mentioned in your last letter?"

"Yes, they're right here." Cristaden reached into the inside pocket of her white cloak, pulled out a purple satchel, and held it up. "I can't wait to plant them. Hopefully they survive in this climate. My old botanist teacher told me they would not."

Hamilda laughed. "I'm sure you've noticed that anything you plant can survive in any weather."

Cristaden reflected on the fruit trees she planted years ago that produced fruit even during blistery cold winters and smiled. "I hope you're right about these."

Hamilda looked back at the others. "We're going to have a lot of practice time this year. General Komuh has requested that you take only three other classes this semester and use the rest of the time to enhance your abilities. Three years is really not a long time and we've been progressing at a snail's pace, which is not good enough if we are going to put an end to this war." She sighed. "I'm sorry to say, but the pressure is upon us now." Her students looked down at the ground. She could feel their fear and uncertainty. "I still believe our goals will be reached because all of you have great potential. Just have no fear. Concentrate on each ability you are learning and you will succeed."

The determined group approached a heavy gate, boarded up with the words 'NO TRESPASSING' written across it. Fajha turned the locks on the other side of the gate without so much as changing his position. Atakos then raised his arms, causing the gate to lift seven feet above the ground. The group passed underneath it and, with the help of Fajha, Atakos brought the gate down to its original position and Cristaden turned the locks manually.

They walked through a dense brush and stepped into a two acre clearing. It was a vacant, eighty-six year old ranch that was once used for the school's horseback riding activities. The ranch had a big, red stable and a beautiful fishpond with a small garden next to a large chorale. Cristaden used a small shed near the pond as a hospital to repair broken bones of animals found in the woods. The ranch was the best place to execute their lessons without the risk of being seen.

Hamilda suddenly shouted something they were not expecting to hear so soon. "Your lesson begins—now!"

CHAPTER 4

Abruptly, a low whistling sound could be heard sweeping through trees and the five teens immediately turned their heads towards it. An enormous rock flew out of the forest, seemingly in slow motion, and headed straight for them. They knew they only had a moment to react before it reached its target.

Cristaden stood frozen, wishing she had the ability to help her friends, but unable to do anything. Zimi and Zadeia used the wind to encircle the rock, causing it to stop its descent while Atakos and Fajha, uniting their strength, pushed it away until it sailed over the trees, back to wherever it came from.

"Very good!" Hamilda said. "That was fine handling one object as a group, but how about individually, with multiple objects?" She told Cristaden to stand next to her, stating that the situation might get dangerous as the others formed a circle and turned their backs to one another, looking cautiously up at the treetops.

The attack surprisingly came from the ground. Rocks hurdled toward the group from all directions. The twins fought to push them away with their wind power, which was not an easy task. Atakos and Fajha always had a set plan: Fajha would handle the small ones while the big ones were left to Atakos, the stronger one. Some rocks that were pushed away would retract and fly back at them, catching them off-guard. Zimi got hit on the arm by one of those particular rocks, causing him to get angry, which made him lose focus. Because of this, he got hit two more times, which infuriated him even more. Seeing what happened to Zimi, Fajha began to doubt himself and tried to duck when the next rock came at him instead of pushing it away. What was worse, because the two boys were losing their concentration, Zadeia lost Zimi's help and Atakos began to get hit by both large and small rocks.

Just then, a large amount of water from the pond rose up over them. Unable to control elements, Atakos and Fajha were powerless against it, their efforts only going through it and not pushing against it. Zadeia and Zimi realized there was not enough time to regain their focus to control it. A second later, they were all drenched with water.

The teens were ashamed to see the look on Hamilda's face so they kept their eyes down. Cristaden scrambled to pick up the fish that were flapping on the ground around them and put them back into the pond. She then went to her shed to collect towels for her wet friends.

Hamilda could not hide her frustration. "Had this been a real fight, all of you would have perished. You must gain and maintain control of the situation in order to succeed. If one person loses control, you will all fail. No matter what happens, if you are injured or afraid, you can never give in to those emotions. They will ruin you and destroy the rest of the group as well."

Hamilda walked over to Zimi and he slowly lifted his eyes to look up at her, water dripping down his face. "Zimi, you cannot allow one mistake to affect you in any way. Do not lose your focus. Learn from that mistake and try to prevent it from happening again." Hamilda looked at the rest of the group. "If you had one hundred thousand men coming at you from all sides and one person goes down, his or her attackers will hit you from behind while you are fending off the ones in front of you. Must I remind you that this is *not* a game? Do not be deterred by one rock because one rock could mean the difference between life and death.

Right now, I would like each of you to practice on your own after you have dried off. I will be walking around giving evaluations and advice, if needed." Hamilda turned to Cristaden, who was handing them the towels. "You may choose to do the evaluations with me or plant your seeds."

"I think I will plant my seeds." Cristaden patted her pocket and glanced toward the shed. She didn't want to go through the evaluations because they reminded her of all the abilities she could not do but always wished she could. Her abilities were meager compared to the others. She could sense things that no one else could. She had the uncanny ability to talk to animals and actually make them understand her. She could fix things, like broken animal bones, but she was no healer. It was a trick that no other Dokami was documented to do. But it still could not rival against moving objects without touching them or manipulating fire, water, and air. With her abilities, she felt helpless when it came to fighting.

Cristaden thought of her home in Laspitu. She never did want to stay when she went back there for vacations. She loved her parents but, as much as they tried to understand who she was, they could never relate to her and conversation with them always seemed to fall flat. Her nine-year-old brother was the same complexion as her parents with brown hair and brown eyes. He constantly teased her, telling her she was adopted and how her uncanny ability to sense things was 'weird'. Every morning, while everyone was still sleeping, Cristaden would walk through the forest towards the sea. It was a glorious feeling to watch the sun rise and to just be alone. She longed for that feeling as she dumped the damp towels next to the shed and continued walking towards Sheidem Forest.

Hamilda watched Cristaden walk away and felt her pain. She always encouraged her to expand her power, to go beyond only being able to fix broken bones, to actually mending wounds back together. Cristaden lacked confidence, a vital key to accomplishment, which Hamilda knew all too well. She hoped that one day Cristaden would find the courage she was looking for and grow stronger. For now she was not going to push her because she knew abilities took time to develop. She was constantly reminding Cristaden that even she did not reach her full potential until the age of seventeen. Sighing, she turned her attention to Zimi and Zadeia, who were standing by the pond discussing their next exercise.

Zadeia always looked up to Hamilda and hoped that, one day, she would be just like her. A confident and strong person. Someone who always managed a smile when times were rough. She remembered following her around as a child and doing everything that Hamilda asked her to do. Her friends teased her and called her a teacher's pet, but it did not matter, for Hamilda was more than just a teacher. She became a second mother to her and she loved her as much as she loved her own. She constantly worried that, in a few years, when their training was over, she would never see her again.

Zimi, on the other hand, had a fear of not being good enough to fight when the time came. His father, in pure military style, never failed to tell him that he wouldn't amount to anything. He constantly reminded him that he will be going into battle and one false move could cost him his life. When Zimi didn't do something right, his father made him feel like less of a person. He tried to cover up his anguish with sarcasm so no one could see how hurt he truly was. Although he got the worse end of things back home, when he was at school he tried to work to the best of his ability. He wanted to one day be better than his father ever was and prove him wrong.

"Okay," Hamilda said. "Let's work on picking up water from the pond and sprinkling it on Cristaden's flowerbed over there by the chorale. I know it seems tedious, but sometimes doing the little things takes more work than doing something big. This will help you gain some control." The twins nodded and got to work.

Atakos was a little annoyed with the circumstances of their practice. He had so much hope for the group. Closing his eyes, he tried to think of something else to ease his mind but his thoughts brought him back to Pontotoma. When he went home for the summer, he learned that his mother was gravely ill. He insisted on staying after the summer was over to help with her care but his father would not allow it. His father assured him that everything was going to be okay, that his mother would pull through, and that the task he was assigned to was far more important than anything in his personal life. They were harsh words his father spoke but he knew his mother would not have been happy if he allowed him to stay and risk causing a collapse in the mission. It was their dream to see Atakos as head of Pontotoma and a spectacular general. Nevertheless, he was still bitter and hoped that his mother would pull through from the sickness that plagued her for many months.

Shaking his head to clear it, Atakos looked around and spotted a tractor within a small field of overgrown grass and he made his way to it in an attempt to lift it and place it on the other side of the field. He had always tried to lift it in the past but was never able to move it. He hoped that, with all the practice he got during the summer, he could finally reach his goal.

Fajha decided that he wanted to go somewhere so as not to be disturbed. Making his way to the stable, he sighed, frustrated that he was one of the reasons why they failed their lesson. He could not understand why he lost his confidence and backed down.

Entering the stable, Fajha went to a small area, inside a horse's pen, where he could sit and meditate. As a descendent of Vermu royalty, he was brought up with their traditions and values. These traditions and values he took with him wherever he went. He was always taught to have proper mannerisms and to keep his head high during dire situations. Instead of taking his anger out on someone or something, he was taught to find a quiet place and meditate, focusing his anger on building strength and perseverance.

Fajha sat cross-legged on the dusty floor and closed his eyes. He pictured himself in the vast garden located at one of his grandfather's summer estates, walking through a maze of tall hedges. He was trying to focus his energy into finding a way out. He began to fall deeper and deeper into a trance. In his dream, he was just about to exit the perplexing maze when he noticed a dark path leading out of the garden and into a gloomy forest. He never remembered seeing the path before so he was curious to see where it led.

Upon entering the forest, he noticed that everything was still. There was no sound. *That's weird,* he thought, *usually there are sounds of animals or even the sound of the wind rustling the leaves in a forest.* He stopped and looked around. Then, as if to answer his thoughts, the branches in the trees began swaying rapidly. Leaves were swirling all around him and unrecognizable animals jumped out at him with high-pitched squeals. He immediately threw his arms over his face in an effort to protect himself. Then everything went quiet. With his heart beating rapidly, he slowly lowered his arms. A dark cave loomed in front of him. Instantaneously, a bright light shined over the cave and blinded him.

Fajha snapped out of his meditation and opened his eyes. As he looked around, he noticed that all the hay in the stable were floating in mid-air. He blinked once and they dropped.

Wow, he thought, *I've had weird dreams before but this one had to be the most extreme.* He tried to interpret it but could not come up with any answers.

Taking a deep breath, Fajha left the stable to get some air. He saw Zimi and Zadeia having a discussion by the lake. Atakos had an old tractor two feet above the ground and Hamilda was encouraging him to lift it higher. Sighing, Fajha decided to go to the shed to see what Cristaden was up to. Upon reaching it, he saw that she was not there.

"Hey guys, have you seen Cristaden?" he said to the twins.

"I haven't seen her in over a half an hour," Zadeia said. She looked at Zimi and he shrugged his shoulders. "I wonder where she is."

A half an hour? Fajha shuddered at the notion of being in his trance for that long. It felt like only a matter of minutes. "We'd better go find her. We have to be getting back soon."

"Fajha, can you try and locate her?" Zimi asked as he and Zadeia walked over to him.

"I'll try." Fajha closed his eyes. The cave from his dream came to mind then and startled him. Letting out a small chuckle to hide his surprise, he tried to refocus until it became clear to him. "She's in the forest," he said. "I think I can find her."

Cristaden stood still in the middle of a clearing. With the sun peeking out here and there with each sway of the tree branches, it seemed so magical to her. *Sheidem Forest,* she thought. She heard stories of the forest being enchanted and how dangerous animals dwelled deep within it. She was not sure of whether or not it was true but she knew, for the many years that she had come to the clearing, she had never seen, heard, or even felt anything out of the ordinary. To her, the forest was pure tranquility.

Taking a deep breath while looking around, Cristaden froze when she saw something move. She peered through the trees at the dense forest ahead of her. To her astonishment, she sensed that something was definitely there. She couldn't make out the shape and wasn't sure if it was man or beast but was absolutely sure it was not friendly.

It was staring at her.

Cristaden took a step back and it was gone. Just like that. No animal sounds came from the forest and the birds still sang sweetly.

Nothing there but trees.

Could I have imagined it? Cristaden asked herself.

A twig snapped, causing her to gasp and turn around, prepared to fight. She then sighed, relieved to see her friends standing behind her.

"What's wrong, Cristaden?" Zadeia said. "You look as though you'd seen a ghost."

"Oh, it's nothing," Cristaden quickly said. She didn't want her friends to think she was crazy. "You're getting a lot better with that location ability, Fajha," she said, changing the subject.

Fajha laughed. "It's easier to pinpoint exactly where my target is, but only if it's within a mile of me. I still can't go further than that."

"We have to get going," Zimi said. "We must get back to school and change before the next class starts."

"Yeah," Cristaden said, shaking off the feeling of being watched. *Let's get out of here.*

CHAPTER 5

"This is unacceptable," King Tholenod said, removing his golden crown from his speckled-gray, black hair. He then pounded a tanned fist against his leg and let out a curse that rang out in the entire candlelit hall, causing some of his finest soldiers to suddenly flinch and glance his way.

His straggly advisor, Menyilh, took one step back. He was always disheveled and cared less about his appearance. With missing teeth, he wore the same tattered clothes every day and smelled as if he hadn't bathed in years. He was a necessary adversary for the king though, being able to blend in with their enemies, spying on them without their realization. "Sire," he hissed. "They grow weaker with each battle. We will succeed."

King Tholenod raised his eyebrows, his dark eyes shining against the light from the candles. "Weaker? *Weaker?* If they grow weaker we should be able to defeat them." He rubbed his graying beard. "We will have to send more soldiers. We have to get them at their weakest point in order to breach their security."

Menyilh leaned in closer. "I have a plan, but it will take some time."

King Tholenod grunted. "What have you devised this time?"

"Well, Western Omordion is powerful as a whole. If we were to attack them many times, simultaneously, in different parts of their land…"

"Then they would be in one place and not expect us to attack elsewhere." King Tholenod sat back. "That's not an easy task. We would need the help of the Alliance," he said with annoyance. When he finally gained control of the West, he will order the deaths of all the leaders, including the other kings of the East, the very ones who formed an alliance with him to help defeat the West. He will be the *only* ruler of Omordion.

"I will inform them right away, sire." Menyilh smiled, revealing his slimy, brown teeth. "We will begin immediately."

A young girl slowly climbed up a small hill and allowed her green eyes to skim over her village. She was completely covered in dirt and ashes. Her cheeks were smeared with fallen tears. Looking up, she could not see the rising sun that awoke her each morning. The sky was darkened with the smoke from her devastated village. Tears filled her eyes once again as she observed the destruction all around her. In all her fourteen years she had never witnessed such devastation. Among the charred ruins were the dead—she had to turn away. She wanted so much to observe and remember, to feed her anger, but it hurt too much to see them. Her friends. Most of them were *dead*. Others were taken prisoner, led away in the night by a band of ruthless soldiers.

Closing her eyes, the young girl recollected the dreadful night that passed. It began with a fire. A home very close to hers had burst into flames. As the villagers ran towards the fire to put it out, they were attacked by soldiers from the East. She remembered her mother's frightened voice telling her to run and hide. Go to their secret hiding place. Her mother's screams echoing in the night as she was dragged away by the armed soldiers.

The young girl had taken off, quickly dashing over the small hill behind her village to an old stone furnace hidden among the trees and dense brush of their forest. She crawled into the small opening, staying hidden throughout the terrifying night that followed. She heard screaming and children crying. Loud explosions rocked the ground beneath her. She had covered her ears with her hands, attempting but not succeeding to block out the horrific sounds, while the fear of being discovered plagued her heart. She cried for her mother, knowing full well that she may never see her again.

The malicious soldiers had left before the sun rose.

There was nothing left now but the devastation.

A noise from the forest made the young girl crouch down so as not to be seen. She saw the black uniforms through the trees and heard the general barking orders. Realizing who they were, she stood up so the soldiers of the West, who entered the village, could see her.

The Southern Udnaruk branch of the Western Army got word of the attack of their eastern villages. The army had soldiers stationed at the shores of Udnaruk, where the Rostumik Pass separated their country from the eastern country of Feim. Those soldiers had been slain before a warning to evacuate could be issued to the isolated villages. The army only learned of the devastation from a few villagers who managed to escape and make their way to the base ten miles away. A few hundred soldiers descended upon the villages, examining the severe damage caused by the unending rampage of the Eastern Army.

"Oh, my …," one soldier muttered under his breath as they entered the clearing of Rostihme Village, the third one they were to explore, tracking the path of their enemies. It was apparent that the entire village was set ablaze during the night and the overwhelming smell of burning flesh slowly enveloped the soldiers as they got closer. The determined soldiers remained on their guard in case of an ambush.

One soldier noticed a young girl standing at the top of a small hill. She was obviously attempting to appear brave and stand tall but he could see how the night's onslaught had taken its toll on her. Her cheeks appeared sunken and her green eyes were red from crying. The tightened fists she made with her hands were quivering and she seemed almost on the verge of collapsing.

"Captain Lughm!" the soldier called out to his superior, pointing to the girl.

Captain Lughm held up his arm in a motion for the troupe to stop marching. "Lieutenant Emyu," he said to a tall man standing in the middle of the first row. "Take one of our men. Go back to the base with the child. After doing so, return here at once. We have to find those Feim soldiers and drive them out. We need all the help we can get."

Lieutenant Emyu looked sadly up the hill at the girl who was staring back at him with tearful eyes. He then motioned for Private Hodin to come with him. Private Hodin was an excellent soldier who won many medals for his bravery in combat. He had a private meeting that day with Major Garunburj, major of the Udnarukan Army, to discuss a change in his rank. That meeting, because of the surprise attack, was cancelled and would not be rescheduled until further notice. He was still deeply upset because he had been waiting for that day for several months. Angrily balling his hands into fists, he went up the hill to assist with the traumatized girl.

Emyu lifted his hand towards her. "What is your name?" he said. The girl spoke but her voice was barely audible. She then seemed as if she did not have the strength to speak anymore, looked back down at her village, and began to cry.

"Come now. We're going to take you someplace safe, away from harm. You must trust us."

The young girl slowly nodded her head and took the hand of the lieutenant and squeezed it, afraid to let go. He, in turn, picked her up and carried her down the hill towards the other soldiers. As they were walking back up the path in which they came, an explosion rocked the ground. Everyone immediately looked around.

"We're under attack!" a soldier cried.

"Take cover!" another one shouted.

Another explosion occurred, this time much closer, killing a few soldiers on impact. The Eastern Army had definitely set a trap for them.

"Take the child and run," Captain Lughm yelled at the two men. "You must warn the major. Go quickly!"

Emyu and Hodin did not hesitate and ran deep into the forest. The young girl buried her head in Emyu's chest and started screaming. She felt as if she was going insane, that the fighting and dying would never end.

As they ran, Hodin did not speak to his commanding officer but knew what the other man was thinking. He knew that the chances of the soldiers they left behind surviving that surprise attack was very slim. Their fellow soldiers were not ready to fend off such an attack. The entire platoon would most likely be killed. They would have to bring in reinforcements from the other western countries if they were going to drive them out.

Emyu put his arm out to stop Hodin from running any further. He had seen movement in the trees. He motioned for Hodin to get down and placed the girl in the brush, putting his finger to his lips in an effort to silence her. Seeing the desperate look on his face, the young girl could not help but to whimper in fear.

Suddenly, four Feim soldiers jumped out from behind several trees. They went towards the men with fire in their eyes. Both men pulled out their swords from behind their backs. They instantly killed two of them but the other two were already upon them. Emyu turned his sword around and bashed his attacker on the side of his head with the hilt. As the soldier was going down, he swung his leg around and caught Emyu in his shin, causing him to fall on his back and drop his sword. Emyu immediately pulled out his pocketknife and stabbed the soldier in his chest, killing him instantly.

The young girl screamed. Emyu turned just in time to see the other Feim soldier pull out a dagger and fling it at Hodin. The dagger made contact and Hodin fell back, clutching his chest. Angrily, Emyu picked up his sword, charged at the Feim soldier, and decapitated him with a single swing. With a thud, the soldier's body fell to the ground.

Emyu rushed to Hodin, who was still breathing. "Hold on, I can help you."

"It's no use. I'm not going to make it." Hodin looked over at the stricken girl. "Make sure you take that girl to a safe place and don't let anyone or anything stop you. We have to let them know. We have to let them know what —" He convulsed then and his eyes rolled back into his head.

Emyu put his hand over his comrade's face to close his eyes. "Goodbye, my friend," he said. Then, without hesitation, he picked up the young girl and, while keeping to the thick brush of the forest, ran without stopping. Even when he felt that his heart was about to give out and he could not run any further, he kept going despite the rise in temperature. He ran past two villages that were destroyed in the rage of the previous night, fearing all the while that they would be ambushed again.

When Lt. Emyu made it to the unpaved road, he was able to relax a little. The army vehicles the troops had left were still there, unscathed by the enemy's touch. Helping the young girl into the closest vehicle, he pressed a button on the control panel to start the engine and quickly sped off. As he was driving, he sucked in a lung full of air and slowly released it, feeling the tension escaping his body. "Are you okay?" he said to the girl. She stared straight ahead and appeared to be in shock, too devastated to answer his question.

"What's your name?" Emyu said, hoping to get her to start talking. When she did not respond again, he decided not to ask her any more questions. Instead he reassured her that she was going to a safe place where she would be taken care of.

After a few minutes of silence, a little voice spoke. "Kireina," the girl said softly, looking down at her hands.

"Kireina. That's a very unique name. My name is Lieutenant Emyu. May I ask how old you are?"

"I'm in my fourteenth year."

Emyu would not have guessed her to be fourteen years old. She seemed so small and fragile compared to his fifteen-year-old twins, Zimi and Zadeia. In fact, he could see that she was not of Udnaruk origin at all. Unlike the reddish-brown complexion and wavy, black hair of the general population, her curly, black hair was tangled with dirt and leaves and her once golden skin was tinted with ash. In fact she looked like she might have derived from the tumultuous country of Mituwa, where the evil King Tholenod himself ruled.

She must have been a slave who escaped the cruelty in Mituwa, Emyu thought. *I wonder what happened to her parents. Poor thing.*

"Don't worry, Kireina, everything will be okay." While reassuring her again, Emyu tried to focus on the fact that Southern Udnaruk was under attack. If the Feim soldiers were not driven away from their coastline soon, their army base would be attacked also. Hopefully they could get reinforcements from General Komuh as soon as possible.

General Komuh shifted his weight uncomfortably from one leg to the other and let out an aggravated sigh. He glanced at the blinking lights of the control panel and turned away. Clasping his hands behind his back, he began to pace the floor and then stopped to look up at the ceiling. As he tried to keep his composure, a drop of sweat trickled down the side of his face signifying how nervous he really was.

An urgent message had just come from Major Garunburj of the Western Army base in Southern Udnaruk, describing the massacre that was unfolding in the villages in their area. Garunburj informed Komuh of the soldiers who were sent out but have yet to return to the base except for one brave soldier who warned the major of the attack. The major was worried that all his soldiers had been annihilated and that Feim might be planning a surprise attack of the base itself. If that were to occur, they could possibly lose their stronghold and the entire country would be taken over by the East.

They needed reinforcements immediately.

Throughout the entire length of the war, there had never been a need for reinforcements. Through hard work and determination, the Western Army was always able to drive back the forces of the Eastern

Army. This worried General Komuh. At the present moment there were no reinforcements to send to fend off this kind of attack. Because of the simultaneous attacks by the East at the borders of all the western countries, every branch of the military was at their posts protecting their own country by any means necessary. The new recruits were in training and could not possibly be prepared to handle such an attack.

There was only one alternative and it was not a move that Komuh was willing to make. He choked out an exasperated sigh of regret and motioned for the Assistant Controller to get a pen and paper ready.

"I need an urgent message to go out to the retired specialists and soldiers who were given permanent leave to return home. Inform them that they are being drafted to Southern Udnaruk to fight off an attack from Feim that has spiraled out of control. Include that we apologize immensely but this is an emergency so we are left with no other choices." Komuh folded his arms and stared hard at the floor before looking up at the soldier again. "And send a message to Major Garunburj that reinforcements are coming—immediately."

CHAPTER 6

"Jo, have you seen my hat?" Hamilda called out to her husband from the bathroom. "I have to get some reports from Principal Rohjees' office and it's pouring outside."

"Yes, it's on the bed," Jogesh said from the kitchen. He was painting a vase he made from clay the color red. With the freedom he had, he was able to enjoy doing the things he loved to do without restrictions. Most of all, he enjoyed the time he spent away from the battlefront with Hamilda when she was not teaching lessons to her pupils. Sometimes Jogesh would accompany her and watch with pure amazement at all the things the teenagers could do. To Hamilda, they could do better. To him, he thought they were incredible, a hope for their future.

Hamilda marched to the room and grabbed her hat. "It's been raining nonstop all week," she said as she walked over to the large windows. The rain was pouring so hard, she could not see the fifth floor roof below. "This is getting ridiculous."

"I know," Jogesh said, coming up behind her. He put his arms around her shoulders and planted a quick kiss on her cheek. "I'll miss you when you're getting drenched out there."

"Why you—" Hamilda pushed him away and jabbed him in the ribs. "Thanks a lot. And don't touch me with paint all over your hands. I'll have to change my clothes again." She gave him a playful pat on his arm, then a kiss, and headed towards the door. "I'll see you later," she said. "Don't miss me too much."

"I won't."

Hamilda opened the door and, before she had a chance to say something smart back, she spotted a young soldier, wet from the rain, approaching their door. She instantly got a really bad feeling.

"Good morning," the soldier greeted with a bright smile. "You must be Mrs. Shing. I have some urgent news for Captain Jogesh Shing sent by General Komuh of the Western Army."

"Urgent news? Don't tell me ..." Hamilda's voice trailed off and she looked back at Jogesh.

"Who is it, Hamu?" Jogesh said, joining her by the door. Hamilda stepped aside and he saw the soldier. "What is it?" he quickly implored. "What's going on?"

The soldier handed him a letter. "You are ordered to report to the battlefront in Southern Udnaruk."

"By whose command?"

The young soldier cleared his throat. "General Komuh, sir."

"General Komuh has relieved me of my duty. You expect me to believe he has requested me to go back into battle? It's been *five years.*"

"This is not a request. It is an order, sir. You are to report to Army Headquarters in Sheidem City at once for your immediate departure to Udnaruk."

"This isn't right!"

"There is a vehicle waiting outside to take you there," the soldier said. To Hamilda, he tipped his hat. "Good day, madam." He then turned on his heels and briskly walked away.

"Good day?" Jogesh said. "What a good day this is turning out to be." He looked down at the letter and opened it.

Dear Captain Jogesh Shing,

We regret to inform you that, due to recent attacks in Southern Udnaruk by the eastern country of Feim, we have no choice but to draft those soldiers that have been relieved of their duties. Our soldiers are currently detained all over Western Omordion's borders to prevent such surprise attacks but the assault on Udnaruk has been so severe, we need experienced soldiers to drive the enemy out. We cannot afford to lose Udnaruk. Please report to Army Headquarters as soon as possible for you will be departing

for Udnaruk today. We apologize for the inconvenience
and wish you the best.

Sincerely,
General Komuh
The Western Army
Sheidem City Branch

Jogesh crumpled the letter and turned to look at Hamilda. She appeared to be in shock. Her eyes were stricken with fear and her breath came out in short gasps.

"Hamil—," Jogesh began, reaching out for her.

Hamilda took a step back. "There must be something you can do," she said deliriously. "There must be some way you can convince them that you don't have to go. You must talk to General Komuh and explain to him that they don't need you. The army has so many experienced soldiers who can fight for them! One man is not going to change the outcome of this war. They don't *need* you."

"Hamilda," Jogesh grabbed her arms and pulled her close to him in an effort to calm her down. "I can't beg the army to stay here, that's dishonor—dishonor to us and to them. If I don't go, I could be facing imprisonment. Besides, they *do* need me. I can lead those men into battle and come up with a strategy to win, like I have done so many times before."

"Then I'll go with you. I'll meet you there and I'll *help* you—" Hamilda then burst into tears.

Jogesh squeezed her tighter. "Honey, you know it's too dangerous, and besides, you have to stay here and fulfill your mission. You can't leave because of those kids. You *know* that."

"I won't let you go."

"I know this is hard and I do not want to leave you, not in a million years. But you have to be strong for us. It was my sworn duty to be available whenever the army needs me, even after I am retired." Jogesh slowly let her go and walked into the bedroom to pack a small bag. He then removed his clothing and put on his black uniform, all the while pretending not to notice Hamilda crying by the doorway. It hurt him just as much as it hurt her that he was leaving. He fought back the tears that were building up in his eyes, knowing it would be hard for both of them if he broke down as well.

When he was done packing, Jogesh finally went towards Hamilda. He put his arm around her shoulders and motioned for her to walk with him. She buried her head in his neck and cried relentlessly as they walked to the elevators and went down to the first floor.

Upon reaching the front door, Jogesh stopped and faced Hamilda. He planted a kiss on her forehead, on both eyes, and finally, on her mouth.

Hamilda wrapped her arms around him. "My prayers will be with you," she said. "You are my heart and soul. The one reason I live. I love you so—" She could not continue.

"I love you too, Hamu," Jogesh said, embracing her tightly. "I promise I will come back to you."

"Promise?"

"Promise."

With that, Jogesh opened the door and walked out into the pouring rain.

CHAPTER 7

Zimi ended the chapter he was reading in his mystery book. He looked through the window by his desk and sighed. The real mystery was how the rain seemed never-ending. It had not stopped for seven days. It seemed as if the school would eventually be immersed in water if it were to continue. There was already some flooding issues in the basement and a pump had to be used to prevent the problem from getting worse. They were lucky their rooms were on the fourth floor.

"We haven't been able to get in some real practice outside lately," Zimi said, turning to look at his two roommates. "What do you think Hamilda's going to have us do?"

"I have no idea," Atakos said from his side of the room. He was folding his newly washed uniforms and placing them neatly in the drawers of an antique dresser by his bed.

"Hm," muttered Fajha, who was lying down on his bed with his nose buried in a physics book written in the Saiyutan language.

"I don't think he heard us, Zimi," Atakos said. "He's lost himself in one of his many science books."

Fajha glanced at Atakos and then looked back down at his book, ramming his glasses back up his nose. "Please don't be upset that I know eight different languages and I spend my time soaking up as much knowledge as possible. A feat that I'm sure seems impossible for you to manage."

"Can you fine tune a radicirculatem on a GDFP 36 model automobile?" Atakos said slyly.

"What is that?"

"My point exactly."

"Hey you two, cut it out," Zimi said. "You're both proficient in your own areas of expertise so your comparisons are senseless."

Both boys glanced at Zimi, gave him a weird look for the use of so many big words in one sentence, and then went back to what they were doing. Zimi sighed and shook his head before returning to his book.

A soft knock came at the door and Atakos jumped over his bed to open it. Cristaden glided into the room wearing a white lab coat over her uniform, her hair swept up into a bun. Zadeia followed behind her, wearing her hair in a similar fashion, with only the school uniform on.

"Good afternoon," Cristaden sang. "How's it going, guys?" All she got from the boys were measly grunts of boredom.

"Come on everyone, we have to go meet Hamilda for our next lesson," Zadeia said, sniffling. She looked like she had been crying, which was not uncommon for her.

"Is it that time already?" Zimi said, standing up to stretch and yawn.

"We're going to be late if we don't hurry," Cristaden said.

Fajha pushed himself off the bed, stood up, and yawned.

Cristaden shook her head. "You boys are so lazy."

"We're not lazy," Atakos said. "We are simply bored out of our minds when we can't go outside and do some recreational activities. I, for one, need a good physical workout every day to burn some energy." He flashed a handsome smile at her.

"We burned a lot of energy with the practice we had with Hamilda last week," Fajha said as he brought his black shoes out from under his bed and put his feet in them, lacing them without so much as getting off the bed or bending down. "But it's been raining ever since."

Cristaden sighed. "I know. I wonder what our next lesson will be. It's not like we can go outside to practice and we can't practice inside, someone's bound to spot us."

Zadeia sniffled again. "Well, let's not waste any more time and go," she said. "She asked us to meet in the faculty conference room."

"What's wrong, Zadeia?" Zimi teased. "Are you still missing mom and dad?"

Zadeia turned away from him and started crying.

Cristaden frowned at Zimi. "You know, you can be so *insensitive*."

"Oh, come on," he said. "She'll get over it. She always does!"

After Cristaden gave him another angry scowl, he spent the whole time riding the elevator to the sixth floor conference room apologizing to his sister.

Hamilda was seated in the conference room at the head of a circular table with eight intricately designed chairs surrounding it. She was lost in her thoughts once again, worried about Jogesh. For an entire platoon to be annihilated by the Feim Army meant that the destructive enemy was getting stronger, smarter, and developing new ways to penetrate their defenses. It was sure to be a tough fight for the men that were sent there to drive them out. Hamilda hoped that those men would accomplish what they set out to do and Jogesh would return to her safe and sound. She was just on the verge of tears when she heard the doorknob turn and her students suddenly filed in one by one. Standing up to greet them, she quickly wiped away the wetness in her eyes so they would not notice her impending tears.

"Welcome my children." Hamilda gestured towards the chairs. "Please have a seat."

"Good afternoon," Zadeia said. She was wiping her eyes with a tissue and taking deep breaths to try and stop the tears from flowing.

Hamilda, knowing why she was sad, thought it best not to make a big deal of it and only smiled back at her. "How is everyone?" she said, trying hard to disguise the sadness in her own voice.

"Great!" Cristaden said.

"How is your medical class going?" Hamilda asked her, taking notice of the white lab coat.

"Wonderful. We are learning about animal organs. Today, we dissected a Montapu lizard found in the Suthack Desert."

"Oh yes," Fajha said, "I've studied those. They are the color of sand to camouflage with the desert and are very poisonous." He smiled, ridiculously proud of himself for knowing everything.

"It was incredible," Cristaden continued. "We actually learned how to pinpoint their poison gland and successfully remove it."

"That's very interesting, Cristaden," Hamilda said laughing. "Hopefully you won't have to encounter a live one."

"Don't worry," Atakos leaned forward to make eye contact with Cristaden. "I'll protect you if we happen to run into one." He then sat back in his chair and folded his arms behind his head with a sense of satisfaction.

Zadeia took one look at him and rolled her eyes. "It just so happens that we're never going anywhere *near* the Suthack Desert."

"Has anyone ever wondered why Sheidem Island has a desert on the other side of it?" Zimi said. "I heard the temperature fluctuates so frequently, you can't wear the same clothes in one single day."

"It doesn't fluctuate that much," Fajha said. "I just learned about it from my geography teacher. It's really hot during the day and gets cold at night, when the sun goes down. It is said that it used to be a forest much like the rest of Sheidem Island but a strange, cataclysmic event happened there a few hundred years ago that changed the environment. All the trees dried up and everything turned into sand on that part of the island."

"Interesting," Zadeia said. "I wonder what might have happened."

"Geologists have never been able to pinpoint what exactly happened. Even to this day."

"Eh hem." Hamilda cleared her throat, interrupting their thoughts. Her students sat up in attention. Looking at each of them, she contemplated telling them about Jogesh but decided otherwise. It was best not to worry them also. "I'm sure you're wondering why I brought all of you here today." The teens nodded. "We haven't discussed our heritage in a while so … I'm giving you a test," Hamilda said.

"Awesome," Zimi said sarcastically. "Where's the pen and paper?"

"Not a written test. A verbal one. I want to see how much you remember. You can take turns telling me parts of our story from the very beginning. Starting with you, Zimi, since you're so enthusiastic about it."

Ignoring the snickers from his friends, Zimi cleared his throat. "Okay. Our story began thousands of years ago. A race of people, who called themselves the Dokami, lived on a planet that, of course, no one knows the name of or where it was located. Dokami, in their language, meant 'the peaceful'. They gave themselves that name because they were against all aspects of war and anger. They were few in numbers, very intelligent, and gifted. They had amazing abilities but … no one knows how this came about. What is known is that they could not form a bond to stay together so, through breeding with other races and moving to other planets, their race eventually died out."

"Good job, Zimi," Hamilda said. "But you did get a couple of things wrong. They did not give themselves the Dokami name. The people who bore witness to their way of life did. So they adopted the name they were being called as their own. And you didn't explain why they had to move to other planets."

Zimi sighed. "I forgot. They're planet was destroyed."

"Exactly. There is still so much we don't know about the ancient Dokami but it's good to go over the facts we do know. So we won't forget." She looked around. "Who wants to continue?"

"I will," Fajha said. He began telling the next part as if he were an old story teller, making it sound as dramatic as possible. "Five hundred years ago, during an age of interstellar wars, the planet Shaerga, fifth planet from the Sun, became devastated and uninhabitable. Before their planet was completely destroyed, the remaining Shaergans fled in every spacecraft they could find and went to Jmugea, the eighth planet from the sun and the closest planet not affected by the devastation of war. The Shaergans and the Jmugeans came to a peaceful agreement. The Shaergans were allowed to stay. It was not long before they began to get together and marry. Because their erratically different DNA mixed together, their offspring were—different. They were always born beautiful. So beautiful that some members of the Jmugean clan came together with the Shaergans just to produce such offspring.

These children were nice and nonjudgmental, very peace-like, avoiding conflicts as much as possible. As they grew, the people of Jmugea noticed something very strange about them. From an early age, they bonded with each other and came together to discuss matters in private many times. They had a 'knowing' of who was a part of their race and who wasn't. Little did they know, by mating together the Shaergans and the Jmugeans, they had unleashed the ancient Dokami race that had died out centuries before. They were born with the knowledge that they were the old Dokami race. They *remembered*. Ancestors of the Shaergans and the Jmugeans were of Dokami descent. Mixing the two together sparked an evolutionary miracle. The Dokami began to demonstrate precognitive abilities, which did not please most 'normal' people.

Seeing the result of the mating of the two species, the Jmugeans decided it was best to forbid any more marriages. They believed the Dokami were evil because of their ability to read minds and do strange things so they decided to outcast them. Our ancestors were driven out of the city and forced to live in an enclosed reservation to 'protect' them from angry Jmugeans who sought to kill them. It wasn't long before the reservation began to feel more like a prison than protection.

One day, a Dokami female displayed too much knowledge about a secret operation to drive out the Shaergans. She was maliciously killed for the public to see. The Dokami mourned her death and decided that it was time to leave their beloved planet and go somewhere far away from civilization to live out the rest of their life in peace. During the night, leaders of the Dokami clan stole a spacecraft and took their people out of Jmugea to find a distant planet to inhabit, which was no easy task, considering the complete destruction of several planets at that time.

Miraculously, they found a small planet that was still intact and very inhabitable. This planet had a nice climate, lush, green forests, and large bodies of water. The previous inhabitants had long since evacuated, fearing that their planet would be destroyed much like the others in close proximity of it. In fact, in the sky, the Dokami could still see the remains of a devastated planet. It was a harsh reminder that as long as there were wars to conquer planets, they were not entirely safe. They named this planet Dokar, meaning 'peace and tranquility' and adopted it as their own."

"Thank you, Fajha," Hamilda said, waking up Atakos who had begun to fall asleep. "That was amazingly … detailed."

Fajha was very proud of himself. "When you told it to us, I wrote it down and study it all the time."

"That's wonderful! I have faith that our story won't be forgotten. At least in the next generation. Who wants to continue?"

Zadeia spoke up then, no longer on the verge of tears. "Decades passed and, with the freedom to do as they pleased, the Dokami strengthened their powers and numbers. Word spread that the Dokami had moved to a small deserted planet and, because their abilities were well known by the inhabitants of Jmugea, somehow the notion came about that they could be controlled, that whoever could make them their slaves could use them to win the interstellar wars. But the Dokami were not easily controlled.

When the spaceships of soldiers from Jmugea landed on their planet and attacked them, what was once a peaceful clan fought and killed those who tried to take them prisoner once again. When the last of those soldiers were destroyed, and before the Jmugeans could make another attempt, the Dokami devised a plan to prevent more devastation and loss of life.

By now, the Dokami were fairly strong and had multiplied from being only a few hundred, to having a population of over five hundred thousand inhabitants. They mentally communicated around the entire planet, instructing each and every Dokami to use their powers to move Dokar. This was very difficult to achieve but, after a few failed attempts, their planet began to move. They located a dead planet called Rute, which was five times as big as their own planet and moved Dokar behind it. The climate was colder on the other side of Rute and they saw little of the sun but the Dokami clan lived in peace for fifty years."

Atakos stepped in then to continue the story. "They were at peace until scientists from the planet Dre-Ahd discovered Dokar. They went back to their planet to form an army strong enough to overcome the incredible strength of the Dokami. The Dre-Ahds declared war against them in an attempt to capture them for their own evil purposes.

When they were hit with the worst attack ever recorded in their history, the Dokami fought back but were not strong enough to withstand the ferocious army of demon Dre-Ahds. Thousands of Dokami and Dre-Ahds died during that war and there were only several hundred Dokami left in captivity while thousands of Dre-Ahds remained, determined to bring them back to their planet and use their powers.

In the night, while the Dre-Ahds celebrated, the remaining Dokami went underground and boarded their only working spacecraft, and, at a speed so fast, they left their beloved planet. Upon reaching outer space, so as not to be followed, the Dokami used their abilities to destroy Planet Dokar along with the entire remaining Dre-Ahd Army. They then traveled millions of miles before deciding to land on Omordion when they were about to run out of fuel."

"Great job everyone," Hamilda said. "I have to say, I am impressed!" Her students looked at each other and smiled. "I will finish the story because I know you have classes to get to. When the Dokami landed on Omordion, it was recorded that Tre-akelomin Gre-ashyu, was their leader. It was his idea to land on Omordion and, for their protection, separate to different parts of Western Omordion. He appointed himself Master Wise Man and recorded every name and dates of birth of all the Dokami before they went about living their lives in freedom. He felt it best to separate because together, as a clan, they stood out as very odd people. Tre-akelomin also appointed assistants who would reside near every Dokami colony to offer advice for the growing families. Those assistants eventually came together and formed what we know today as the Dokami Council. Tre-akelomin stated that every fifty years, there would be a new Wise Man chosen to carry on the stories and the legacy of the Dokami clan.

The next Wise Man appointed after him was a female Dokami by the name of Maes Minat. She was the one who developed our system of restraint, teaching every Dokami how to resist the temptation to use their powers, convincing them that they had no need for them. She had a great fear that they would be discovered if one Dokami were to use his or her powers accidentally in front of a stranger. Maes did not want her people to be attacked or held captive again. At that point they had been through so much and wanted to just be free.

We Dokami lived in peace once again, mixing with the inhabitants of Omordion, for three hundred years. The Dokami Council is said to have a record of every Dokami born since then except for a few 'lost ones' who managed to stay off their radar. I'm not sure what became of them, but our secret still remains so they must be doing a good job of keeping it."

Hamilda glanced around the room at her pupils. "And that, ladies and gentlemen, is where we end our test of the Dokami clan. Any questions?"

"I have a question," Fajha said. "When the Dokami were reborn, how did they remember about their ancestry?"

"Yes," Zadeia said. "How did they know their kind used to exist and how did they know who was a member of their race and who was not?"

"Not much is known about the Dokami. I have only reiterated what was told to me. I do know that we Dokami, in general, have an amazing sense of who we are and, if tapped into it, we have the ability to 'feel' people out and discover who they really are." Hamilda sighed. "I am not sure how they were able to remember the past lives they lived. That is an ability that I do not possess. Do you have any other questions?"

"Why did Bontihm decide it was best to eventually expose us to the world and, potentially, to the entire universe?" Atakos said.

"Bontihm made that choice with the Dokami Council. If Eastern Omordion were to take over our side, they would capture all of us and, if that were to happen, under their control they would discover who we are and use us for their own evil purposes, much like the Jmugeans and the Dre-Ahds attempted to do long ago. Because there are millions of Dokami descendants living in all parts of Western Omordion, it would be impossible to relocate, especially since many of them have married and have children with Omordions. They have lived a very normal life, not even knowing about their ancestry."

"What are we going to do if, when we end this war, other threats come, possibly in Omordion itself?" Zimi said.

"We have signed an agreement with Western Omordion to leave us at peace when the war is officially over, but if there are others who seek to control us, we will have to fight until we are free."

"What if we don't win the war?" Cristaden asked in a small voice.

"That, my children, is an impossibility."

Silence fell over the entire room as the friends glanced at each other. It was a tremendous amount of pressure.

"But let's not worry about that," Hamilda said, sensing their fear. "We still have a long way to go if we are going to win this war. You are dismissed to go to your scheduled classes. I will let you know when we are going to meet again."

The teens got up and filtered out of the room.

"Have a nice day Hamilda," Zadeia said, turning back to look at her. "Tell Jogesh I said hello."

"I will," Hamilda said with a big smile. "See you tomorrow."

When the five teens left the room, Cristaden voiced a concern. "Did anyone realize that Hamilda was not herself today?"

"I did pick that up," Fajha said. "She seemed almost ... depressed. Not at all like her usually happy nature."

"Maybe it's the weather," Zadeia said. "It puts a damper on my mood when it's dark, wet, and gloomy outside."

"Your mood is always damp," Zimi said.

Cristaden shook her head as they entered the elevator. "No, it seemed like it was much more than the weather. Like her mind was somewhere else. Even as she spoke, it did not seem like she was really enjoying what she was talking about. I got a weird vibe from her."

"I don't know what it could be," Atakos said, "but if it were something important, don't you think she would have told us? There are no real secrets between us."

"That's true," Zimi said. "It's probably something very minor. Nothing to worry about."

The elevator reached the ground floor and the five teens got out.

"You're probably right, Zimi," Fajha said. "Anyways, I would love to stay and chat but I have to run to my geography class. See you all later."

"Hey, wait up," Atakos said. "I'm going that way to mechanics. Are you coming Zimi?"

"Yeah, my environmental science class is in the same building, remember? Bye girls, we'll see you after class," Zimi said, racing out the front door with the other boys.

"Bye guys!" Cristaden and Zadeia said.

Cristaden sighed. "I still think there's something seriously bothering our teacher."

"Yes, I'm really worried about her," Zadeia said. "But I guess if it was really important, she would have told us."

Cristaden looked worried. "Her mind was closed off. I could not read her."

"That's odd," Zadeia frowned.

Cristaden sighed. "I guess we'll find out when she wants to tell us. Come on. Let's clean up that messy room of ours," she said, smiling.

"You say it as if it's a fun thing to do," Zadeia said.

"It is! What do you suppose we do to pass by the time?"

"Something a little spontaneous wouldn't hurt," Zadeia said sarcastically. "Even throwing rocks at a wall is better than that."

Cristaden laughed as they took the elevator back up to the fourth floor.

When her pupils left the conference room, Hamilda sunk down into her chair and put her face in her hands. She wept for a while before deciding to return to her apartment.

Upon reaching her door, Hamilda saw a letter sticking out of the bottom. She slowly picked up the letter and read the words on the envelope. In big bold, red letters, it said:

Mrs. Hamilda Shing
URGENT

Hamilda was afraid to open it but, instead, held it tight in her hand, fumbling to unlock the door with her key. She stepped into the living room and made her way to the window seat in the bedroom and sat down. The world outside her window seemed dull, gray, and depressing. She just wanted to curl up with her soft blanket and sleep the days away, forgetting all her worries.

Sighing, Hamilda decided to open the letter. It was best to find out what it said sooner rather than later. Tearing it open, she saw that it was written in Jogesh's handwriting. A sense of relief flooded her heart and she let out the breath she was holding. He was still alive. She smiled and read his letter.

> *My Dearest,*
>
> *Even though it has been a little over a week since I've seen you last, it feels like an eternity. I'm writing this to inform you that we have infiltrated the largest band of Feim soldiers here in Southern Udnaruk. We snuck up on them in the night and ambushed them. It was fairly easy to take them out but we had several casualties on our side, which was small compared to what we did to those horrific soldiers.*
>
> *We are currently at the Southern Udnaruk army base awaiting orders to attack a few more pockets of the enemy's operation and take the rest of them out. This mission should be even easier than the last one because they are in smaller numbers. We are sending a messenger to update General Komuh on our progress so I will send this letter with him, hoping that you will read it and know that everything is okay. As soon as we are done, I will be coming home to you for good. Our new, younger soldiers should be ready to fend off any new attack after this one so the army will have no more need for us retirees.*
>
> *Don't worry for me, my darling, I will return to you as soon as we are done with this mission and we will be together forever—nothing will take me away from your side again.*
>
> *Love Always,*
> *Jo*

Hamilda clutched the letter to her chest, tears streaming down her face. It was strange how Jogesh had only been away from her for a short period of time but she felt like she was dying a slow death. There were times, throughout the war, that she would not see him for a year or more but was always confident that he would return home safely, which he always did. Yet this time was different. She wasn't as confident as she had been in the past.

Hamilda stood up and walked over to the bed, still clutching the letter as if she were afraid to lose it. She then placed her head on her pillow and pulled the blanket over it. She allowed herself to drift into a deep sleep, hoping that she would forget her worries while she slept, even if it were only for a couple of hours.

CHAPTER 8

Specialists of the Western Army crouched silently in the bushes outside of Chrulm Village, waiting for their chance to strike. It had been a tough battle to get to their final destination. These bands of Feim soldiers were ruthless, unlike anything they had ever seen before. Their fast, almost demon-like movements were one of the reasons why they overtook the Southern Udnaruk Army with such ease. They wore heavy, gray armor made of some kind of special metal that could not be easily penetrated. The masks they wore resembled demon faces with big, angry eyes and a mouth with sharp teeth that extended from ear to ear in a devilish grin. Those who had their masks off appeared to look like demons without it. Their faces were distorted and full of rage and they spoke very harshly to each other as if they were monsters that did not have an ounce of kindness in their bones. To stare one down in battle was to stare at the ultimate face of evil.

A face one would never forget.

Night fell.

Jogesh signaled to the seventy-three men crouching around him that it was the time to attack but to stay low and be quiet. Most of the Feim soldiers were asleep on the ground and in tents, except for a few night watchmen.

Jogesh motioned for the men to quietly follow him. They pulled out their weapons and moved silently through the trees, careful not to alert the enemy. All was quiet in the forest and in the enemy camp that it seemed as if they would launch their attack undetected and the battle would be over fairly quickly.

Once they reached the outside of the clearing, Jogesh put his hand up to signify them to halt. It was still very quiet. There was not a stir from any of the sleeping soldiers and, under the cover of darkness, the watchmen still had not spotted them. With one more glance around the entire clearing, Jogesh put his arm down to signal the men to move in.

They ran a few steps ahead into the clearing but halted when the Feim soldiers suddenly stood up with their swords drawn. They were feigning sleep, awaiting the attack they knew was eventually coming. Taken by surprise, Jogesh stopped his men.

One extremely hideous soldier stepped forward. Since his armor was the only red and gold one, Jogesh assumed he was their leader. "Good evening, soldiers of the Western Army," he said, practically growling. "We have been awaiting your attack for a few days now. When you first came to spy on us."

"If that's so," Jogesh said, "why didn't you just attack us first?"

The Feim leader laughed. "We like this little game you play. It is fun for us. Besides, it is much more of a challenge if you strike first. It would not be worthwhile if we killed you while you were unaware." He stepped forward and stared down at Jogesh. "Only cowards would do such a thing."

"I'll show you coward!" Jogesh shouted as he moved quickly towards him. Before the leader could take out his sword, Jogesh was already upon him. With one clean swing, he decapitated the demon leader and, without hesitation, swung his sword at the men who were standing behind him.

On cue, both sides began to fight. The soldiers of the Western Army had no mercy for the Feim soldiers and were cutting their way through the camp. Although the Feim soldiers were prepared for their attack, they underestimated the shear strength of Jogesh's platoon. He watched as the enemy knocked a sword out of a comrade's hand. The soldier picked up a heavy piece of burning log from a nearby fire and hit the side of his opponent's head, burning him and knocking the hideous demon mask off. Blood poured from the enemy's mouth, which he wiped away as he stood back up. The western soldier swung the log harder, this time knocking him unconscious. He then picked up his sword and drove it through the Feim soldier's heart, insuring that he was dead.

The battle ensued for a couple of hours. The few remaining Feim soldiers were trying to hold their own against the fifty remaining western soldiers but they were fighting a losing battle. One by one, they went down.

Jogesh knocked down a Feim soldier and plunged his sword into his heart, killing him instantly. He took a moment to survey the area and watched as every last Feim soldier was brought down and killed. He felt triumphant. Another battle won under his command.

Jogesh had no time to react. He let his guard down too soon. He did not hear the hidden Feim soldier that ran out from the trees behind him until it was too late. The merciless soldier ran up to Jogesh with his sword over his head and brought it down, slashing a deep, diagonal wound from his left shoulder, through his back and all the way to his right hip. Jogesh dropped to his knees and then fell onto his side. His fellow troops noticed what was going on and ran over to assist him but they were too far to reach him in time. All Jogesh saw was the enemy getting on top of him, raising his sword, and bringing it down quickly.

Jogesh belted out a high-pitched cry. "HAMILDA!!!"

Drenched in sweat, Hamilda suddenly woke up. It was dark in her room, the only light coming from an orange full moon outside her window. She was having a dreadful dream about soldiers being killed left and right by gruesome looking demons. She then thought she heard a loud cry of her name coming from a voice sounding much like Jogesh.

Breathing heavily, Hamilda ran to the window and opened it, taking in deep breaths of cool, night air. She was terrified and hyperventilating, her heart beating so fast she could not breathe. It felt like the world was closing in around her and she began to sob uncontrollably. She hastily did her routine, silent prayers that Jogesh was okay, that he was well protected and would come back to her safely. She hoped that it was only a dream, that it was not the present or the near future because, if it were real, it would mean that Jogesh did not or will not make it out alive. All she could do was hope that it wasn't so.

Hamilda paced back and forth in her bedroom and decided that she could not possibly go back to sleep. She feared that, as soon as she closed her eyes again, she would see those awful faces and hear the cries of dying men. She went into the kitchen and spotted the unfinished pottery that Jogesh was painting right before he left and she decided to finish it. It would be a very lovely red vase full of flowers for him upon his return, she vowed.

Upon his return, Hamilda thought confidently.

The following morning, Hamilda was making breakfast when a knock came at her door. Wiping her hands on a towel, she stole a glance at the finished vase on the kitchen table. She smiled to herself, knowing that she had accomplished what she had set out to do.

As Hamilda approached the door, she began to get a sinking feeling in the pit of her stomach. The aura coming from behind the door was not necessarily a bad one, but it seemed very sad and heavy. She hesitated to open the door.

"Who is it?" she said slowly.

A deep, masculine voice came from behind the door. "I have a message from General Komuh, madam. It's very important."

Hamilda's body became rigid while her heart skipped a beat. She opened the door with a shaky hand.

"Good morning, madam," the tall, young soldier greeted. "My name is Lieutenant Gaojh. I am sorry to disturb you at this hour but I was told to give you a message personally and immediately. General Komuh wanted to come here himself but he is not in the area at this present time."

Hamilda wanted to rush the soldier but decided to let him take his time with the news. She was hoping that it had something to do with her mission and not Jogesh.

"I am pleased to inform you that, during the night, the remaining soldiers from the Feim army were annihilated by our team of specialists and the battle is now over." He tipped his hat at her satisfyingly. "But I …"

Hamilda wanted to grab him and shake it out of him. "Go on."

"But I regret to inform you that Captain Jogesh Shing, of the Western Army, who fought bravely and heroically throughout the battle, has been killed by the enemy last night during …"

Hamilda didn't hear or want to hear the rest of what he was saying because she already knew what took place the night before.

"Thank you," Hamilda said, cutting the soldier off. She shut the door abruptly and leaned against it. She could hear the soldier's footsteps walking towards the elevator where he met Principal Rohjees. She heard the two men mumble a few things to each other before entering the elevator. They were most likely discussing leaving her alone to grieve. She closed her eyes and waited until there was complete silence. Again, just as the night before, she felt as if she could not breathe. The tears did not come immediately though. She was more in shock than anything. In shock that Jogesh would, indeed, not be returning to her.

"He's not okay," Hamilda mumbled. "He's not okay." She repeated it to herself several more times as if she was trying to make sense of those three words. As if it could not possibly be true. She tried to walk forward but her knees felt weak. She leaned back against the door and sunk to the ground, then hugged her knees. Staring off at the opposite wall, she was afraid to blink and react. An image of Jogesh floated to her mind and she finally broke into a fit of tears. The tears turned into cries of pain and devastation. "Jo," she said. "You just wrote me a letter. You were *fine*. Why did this have to happen to you? How could this happen? You *promised* me you would come back."

Hamilda buried her face in her arms while her fallen tears soaked the carpet. Her cries became louder until she was practically screaming. She sunk down to the carpet and cried for a long time, curled up in a fetal position. She felt as if she was slowly dying, as if the world was somehow weighing itself upon her heart. Her insides felt as though they were about to burst and her stomach was twisting in pain. She dreamt that Jogesh was lying next to her, holding her hand, but it was not true. He wasn't there and he would never come back to hold her again.

Hamilda began to think random, crazy thoughts. She thought that if she had been there to help him, he would not have died. She would have protected him from a distance. The army would not have known she was there. No one would have seen her use her power. She could have crushed the enemy's skulls with her mind. They would not have known what hit them. But no, she could not have helped Jogesh because she had to stay and do her duty teaching the children.

Duty? It was that 'duty' that caused her to let her husband fend off monsters by himself. It was that 'duty' that kept her from having children of her own and carrying on Jogesh's legacy. It was that 'duty' that confined her to stay within the walls of Lochenby, a school she resented, ten months out of the year for the past ten years. It was that 'duty' that caused her to lose the one thing in her life that meant more to her than life itself. She lost her companion, her lover, and the man who helped her through the hardest times in her life. He was gone. All because of that 'duty'.

Hamilda's sadness began to dissipate and was replaced by anger. She began to feel resentment towards her mission, resentment towards the leaders of Western Omordion, including General Komuh. Resentment towards Lochenby, and even resentment towards her students, the ones she loved as if they were her own. If it wasn't for the decision Bontihm made, she would not have remained there to teach them everything she knew. She would not have wasted years of her life dedicating herself to a useless cause—

No, this isn't right, Hamilda thought. *I should not hate the cause or anyone involved in it. Especially my apprentices. What is wrong with me? This isn't their fault. What if what happened to Jogesh was his destiny and things are this way because they're supposed to be?* She frowned. *I can't believe that. I could have* done *something. This time, I could have stopped it. This time—*

The accident. The memory of it came back to Hamilda then, hitting her like a freight train. It was enough to send her into a fit of rage. She started pounding her fists on the carpeted floor and belched out a horrifying scream.

CHAPTER 9

"Atakos," Coach Mulhn said, "it's your turn to spar with Len."

Atakos rose from his seat in the bleachers and glanced at Len. The only other student in the entire school who could beat him was his friend, Bho. Even with his jumpsuit on, Len still looked big and muscular which was incredibly scary to Atakos. He looked down at Rhokh, who was sitting next to him, and gulped. His friend only shrugged his shoulders while shaking his head.

For the past month, his combat class was learning the art of fencing which Atakos began to detest, unlike the other courses in combat. It didn't help that Len was Coach Mulhn's assistant.

Taking their place on the mat in the middle of the floor, the boys zipped up the top of their green and black, protective jumpsuits and put on their masks. They lifted their foils and stood en garde. The distant cry of the coach to begin was barely audible over the roar of the other students. Atakos lunged toward Len who did a quick retreat backwards. Before Atakos could recover back into an en garde position, Len did a quick forward advance with a lunge at his torso. There was a loud uproar of whistles and applause when his foil made contact.

Just as the boys retreated to an en garde position once again, the gymnasium door flew open, silencing the students.

Principal Rohjees walked in, a solemn look on his aging face. All eyes were on him when he approached Coach Mulhn and whispered something to him. Coach Mulhn turned to look at Atakos and motioned for him to go with Rohjees.

Wondering what it could possibly be about, Atakos looked at Rohjees, hoping to find some answers. Rohjees only turned to walk out of the gymnasium and Atakos trailed behind him, deciding not to ask any questions but fearing that it was very bad news.

"Can anyone tell me which part of the brain is responsible for visual processing?" the anatomy teacher, Mrs. Noume, asked.

Cristaden did not want to respond. She was always raising her hand with the right answers, which made most of the students in her class seriously dislike her. They were even more upset because she was a full year younger than them, having scored very high on all the placement tests. As if to make matters worse, her teacher always called on her when no other student raised their hand.

"Cristaden? Do you know the answer, dear?" the gray-haired teacher asked sweetly.

Cristaden sighed but was interrupted when a spark ignited in her head. She immediately looked up at the closed door expecting to see someone standing there. There was no one.

What was that? Cristaden thought before looking back at Mrs. Noume.

Just then, the door opened and Principal Rohjees stepped into the classroom. *That explains it.* Cristaden often received a forewarning before someone of importance comes into a room. Rohjees quickly glanced around before bringing his attention to Mrs. Noume. He spoke to her quietly, keeping his voice low so the other students would not hear.

"Why of course she's here," Mrs. Noume ignorantly said out loud. "Cristaden. Come here, dear. You have to go to the principal's office right now. He has some important matters to discuss with you."

Rohjees brought his hand to his temple, trying to hide his annoyance with the teacher.

What does he want me for? Cristaden noticed he was sad about something, though, but did not have time to pinpoint exactly what it was. After she gathered her books and walked up to the principal, he ushered her out of the room very quickly and closed the door behind them, meeting Atakos in the hall. When Cristaden saw him, her worries turned to fear. They exchanged glances and Atakos shrugged his shoulders and mouthed the words 'I don't know'.

Zimi and Zadeia were in their Biology Lab class, wearing their protective goggles, dissecting a species of the rodent family. The students were separated into groups of two and were so focused on their dissections that they did not notice when the door opened and Principal Rohjees came in to talk to their teacher.

"Zimi, Zadeia, please come up to the front of the room," Ms. Leit, the young, brown-haired biology teacher said. "All other students continue with your work."

The twins frowned as they immediately removed their goggles and lab coats and followed Rohjees. When they stepped out into the hall, they were astonished to see Cristaden and Atakos standing there, looking just as bewildered as they were.

"I just have to make one more stop," Rohjees said. He crossed the hall and entered Fajha's Geography Lab class. The students were in one large group, surrounding a center island filled with different types of soil, sand, and dirt. Each student had a notepad and pencil in their hands and they were slowly circling the table writing down which area each pile of earth most likely came from. The teacher was not in the classroom at the moment and a senior student was left in charge.

Rohjees informed the student that he needed Fajha to run an errand and that he would most likely not be returning for the rest of class. He then got Fajha's attention and told him to get his things.

Astonished, Fajha's classmates all turned to look at him, thinking that he was in some sort of trouble. Fajha knew there was nothing he could be in trouble for but still searched his memory to try to come up with a conclusion. Moments later, he stepped out into the hall and, upon seeing all his friends patiently waiting, he realized the situation was much bigger than him.

The teens went into Rohjees' office near the entrance of the school and were asked to sit down. They exchanged glances with each other as Rohjees leaned against his desk and folded his arms over his chest. The look on his face told them it was going to be very bad news.

Rohjees cleared his throat. "As you all know, I have called this meeting today to discuss an important matter." He paused and continued. "It is my unfortunate duty to inform you that Captain Jogesh Shing has perished in battle."

The confused eyes of his audience opened wide in astonishment and Cristaden brought her hands to her mouth. After a moment Zadeia began to cry. Fajha frowned and spoke up. "What do you mean he perished in battle? Wasn't he retired?"

"Indeed he was. But the retirees were called back to battle to resolve an important issue in Southern Udnaruk about two weeks ago. It was very last minute and the battle has in fact been resolved. The loss of life since the battle began was tremendous."

"How is Hamilda?" Atakos said. "Can we go see her?"

"She is grieving. You cannot see her right now."

"Why? We must see her," Cristaden demanded, standing up.

"Please sit down," Rohjees said in a soft voice. He looked at each of them before continuing. "Hamilda is in isolation right now. She asks that no one disturb her for a little while. She is trying to deal with her loss the best way she can. She has requested to withdraw from her classes to allow some time to heal. Although it would most likely take more than a week to grieve, maybe months, we cannot allow her to be away from her mission for that long. She has a duty to continue with this mission regardless of unfortunate circumstances."

"*What?*" Atakos blurted out. "Are you trying to tell us that you are only giving her a *week* to grieve the death of her husband?"

"Hamilda has a contract with the Western Army and it specifically states that, in spite of the fatalities of family members and personal issues, the mission has to be carried out as planned. Hamilda understands this fully and has agreed to do what she must." Rohjees then raised his voice. "I feel sorry for her and I wish I could take her pain away but we are still in the midst of an ongoing war. We cannot allow outside influences to sidetrack us."

"Outside influences?" Zadeia said between sobs.

"But that is ridicu—" Zimi yelled before he was interrupted.

"Enough." Rohjees stood tall. "That is all regarding this matter. You are dismissed and may go back to your rooms for the remainder of the day. I ask that you keep this information to yourselves and do not discuss it with each other any further. Your regular meetings with Hamilda will resume at the beginning of next week."

With that, he ushered them out of his office and closed the door behind them.

"What was that all about?" Zimi said as they walked out of the building. "It seemed like he was about to chew our heads off."

"He's grieving too," Cristaden said. "He just didn't want us to see it. Maybe he thinks it would be harder for us if he broke down as well."

"Poor Hamilda," Zadeia said. "I can't imagine what she must be going through."

Atakos threw his arms up. "I can't believe they're only giving her a week to grieve. That's insane."

"Do they honestly think she would be in her right mind to teach us *anything* next week?" Zimi said.

"Why didn't she tell us Jo went back to the battlefield?" Zadeia said, wiping her eyes.

Fajha shook his head. "She probably wanted us to focus on our studies and not worry about her situation."

"But why doesn't she want to see us?"

"There are so many questions that we're not going to find answers to by asking each other," Zimi said. "All we can do is hope she'll be okay."

"Yeah, but she'll never really be okay," Cristaden said.

"No kidding," Atakos agreed.

For the first time in over a week the sun had finally began to peek out of the gray clouds but darker clouds were steadily approaching once again. A roll of thunder could be heard from a distance. As a steady rain began to fall again, silence fell among the group as they walked to the dormitory, allowing themselves to get wet.

After a short time, Cristaden cleared her throat. "Well then, it's up to us to help her through it, isn't it?"

"Right," Atakos said.

CHAPTER 10

A seven year old Hamilda walked through the woods behind Lochenby. It was a calm, clear night, with the bright moon lighting her way.

She was alone.

Little Hamilda did not know how she got there nor where she was going, but she kept walking further and further into the woods.

In slow motion, two people were suddenly running through the trees ahead of her. They were holding hands and smiling, seemingly in love. She didn't see where they came from but she knew them very well.

They were her parents.

Hamilda tried to cry out to them, to get them to stop running away from her but they did not hear her. She ran after them, hoping they would stop and turn around. It wasn't until she ran pass the man with the black robe did she notice he was standing there, pointing at her parents, shouting words she could not understand.

Hamilda saw her parents turn around. They weren't smiling anymore. They were screaming and fearful for their lives. Tears were rolling down her mother's face.

Don't cry mama, little Hamilda begged. *Please don't cry.* But they didn't hear her.

Her eyes grew wide when she saw the beasts charging at them. There must have been twenty of them bent on killing her parents. All she could remember about them were the teeth. So many sharp teeth in their grotesque mouths. It wasn't until they were tearing her parents apart that she woke up screaming, drenched in sweat.

When the principal and a grief counselor came to Hamilda just moments later with the terrible news, she was in complete disbelief.

It *wasn't* a dream.

They told her there was a boating accident. That her parents had drowned. But she knew it was no accident. No words could leave her mouth to tell them that she knew they were lying. She was in shock. Someone ordered her parents dead. But even they would not know that. They were probably convinced it was a vicious animal attack of the worse kind.

When the two men left her room, Hamilda became very upset and the tears would not stop flowing. Her parents, who had left her in the care of another teacher to go out for an evening stroll, were not coming back. The more she thought about it, the more upset she became. She then started noticing objects flying across the room. She stopped crying, unsure of what was happening, and everything dropped simultaneously.

At first Hamilda did not think she had caused them to rise, but with careful consideration, she tried to move her porcelain doll, which was sitting on her pink bed, without touching it. Shocked, she watched as the doll flew to the opposite wall and broke into pieces. Besides the pain she felt because of her parents' death, she was horrified. What was *wrong* with her? For fear of what might happen to her if anyone were to find out, she remained quiet about her new discovery. Unable to control her emotions and her ability, she did not leave her room for a couple of days and refused to eat.

The day of her parents' funeral, after crying relentlessly for hours, Hamilda had fallen asleep. A hand touched her shoulder and she looked up to see what appeared to be an angel sitting next to her. She wiped her green eyes and opened them again to see if the vision would disappear but it did not. The angel was beautiful with long, blonde hair, and piercing blue eyes. White wings spread out behind her. She told Hamilda that her parents would always be with her and to not despair. Hamilda hugged the angel and felt an overwhelming sense of love and relief, as if her parents were the ones holding her. Upon opening her eyes, she saw that her room was empty once more, leaving her to wonder if it all had been a dream.

Hours later, the school principal introduced Hamilda to an old man, whom her parents had named as her only living relative. She was to leave Lochenby, because she could no longer afford to stay there, and live with the old man in the village of Hortu, which rested in the outskirts of Sheidem City. The old man, Bontihm Fhakaemeli, was not a relative at all. One of his responsibilities as Wise Man included the placement of orphaned Dokami children to good Dokami families.

Upon realizing how much strength Hamilda had, Bontihm took her under his wing as his apprentice, hoping she would one day be elected as the next Wise Man when his fifty year term was over. He taught her everything he knew about their heritage and encouraged her to increase her strength and abilities rather than suppress them. Hamilda, on the other hand, was not confident in herself, especially when she had trouble performing the tasks given to her by Bontihm.

All that changed when she met Captain Jogesh Shing of the Western Army. A descendant of the Dokami clan who had no abilities due to generations of restraint. He had given her the confidence and love she needed to increase her ability and become a very powerful Dokami. With him, she was able to push aside her dark memories of her parents' death and finally be able to live.

They married not too long after they met.

She had never been so happy.

Hamilda was sitting on the window seat by her bed. The rain outside was coming down so hard, she could barely see the fifth floor roof below. Pulling herself away from her awful and bittersweet memories, she tried to regain focus of her jumbled thoughts. She felt so much anger and hatred. Emotions that she had not felt since her parents died twenty-five years ago. She dreaded returning to her normal schedule the next day to teach those teenagers.

Looking up at a silver glass figurine of a dancing couple sitting on her nightstand, Hamilda allowed her eyes to water again. Jogesh had given it to her long ago. Without as much as changing her position or expression, she threw it against the wall, shattering it into a thousand pieces. The same was done with everything else in the room until there was nothing left to break.

Bringing her hand up to her forehead, Hamilda squeezed her eyes shut. The pressure in her brain was so unbearable, she felt as if she would never recover from it. It seemed as if there was a thick, dark cloud that had descended upon her room and wrapped itself around her. At times, she even thought she could see the cloud.

She was losing her mind.

Hamilda had not spoken to anyone or left her room in two weeks. For several days, she had neither showered nor eaten. She stayed at the window mostly, sinking into the greatest depression of her life. She felt like she had nothing to live for anymore. Looking down at the fifth floor roof, she began contemplating the worse. The ground seemed so far away. Five stories. It would be a long way down. The dark cloud began to descend upon her once again and she just wanted to escape it. She wanted to see Jogesh again. She wanted so much for the pain and suffering to end.

Finalizing her eccentric decision, Hamilda managed to stand up and open the window. She then climbed up on the seat and bowed her head to go through it. The falling rain felt so refreshing against her hair, she felt rejuvenated.

The end was near.

A sound behind Hamilda made her sharply turn around. At first she could not understand what she saw. When it finally dawned on her, the fear was so great, she thought she was having an intense heart attack.

It couldn't be.

A violent spasm of screams erupted from her, muffled by a resonating thunder clap outside.

Then everything went black.

CHAPTER 11

"Please come in General Komuh," Principal Rohjees said, motioning for the general to have a seat. "I was just going over the schedule for the upcoming month."

Komuh did not sit down. He removed his hat and got right down to business. "How is the status with Hamilda Shing? Have you spoken to her yet? Did she resume her teachings?"

Rohjees stood up and scratched his bald head. Being a tall man himself, he was still not as big as the general. He felt like a cornered animal that had no choice but to defend itself. "I have made several attempts to speak to her, to get her to come out of her apartment, but I have been given no response. As of right now, she's still in her room—"

"What?!" General Komuh was furious, his thick eyebrows turning down into a scowl. "That is unacceptable, Rohjees. She fully understands what her duties are and there are *no* excuses. Do you have the key to her apartment?"

"Why, yes. I do." The principal rubbed his full beard. He genuinely felt bad for Hamilda and didn't want to disturb her.

"Well, what are you waiting for? Let's get her out of there. If she needs therapy, we'll give it to her. But she can't stay in there any longer. It has been almost *two weeks*."

General Komuh stormed out of the office and met two officers standing in the hallway. Rohjees slowly took the school's only master key from his pocket. He then regrettably unlocked a box in his top drawer that held the keys to all the rooms in the school and located the one marked 1013.

"What's taking so long Rohjees?" the general's voice boomed from the hall.

Rohjees quickly stepped out of his office. "I was just getting the key, sir."

The four men left the school and briskly walked to the dormitory. After days of rain, the sun was finally shining and the weather was unseasonably warm. They entered the dormitory, and then boarded the elevator to the tenth floor. Rohjees took a deep breath upon reaching the end of the hall and knocked on Hamilda's door. "Hamilda? Principal Rohjees again. General Komuh has come to see if you're okay." It was a lie but he felt like he had to say something comforting. When there was no response, Komuh grabbed the key from his hand.

"Wait!"

Komuh frowned at Rohjees and ignored his plea. "Hamilda, we're coming in whether you like it or not!" he yelled. He then fumbled with the key and unlocked the door, opening it slightly.

From the tiny crack of the opened door, the general saw something he was not expecting to see. He opened the door wider and stared in disbelief. The entire living room and kitchen were in disarray. Broken plates and bowls littered both rooms. A hand painted, red vase lay cracked on the floor in front of them. The four men slowly walked in to survey the area with caution.

A weird feeling began to form in the pit of Komuh's stomach. "Hamilda?" he said. He received no response. Making his way to her bedroom, he was reluctant to go in, fearing what he might see.

"What happened here?" Rohjees whispered from behind him, not expecting to get a response back. The other two soldiers were on high alert. This was not a normal situation.

The door to Hamilda's room was closed and Komuh signaled to the other soldiers to get ready for anything. Upon opening the door, he and the other three men saw something even more astonishing.

"She's gone!" Rohjees said.

Komuh surveyed the area. The bed sheets were off the bed and there was a broken lamp and several other broken figurines, all of which looked as though they were thrown up against the wall. The large mirror sitting on the dresser was also broken but there was nothing to indicate what broke it. The window stood wide open and the general went to it, looking down to the fifth floor roof. No body. There was no sign of life anywhere in the apartment or on the ledge. All of Hamilda's belongings were still there, even a pair of shoes that was on the window seat.

"Do you think she ran away?" Rohjees asked.

"No," Komuh said, surveying the room. "Look, her key is on the nightstand. She would have needed it to lock the door behind her if she had run away. Isn't that right?"

"That's true, but ..."

"Also, if you notice, her essentials are still here. There's currency and jewelry on her dresser." He opened the dresser and then the closet. "Her draws and closet still appears full, so she must not have taken any or much of her clothes."

"Sir!" one of the soldiers cried out.

Komuh rushed to his side. The floor at the base of the window was discolored. He couldn't believe he didn't see it before. As he surveyed the area around the window, his breath suddenly began to come out in short gasps and the color drained from his face.

"There has been a struggle here."

"How do you know?" Rohjees said, quickly coming to look at the stain.

Blood. Lots of blood. There were tiny droplets here and there along the wall and window and even on Hamilda's shoes.

"You two," General Komuh said, pointing to his soldiers. "Go down to the fifth floor roof. Check to see if there's any evidence of blood or a body that has been removed." He rushed out of the room, signaling Rohjees to come with him.

"Where are we going?" Rohjees said.

"We have a murder or a kidnapping on our hands and as far as I know it, those kids are in danger."

CHAPTER 12

Something was very wrong.

In all the years in Lochenby, General Komuh never pulled the teens out of their classes in this manner. The sense of urgency was definitely high when they and their principal were ushered into the two army vehicles awaiting them in front of the school. The general looked upset, shocked even, and didn't say much about where they were headed or why they were leaving.

After a short drive, the tall buildings of Sheidem City came into view, their high arches and towers seemingly grazing the sky. It was a rare sight. Only during few occasions were they allowed to exit the premises of the school with their families and accompany them to any one of the city's seven luxurious hotels. They now took in the atmosphere they so longed to be a part of, away from the day-to-day activities of Lochenby and the stresses of doing what was required of them. Along the way, people stared at the passing army vehicles wondering what kind of trouble the students from Lochenby were in.

Before they knew it, they had turned off the road at a sign that read 'Western Army'.

"What's going on?" Zadeia whispered when they passed the secured gates of the base. "Why are they taking us here?"

"I don't know," Cristaden said, "but I have a strong feeling it has something to do with Hamilda. And it's not good." Zadeia burst into tears and Cristaden put her arm around her. She wanted so much to reassure her, to tell her that there was nothing to worry about, but she couldn't lie. She knew it wasn't true.

The vehicles stopped outside a building marked 'Army Headquarters'. The three men ushered the five teens and Rohjees out of the vehicles quickly and entered the secured building. They passed a door that read 'General Komuh' but the general directed them to the conference room next to his office. The two soldiers did not go in but instead stood outside as if they were standing guard.

The five friends sat around the large oval table, nervously looking between Komuh and Rohjees for answers. Their principal seemed terrified, the color drained completely from his face.

"Ok," Komuh said, "I wish I could have brought you here under different circumstances. But..." He cleared his throat and took a deep breath. "Your principal and I took it upon ourselves to enter Hamilda's apartment today after not hearing from her for nearly two weeks. When we went in, we were discouraged to find that she was not there. Furthermore, with evidence, I have ruled her disappearance as a kidnapping."

"Kidnapping?" the teens asked in unison.

"How are you so sure she was kidnapped?" Fajha said. "What kind of evidence did you find?"

"Hamilda left everything behind, including her keys, which is needed to lock her door. Her door was *locked*. We saw splatters of blood in her room but nowhere else in her apartment or on the fifth floor roof. No body was found. The only thing we haven't figured out was how they did it without being seen. They would have had to climb the building to the tenth floor. And leave the *same way*. With Hamilda." Komuh looked at Rohjees. "Was there anyone with a key to her apartment?"

"The only other person who had a key besides me was Jogesh."

"It could not have been done with Jogesh's key. His body is still at the Southern Udnaruk base, awaiting a proper burial, along with all of his belongings. It had to be someone at Lochenby."

Rohjees fumed. "Are you suggesting that this was an inside job, that there has been some kind of breach of security within the walls of Lochenby?"

"How else could you explain someone being able to kidnap her and locking the door behind them? I don't believe they came in and out through the window. This person must know the ins and outs of the school in order to carry out such a devious plan and not get caught."

Rohjees looked bewildered. "But I keep my master key with me at all times and all the dormitory keys in a *locked box.*"

Komuh shook his head and sighed. "Right now, we have no suspects," he said, turning to the teenagers. "Whether or not this person knows about the mission, I do not know. But if Hamilda was kidnapped, there's a big possibility that they do. There is no other motive. Hamilda has no fortune and she is not set to inherit anything. As far as I know, the five of you are not safe as long as this kidnapper and whomever they're working with is still out there. Currently I have army investigators looking into this situation as we speak. Until this is resolved, all of you have to be under direct surveillance at all times."

"But that could be months," Rohjees complained. He shut his mouth quickly when the general shot him a suspicious look.

Komuh then directed his attention back to the teens. "I will contact your families immediately to inform them of the situation. Each of you will be given a chance to speak to them. Are there any questions?"

The teens glanced at each other. This was something they needed to discuss without the presence of the general. Collectively, they decided not to say anything.

"That's fine," Komuh said. "When questions arise you should feel free to ask me anytime. Right now I will contact your families after I have a word with your *principal.*" He glowered at Rohjees before leaving the room, prompting him to follow.

Once the two men left the room, everyone turned to look at Cristaden.

"Did you get anything from what the general was thinking?" Atakos asked her.

"I got very vague impressions from him. Remember, I can't totally read minds, I can only hear a few words here and there and get a 'feel' of his emotions." Cristaden lowered her voice. "I do know that he suspects Rohjees."

"That's obvious," Fajha said. "What did you get from Rohjees?"

"The man is completely innocent," Cristaden said. "He knows nothing. He is very fearful because he knows that everyone is a suspect until proven innocent. Especially him."

"Of course," Zimi said, "he is the primary suspect. He's the only one who has direct access to all the rooms."

"Exactly. I'm pretty sure he's already under investigation and does not even know it yet—which worries me."

"Why?" Zadeia said.

"Because if they are investigating him, they are not looking where they should be," Atakos answered for Cristadan. "Which means—"

"They won't find Hamilda," Fajha finished.

Zadeia wiped her red eyes and sniffled. "Well then it's up to us to find her."

The group fell silent. It seemed like an impossible feat.

"She's right," Atakos said after some thought. "If Hamilda is not found right away, she could be killed … if she hasn't been killed already."

"It seems like the best possible solution," Cristaden said. "But, if you haven't noticed, we are surrounded by soldiers on a secured *military base.* How are we supposed to get by them?"

"And even if we *do* manage to escape, how are we going to find Hamilda?" Zimi said. "Where would we begin?"

"We can't commandeer a vehicle," Atakos said. "Who here knows how to drive?"

With no response, the group fell silent again. Just then General Komuh came back. *Without Rohjees.*

"Fajha," Komuh said, "I have your parents on the communicator in my office. The rest of you will get a chance to speak to your parents one at a time." He motioned for a soldier to come into the room. "For your protection." He smiled at the remaining four and left with Fajha.

With the soldier standing at the doorway, the teens couldn't say anything more regarding the situation. Instead, they talked about their classes and activities, all the while hoping the soldier would be told to leave. But he did not leave. As each of them was sent out to talk to his or her parents, he remained grounded, staring straight at the opposite wall without blinking.

When Zimi and Zadeia came back into the room, they explained to their friends how their father had been caught up in the ambush that prompted the army to send Jogesh and the other retirees to Southern Udnaruk. They were all relieved that he had escaped and was still alive. Sadly, they wished Jogesh had escaped unharmed as well.

"How's your mother doing with her sickness?" Cristaden asked Atakos when he returned from talking with his parents.

"She's not feeling any better," Atakos said sadly. Then he narrowed his eyes. "Hey, I don't ever recall telling you about her, did I?"

Cristaden's eyes widened and she suddenly glanced nervously at the soldier who never blinked. "Well … yeah, of course you did. You don't remember that time …" She made a motion towards the soldier with her eyes.

Atakos then realized Cristaden had made a mistake bringing up his mother around the stranger. He never did tell her, she 'read' it off of him and, without realizing it, brought it up, trying to make casual conversation. "Oh, yes. Now I remember … Your birthday is tomorrow," he said, trying to change the subject.

"Yeah, I guess we're not going to have that party we were planning on having for you," Fajha said.

"You were planning a party for me?"

"Of course, but it was just going to be something small," Zadeia said.

"That's really sweet." When hearing about the party that will never take place, tears filled Cristaden's eyes. "Thank you," she said sadly.

Zimi, who was sitting next to her, reached over and gave her shoulder a squeeze. The atmosphere turned sour as the friends realized that they were going to be at the base for a while until they could make their escape. For how long, they did not know.

General Komuh walked in and dismissed the soldier. "Sorry to keep you waiting ladies and gentlemen. For the time being, we have arranged sleeping quarters for you. I'm afraid it's one room for all of you, girls and boys. We cannot risk separating you in case of any undesirable situations."

"What kind of 'undesirable situation' could happen on an army base?" Fajha asked.

"Well, if you haven't forgotten, we are in the middle of a war. So far, the Eastern Army has not come to this region at all. But that does not mean we are not subject to any surprise attacks. I will personally escort you children to your room in the barracks."

As they followed the general, they saw the sun setting in the bright orange sky. Freshly fallen rain made the sidewalks sparkle like little diamonds embedded in the ground. They must have been in the headquarters for a long time. It was way past dinnertime.

"You will be given food when you reach your room," General Komuh said, as if reading their minds.

"What about our clothes?" Zadeia asked him.

"I have already made arrangements to have those picked up tomorrow by my soldiers."

"Are they getting *everything*?"

"Of course not, only your essentials."

Zadeia saw an opportunity. "But how will they know what our essentials are? How will they know what we need?"

"I'm sure they could figure it out," Komuh said bluntly. "It's not that difficult."

"What I consider an essential may not be the same for *normal* people," Zadeia said, taking advantage of the general's ignorance.

Cristaden caught on to what she was trying to do. "Yes. For instance, I have two different kinds of toothpaste. One I use in the morning, and one I have to use at night for my 'special' teeth. What if they grab just one? I'll lose all my teeth!"

General Komuh frowned at her. "Just write it down, I'm sure they can read."

"I have medication," Atakos chipped in. "It's in an enormous box that only I can open. It doesn't have a key."

The general glared at him.

"I have special shampoo I have to use every day. If they can't find it, I'll lose all my hair!" Zimi cried out.

The general glared at him, too.

Oh, great, Atakos thought, *now he's never going to believe us.*

General Komuh considered it for a moment, rubbing his horseshoe mustache. "Okay. Tomorrow morning you will be escorted back to the school to collect your belongings and 'special' things. But you can only fill one bag and you will have only five minutes. That's it."

Atakos let go of the breath he was holding. *Thank goodness.*

When they reached the largest building in the center of the base, they overheard General Komuh telling three soldiers to stand guard outside their room throughout the night. Three more soldiers would come before dawn to relieve them. Then they were taken to a long, narrow room with five small beds on the second floor. The walls were a dull green color that matched the bed sheets but the floor was sparkling white. The one window in the room was tiny with three bars running across it.

"Okay kids, you will find temporary night clothes in the closet next to the bathroom so you don't have to sleep in your uniforms. Toothbrushes and paste are in the bathroom," he then looked at Cristaden, "for those of you who can brush your teeth. Your food will be here within the next half hour. I hope you have a nice night and I apologize for the inconvenience." With that, he left them alone in the room, shutting the door and locking it behind him.

"Is this protection or jail?" Zimi said, sitting on the first bed.

"Shhh," Fajha said. He pointed towards the door and began to whisper. "We have to keep our voices down so *Ligmi*, *Tigle*, and *Dwet* don't hear us."

"How do you know their names?" Zadeia whispered.

"He doesn't smarty," Zimi said.

"Oh."

Atakos looked at Zimi. "Thanks for that thing about the shampoo. I thought we were done for sure," he whispered sarcastically.

"What? And the amazing box that only *you* can open was better?"

"Actually, it was."

"Boys, enough useless chatter," Cristaden whispered. "We got what we wanted and that was a way out. Good job Zadeia."

"Not a problem," Zadeia whispered back.

"And," Cristaden dropped her eyes, "there's something else you should know."

"What is it?" Atakos said.

"They arrested Rohjees."

"What?"

Zadeia burst into tears.

Zimi sighed and gently took her hand to reassure her. "It's not like we didn't see that coming," he said.

"I know," she said, sniffling.

There was silence among the group for a few minutes until Fajha broke it. "When we go back to Lochenby tomorrow, we are definitely going to be heavily guarded," he said.

"Right," Atakos said. "We will have to figure out a way to elude the soldiers who accompany us."

"That's going to be difficult," Zimi said, "considering our rooms are on the fourth floor. And even if we do manage to escape, where do we go? How do we know which direction to take?"

Cristaden, Zadeia, and Atakos turned to Fajha.

"Oh no," Fajha whispered. "You can't expect me to pinpoint where Hamilda is. I'm sure she is not even in the vicinity. And my power doesn't go very far."

"Fajha, you're our only hope," Cristaden whispered. "Even if you think you can't, you have to at least *try*."

"I'll try. But it may take a while and probably won't be successful."

"We have all night."

CHAPTER 13

As the sun slowly rose over Hortu, Bontihm Fhakaemeli stepped out into his garden. He had not seen or spoken to Hamilda for several months. When he inquired about her a week ago, he was told that her husband died and she was in seclusion. Not seeing or speaking to anyone. In the very late hours of the night, he received a message from General Komuh informing him of Hamilda's kidnapping and a need to be advised on what to do with the teenagers. The general requested that he meet with him at the Western Army Base around noontime to devise a strategy.

Bontihm was so distraught and disturbed over the news of his kidnapped apprentice that he could not sleep. She was like a daughter to him and it killed him that any harm could have come to her. As for the five teens, he did not have a backup plan for the mission. At his age, he was getting too old to teach them efficiently and he could not move as fast and with as much agility as he used to when he was younger. It could take months, maybe even years, before he can locate someone worthy enough to teach them. If such a person existed. The Dokami have all been taught to restrain their powers, except Hamilda, himself, and a few outsiders who could not be trusted.

As Bontihm walked around his garden, he shook his head in disgust. He wondered who could do such a thing and what their reasoning behind the kidnapping was. Afraid for the Dokami civilization, he considered the possibility that their time at peace was coming to a horrific end because of his decision to expose them.

He had to keep reminding himself that it was a mission to save lives, not to put them all in danger. Nevertheless, he was distraught.

Bontihm walked slowly down the winding walkway and stopped next to a cherub fountain. The little angels sitting on the ledge looked as if they did not have a care in the world and that love was their only obsession. He wished for a moment that the species of the universe were just like them yet he knew that greed was an incurable disease. There will continue to be wars as long as it existed.

Taking a deep breath he went back to his house to get ready to leave for Sheidem City, all the while hoping that Hamilda was found sooner rather than later.

Cristaden opened her eyes and looked around the darkened room. The only light was a small ray of sunshine beaming through the tiny window over her head. The others were still sleeping, having just crawled into their beds a couple of hours beforehand. They spent the better part of the night trying to devise a plan to escape and convincing Fajha to keep trying to locate Hamilda. Their efforts failed. As much as he tried, Fajha could not pinpoint exactly where she was because she was simply too far away. Cristaden was not so sure there was much of a reason to escape anymore. They did not know where to *begin* looking for Hamilda.

There was a knock at the door and Cristaden realized it was what had woken her from her deep sleep.

Fajha rolled over and looked at the door. "Who's that?" he said groggily.

Cristaden shrugged as she took the drab, green sheet off of her. She climbed out of the small bed and dragged her feet to the door. Barely awake, she managed to get out a few words. "Who is it?"

"It's Lieutenant Gaojh, miss. General Komuh has instructed me to awake you. We will be leaving for Lochenby in precisely one hour."

"Thank you." Cristaden turned to the others. Fajha was already sitting up in bed and Zadeia was looking at her. "Come on, guys, we have one hour."

Atakos lifted up his head and opened one hazel eye. "Come on, give me another hour. Please?"

"We only have an hour to get ready," Fajha said. Atakos groaned and rolled out of bed. As Cristaden awoke Zimi, Fajha immediately grabbed his folded uniform off his bed and went to the bathroom. As he got ready, the others got their clothes together and straightened the sheets on their beds.

"I'm so disappointed," Zadeia said. "How are we ever going to find Hamilda?"

"I don't know, but we have to start somewhere," Atakos said.

"He's right," Zimi said. "We can't just do nothing."

Cristaden was quiet, lost in her thoughts about their escape plan. She looked up and saw Fajha coming out of the bathroom with his uniform on and his usually untamed black hair brushed and pulled back into a short ponytail.

"I'm all set," he said, putting on his glasses and going to his bed to tidy it.

Zadeia went to the bathroom next and the others sat down on the beds to wait.

"How are you feeling, Fajha?" Cristaden said.

"I'm doing okay," he said. "Just a little tension in my head, that's all."

"Sorry to put so much pressure on you last night."

"It's okay. We all serve a purpose and I was just trying to do what I do best." Fajha sat down on the bed and sighed. "I only wish it worked."

"Don't worry, we'll figure something out," Zimi said. "We are 'Omordion's Hope' aren't we? In a few years, we're supposed to take down the entire Eastern Alliance. We have to be able to find *one* person."

"Sure," Fajha said but he wasn't so sure. Feeling more pressure on his head, he crossed his legs and removed his glasses. "I need a few minutes of complete silence. I have to meditate in order to clear this pressure in my head so I can think better."

"No problem," Atakos said. He looked up as Zadeia came out of the bathroom and he quietly took his turn, explaining to her what Fajha was going to do on his way in.

Zadeia smiled at Fajha and nodded, sitting down next to Cristaden on one of the beds.

Hearing that everything was quiet, Fajha closed his eyes and pictured himself in the garden located at his grandfather's summer home again. It was what he used to get into a deep trance because it was so calm and peaceful. He imagined the maze of green hedges. This time he added bright red roses to them because they were his favorite. As he began to fall deeper and deeper into a trance, he began losing all sense of reality. He didn't even hear Atakos come out of the bathroom and Zimi go in to change.

The maze was beautiful and the sky overhead was a clear blue. The sun was shining so brightly, he could practically feel its warmth on his neck. Without even knowing it, he had made his way to the end of the maze. In front of him was a grassy hill that led down to a forest. Again, just like the last trance he was in at the stables, he saw a dark path leading into it. He wasn't so sure he wanted to go in there again but something was telling him that he had to do it.

Fajha went down the hill and stopped at the foot of the path. The forest was quiet, like before, and there were no birds chirping or wind rustling the leaves in the trees. Everything was still. He stood there for a while before deciding to enter. The trees seemed calm, the forest inviting. He loved the way the sun filtered through the leaves of the trees, casting pockets of sunshine on the forest floor. The beauty of it all convinced him to step in and walk down the leaf-ridden path.

As soon as Fajha started walking, just like his previous vision, the trees started to move ferociously, twisting and turning, roots groaning under his feet as they tried to pull themselves out of the ground. He bent down to hug his knees and cover his ears with his hands, attempting to block out the horrifying sound. But then he heard the loud shrieks of animals directly behind him. Without turning around to see what they were, he stood up and ran as the trees reached out to him, trying to grab him. He heard the ferocious beasts pounding the ground as they chased him. By their footfall, he knew they had to be really big. At the end of the darkened forest path, he saw a bright light. It seemed like his only way out so he ran towards it.

Upon reaching the bright light, the sounds of the animals disappeared and the trees stood still behind Fajha, as if they had never moved at all. In front of him loomed the giant, dark cave he saw before. But this time the vision had changed. He heard a whisper coming from inside the cave. It shocked him at first but he strained his ears to hear what it was saying. It sounded like a woman whispering. The word 'Ardomion' reached his ears before it was carried away with the wind.

Then suddenly someone was calling his name. It sounded like it was deep in the forest behind him. Turning around, he didn't see anyone. *No*, he thought, turning back around. *I have to go into the cave!* The voice got louder and louder until he felt himself being sucked back into the forest towards his name as if he were liquid in a straw.

"Fajha!"

Fajha opened his eyes. He was lying on his back, on the floor, on the other side of the room. His friends were crowded around him, trying to wake him.

"How did I get here?" Fajha said. His head hurt even worse than before. "What the …? Ohhh," he moaned softly.

Cristaden helped him to his feet and led him to the closest bed so he could sit down. "You jumped up from the bed screaming and ran to the other side of the room. When you got to the wall, you just fell backwards and stayed there, not saying anything and breathing heavily."

"Your eyes were open," Zadeia said. "All we could see were the whites of your eyes! We were so scared. We tried to wake you—"

"But it didn't work," Atakos said. "The soldiers heard you scream and they were about to come in but we convinced them that we saw a spider and you freaked out."

"How long was I out for?" Fajha said.

"About half an hour," Zimi said.

"That long? It seemed like it was only five minutes." Fajha shook his head.

"What did you see?" Cristaden said, searching his eyes. "What made you scream like that? You looked really scared. Everything in the room began to float—even the beds."

Still in shock, Fajha shook his head to clear it. "I had a vision," he said, trying to recall everything. "I've had this vision before, but this time it was much more real."

"What was it about?" Atakos said, visibly worried.

"Well. I always start my meditation in my grandfather's garden. At the summer estate we visit every year. I was walking through a maze and when I got to the exit, I saw this dark path leading into a forest. I went into the forest and it's the same as before. Everything is calm and then the trees start to move and wild animals are chasing me, trying to attack me. I run to the end of the path and in front of me is this giant cave and in my last vision a bright light came and blinded me."

"Whoa," Zadeia said.

"Only this time the vision changed." Fajha looked up at each of them. "I followed the bright light to the cave this time. Then I heard a voice."

"What did it say?" Zimi said. "Do you remember?"

"It was a whisper and I heard it very clearly. It said 'Ardomion'. The voice. It sounded like *Hamilda's*."

Stunned, his friends held their breath.

"Are you sure?" Cristaden said. "Are you positive it was *her* voice?"

"Yes, I would recognize it anywhere."

"What is…Ardomion?" Zadeia said slowly.

"Well, the only Ardomion I can think of are the Ardomion Caves on the island of Paimonu." Fajha frowned. "I just learned about them in my geography class. We were learning about different types of earth. Come to think of it, the earth from that region is black, similar to the cave I saw in my visions."

"Could we get there on foot?" Atakos said.

"There is a very distinct path to get there—" Fajha paused when he said the words 'distinct path' and his eyes opened wide, remembering the path into the forest from his visions. "We would have to go through Sheidem Forest."

"Could it be the same forest from your visions?" Zimi said.

"It couldn't be," Zadeia said. "I've gone into Sheidem Forest and it's not scary at all."

Cristaden frowned at her friend. She remembered the feeling of being watched. Sheidem Forest definitely seemed very scary to her.

"True," Fajha said. "There are tales about evil creatures and ferocious monsters living there but my textbooks tell me otherwise."

"I believe it," Cristaden said.

Zimi shook his head. "Those tales were told to scare children and keep them from wandering and getting lost in the forest."

"Whatever. I still believe it."

"Whether it's true or not," Fajha said. "Sheidem Forest is our only direct path to get to Paimonu. We would have to go through the forest, pass Osmatu, then the Suthack Desert, and finally cross the Hejdian Sea to reach the island of Paimonu. Just to get to the Ardomion Caves."

"My goodness, that sounds like it could take *days*," Zadeia said.

"It would be a long journey. But our only choice is to go by foot to decrease the risk of being seen."

Zimi crossed his arms. "How do we know this would not lead to a dead end?"

"It's a chance we're going to have to take," Atakos said. "We have no other leads. We know that Fajha doesn't sense Hamilda anywhere near here so she would have to be someplace really far. And maybe his visions are just another branch of his power. Regardless, we have to start somewhere and sitting around thinking about it is not going to help Hamilda."

"As much as I don't want to go in that forest," Cristaden said, "Atakos is right. Let's get our things together before General Komuh wonders where we are."

"I hope my visions are correct," Fajha said aloud to himself, standing up and putting his glasses back on.

"I hope so, too," Zadeia said, reaching out to squeeze his hand. "Don't worry, we believe in you. We'll find her."

Fajha nodded and walked to the door. "We're ready," he said.

CHAPTER 14

General Komuh sat at his desk, his head in his hands, trying to make sense of his jumbled thoughts. *How could we have allowed this to happen? Rohjees is the only one at the school who knew about the project and he has the keys to all the rooms. I have to figure out who he's working with. Those kids must be watched at all times. We cannot allow them to get into the wrong hands if we're going to use them to take over the—*

Just then a knock came at the door, interrupting his thoughts.

"You may enter," Komuh said wearily.

Lt. Gaojh immediately saluted him after coming in to the office. "Sir, they are ready to leave," he said.

"Good, I will accompany them as well."

The teenagers were waiting in two army vehicles. General Komuh took the seat next to the soldier driving the first vehicle much to the surprise of his guests. How could they assume he would not be going with them? They did not have to look at each other to know what everyone was thinking. It would be very difficult to elude him. He suspected everyone.

As they began the journey back to the school, Cristaden closed her eyes and did a short prayer for a way out of their mess. Driving through Sheidem City, Zimi's hands started shaking so he tried rubbing them together to steady his nerves. Atakos stared straight ahead, trying to focus on their objective but also feeling very scared. Fajha kept going over the vision in his head so he would not forget the fine details of it and Zadeia was just plain frightened. Luckily, the soldiers and General

Komuh never turned around. The teens looked as if they were ready to pass out, panic, or worse. It was the longest twenty minutes of their lives.

Before long, the wrought-iron gate that read 'Lochenby' came into view. The vehicles winded down the long driveway and halted in front of the school. General Komuh got out first and motioned for the other three soldiers to join him at the front door. Cristaden strained to hear what he was saying, but all she could get was 'Rohiees' office' and 'out of your sight'. He then walked back to the vehicles and told the teens to get out.

"I will be leaving you in the company of Lt. Gaojh, Lt. Hodlin, and Lt. Fohln," Komuh said, taking the collective sighs of relief he heard as sighs of disappointment. "Don't worry, you are in good hands. You have five minutes to grab what you need and nothing more." He then walked back towards the school.

"Okay," Lt. Gaojh said. "Lt. Fohln will go with the girls and Lt. Hodlin and I will go with you boys. We don't have much time, so let's move."

The group walked into the dormitory and took the elevator to the fourth level. It was so quiet that one could hear a pin drop on the marble floor. The students at Lochenby were still sleeping soundly, having no idea that soldiers from the Western Army were in their building. The teens glanced at each other and nodded, knowing what they must do. They then separated, the girls taking the right out of the elevator towards their room and the boys going left towards theirs.

Cristaden and Zadeia had an easy time convincing Lt. Fohln to wait outside, giving them their privacy to change into fresh clothes.

The boys were not so lucky.

"We have specific orders from General Komuh to not let you children out of our sight," Lt. Gaojh said. "There is no reason for you to need privacy."

"There's a very good reason," Atakos said.

"And what would that be?" Lt. Hodlin said, frowning.

"It's top secret. I can't disclose that information. But I can tell you that I have to get something out that no one is meant to see." Atakos hoped that it was believable.

"Yes," Fajha said. "General Komuh will be very upset to learn that this important object was left behind."

The soldiers exchanged glances. "What could happen on the fourth floor?" Lt. Gaojh asked his comrade.

"Alright," Lt. Hodlin said. "You have five minutes to pack up your things or we're coming in."

"That's all the time we need," Fajha said and went into the room with the other boys, closing the door behind them and slowly locking it, careful not to make it click.

The three boys made a mad dash around their room. They grabbed backpacks to put their necessities in and packed an extra uniform. All three threw on their dark green, hooded cloaks so they could blend in with the forest and put on black pants. At the last minute, Fajha remembered that they needed provisions so he pulled out a large plastic bin from under his bed and started stuffing bottles of water and packages of dried foods into his backpack. His two friends frowned at him, wondering why he had all that stashed under his bed. Fajha shrugged his shoulders and mouthed the word 'emergency' and closed his full backpack. Atakos and Zimi grabbed the remaining provisions and stuffed them in their backpacks as well.

Just then the doorknob began to jiggle and they heard Lt. Gaojh shout. The boys knew they had only moments before the soldiers would break down their flimsy door.

"Ready?" Zimi asked and his friends nodded.

"Are you girls ready?" Lt. Fohln said through the closed door.

"Just a minuuute," Cristaden said in her sweetest singsong voice. After changing their uniform skirts into black pants and packing extra uniforms, the girls threw their green cloaks on and made their way to the large window.

"Almost dooone!" Cristaden said. She then climbed the windowsill and looked back, nodding at Zadeia.

"Go," Zadeia whispered.

Cristaden took a deep breath, looking down at the sheer drop of four flights to the ground. Taking another deep breath, she leapt out of the window. Zadeia threw her arms out and immediately the air around Cristaden tightened, suspending her in midair as if she were in a bubble. She was then slowly lowered to the grass below.

Zadeia climbed out of the window, shutting it behind her. She then effortlessly glided to the ground with the help of her wind power and, upon touching it, broke out into a run with Cristaden. The two girls forged their way into the thick brush, heading towards the lake, all the while hoping the boys made it out okay.

While Atakos picked up his desk and placed it in front of the door with his mind, Zimi enveloped Fajha with wind and eased him down to the ground. He then tapped Atakos' shoulder and pointed to the window. Atakos did not hesitate and, after getting up on the windowsill, took a giant leap into the air. He went so fast that Zimi almost did not catch him but, just when he was about to hit the ground, he finally managed to soften his fall by suspending him in air for a moment and then releasing him. Atakos landed on his back but was okay.

Crack.

The door opened slightly as the soldiers tried to push the desk with their weight.

Zimi quickly leapt out of the window and conjured up the winds to carry him down. "Run!" he said as he touched ground. The three boys ran towards the thick brush. Once inside the brush, they breathed a little bit easier. They knew the soldiers would not be able to see them from the window because of their green cloaks.

They had escaped.

Lt. Gaojh and Lt. Hodlin finally managed to push the desk aside and enter the room. They looked around and realized the boys were not there. Lt. Hodlin quickly ran to the window, seeing nothing below but thick, overgrown brush.

"How did they escape through this window?" Lt. Hodlin asked his comrade.

"Yes, and on the fourth floor," Lt. Gaojh said. "They must have had some kind of rope—" He then looked at Lt. Hodlin. "The girls!"

Both men rushed out of the room and raced down the long hallway, sidestepping students who were coming out of their rooms to see what the commotion was about. A sandy-blonde haired boy tried asking them a question about his friends as they passed but they ignored him. Upon turning the corner at the end of the hall, the soldiers spotted Lt. Fohln waiting patiently in front of the girls' room. The oblivious soldier frowned at them as they quickly approached. Before he could ask any questions, the two men shoved him aside and forced the door open.

"Hey, they're not read—," Lt. Fohln began but stopped short when he looked into the empty room.

"This can't be happening," Lt. Hodlin said.

"We have to alert the general," Lt. Gaojh said, running out of the room, followed by the other two men.

The three soldiers took the elevator down to the first floor, running right into General Komuh, who was just entering the building.

"Where are they?" General Komuh's voice boomed throughout the lobby.

"They're gone, sir," Lt. Gaojh quickly said.

"What do you mean they're *gone*?" Komuh's face grew red with anger.

"We did exactly what you told us to do. We were tricked into giving them privacy."

"Didn't I tell you not to let them out of your sight?"

Lt. Hodlin stepped forward. "We had no idea they had a plan to escape or *could* through a fourth floor window," he said.

Exasperated, General Komuh led the men out of the building. "Those kids are capable of anything. I should never have left the three of you alone with them. Come on, we have no time to waste. They must be on the grounds still."

General Komuh got the school's secretary, a plump, old woman with bluish gray hair, to go over the layout of the school with him. The four men spread out across the campus. They searched the courtyard and the gymnasium. They circled the entire school and even ran down the path to the lake. There was absolutely no sign of them.

When they met up again at the front of the school, General Komuh shook his head. "They're not on the grounds anymore. We will search the woods by the lake. If they're not found, then we'll get every soldier to join us in the search. These children must be found!"

When Fajha, Atakos and Zimi got to the hidden path into the woods by the lake, they began to slow down a bit.

"Whew, that was close," Zimi said. "I thought we were going to get caught."

"Me too," Atakos said.

"What was with the frost you used to bring us down, Zimi?" Fajha said.

"What frost?"

Atakos shivered. "It was so cold, I thought my fingers and toes were going to fall off."

"All I was doing was conjuring the winds around us. It should have been the same temperature as the air."

"Trust me, it wasn't," Fajha said.

"That's weird." Zimi looked down at his hands. "I didn't feel it."

"Boys. You made it!"

The boys looked up and saw Cristaden and Zadeia waiting by the boarded up gate of the ranch. "Alright!" Cristaden said.

"We barely escaped," Atakos said when they reached the girls, trying to make it sound as dramatic as possible. "It was awful."

Zadeia laughed but Cristaden threw her arms out and gave him a hug. When she pulled away, Atakos was smiling at her. Feeling her cheeks grow hot in embarrassment, she quickly gave the other boys hugs to justify that the affectionate way she hugged him was friendly and nothing more. She wasn't so sure it worked because Atakos was still staring at her strangely when their eyes met again. He then quickly looked away.

The teens were startled when they suddenly heard voices. Feet rapidly hitting the forest floor only meant one thing. General Komuh and his soldiers were headed their way. Fast.

Without a moment's hesitation, they ran up to the boarded gate of the ranch. Fajha, trying to steady his nerves, unlocked it from the other side with his mind. Atakos quickly lifted the gate and held it in the air until all of his friends passed through and then he let it fall gently back into place. Cristaden locked the gate while Fajha brought leaves and branches up from the other side, covering the gate and their tracks completely, hoping that General Komuh and his men would assume no one had passed through there in a long time.

The teens crouched down within the dense brush behind the gate and waited, their anxiety building with every passing second. What if they were caught? Will they have to take a stand and fight? Or will they be forced to surrender? As the four men got closer, they knew they did not have long to wait for the answer to their questions.

"There's a gate here, sir," Lt. Hodlin said.

"What is this doing here?" Komuh said. "It's not noted on the map."

"Do you think they might have come through here?" Lt. Fohln said.

"Anything is possible."

Cristaden looked at her friends with wide eyes. Atakos' hands were balled into fists, preparing to take action. Zimi reached over and grabbed Zadeia's hand, seemingly to comfort her but she had a feeling he was trying to comfort himself, too. Fajha had his back to the gate, trying to calculate how long it would take them to run through the ranch and into Sheidem Forest before General Komuh managed to break it down. Cristaden's eyes met with Zadeia's. She shook her head slowly. This did not look good.

"General Komuh!" they heard Lt. Gaojh shout.

"What is it, lieutenant?"

"Their tracks do not continue there, it ends here. I think they're trying to fool us."

Komuh let out an exasperated growl. "Spread out! They can't be too far from here."

As the general and his soldiers moved away from the gate, Fajha motioned for everyone to stay low and follow him. They moved as quickly as possible through the ranch and breathed easier once they entered Sheidem Forest. They could not risk being taken into custody again. It was detrimental to their plan of finding Hamilda.

Heading east towards Osmatu without hesitation, the teens had no idea escaping General Komuh would probably be the easiest thing they had to do.

PART TWO
SHEIDEM FOREST

CHAPTER 15

"Those rotten inhabitants of the Western world are trying my patience," King Tholenod hissed, his dark eyes narrowing. He leaned over the balcony of his chamber and allowed his eyes to roam over the countryside of Mituwa in Eastern Omordion. The sky was dark with smoke from the furnaces that kept the digging machines running. If his slaves were not working the fields, they were deep in the mines, digging for stones and coal.

Tholenod frowned when he noticed a young boy had fallen over as a group of slaves were being led past the castle to the fields. He was most likely dead from exhaustion and starvation. It would definitely slow down production that day.

"But sire, they are getting weaker with each strike," his assistant Menyilh said. He slithered over to Tholenod and stood beside him. "Their recent victory from Feim was brought upon by *retirees*. They are destined for failure."

"Menyilh. I have heard you say that very phrase for over ten years now. It's not enough. Our victory is taking much too long to accomplish." Tholenod grunted. "As we speak, they could be training hundreds of thousands of new recruits to bring us down any day now. We need to find a way to destroy them before that happens."

Menyilh offered a sly smile. "I may have exactly what you're looking for."

"And what might that be?"

"Throughout my wanderings, I have discovered something rather interesting." He leaned in closer. "Something that might help us win this war—"

"You are trying my *patience*, Menyilh. This had better be good."

"Aah yes, my lord," Menyilh hissed, revealing his slimy teeth. "I think this news will please you indeed." He rubbed his hands together as he informed Tholenod of a very powerful old wizard he had located in the mountains of Effit. He explained that the old wizard had isolated himself in a cave, built into the side of a mountain many years ago. It was surrounded by a dead forest, destroyed by him because of his hate for all living things. If they were to win the war, the wizard would be a powerful adversary. All the king would have to do was to convince him to be his ally.

Tholenod thought long and hard. *An old wizard?* He never believed the ancient stories of witches, wizards, and magical creatures. Nevertheless, he trusted Menyilh. Fearful of his wrath, his assistant always made sure whatever he had to say was the absolute truth. *The wizard must be real.* Tholenod shook his head. He was not fond of the idea of bringing another party into his operation. He already had to deal with the impertinence of King Huadmont from the northern country of Srepas, the sheer stupidity of King Gomu from the southeastern country of Effit, and the rivalry of King Basapanul, from the southwestern country of Feim, who were always trying to surpass him. But if he convinced the wizard to help him, he may be able to do away with the other kings once and for all.

Grumbling, Tholenod walked back into the chamber, with Menyilh following close behind him, and sat on his throne. The heavy doors of the chamber opened and his son, Aillios, wearing his gray suit of armor, forced his way past the two soldiers standing guard by the door. He quickly removed his helmet, revealing his full head of black hair and hard blue eyes. His square jaw was tight as if he was clenching his teeth and his eyebrows were drawn into a scowl. It was obvious he was upset.

"Father," Aillios said, approaching the throne.

"I hope this is important, Aillios," Tholenod scowled.

Menyilh sneered at him but did not greet him.

When Aillios was a young boy, he lost his mother when she was met with, what his father had described as, 'a tragic end'. He was so young that he barely remembered what she looked like and how it felt to be in the arms of a loving person. Instead, he was subject to the impossible goals his father set before him and the severe punishment he received if they were not fulfilled. Under the strong hand of his father, highly skilled tutors worked with him day and night, fine tuning his education and combat skills, which were so magnificent, he has not found a match in the battlefield.

"I have just received a report that there have been nineteen deaths in the commons this week alone," Aillios said.

"Once again, you are wasting my time with this senseless chatter."

"But father, if this continues—if people keep dying—"

"Are you telling me that you *care* for these people?" Tholenod peered at his son.

"Well… I …"

"What are you saying then? That these animals should be cared for and allowed to feed off the riches of our land? If I allowed them to live freely, they would have overthrown us by now. If I show them any ounce of kindness, they will become strong enough to achieve what they have sought out to do for centuries."

"Don't you fear they will rebel against us again *because* we are cruel to them and offer no kindness to them?"

"By keeping them weak and brainless, we reduce that chance indefinitely. You can't expect me to cater to these creatures. They are lower than us. They deserve *nothing*."

"They are not animals, father. They are people. Just like you and me. They have brains to think for themselves."

"That is exactly why I did what I had to do. The monarchy was dying. Our resources were being depleted—eaten up by those *things* out there and you expect me to have pity on them? If I were dying in the fields, do you think they would have taken pity on me? They want what we have and they would have stopped at nothing to attain it. You were there when they retaliated! How can you forget?"

Aillios looked down. It was hard to forget. Those men. Fighting for their freedom. And Aillios. Taking them down one by one. Convinced by his father that he had to fight back and kill whomsoever crossed his path because they were the ones who killed his mother. It wasn't until Aillios started visiting the villages did he realize that if they had killed his mother, he couldn't find it in his heart to blame them. He blamed his father.

"Let them die," Tholenod said. "If they all die, we wouldn't have to deal with them anymore."

"Father, you are being unreasonable—"

"Every week, you come to me with these nonsensical theories and you say I am being unreasonable? You seem to forget that they were the ones who killed your mother! If I hear this talk one more time, I will banish you from this castle. You will meet the same fate as those *things* out there since you care about them so much."

"But father—"

"Now get out of my sight. I will hear no more of this insubordination from my own son." Tholenod waved his hand and turned away from him.

Aillios glared at the king and then stormed out of the chamber with increasing fury. Unbeknownst to his father, he spent most of his days in the fields, offering water to the thirsty and attempting to care for the sick and dying. The people liked him but knew he could not free them because of his father. They knew he was just as much in harm's way as they were. His father warned him, when he was caught freeing some commoners, that if he helped them escape again, he would personally behead him. Aillios knew Tholenod would not hesitate when it came to safeguarding his rule over Mituwa.

Aillios climbed the stairs and entered his chamber, throwing his helmet on his large bed. With an aggravated sigh, he sat down on a big armchair near a window and stared out into the fields. He could see the smoke rising from the furnaces on the other side of the hill next to the castle. At night, he could barely sleep. The crying from the orphaned or injured children kept him from closing his eyes. The overseers were cruel and often beat anyone who showed signs of slowing down production. The majority of the slaves were attached to each other with chains on their ankles. At times, when a person died, the body had to be dragged around until the guards picked it up. They carried the deceased to the marshes, which had become a mass grave. The stench coming from there was so overpowering that the soldiers did not go there every day. They made the trip once a week, leaving some of the dead to be dragged around in the meantime, driving the slaves to near insanity.

Aillios stayed in Mituwa to care for his people but at times, he wished he could just escape, to be free of the harshness and cruelty. But if he left, he could do nothing to help his people and he would have to forget who he was. It was a hard decision to make. He didn't know which way to turn.

Tholenod stared at the door after his son left. He was beginning to lose hope that Aillios would change. If he fell ill, how could he trust that his son would carry on his legacy? The minute he lost his bearings, his son would free the slaves and allow the monarchy to die. He would much rather leave the kingdom to Menyilh than to leave it in the hands of his son. But his son was right about one thing. If the people died, there would be no more slaves to work the lands for them. He could not risk that happening. If he could gain control of Western Omordion, millions of slaves would be at his disposal. The thought brought him back to what Menyilh offered. An alliance with the old wizard.

"Menyilh," King Tholenod said, bringing the assistant to his full attention.

"Yes, sire?" Menyilh hissed.

"I think we shall pay that wizard a visit."

"Wise choice, sire."

"Guards."

One of the soldiers opened the heavy door. "Yes, sire?"

"Tell my handmaid, Frolemin, to prepare my things. We will be taking a trip to Effit and I want everything ready. Tonight."

CHAPTER 16

In Laspitu, the forests were just trees here and there, which hardly made them seem like real forests at all. Cristaden finally felt like she was in a real forest, barely having any room to walk, having to step over or push aside plants and bushes just to get around the hundreds of thousands of closely knit trees surrounding them. Everything was so green and vibrant and the air smelled fresher than anything she had breathed before. Smiling as she brushed a leaf off her face, her initial fears of the forest slowly slipped away. "It's so beautiful here," she said.

Fajha ducked under a low branch and sighed. "Yes, nothing at all like my visions."

"How long have we been walking today?" Atakos asked, looking up at the sky.

"It feels like it's been almost the whole day," Zimi said. "We would have to find a place to rest before the sun goes down."

"How is that going to be possible?" Zadeia said. "We hardly have any room to sit down."

"Perhaps we can make our own clearing," Fajha said.

"Oh sure," Atakos said, pulling his cloak free from a thorn-ridden branch. "Who brought the saw? I know I didn't."

"If we pull together, we can uproot some of these bushes. It shouldn't be too hard."

"Well, I guess we have no choice. If the forest continues to be this congested, we'll have to do something." Looking up ahead at the never-ending forest of trees, Atakos thought of how his father would encourage him to be a leader. At his age he hadn't come close to being good at anything he did. He felt unworthy of his friends, afraid that when a conflict rose, he would not be able to protect them. If anything were to happen to them… he tried not to think about the possibilities. "Let's just keep going until the sun starts to go down," Atakos said, trying to motivate his friends. "Who knows, maybe we will run into a nice clearing before that happens."

The others nodded and forged ahead, hoping to cover as much ground as possible before the sun began its descent.

General Komuh stormed into Army Headquarters, letting out an exasperated growl. "Those foolish kids," he said, pounding his fist into his hand.

A young soldier quickly saluted him. "Sir."

"What is it private?" Komuh said with pure agitation.

"Mr. Bontihm Fhakaemeli is here for his appointment, sir. I let him into your office."

"This is very bad timing." He had forgotten about the appointment he set up with the man upon Hamilda's disappearance. Treading wearily to his office, he took a deep breath before opening the door.

Bontihm was standing by the only window. He was staring despairingly outside, watching the activities of the base. He hardly noticed when the general entered the room.

Komuh hesitated for a moment and studied the old man. He seemed more hunched over than he remembered and his graying hair had turned a stark white. His pale skin was now speckled with brown age spots and so were his hands. "Sorry to keep you waiting," he said. "We have a situation on our hands."

Bontihm turned to look at him and frowned. "What *kind* of situation?"

"Would you please have a seat?"

"No, thank you. I would much rather stand."

"That's fine." Komuh leaned against his desk and folded his arms.

"What is this situation that concerns you?" Bontihm searched his face for answers. And then it dawned on him. "Where are the children?"

"The children, Fhakaemeli, have escaped."

Visibly upset, Bontihm took a step towards him. "Escaped? What you mean by escaped? Were you holding them captive?"

"Absolutely not," he quickly said. "We were protecting them. Whoever took Hamilda could come after them. Desperate measures were taken in order to prevent them from meeting the same fate."

Bontihm thought for a moment. "I suppose you're right. If they were taken, Omordion could be in peril."

"Exactly. But now they have run away from our protection."

"Why do you think they ran away?"

Komuh shrugged. "Perhaps they know something about the kidnapping they were not telling us. Perhaps they were scared and didn't want us to find out their secrets. We do not know."

Bontihm turned towards the window again and watched as soldiers ran towards the center of the base as if preparing for a major battle. *Must be the search party,* he thought. Sighing, he looked back at the general. He knew the reasons he was given about the teens running away did not make any sense. He knew the reason why they would run away. If he was younger, he would have done the same.

They went to find Hamilda.

"We are gathering a search party as we speak." Obviously confident in his impending success, Komuh's eyes sparkled when he spoke.

"Where are you going to begin your search?"

"We believe that they are headed towards Osmatu. It's the only direction they would go if they were trying to evade us. We will find them at any cost."

An alarm went off in Bontihm's head. He knew that Komuh's suspicions were true. The teenagers were headed towards Osmatu. He did not know how he knew, or why they were headed that way, but he was filled with sudden dread. It occurred to him that he had to stop the search party from going after them. He brought his hands to his temple and frowned as if he were deep in thought.

"What are you doing?" Komuh uneasily asked.

"I am conducting a search for them." Bontihm squeezed his eyes shut, knowing full well he did not have the location ability but hoping Komuh did not see through his deception. He then opened his eyes wide. "Ah. Yes. They are indeed traveling through Sheidem Forest, but their destination is Hortu, not Osmatu as you have perceived. I assume they are headed to the only place on this island where they feel the safest. My home."

"You are sure of this?"

"Absolutely. You should head west."

General Komuh thought for a moment. "We will do as you say. But mark my words, old man. If you are lying, I will personally hold you in contempt."

"Do not be concerned. I assure you that I want those teenagers found more than anything. You understand. For their protection."

With that, Komuh grunted and stormed out of his office.

Bontihm turned toward the window one last time and brought his eyes toward the sky. *Good luck, children.*

"It feels like we've been walking in circles," Zadeia said, looking up at the tall trees. "These trees look so familiar."

"They all look the same," Atakos said and frowned at her. "They're trees. We've been walking straight, so there's no way possible we could be going in circles."

Cristaden looked up at the trees. It was the third day of their journey and they were confused. Nothing much about the forest had changed since they had started their mission. Zimi suddenly stopped short and she walked right into him. "Hey!" she cried.

"Look," Zimi said, pointing straight ahead. The path in front of them was trampled, the brush leaning to either sides of the path as if they were pushed aside.

Something big had gone through there.

Atakos felt heat rise up to his ears and his heart began to race. "I thought there were no large animals here," he said.

No one responded as they stood frozen, gripped in fear. They were holding their breath and listening closely to the sounds of the forest for any evidence that they were not alone. All they heard were birds singing and the wind rustling the leaves overhead.

"What could have done this?" Cristaden said.

"Maybe it *is* an animal," Zimi said.

"The animal would have to be very big to make that kind of path," Fajha said. "And if it were a large beast, we would have at least heard it by now. The path seems as if it was freshly—"

Cristaden suddenly grabbed Fajha's arm, interrupting him. "This doesn't appear to be a path made by animals at all. It seems too perfect. Almost like it was made by *humans*."

Fajha shook his head. "That's impossible. There are no humans out here. I've studied Sheidem Forest at school. The soil is not good for planting, the plants can be poisonous, and there are no animals to hunt. Something about that cataclysmic event that happened hundreds of years ago. Besides the birds flying overhead, I haven't seen any ground animals since we started this journey, have you?"

"Well what do we do?" Zadeia said, beginning to panic.

Fajha stepped up to the path and bent down to examine it, hoping to find any evidence that it was an animal. The others joined him as well, looking for any clue as to what may have walked through there.

"I don't see anything," Atakos said, standing up. "What exactly are we looking for anyways?"

"Wait," Zimi said. "Come see this." He was pointing at a tree. As the rest of the group came closer, they only became more confused.

"It's a broken tree," Atakos said sarcastically. "How is that supposed to help us? There are hundreds of those here."

"No, I *remember* this tree," Zimi said. "I remember it because *I* helped it break."

"Are you sure about that?" Zadeia said.

"Yes. Look at it. It's thick and gnarled with roots sticking out of the ground and curling around its trunk. When we were walking, I noticed that it was dying and already breaking in the middle. I gave it a little push and it fell onto its side, like it's lying right now."

"How long ago did you do this?" Cristaden said.

"Hmmm…sometime yesterday."

The teenagers stared at the tree, not wanting to believe what Zimi was saying. If he was right, it would mean that they had gone in a big circle over the course of one day. It was disappointing to think that all of those hours spent walking had been a waste of time.

Atakos looked away from the broken tree and walked a little further down the path, studying the trampled plant life and trees as he went along. "I think he might be on to something. The other trees don't look like that. They go straight into the ground."

"But that would be impossible," Fajha said. "That would mean we did a full circle while we were walking straight."

"I knew it," Zadeia said. "We were walking in circles."

"Fajha, can you take out your compass so we can see which direction we're going?" Cristaden said, trying not to show her disappointment.

Fajha removed his backpack and set it on the ground. He fished through the contents of it and grew frustrated when he could not find the compass. "It has to be here somewhere." He emptied out a side pocket and his hand closed around what he was looking for. Putting everything back in the bag, he stood up. He then looked at the compass and frowned. "That's weird," he said.

"What's wrong?" Cristaden said.

Fajha shook the compass and tapped the glass. "Look at it." He held it out so the others could see. The compass, which usually only pointed North, was spinning crazily in every direction, left to right, right to left. "I've never seen it do this. It's supposed to point to where North is at all times." Fajha looked extremely worried. His unusually sweaty hands closed around the compass and he put it back in his backpack.

"We're lost," Zadeia said in a small voice. "I'm scared."

"Don't be scared, Zadeia," Zimi said, putting his arm around her shoulders. "We'll find a way out of this mess."

"So how are we going to get out of this forest?" Cristaden asked, her stomach twisting in knots.

"I have a plan," Atakos said. All eyes shifted to look at him. He suddenly felt a bit of anxiety and did not want to give his suggestion in case his friends did not approve. "Well ... I think we should go another direction." He pointed to the dense forest on the right of the path. "Let's not go straight anymore. We can also keep an eye on the direction the sun is setting and keep it behind us in order to continue going east."

"That's a great idea," Cristaden said. "I can't believe we haven't thought of this before."

Atakos smiled. Cristaden was always good at making everyone feel better about themselves.

Zimi shuffled his foot in the dirt. "A whole day. Gone. Just like that."

What a waste, Zadeia thought, and began to cry.

"Well it's a good thing we found out sooner than later," Atakos said, trying to cheer up his friends. "We don't have many hours of daytime left, let's keep moving." He stepped over the broken, fallen tree and forged his way through the dense brush with the rest of the group following close behind him.

As they walked, the five friends were quiet. They were listening for the sounds of the forest and studying their surroundings. Feeling as though they had been careless for three days, their spirit and confidence shrunk to the point where they did not want to continue the journey. Yet they knew they had set out to find Hamilda and were not turning back until she was found. No matter how weary and disheartened they felt, they had no choice but to forge on.

When the sun began its swift descent, the group adjusted their direction slightly so they were walking away from it. With Atakos' brilliant suggestion, in no time they were heading east towards the heart of the forest. The sun was still shining brightly and the sky was a beautiful clear blue so they had a few more hours of ground to cover before stopping to rest.

"This is the perfect weather to go for a nature hike," Fajha said, snickering.

Zadeia burst out crying.

Zimi groaned. "Oh, not again."

"I can't help it," she said between choked gasps. "I miss her."

Fajha looked back at the sun once more and was about to tease Zadeia when he felt something touch his forehead. Wiping his head, he looked down at his hand. "Water?"

"What did you say?" Atakos said.

"Water," Fajha said as another drop touched his nose.

One drop fell on Cristaden's cheek. "Rain?"

"There's not a cloud in the ..." Fajha didn't finish his sentence. He looked up and saw dark clouds moving in fast, threatening to block out the sun.

"Where did those come from?" Zimi said. "They weren't there a second ago."

"I just looked up and the sky was bright blue."

"This is not good," Cristaden said, watching the heavy, dark clouds roll in and the forest grow very dark.

"Do you know what this is?" Atakos said angrily as the sun disappeared behind the clouds. "This is just plain outrageous."

"It's as if someone or something is trying to prevent us from reaching our destination." Cristaden was beginning to feel afraid again and shifted her eyes around the darkening forest. She felt no other presence besides their own.

"Whatever it is, something's got to give," Fajha said.

As if to respond to his request, lightning then struck and a torrential downpour of rain descended through the trees.

CHAPTER 17

The now irritated teens barely managed to pull their hoods over their heads before the heavy rain slammed them with a force so strong, they could barely keep their eyes open. They struggled to walk on the increasingly muddy forest floor, their hope diminishing with every step they took.

"We'll have to stop and make camp until this clears up," Fajha said.

Zimi shook his head. "If we do that, we will be wasting more time."

"But we don't know if we are even going the right way," Atakos shouted as thunder rolled across the sky. "For all we know, we could be going in a giant circle as we speak." He shuddered at the thought. To make the same mistake again would be disadvantageous to their search. They had no choice but to stop marching through the thick brush if they wanted to make sure they were going east.

As they continued walking, Cristaden took a moment to observe the trees, noticing a definite change. They seemed smaller to her compared to the tall trees she was getting used to seeing throughout the forest. It was either they were smaller or she could not see the tops of them fully because of the fog that had spread itself over their heads. As she was bringing her eyes back down to look ahead, she thought she saw something move. Startled, she gasped. "Did anyone see that?"

"See what?" Zadeia said.

Cristaden looked closely at the tree she saw the movement on as they walked past it. The branches were still and there was no sign of anything on or around it. Just the rain falling on the green leaves. *I must be tired,*

Cristaden thought, frowning. "Never mind," she said. "Must have been my imagination."

They walked on ahead, looking for a place to set up camp.

"There," Atakos said. He was pointing to an area to their left, were the brush was less dense and there were no trees.

"Looks good to me," Zadeia said. "My feet are getting tired."

"I think we should keep moving," Zimi said.

"You suggest we leave an area this perfect?" Atakos said. "All we have to do is pull out those bushes and set up our tent."

"I definitely think we would be safer stopping," Fajha said, agreeing with the others. He pointed at the sky. "The rain does not seem to be stopping anytime soon and we don't know which direction we're walking. Also the water under our feet is accumulating very fast. How will we ever be able to walk through this any longer?"

"I guess you're right," Zimi said, embarrassed he made the suggestion to keep moving.

As they pushed their way through the brush to reach their destination, Zimi thought he saw a figure reaching out for him at the corner of his eyes. "Aah!" he yelped and crashed into Zadeia.

"What is it?" Zadeia said, trying to keep from falling over.

"What's wrong, Zimi?" Cristaden said.

Zimi squinted at the broad, gnarled tree closest to him. "I thought I saw this tree move," Zimi said, his heart still in his throat.

Atakos couldn't help but laugh. "You're seeing things. Trees don't move."

"Yeah, you're definitely hallucinating," Fajha said, while allowing his eyes to examine the perfectly still tree.

Cristaden wasn't so sure he was hallucinating. She wondered if it had anything to do with what she thought she saw earlier. She peered at the tree, looking for any signs of life but saw none. Something was not right about it though but she couldn't pinpoint what it was.

The friends set their backpacks down and began to pull at the bushes. They yanked and twisted but the bushes wouldn't budge. They even tried coming together and pulling one bush at the same time, but it still did not work. Zimi used his technique of kicking the base of the bush, which did break it, but left a stump protruding out of the ground so high they would not feel comfortable resting on it.

Fajha was distracted. He kept looking up at the trees surrounding them. "Does anyone have the feeling we're being watched?"

"Now Fajha's hallucinating," Zadeia said, giggling.

"No," Cristaden said, wiping the rain from her eyes. "I feel it too. I thought I was going crazy. I've felt this way before but it turned out to be my imagination. This time, I'm not so sure."

Atakos nodded. "I didn't want to scare anyone but I feel it too. It's as if we are being watched. Not just from one place but *all around us.*"

The group stood up and examined the broad trees around them. Besides the falling rain jostling the leaves, there were no other signs of movement.

Yet the feeling *was* there.

"This is bizarre," Zadeia said. "I feel it too."

"Maybe the forest is getting to us," Fajha said. "We've been out here for too many days. It's called mass hysteria. Sort of like when you're in a hot desert and everyone begins to see mirages of things that are not really there."

"I don't think that's it, Fajha," Atakos said. "Cristaden. Are you picking up anything? Or anyone?"

Cristaden looked around. "Nothing," she said, turning back to her friends. "If there was someone here, I would have picked up on their presence a long time ago. I feel like we are being watched but it's as if there is a wall here that I cannot break through. A wall of emptiness. Like there are no living creatures here at all."

The teens looked around them again, listening to the sounds of the forest. The only thing they heard was the rain pitter-pattering on the leaves and on the muddy ground beneath them. All else seemed still, including the wind, which ceased to blow.

"I told you guys to keep it moving," Zimi said. "But does anyone listen to me? N—"

"Does anyone hear that sound?" Zadeia suddenly said, cutting him off. "It sounds like it's coming from over there." She pointed straight ahead.

At first, all her friends heard were the heavy drops of rain. Then, one by one, they heard a different sound.

"It sounds like rushing water," Zimi said.

"Kind of like a river or a stream," Fajha said.

"Do you remember anything about any rivers in you studies of Sheidem Forest, Fajha?" Cristaden said.

"No, I don't recall there being any body of water."

"But don't all streams lead to or from a larger body of water?" Atakos said.

"Most of the time."

"Could it have been caused by the rain?" Zimi said.

"It's possible."

"I'm all for getting away from here and checking it out," Cristaden said. "Does anyone else want to find this stream?"

It was a unanimous vote to begin moving again. No one wanted to stick around. As they were walking, the sound of the tumbling water got louder and louder with each determined step. Their hope was to find a clearing by the river or stream big enough to allow them a chance to sleep for the night. Nighttime was at an early surrender with dark clouds looming overhead. It would not be long before they could not see anything at all.

They passed a row of broad trees and there, directly ahead of them, was a stream about ten feet across, rushing wildly downstream with added water from the rain. It was clear, fresh water, littered with fallen leaves, branches, and large rocks.

"I think we found exactly what we're looking for," Atakos said, pointing to an area a little ways downstream across the water. It could not have been a more perfect clearing. The land was flawlessly flat and surrounded by trees in a semicircle.

"Excellent," Cristaden said.

Zadeia looked up at the darkening sky. "Let's go before we can't even see what's in front of us."

They walked down to a patch of large rocks and hopped from one to another until they reached the opposite shore. The earth was solid beneath them, not muddy like the rest of the forest. Pitching the only tent they had, they removed their wet cloaks before going inside. Just as they were trying to crawl in, the tent collapsed.

"Nice, Zimi," Zadeia said. "Where did you get this cheap tent from?"

"Well, it really was a one-time-use-only tent," Zimi said. "This is the third time we've used it."

"Just another thing to add to our bad luck," Atakos said, sighing.

Zadeia's eyes welled up with tears at the sight of the broken tent. The enthusiasm they had when they started their journey was slowly fading away. Now they were stuck in the middle of a forest, drenched, with no promise of finding their way out or even finding Hamilda.

"We'll get through this, Zadeia," Cristaden said when she heard Zadeia sniffle. "We're all in this together."

"I miss Hamilda, Cristaden," Zadeia said. "I miss the good times we had together before she was taken from us."

"With the death of her only love, I think she was already taken from us before her kidnapping. All we can hope now is to get her back safely and restore some of her lost happiness." Cristaden hoped that after a good night sleep, they could wake up refreshed and start their journey all over again with renewed confidence. "I only wish it wasn't raining and we could sleep under the moon and stars."

As if to answer her wish, a bright, orange moon peeked out from a dark cloud in the horizon and shined its light on them.

"A full moon is rising," Zadeia said, happy to see it. "How beautiful." Along with the appearance of the moon, the clouds rolled by and, within a few moments, the rain stopped.

"Incredible," Atakos said and looked at Cristaden. "Why didn't you ask for the rain to stop sooner?"

Cristaden shrugged. "I had nothing to do with it," she said, laughing.

"But those rain clouds left as fast as they came," Fajha said. "That's just too strange."

"I don't care," Zimi said as he and Atakos shook the tent free of rainwater. "As long as it doesn't come back any time soon, I don't care."

Cristaden took a deep breath. The rain coming and going so quickly wasn't the only thing that was strange about the forest. She glanced around. In the light of the moon, the trees around them stood in an almost too perfect semicircle. They all seemed to resemble each other completely from the directions their branches were facing down to the way their roots poked out of the ground slightly as if the earth beneath them was slowly washing away. Surprisingly, despite all the oddness around her, Cristaden did not get the feeling they were being watched any longer. She felt safe.

"It's best if we just lie down on the tent and cover ourselves with our cloaks," Fajha said. "If it rains again, I really don't know what we're going to do." He then pulled out food for them to eat from his backpack. They ate beans from a can, bread, and dried fruit. Finally, they drank fresh water from the stream.

"That was the most disgusting but best meal I've ever had," Zimi said, letting out a foul-smelling burp.

"You. Are. Disgusting," Zadeia said.

Just then, a twig snapped from somewhere within the forest. The friends jerked their heads towards the sound. With their eyes opened wide, they looked for anything that could have created it. Everything was perfectly still.

"It was probably some little creature," Cristaden whispered.

"Yeah, one of those little creatures we haven't been seeing all day," Zimi whispered back.

"Maybe they live on this side of the stream," Zadeia said.

"Whatever it is," Fajha said. "It probably won't harm us. Sheidem Forest does not shelter dangerous animals. It's not documented in my textbooks. And what my textbooks say, I believe." When no one said anything, he laid down on the tarp and, using his backpack as a pillow, pulled his cloak over his head and closed his eyes. "I'm going to sleep."

A few moments later, when they didn't hear any new sounds, Zimi sighed. "I'm with Fajha on that one. I don't even want to know what it was." He closed his eyes when his head hit his backpack. Cristaden and Atakos did the same.

"But shouldn't someone keep watch?" Zadeia said.

"Goodnight, Zadeia," the others said in unison. They were all very tired and just wanted to end the day.

"Alright then. Don't say I didn't warn you." Zadeia laid her head on her backpack and shivered. The tent was still a little wet from the rain and the cloak barely provided any warmth but it would have to do. She was about to make some sly remark about animals attacking them in their sleep but as soon as her eyes closed, the sound of the rushing water helped her immediately fall into a deep sleep. The last thing she remembered thinking was how she hoped Fajha was right.

Crack.

"What was that?" Atakos said, rubbing the sleep out of his eyes. The moon was still high in the sky, providing some light in the clearing.

"Shhh," Fajha said.

Atakos looked around and saw that everyone's eyes were open and staring out into the trees. They were trying not to move.

Snap.

Zadeia gasped. They actually felt the snap as if it were something being pulled from the ground beneath them.

"Do you think it's an earthquake?" Zimi whispered.

"No, the ground would be shaking, you idiot," Fajha said through his teeth.

"How about a landslide?"

Fajha wanted to remark on the fact that they were not at the bottom of a hill but held his tongue when they heard another loud crack that sounded more like someone stepping on a branch and breaking it.

"There's someone or something out there," Cristaden said. She was horrified.

Another loud snap caused them to jump. Then a crackling sound started. It sounded like corn, popping on a hot stove. Except they felt every pop in the ground beneath them. And then the popping sounds grew louder and louder until it suddenly erupted into a chorus of crackling and snapping as if someone were pulling the trees right out of the ground all around them. There was so much noise the ground began to shake.

"Oh!" Zadeia said.

"What the—?" Fajha said.

"Earthquake!" Zimi said, screaming.

"Remain calm," Cristaden said. "We have to keep our minds open in case we have to fight—" She couldn't believe what happened next.

They saw movement around the outside of the semicircle they made their campground. It was so dark, the teenagers could not see exactly what they were looking at. It seemed like tall figures were moving, and they had what appeared to be many arms. They were doing an eerie dance, swaying from side to side. Then they suddenly picked up speed, swaying rapidly, causing the teens to jump up and step back. The rumbling of the forest floor got louder to the point that it was almost deafening.

Cristaden started trembling in fear. Her heart felt as if it were going to jump out of her chest. Zadeia grabbed her arm and held fast to it, squeezing it tightly. She, too, was trembling with goose bumps forming up and down her arms. The boys were staring straight ahead, poised and ready for an attack but they were deathly afraid also, trying not to let the fear consume them. The sight in the woods, although they could not see it well, was the most frightening thing they had ever witnessed.

We are not prepared for this, Atakos screamed in his head. *All these years of training did not prepare us at all.*

As they began moving forward, the beings let out loud groaning sounds as if they were monsters awakening from a century-long slumber. Cristaden watched them very carefully to see if she could tell what they were. She gasped when one finally stepped into the moonlight. "They're *trees,*" she said.

The others saw it too. The trees, which made up the perfect semicircle around their camp, were moving towards them. The crackling sound they heard was coming from their roots, pulling out of the ground, allowing them to move. The teens could barely make out the evil faces carved on the trees but they saw the red, angry eyes that stared back at them.

"Just like my vision," Fajha said. "We have to get out of here. We have to run." He turned to run and Atakos grabbed his arm.

"No," Atakos said. "We are not cowards. We stand and fight." As he clenched his fists and put himself in a defense stance, the trees suddenly stopped moving and all went quiet.

"Why did they stop?" Cristaden said.

"I don't know," Fajha said. The air around them was thick with tension and they could feel their hearts beating hard against their chests.

"AAAAAAAAH!!!!" Zadeia fell onto her back. A tree root had a hold of her ankle and was dragging her along the ground, towards its gaping trunk. She belted out a scream again and turned, trying to dig her hands into the ground to stop from going any further.

Zimi reached out for her. "Zadeia!" His scream virtually woke up his friends who had been frozen in terror, unsure if what they were seeing was real.

As the four teens ran forward, Atakos tried to pull Zadeia towards him with his mind but the tree was simply too strong.

"This can't be happening," Cristaden said.

Fajha attempted to pull Zadeia with his mind power also, but he was knocked over by an invisible force. He landed flat on his back, several feet away. As Zadeia neared the tree trunk, everyone began to get desperate. Atakos picked up heavy rocks and threw it at the red eyes of the tree but it didn't seem to affect it. Zimi felt he had no useful power against the tree. All he could picture was his sister being gobbled up and never seeing her alive again. In his confusion and anger, he tried to use his wind power just to try anything. With all his strength, he pushed the wind against the tree, practically knocking it down. After doing it the first time, he noticed some icicles hanging off some of the leaves. He pushed himself to do it harder. In an instant he had turned the entire tree, down to its gnarled roots, into a block of ice. The tree stopped pulling Zadeia. She kicked the frozen root off her leg, smashing it to pieces.

Just as Cristaden was helping Zadeia to her feet, she noticed that, in the confusion to free their friend, the other trees had moved closer to them until they were just a few feet away. The five teens slowly backed up, knowing that if they backed up too far, they would be in the stream. It was too dark to see the rocks they used to cross it.

Zadeia began to cry again as horror gripped her.

"Listen to me everyone," Atakos said. "We fight until the last tree has been destroyed."

Cristaden glanced at him and thought of how, under different circumstances, she would have been furious at the very notion of destroying trees. Trees were supposed to give life, not take it away. But these were different circumstances. Their lives were in danger.

At that moment, all the branches from the trees moved quickly, reaching out for them. It happened so fast, the five teens didn't have a chance to use their powers against them. The tree that grabbed Zadeia melted quickly and shook off the icicles clinging to its body, advancing towards them with an eerie shriek. Cristaden let out a squeal and the group backed up so fast they almost fell into the stream.

"That's enough!" a woman's voice echoed from behind them.

The friends turned and stared in disbelief. A brightly glowing woman walked past them as if she had come from the stream. She had long white-blonde hair with a beautiful pale face. She wore a long, flowing white dress trimmed with gold. She was holding her hands up to the trees, commanding them to stop. As if to obey her, the trees froze in midair, immediately stopping their violent attack.

CHAPTER 18

Atakos, Cristaden, Fajha, Zimi, and Zadeia stared at the glowing woman that walked past them, commanding the trees to stop their incessant attack.

"I beg you to allow these children safe passage through the forest for they are innocent," the woman told the trees in a calm voice. "Please resume your places and be at peace."

The teens watched in amazement as the trees immediately began to withdraw. Their angry, red eyes and faces faded as their branches retracted. With a long grinding sound, the trees backed up until they came to a rest at their original spots, once again creating the perfect semicircle around the clearing. Their roots dug into the ground, searching for a place to rest and once they found it, all was quiet.

The glowing woman then turned to the teenagers who were still on their guard. "Those are the guardians of the forest," she said. "They watch over us. When they feel like the forest is in trouble, they launch an attack to get rid of the problem." She noticed the group's stance and smiled, her pale silver eyes sparkling in the moonlight. "You may relax, I won't hurt you."

"Who are you?" Cristaden said, stepping out from behind Atakos.

"My name is Queen Lhainna. Welcome to my forest. All you see here belongs to me and my people."

"Your people?" Fajha said. "Why haven't we seen any of your people since we've been in this forest?"

"Oh, but you could not have seen us even if you tried." Lhainna took a step forward. "We do not show ourselves unless we want to be seen. It would be too disastrous."

"How so?" Zadeia said.

"Because of what we are. Fairies." She said the word as if it was the most natural thing to say.

"Fairies?" Atakos said. "But fairies don't exist."

"Apparently, neither do you," Lhainna said with a slight smile.

"What do you mean by that?"

"I'm sure where you come from people do not know who you really are and what you are capable of doing. Am I correct?"

"But—"

Atakos was interrupted by Cristaden. "How do we know you are what you say?" she said. "Aren't fairies supposed to be tiny and have wings?"

"It is understandable that you do not believe me. We fairies can change shapes. I chose to be human-like to speak with you. In fact, I am typically very small and I do have wings." Lhainna saw that they were still skeptical. "We are protectors of this forest. We help the forest stay alive and vibrant as it were many centuries ago. We are the last of our kind and we would give our lives to ensure the survival of our species." Seeing that the teens were still on their guard, she bent down on one knee and placed a glowing hand on the ground in front of her. The ground turned bright white and, as she lifted her hand, they saw a small seedling rise out of the brightness. It grew until it was a two foot tall plant. Its branches spread out and leaves grew all around it, until it became a small tree. Then it grew a bud, which blossomed into a magnificent magenta flower. It was the most amazing thing they had ever seen.

"We have the power to make things grow," Lhainna waved her hands over the little tree, "and the power to cause its destruction." The tree turned brown and shrunk until it was ash at her feet and the bright light disappeared.

The teens were shocked.

"Wow," Zadeia said. "Fairies do exist."

"What about the trees?" Fajha said. "If you are all about retaining life, why did they attack us?"

Lhainna glanced at the trees. "The trees would do anything to protect the well-being of this forest. I made them that way."

"You fashioned them to kill?" Cristaden asked.

"I fashioned them to protect this forest at all costs. They attacked you because they viewed you as a threat. I instructed them to observe before they bring on an attack and if they find a reason, they *will* eliminate the danger."

"That would explain why we felt like we were being watched," Fajha said. "It was the trees."

"But what did we do to give them reason to kill us?" Atakos said.

"The trees are not instructed to kill humans. Many humans have passed through here unharmed. But you are of Dokami blood. They sensed your power. The power you have brewing inside of each of you. Dokamis who have passed through here in the past never exhibited your incredible strength. They viewed your power as a threat to my people."

Five pairs of eyes widened in response to her statement. Besides the members of the Dokami clan and the rulers of Western Omordion, no one was supposed to know of them. For her to tell them she knew what they were was an absolute breach in their security.

"How did you…?" Atakos said.

"I know all your secrets."

"If you know our secrets," Zimi said, "you should know we wouldn't harm anyone."

"I know you wouldn't, but the trees did not. They would not have stopped their attack until you were dead."

Zadeia gasped, thinking of how she was almost killed by the tree that grabbed her.

Queen Lhainna noticed her frightened look. "Don't worry. I would not have allowed that to happen. They did what they were taught to do and I will give you a very good reason why. But right now let me introduce you to my people."

"Where are they?" Fajha said, looking around with his friends. The only one there besides them was Queen Lhainna.

"They are all around us." Lhainna stepped back and raised her arms.

Suddenly, hundreds of tiny lights came out from behind the trees in the forest. They resembled fireflies, bobbing and weaving as they flew, their little wings making buzzing sounds as they came closer. When they got close enough for the teens to get a better look at them, they no longer looked like fireflies but instead like tiny humans with wings, wearing white dresses, much shorter and so unlike the queen's long flowing one. The majority of them had blonde hair and light eyes and, from what the teens could see, they were all female.

"This can't be real," Cristaden said.

"Oh, but it is." Lhainna stepped back again to allow the fairies a closer look at the stunned teenagers.

"Amazing," a tiny voice said, "it's been a long time since I've seen one up close."

"Don't get *too* close," said another. "They look dangerous."

One fairy did not heed that warning and went straight up to Cristaden's face. She was one of the only ones who had fiery red hair and light purple eyes. Cristaden's natural reflexes made her take a step back from the tiny creature. The fairy suddenly opened her eyes wide in astonishment, bringing her hands to her mouth. "Oh. Why does she...? She looks... Almost as if she were—"

"That's enough, Kapimia," Queen Lhainna said, her voice rising over the buzzing of fairy wings. "You may all leave us now and return to your homes, please. I have some important things to discuss with the children."

The fairies appeared sad but fluttered away immediately, illuminating the forest on the way back to their homes. When all was quiet again, Lhainna turned to the teenagers. "I came to you today not just to save you from our guardians but because I have to tell you some things I think you should know."

CHAPTER 19

The sky transitioned to a dark shade of purple as the warm, early morning sun began to rise. Besides the sound of rushing water, there were neither birds chirping nor small animals scurrying about, looking for bits of food to eat. The forest seemed devoid of life except for the radiant queen, the aura surrounding her providing a light in the mist of the dark forest as if she were an iridescent candle.

Growing up in Omordion, the Dokami friends had adapted to being 'the secret', assuming they were the only living things on their planet that had to live life with precaution and lies. It was apparent they were very wrong.

Queen Lhainna gestured to the tent and asked them to sit. The teens did as they were told as she sat down with them, her long, white dress billowing around her. "There are things about Omordion that you do not know," she said. "Long ago, magical beings resided on this planet much like we do now. They lived happily and were so full of life. We were at peace, away from the interstellar wars fought between the other planets. Omordion was a safe haven." She looked down at her hands and clasped them together. She then opened them slowly to reveal images in a spherical form. Within the sphere, the teens saw fairies dancing around the forest, helping trees grow and healing injured animals. Little people were in the fields planting fruits and vegetables, using magic to develop potions and medicine, and building their little homes. They rode magnificently large blue birds, whose wings were brilliant colors of the rainbow and whose eyes shined bright like jewels. Yet it was the people of the sea who astonished the teens the most. Resembling humans with a hint of green skin, they had patches of dark scales with little protruding fins that helped them swim. When they swam, they were powerful, much faster and stronger than the largest sea creature. With eyes the color of the sea and hair the vibrant colors of green, pink, blue, or purple, they were magnificent to behold.

"What are they?" Cristaden said.

Lhainna smiled warmly but the teens could see the sadness in her eyes. "The little people were *flitnies*. They helped tend to the land along with us fairies and they used *chlysems*, the birds you saw, to get around faster. The birds were so beautiful...they could breathe fire as well, although we didn't realize it until..." Lhainna frowned and paused, then continued. "The sea people were called *ceanaves*. They cared for the plants and animals of the oceans, lakes, and rivers."

"What became of all of them?" Fajha said. Of all the magical creatures in the fairytales he had read, he never heard mention of any of the ones Lhainna spoke of.

"I will show you."

Lhainna told her audience to remain seated while the sphere-shaped images in her hand grew until it enveloped the entire clearing and they were seated right in the middle of it. The images were so clear and real, they felt like they were actually there.

"A group of human nomads landed on our planet five hundred years ago and we immediately welcomed them," Lhainna said. The teens saw the image of a spaceship and ten people being welcomed by many of the magical creatures. They then saw the humans eating and laughing with them. "We became great friends. But there was one who did not warm up to us. His name was Brulok." The images showed a man, with dark features, set apart from the rest and watching all of the creatures with devious curiosity. He was a beautiful man, with dark hair and bright blue eyes that shown in the sunlight when he looked up. "He was not like the others. He did not speak much, he only watched us. We asked the other humans about him and they only said he was a mute. All they knew was that he had suffered a great loss at a young age and had not spoken since. We ignored him but had no idea what he was planning to do until it was too late." The images showed Brulok shouting inaudible words at the peaceful creatures and bringing his arm forward to point at them. Just then the ground began to rumble so violently that the teens stood up in fear.

"Remain seated, children," Lhainna shouted over the deafening noise. "This is *not* real."

They sat down again in time to see monsters run out of the forest and barrel towards the inhabitants of the planet. These monsters were ferocious and brutal. Some were in the shape of animals and beasts and others were in human form. They were ugly, with dark, slimy, contorted bodies and faces. There was so many of them they practically covered the planet. The images showed them eating and ripping apart the fairies, the flitnies, and the chlysems. It showed Brulok releasing a poison into the oceans and the lakes, which made the ceanaves have no choice but to come out of the water to meet their deaths. The images were so real that at one point, a ferocious beast ran towards Zimi and he rolled out of the way to avoid being eaten. He turned to see it snag a flitny and pin it to the ground, gnawing on its head. Zadeia had her eyes shut. She did not want to see anymore. As fast as the images came, they suddenly disappeared, and the forest was serene once again. With hearts beating fast, the teens saw that Lhainna had closed her hand. There were tears in her eyes when she looked up at them again.

"That was when all we knew came to an end," Lhainna sadly said.

"You say 'we' as if you were there," Atakos frowned, trying to catch his breath.

"I *was* there. I am over seven hundred years old, although I lost count many years ago. I witnessed all of this brutality. That's why I am able to share it with you today."

"Are you immortal?"

Lhainna laughed. "I am not. We fairies can be killed but I do not know how long we can live without harm. It was not normal to keep our children close to us back then. I never knew my mother. She moved on to another part of Omordion when I was young. I believe she perished in the slaughter. All of the fairy men died too. They were the first ones who tried to defend us. Since that time, I have kept my children very close."

"Why did Brulok want to kill all the creatures of this planet?" Cristaden said.

"Brulok did not like happiness. It irritated him so much that he could not bear it any longer. I assumed he must have been raised with pure evil and malice in his heart. Where the beasts he conjured up came from, we do not know, nor do we understand why he felt that it was necessary to kill us. He could have left if he did not like our planet but he chose not to. Instead he chose to take out his anger on us."

"What became of the humans he came with?" Fajha asked.

"They were the first ones killed. In their sleep, the night before Brulok attacked us, he killed them all. We were so angry and tried to stop him from killing again. That was when he released his beasts."

"That's horrible," Zadeia said with tears in her eyes.

"What happened afterwards?" Cristaden said. "What stopped the attacks?"

Lhainna took a deep breath as if reminding herself to breathe. "Along with the flitnies, we developed spells to protect this forest. We managed to provide a safe haven for the survivors. Using temporary cloaking spells, it took us a long time to gather the survivors without getting ourselves killed in the process. Having once overrun this planet, we were down to a few thousand fairies, flitnies, and ceanaves. The chlysems had disappeared. We never heard from them again. Once in a while, I would sense their presence but it would only be for an instant. With a blink of an eye, the feeling always disappears.

For many years, we hid behind our protection spells and Brulok grew tired of trying to force his way through. He isolated himself somewhere on this planet. I don't know what became of him. His beasts still roam Omordion to this day though, although not the great army they were before. We were still so very frightened to come out of hiding that for fifty years we remained in this forest, hidden from the world. When we finally decided to venture out, we realized that Brulok had left traps behind. He designed lovely creatures to lure us into an ambush by his minions whom he left behind to kill us in the event that we were to leave the forest. We fairies have a tendency to fall under a deep spell when presented with something extraordinarily beautiful. Because of that reason we cannot leave this forest." Lhainna sadly looked around at the trees and stared longingly into the stream beside them. The sky was now a mixture of orange and blue with purple clouds as the sun continued its triumphant rise into the sky. "I invoked spirits of lost fairies and instructed them to control the trees of this forest. I trained them to kill. But now you know why it was absolutely necessary. Brulok's minions do not dare enter the forest because of the tree spirits but they lurk just outside my jurisdiction, waiting for a chance to lure us out and eliminate us. As long as those beasts roam this planet, we have to remain here." She seemed lost for a few moments in some distant memory.

The friends became thoughtful too, taking in everything the queen had told them.

After a long pause, Zimi broke the silence. "We haven't seen or heard of any of these beasts. Are you sure they still exist?"

"Yes," Lhainna said. "They are still here. Occasionally there are *incidences*. Humans from a distant planet, intent on escaping the wars before it reached their home, came to live on Omordion. For some reason, Brulok let them live. He continued to stay in hiding. He must have instructed his animals to kill only magical creatures because the attacks on humans were very few. The humans were allowed to live on this planet and make their own rules without much interruption. There were some incidents when the beasts were confused and killed humans but those cases are still unsolved with only rumors to coincide with them. To this day, the humans on this planet are unaware of its history and the secrets that lie within its very core. I believe that it is better that way and I am sure Brulok feels the same way. If the humans were to discover him and our secrets, he would have to kill them all and start the war all over again. Because he has not declared war on them all this time, I don't think that is what he wants. He is more interested in destroying us. Perhaps he feels threatened and believes that we could somehow destroy him if we ever find him."

"What happened to the ceanaves and the flitnies?" Cristaden said.

Lhainna sighed. "For a long time, they remained here in the forest, but the fresh water of the stream was not good for the ceanaves and they decided that the ocean was the best place for them if they were going to survive. I provided them a temporary but powerful cloaking spell. They left my forest hundreds of years ago. I have not heard from or seen them since. The flitnies, on the other hand, fell ill. I tried to heal them but it was not the type of illness that could be healed. They dwindled away because of their sadness and could not be revived. We lost our beloved flitnies one by one until they were no more."

Cristaden looked down at her hands and examined them. If she were a true healer, she could not imagine trying to heal someone incurable. She suddenly felt so helpless and full of despair. She looked up and locked eyes with Lhainna, who was staring back at her. Cristaden realized the feeling of hopelessness was coming from her.

Fajha spoke up then, breaking their momentary connection. "How did you learn of us?"

Lhainna turned towards him. "I have selected foresight. I can see certain things that want to be seen. It is as if the images are being projected to me from all areas of the planet, from people and animals that are in need of help. I saw who your ancestors were and what they were capable of doing. When they landed on this planet, they were in need of great help although they could not ask for it. I saw all of you when you cried at night for your parents when you were at a young age and now, when your teacher has disappeared."

"Yes!" Fajha jumped up. "Hamilda was kidnapped. Did you see her? Did you see who took her?"

"No, I did not."

"But when she was taken, she must have been at a time of great need, wasn't she?" Atakos said. "Surely you would have seen her in your visions?"

Lhainna shook her head slowly. "I cannot see who took her, nor can I see where she is. All I can say is…" She looked at each of the teens with sorrow, as if she already regretted what she was about to say. "Your teacher is surrounded by impenetrable *evil*."

CHAPTER 20

"Impenetrable evil?" Cristaden said. "How is that possible?"

Lhainna's eyebrows lifted. "Anything is possible, Cristaden, as I have just shown you. Everything you see may not be as it seems. This world is full of magic. Good and evil. Your lives at Lochenby have been very sheltered, much like the rest of Western Omordion. The Free Lands are unaware of what is out there and they don't realize what they are really up against." She looked at each of the teenagers before her. "What do you know of the war?"

Zimi, having been briefed by his father many times, spoke up. "Eastern Omordion has turned their citizens into slaves and they are angry that some of them escaped to the Free Lands."

"Yes," Fajha said. "We are also much more technologically advanced than they are so they declared war on us in an effort to gain our resources as well."

"Right but *very wrong*," Queen Lhainna said. "King Tholenod of Mituwa wants Western Omordion's resources, he does not like the fact that we took in some of the Eastern slaves, but those are not the only reasons why he declared war on us. These are just excuses. It is a fight to rule *all* of Omordion. Even after he wins the war against the West, Tholenod will then kill the kings who are fighting alongside him."

"That makes sense," Atakos said. "It explains why he will stop at nothing to win. Even a decade of fighting and losing hasn't slowed him down."

"Exactly." Queen Lhainna sat up and took a deep breath before continuing. "Now. Do you know the real reason why *Western Omordion* is trying to win this war?"

"Real reason?" Fajha laughed. "Why would they want the East to *win*? Western Omordion just wants everyone to be free," he said, recalling what his grandfather, Emperor Vermu had told him.

Lhainna became cross. "No," she said flatly. "The rulers of Western Omordion are after the same thing. They want to take over this planet as much as the Eastern Alliance does. They want to rid this planet of a threat but not to live peacefully as they claim. To proclaim the Eastern slaves as their own."

"That's a lie," Fajha said, his face turning red. "My grandfather would never make slaves out of innocent people. I don't believe that."

"I do not lie," Lhainna said with no emotion. "I have seen this through the very eyes of the Western rulers."

"If what you're saying is true …" Atakos frowned at the queen, slowly putting pieces together in his head. "If what you're saying is true, then that means if we are to fight this war and win, the Western Army will then use us to rule Omordion?"

"That is exactly what will happen."

Fajha put his head down, his eyes filling with tears he did not want anyone to see. He was in denial but he knew the fairy queen was speaking the truth. It definitely explained why they felt like they were being held prisoner at the army base.

They *were*.

Zadeia brought her hands up to her mouth. "Bontihm…the Dokami Council…they've made a terrible mistake."

Queen Lhainna nodded. "I knew of this for some time but could not get this message to you. From my understanding, they want to use you to control all of Omordion when you help them defeat the Eastern Alliance."

"If we knew of this sooner," Atakos said, "we would have run away from the Western Army long ago." He shrugged. "But it would have been too late. They already know what our people are capable of doing."

"But don't you understand?" Lhainna said. "You are still Omordion's Hope. You are the ones destined to bring peace to this planet once and for all. While being under the Western Alliance's protection, you were safe as long as the Eastern Alliance still existed. You owe your training to the people of Western Omordion, to Hamilda, and Bontihm. Even to General Komuh. Without them, you would be helpless against the Eastern Army and you would not be able to protect your families from their relentless attacks. This is why it was necessary for you to stay."

"Now it's not necessary," Zadeia said. "We don't need them anymore."

"In a way, you do. You need their army to fight. Regardless of your strength and abilities, the Eastern Army is too much for you to handle on your own. I'm not sure if you are aware of this but the Eastern Alliance is very powerful. It draws its strength in sheer numbers, one hundred times more than what Western Omordion has to offer. Their leader, King Tholenod, has turned even his slaves into merciless soldiers. I've seen it through the eyes of his people. He has no regard for human life and would stop at nothing to acquire absolute power. Every day he is trying to discover new ways to penetrate Western Omordion's defenses and he won't stop until he does. It is better to use what you have to fight then to go at it alone. When it has ended, you can bring your fight to the core of the Western Alliance."

Fajha was silent, thinking about his grandfather. How could the Emperor put his own grandson in danger? How could he not think twice about the consequences of his actions?

Lhainna saw the stunned look on his face. "The Western Alliance was easily influenced. It is not your grandfather's fault. He had no choice. They picked you out of a large group of children. You just happened to be the best, much to your grandfather's disappointment. There was nothing he could do."

Fajha clenched his fists. "We will find a way not to require *their* help," he said through his teeth.

"If you could, that would definitely be better," Lhainna said. "As for now, it is unfeasible." She glanced at the rising sun peeking through the trees. "It is almost time for you to go."

Lhainna stood up and invited the others to do the same. Before they could completely stand up though, with a few quick strides, she approached Cristaden, causing her to take a step back and almost fall backwards. "My dear, you are very special indeed," she said. "You have the power to make things grow and the gift of healing, which we also have. Your gift can be the most important during dangerous times."

Cristaden shook her head. "I have the power to 'fix' things, not to heal. The seeds I plant grow well because I take care of them. That is all."

"Do not underestimate yourself, Cristaden. You have more power than you could ever imagine. You have the power to make things *happen*. When you were little, you were the reason why no one showed up the day they chose a child from Laspitu. It was you and only you that made that happen. Tap into that power and you can accomplish great things. I believe in you."

Cristaden was bewildered. All her life she always thought she was unworthy to be part of 'Omordion's Hope'. "I don't understand," she said. "How do you know all of this?"

After a small pause, Lhainna smiled. "I can feel it. It is within you. You only have to *find* it."

"But how?"

"I wish I can help you but I can't. For that, I am truly sorry." Lhainna's eyes lingered on her face for a few moments and then looked around at the rest of the group. "Children, you must try and increase your strength as much as possible. What you are going up against is nothing you have prepared for. The Eastern Army will give Tholenod what he needs, even if it means cutting down young people like you. Be careful, the road is going to be long and fierce. You have to have more confidence in yourself to win." Lhainna lowered her voice. "And furthermore, be very careful who you trust. There are many enemies out there."

Lhainna took a couple of steps towards the twins. "You are both very strong," she said. "The elemental powers you possess are truly magnificent." She then smiled at Zimi. "You risked your life to save your sister. What you did today... your father would be so proud."

Zimi shook his head at the mention of his father, who was very stern and expected him to be just like him down to the way he walked, the way he talked, and even the way he wore his hair. Instead he did the exact opposite to defy him. He did not want to be like his father at all. But it still saddened him that in his father's eyes, he would never be good enough no matter what he did.

Lhainna shocked him when she suddenly grabbed his hand. "You don't have to be exactly like your father to be a hero, Zimi. You are your own person and a good person at that. Your father will be proud of your achievements—no matter what they are. I'm sure of that." She smiled at him again and let go of his hand.

Zimi frowned as she walked away. He wanted so much to believe her but it was very difficult.

Lhainna then walked over to Atakos. When she brought her eyes to him, her smile faded and she froze in mid-step. "What ..." She suddenly squeezed her eyes shut and swayed a little, looking as if she was about to faint.

Half expecting to hear the same confidence speech she had given his friends, Atakos was taken by surprise. "Queen Lhainna," he said. "Are you all right?"

She didn't respond.

An eerie silence fell on the forest around them. The wind stopped blowing and everything went still. A slow moan suddenly escaped Lhainna's throat. Atakos stepped forward and grabbed her by the shoulders. Upon doing so, her eyes suddenly opened.

They were completely white.

She started to hyperventilate as if there was no air to breathe and she grabbed her throat. "Atakos–Croit–," she said, falling against him. The others rushed to her side and tried to help Atakos hold her up but they couldn't. She was simply too heavy. They, instead, brought her down to the ground. Still gasping for air, she grabbed Atakos' shirt and whispered his name once again.

"What's going on?" Zadeia said, panicking.

"I don't know," Atakos said. He was terrified. He felt that, for some reason, he had caused Lhainna to react that way.

"We have to do something," Cristaden said, feeling helpless.

"Atakos," Zimi said, "What did you do to her?"

"I didn't do *anything*!" Atakos said.

With short gasps of air, Lhainna pulled on Atakos' shirt and brought him down to her until he was a few inches from her face. "Ata ... Ata ... kos. You ... are ..." She then began to moan again.

A distant light came from the forest and sped towards the horrified teens. When it reached the clearing, it separated into two lights, which the friends could now see were fairies. One of them was the redheaded one Lhainna called Kapimia and the other one was blonde and fair-skinned, with features similar to her mother. They instantly grew to human size, pushed past the teens, and knelt down beside their mother, who still had her eyes closed. Her breath was coming out in short, painful gasps.

"What did you do to her?" Kapimia shot a glance at the teens, her nostrils flaring.

"Nothing," Fajha quickly said. "She just fell into some kind of trance. I should ask *you* what's wrong with her. You know her best."

"I've never seen her like this," Kapimia said and touched Queen Lhainna's forehead.

"You mean she's never acted this way before?"

"Never. This is serious." She looked at the other fairy, who shook her head as if she was reading her mind.

"Well, you have to *do* something," Atakos said. He grabbed a hold of the hands that were still gripping his shirt and looked down at the twisted face of the queen. She was trying to tell him something but could not speak. If only she would finish what she was trying to say.

"Keirak," Kapimia said to the other fairy. She nodded towards the hands that were gripping Atakos' shirt. Keirak immediately went to the other side of the queen and pried her hands off. She then looked up into Atakos' eyes. She appeared to be very young, close to their age even, whereas Kapimia was much older. Keirak's bright blue eyes complimented her pale skin and yellow-white hair and she was very beautiful.

"Please step aside," she said in a small voice.

Atakos immediately stood up and stepped back with his friends. Kapimia placed her hand on the queen's forehead and closed her eyes, whispering something in their fairy language. Keirak did the same but placed her hands on Lhainna's chest. Under their hands, the queen's skin turned a bright white and the gasping subsided. When all was silent, they released their hands and waited for a reaction from their mother.

Queen Lhainna drew her breath in slowly at first and then began to breathe normally. She was no longer moaning and seemed peaceful. Her eyes slowly opened to see the two fairies standing over her.

"What happened?" Lhainna said suddenly. "Why am I—?" She tried to lift her head off the ground but dizziness overcame her.

"Shhh," Kapimia said, putting her hand on her forehead to relax her back down. "You must rest, mother. Try not to move."

"But what happened?"

Atakos stepped forward and explained to her in detail what took place. "You tried to tell me something. Do you remember what that was?"

Kapimia shot him a disapproving look.

"Tried to tell you something?" Lhainna said, searching the blue sky with her gray eyes. "I do not recall. I don't remember anything. Oh, my head hurts so much."

"Please relax, mother," Keirak said. "You've been through an ordeal. Try not to speak."

"I must try." Lhainna slowly lifted her head and, with the help of her daughters, sat up and looked around at the five bewildered teens staring back at her. "I'm sorry. I completely blacked out. You must forgive me."

"Please don't apologize," Fajha said. "It seemed as if you had a vision. I have those all the time."

Lhainna shook her head. "Whatever that was, I can't remember anything." She then looked at Atakos. "I am deeply sorry."

"Mother, we need to take you home so you can rest," Kapimia said.

"No. You two must take them through the forest and to safety. Call Saraimen and Lanchie to bring me home."

Keirak immediately returned to fairy size and raced through the trees, illuminating them around her until her light disappeared.

"Kapimia, you and Keirak must protect them. Make sure they make it safely out of this forest. Our very existence lies in their hands. If I fail to survive, my forest will no longer be protected. Within moments, it will be destroyed."

"Don't speak that way, mother," Kapimia said, tears welling up in her light purple eyes. "You know I cannot bear the thought of death."

"I know, my darling. But you know what you must do."

Just then, the forest was illuminated by dozens of lights with the return of Keirak and more fairies. Two of the fairies and Keirak changed to human form and ran to the queen. The other two fairies had features similar to Kapimia but they were not as beautiful as she.

"Saraimen and Lanchie," Kapimia said. "Take mother back to our home at once."

"Will she be okay?" Cristaden said.

Kapimia exhaled. "I hope so."

Saraimen and Lanchie picked the queen up and stood on either side of her, allowing her to put her arms around their shoulders and her weight up against them.

"Thank you for everything, Queen Lhainna," Atakos said and he bowed to her, prompting his friends to do the same.

Lhainna smiled weakly. "Please be careful who you trust and have confidence in yourself. This planet depends on you. Good luck finding your teacher." The three women then shrunk down to fairy size and quickly disappeared into the forest along with the other fairies.

"We have no time to waste," Kapimia said. "We must make haste and get all of you out of the forest."

The friends quickly packed up their belongings, putting their cloaks into their backpacks before they put them on their backs. When the clearing was emptied, Kapimia and Keirak changed back to fairy size again and flew through the trees with the five friends quickly following close behind, trying desperately to keep up. Although they had fallen behind on their quest to find Hamilda, the sheer urgency the fairies showed to get them out of the forest was almost… frightening.

CHAPTER 21

'*Atakos ... you ... are ...*'

"I am what?" Atakos said softly at the front of the line so only his friends could hear him.

Zadeia looked past Atakos' head at the fairies flying way ahead of them. "That's what I'd like to know. Whatever 'you are', it did not seem good. Even her daughters seemed afraid."

"It doesn't make any sense," Cristaden said from the end of the line. "She looked at you as if she'd seen a ghost!"

"Everything she said and showed us seemed so unreal to me," Zimi said. "Who would have thought magical creatures dominated this planet hundreds of years ago?"

"Yes," Zadeia said, "and vicious beasts who appeared out of nowhere to kill them?" She shivered. "Sounds like the stuff of fairytales to me. Or a bad nightmare."

"Guys, *we* are the stuff of fairytales according to the rest of civilization," Fajha said. "Well. Except for the rulers of Western Omordion." His jaw tightened when he thought of his grandfather and how he knew his grandson's life was at risk. It made him furious but he tried to put it out of his mind.

Cristaden could sense how Fajha was feeling and reached out to pat his back. He turned around and smiled, attempting to hide his disappointment. "Cristaden, why didn't you tell us you were the only one who stepped forward as a child when they were looking for a Dokami child in Laspitu?"

Cristaden sheepishly bowed her head and stared at the leaf-ridden ground. "I didn't think it was worth mentioning. I just figured no one wanted to volunteer."

"Becoming a high official on this planet is every parent's dream for their child," Atakos said. "It's impossible for so many people not to come forward."

Cristaden frowned. It always seemed strange to her but she never questioned it. Her parents did not think anything of it either. They just knew she wanted to go and did what she asked. She suddenly recalled the words of the queen. '*You have the power to make things happen.*' With her second-rate powers, how could that be true?

"Don't worry about it, Cristaden," Zimi said, turning back to look at her. "You couldn't have known there was a greater reason for no one showing up that day." He looked ahead of him in time to see the fairies rushing back towards them.

"We have just a little ways to go before we leave the realm of our queen mother," Kapimia said in her tiny fairy voice. "The forest will become very treacherous after that. Please stay on the path we create and do not stray from it. We will lead you out of here unharmed."

The teenagers nodded. Kapimia and Keirak led them down a steep slope. The sun was climbing high in the sky, making the air warmer with each passing minute. Once they reached the bottom, the fairies communicated to them that they had left the queen's jurisdiction and reiterated to stay in a straight line directly behind them.

At the back of the line, Cristaden looked up at the trees, which were tall once again, and noticed how a steady breeze, nonexistent in Lhainna's forest, had begun to blow. She was glad to be out of that demented forest even if it was well protected. It was not natural. This part of the forest made her feel more at ease. Taking a deep breath in and letting it out slowly, she closed her eyes to take it all in. When she opened her eyes again, something flickered near her face, catching her off-guard. Almost tripping on a rock, she caught herself, turned towards the flickering object, and froze. No one noticed when she stopped. Her friends kept walking, thinking she was still at the back of the line.

Cristaden had never seen anything so beautiful. It was, in every sense, a butterfly. But it was not just any regular butterfly. This one appeared to be glowing. It had big, beautiful wings that were bright yellow, green, and red with a long, black tail. "Hey—," she started to say but was interrupted by another butterfly, similar to the first one, fluttering by her, close enough that it practically touched her face. Cristaden's eyes glazed over with each flap of the butterflies' wings. "How beautiful," she whispered. As the butterflies flew away, they compelled her to follow them, which she did. She walked away from the path made by the fairies, stepping through the dense brush as if they were not there at all.

"Look out for rocks," Kapimia said from the front of the line. "It's best to go around them." Still wet from the previous rainfall, the forest floor became increasingly rocky and slippery with every step they took. The trees and brush became less dense as they made their way out of Sheidem Forest.

Kapimia and Keirak turned around. "Our journey through the forest is coming to an end, children," Kapimia said. "I am afraid we must say goodb– where is the fair-headed one?"

Turning around, the teens were shocked to see Cristaden missing.

"Where is she?" Zadeia shrieked.

"Cristaden!" Atakos called, his heart beating hard in his chest. In response, all he heard was silence.

"I didn't even realize she was gone," Fajha said. "I thought she was behind me the whole time. She shouldn't have been at the back of the line. It should have been me—"

"It makes no difference now," Keirak said. "We must find her quickly before it is too late." She hurriedly flew back the direction in which they came.

As they followed Keirak, Atakos called Cristaden again but still received no response. The others joined in with him, their voices echoing throughout the forest but there was no sound in return, not even the sound of birds or animals. Once again, the forest was still and eerily quiet.

"Cristaden!" Zadeia called, her voice coming out in short bursts as she tried to hold back her tears. There was no sign of her anywhere.

Kapimia flew down to the forest floor and scanned it briefly. "She walked away from us here," she said.

Atakos bent down quickly to see what she was observing. "Footprints. Heading in that direction." He pointed to their right and immediately followed the footprints, with the team following close behind him, calling out her name frequently to no avail.

"We must hurry, she might be in danger," Kapimia said. She looked up ahead, spotted something that flew out from behind a tree, and stopped short. "No. It can't be."

"What is it?" Atakos said.

A butterfly slowly flew past them. "It's a butterfly," Zadeia said, watching the brightly colored butterfly fly up to another tree. It was nothing like any butterfly she had ever seen. "A very strange looking—"

"It's not just any butterfly," Kapimia said. "It is a *Harpelily* butterfly. They are used to distract us, to lure us directly to *oblots*."

Throughout his studies of different species in his Biology class, Fajha never learned of anything called an oblot or a Harpelily butterfly for that matter. "What's an oblot?" he said.

"No time to explain. We must move quickly. She has to be found. NOW!" Kapimia flew away, calling for her sister who was way ahead of them.

The four friends took off running after the fairies and their hearts began beating faster. Whatever an oblot was, it did not sound good.

When Kapimia reached Keirak, she explained to her that they may be dealing with one or more oblots and Keirak became visibly frightened.

"Cristaden!" they called, still following the footprints.

"Please be okay," Atakos repeated over and over as they ran.

Just then her footprints veered off to the left and the group took a sharp turn and followed them. They ran past more butterflies and their fear grew stronger.

"There she is!" Keirak said and pointed straight ahead. Looking up from the footprints, they spotted her. Cristaden was in a large clearing, surrounded by what seemed like fifty or more Harpelily butterflies. They were landing on her shoulders, her outstretched palms, and playing with her hair. Her eyes seemed glazed over yet she was smiling crazily at them, not realizing she may be in serious trouble.

"Cristaden!" Atakos cried out when they reached the clearing.

"They are so beautiful," Cristaden said in a soft voice.

"We must leave," Kapimia said as she approached her. "We have to go."

"Look at them," Cristaden said with a dreamy look in her eyes. "Have you ever seen anything so perfect?"

Kapimia went right up to Cristaden's face and raised her voice. "These butterflies are Brulok's way of luring us out of the forest. The cloaking spell we've developed makes us immune to them. You must snap out of it, Cristaden. They will lead the oblots *straight* to us."

Cristaden did not respond.

Kapimia glanced at Keirak. "We have to get her out of here. Help me carry her."

"It's too late," Keirak said, her voice quivering. "They were waiting for us. We've fallen into their trap."

It did not take long to see what Keirak was observing. Three oblots, as the fairies called them, had the group surrounded. About the size of large bears with black, matted, and slimy fur, they stood just outside the clearing, ready to attack. Red beady eyes glared back at the teens with large ears that pushed up against the side of their nasty, distorted heads. Their paws were gigantic with sharp looking claws. When they snarled, hundreds of razor-sharp teeth could be seen in their large, slimy mouths. They growled ferociously with anticipation, drool dripping down their chins.

"Brulok's beasts," Kapimia said, her voice quivering. "You must run, children." When the petrified teens did not move she yelled, "Run!"

They turned to run but Cristaden was still lost in a trance. Atakos reached for her hand to pull her with him. He didn't even see one of the beasts running towards them with incredible speed until it pounced on Cristaden's back, knocking her face down on the ground.

Cristaden started screaming.

"No!" Atakos screamed.

The others stopped and turned around to see the oblot snarling at Atakos, with Cristaden under its giant paws. It greedily opened its mouth and bent low to bite the horrified girl, eyes still transfixed on Atakos. Zimi and Zadeia immediately used their wind-force to push the oblot off before it bit her. It flew back twenty feet, giving Atakos enough time to yank Cristaden off the ground and push her to the side of the clearing. The other two oblots snarled at them and maintained their positions, as if calculating the group's every move.

It was too late to run. They had to stand their ground.

Atakos, Fajha, Zimi and Zadeia removed their backpacks and threw them to the side to prepare for the fight. Before they had a chance to react, the three oblots charged at them all together. The oblot that was thrown off Cristaden ran directly at Atakos, huffing and puffing like a bull, its sharp teeth glinting in the sun.

Everything happened so quickly that the terrified teens had to think fast. Atakos picked the oblot up with his power. The beast made an agonizing screech as he threw it several feet away. At first, he thought that he might have killed it, but it lifted its head, shaking it from side to side. It then got up and charged at him faster than before, giving Atakos only a millisecond to push it away. This time the creature did not go back as far. It gripped the ground with its claws to come to a halt and prepared to retract.

Cristaden screamed and closed her eyes, bringing her hands to her ears. She was horrified and felt so helpless. It suddenly occurred to her that this was her fault. She remembered the two butterflies. Everything else was a blur. Looking around, she did not see any of them, as if they had performed their duty and left before things got rough.

But the word 'rough' was an understatement. One oblot was charging at Atakos, the second one was playing games with Zimi and Zadeia, running around them so they couldn't aim right with their wind powers. Fajha was on the ground with what appeared to be blood on his head and the third oblot, after knocking him over, ran straight towards Cristaden, looking as if it was ready to have a feast. She opened her mouth to scream but Kapimia and Keirak grabbed each of her arms and, with strength she did not know they had, pulled her up into a tall tree behind them. The sisters managed to get her at a high, thick branch just as the oblot reached them. Enraged, the beast tried desperately to slam against the tree, hoping to rattle it enough to make Cristaden fall. She almost slipped forward but managed to grab a branch to keep herself steady.

"*Do* something," Cristaden said to the two fairies. The oblot pushed against the tree once more, releasing an angry growl from the depths of its massive body.

"We can't," Keirak said. "They want us dead and will stop at nothing to destroy us. Our powers are defenseless against them! There's nothing we can do to help. It's up to your friends now."

The charging oblot came at Atakos fast and pushed him to the ground. He put his arm up and pushed against the side of the beast's head in order to block it from biting him but it kept pushing up against his raised arm, just inches from his face. Atakos could feel and smell the oblot's hot, sour breath and some of the drool from its mouth descended onto his cheek.

The slimy fur made it hard for him to keep his arm from slipping and he began to lose hope that he was going to win the battle with the creature. The beast became more furious every time it tried to bite him but was pushed back. It raised its massive paw and clawed at Atakos' shoulder and arm, tearing through his flesh down to the bone. Wailing in pain, Atakos knew that if he did not do something quickly, the beast would kill him.

Using all the strength he had, Atakos kicked the oblot in the abdomen. As soon as the beast retracted, he channeled all his energy to his hands and, while trying his best to ignore the pain in his arm, pushed the oblot as hard as he could with his ability. The beast flew back, hitting a tree with full force, and hung there, impaled by a thick branch. Wriggling around, it squealed and shrieked, blood pouring from its mouth. And then it was still.

Positive the beast was dead, Atakos turned to his friends. The second oblot was still running around Zimi, Zadeia, and a now standing Fajha with supernatural speed. Zimi tried to freeze it but the creature kept dodging his blows. When the oblot got tired of its game, it charged at Zimi. Before any of the teens had a chance to react, it opened its hideous mouth and grabbed his thigh, clamping down hard, sinking its teeth into his flesh. Zimi screamed as he tried to freeze it but the throbbing pain made it too difficult to concentrate. Zadeia and Fajha immediately brought forth their power to force the beast off of him. The oblot's grip was so strong that his flesh began to tear as it was being pushed back.

"Stop!" Zimi screamed. "STOP!"

"What do we do?!" Zadeia cried as she and Fajha stopped pushing. Fajha felt defenseless.

Zimi's screams were echoing throughout the forest. The oblot raised its head, lifting him off the ground, and slammed him down hard. The blow knocked him unconscious and his screams of pain ceased.

"Over here!" Zadeia called to the oblot, waving her arms, desperately trying to get it to release its hold on her brother.

"Zadeia, NO!" Fajha shouted, but it was too late. The oblot released its hold on Zimi and turned to her with incredible speed, grabbing her arm with its razor-sharp teeth. Zadeia screamed and tried to free her arm but it seemed that the more she struggled, the tighter the hold on her arm became. Fajha didn't know what to do.

Just then Atakos ran up to them, holding a fallen branch he picked up off the forest floor. He broke the branch in half against his knee, making sure both ends were sharp. He then handed one end to Fajha. They looked at each other and nodded, knowing what they had to do. Instantly, they ran at the oblot, raising the stakes high above their heads. Atakos brought his down between the oblot's eyes and Fajha pierced its neck. The raging beast let go of Zadeia's arm and wobbled towards the boys but fell down dead before it could attack them. Seeing the massive amount of blood dripping from her mangled and broken arm, Zadeia started crying and sunk to the ground. The boys stared at the twins in horror. What have they gotten themselves into?

A piercing scream then rang out in the forest.

The third oblot rammed the tree so hard, Cristaden lost her grip on the branch she was holding and slid forward, only managing to grab a tiny branch, which could not hold her weight efficiently. Kapimia and Keirak made an effort to pull her back up while the beast jumped up, trying to bite her leg.

Fajha immediately ran to the beast and used his energy to push it away from the tree but the beast was simply too strong. It retracted quickly and ran to Fajha, snarling and snapping at him. Getting up on its hind legs, it swiped its sharp claws across his face, tearing it open, and then knocked him over with its enormous head. The oblot was about to take a vicious bite out of him when it was suddenly lifted into the air. Squealing like an enormous, crazed pig, its arms and legs flailed in mid-air as its body started bending at an unnatural angle. The oblot's stunned audience watched in horror as it bent in half until its spine cracked loudly, sending shivers down their backs. It then started stretching as if it were being pulled at both ends by some unseen force. Entrails fell out of its body and blood splattered everywhere as it separated into two pieces, its legs and arms still flailing. What remained of the beast fell to the leaf-ridden ground and was still.

Atakos' arms dropped to his side. He wasn't sure what happened or how he did it. All he knew was he had to do what he could to save his friends. Surveying the clearing, he realized that all the oblots were dead, he and his friends were hurt really bad, and the forest suddenly seemed so dark and scary. Somewhere, far away, his name was being called but he could not figure out where it was coming from. His body swayed back and forth for a moment as his eyes rolled back into his head. He did not feel when he hit the ground but suddenly he wasn't standing anymore.

Then everything went black.

CHAPTER 22

As Cristaden observed the horror the oblots left behind, she couldn't help but feel as though her friends had come to a very fatal end of their journey to find Hamilda. Zimi was unconscious with blood dripping from a huge bite on his thigh. Zadeia was sitting on the ground whimpering while cradling her mangled arm and trying not to look at it. Fajha was picking himself off the ground with a hand pressed against the deep wounds on his face to prevent the loss of more blood. Atakos was unconscious with a torn, bloody arm where the first oblot had scratched him.

Her friends were *dying*.

Kapimia and Keirak helped Cristaden down from the tree and they made their way around the dead, ripped apart oblot to Zadeia, who was trying to be brave and not cry.

"Can you help them?" Cristaden asked the two fairies. When they did not respond and just looked at each other, tears sprung up in her eyes. "Please?"

Kapimia shook her head. "I'm sorry, Cristaden. Keirak and I believe you can help them. On your own."

Cristaden scoffed at the idea. "But I can't."

"Yes. You can."

"My friends are dying. I can't heal them. Don't you understand?"

"Just try."

With tears rolling down her face, Cristaden turned to Zadeia. "Let me see." She pulled Zadeia's other hand away from the torn arm and looked at the damage. The bones in her forearm were protruding out of her skin and her hand was hanging limp, unable to move. *I can't fix this,* Cristaden thought. *It's too extreme.*

"Cristaden, you can do this," Keirak said reassuringly.

"All I can do is fix things. Even if I get the bones back together, there will still be an open wound."

"Trust me. Your powers are meant for healing, not for merely 'fixing'. You can do this. We will show you how."

The two sisters instantly grew to human size and bent down next to Cristaden and Zadeia. Kapimia took Cristaden's right hand and placed it above the broken arm.

"Now close your eyes," Kapimia said. "Are you aware of the anatomy of the human body?"

Cristaden closed her eyes. "Yes, I have done extensive research on it."

"Then you must know how the forearm is supposed to look like on the inside?"

"Yes, of course."

"Good. Just focus on how it's supposed to look and bring your thoughts to your hand."

Cristaden concentrated on how the bones and tendons in the forearm should look and she channeled her energy to her hand. When her palm began to grow hot, she instantly lost her focus and stopped. Opening her eyes, she saw no change in the wound. Zadeia began moaning in pain and tears sprung up to her eyes once again.

"It's okay, Cristaden," Keirak said. "Have more confidence in yourself."

"Cristaden, please help me," Zadeia choked through her tears. "The pain. I can't bear it any longer." She looked over at her brother and wondered if he was even still alive.

Cristaden closed her eyes again, determined not to lose her focus. She thought of how the bones were supposed to look and brought her energy to her hand. Her palm began growing hot again but she didn't let it deter her. The sound of bones crunching together disturbed Cristaden, causing her to flinch as Zadeia started screaming in excruciating pain. Fajha crawled over and offered his hand for her to squeeze. As Zadeia's screams grew louder, Cristaden tried hard not to break her concentration. When the sounds of crunching bones stopped, she focused on how the nerves and muscles should be. She slowly opened her eyes in time to see the nerves coming together and the muscle slowly rolling over them to cover the exposed bones. Then Kapimia grabbed Cristaden's wrist and placed her hand on Zadeia's arm. Cristaden concentrated on how smooth the skin should be and Zadeia's arm began turning a bright white. The torn skin came together under her hand and Zadeia stopped screaming.

Cristaden sat back, breathing hard. She couldn't believe what she was seeing. Zadeia's arm was completely healed and she could move her wrist and hands again. The fairies were right. She was a healer.

"You did it!" Zadeia said. She started crying and flung her arms around Cristaden. Then she backed up suddenly. "Oh! You must help the others."

Cristaden turned to Fajha, who was still bent over them, pressing his hand against the wounds on his face. Taking a deep breath, she leaned forward, pulled his hand away, and touched his face as she closed her eyes. His skin turned a bright white beneath her palm as the wounds closed. She then opened her eyes and removed her hand, leaving behind a white handprint which slowly faded away. When she saw that his flushed cheek was completely healed, she breathed a sigh of relief.

"Thank you, Cristaden," Fajha said. For the first time, she could see tears in his eyes.

Cristaden nodded, still in awe about her new power. Feeling as though, at any moment, she might lose it, she quickly stood up and ran to Zimi, who was slowly waking up. Moaning, he brought his hand to his throbbing head. The pain in his leg was so agonizing, he dared not move it.

"Why does it hurt so much?" Zimi moaned. He could not sit up to see the damage that was done. The last thing he remembered was the oblot biting down on his leg. The ripping sensation was enough to send him over the edge. He remembered thinking that their journey to find Hamilda was over, that they were all going to die in Sheidem Forest and no one would know where to find their remains.

"It's okay Zimi, I believe I can help you," Cristaden said. She placed her hand on his thigh and concentrated on putting the torn ligaments, muscle tissue, and skin back together. The gaping wound healed fast, allowing Zimi to move his leg without any more pain. Cristaden then placed her hand on his head where he suffered the concussion and healed any head trauma and nerve damage she thought might be present.

"H-how did y-you ...?"

Letting out the breath she was holding, Cristaden felt more useful now than ever before. To be able to help dying victims was something she had always dreamt about since she started taking science classes. She never thought that she would be able to help them in this way. "The fairies," she said. "They showed me how."

After helping Zimi to his feet, Cristaden looked around. There was a strong odor radiating off the oblots now and they seemed to have shrunk since she last observed them. It was as if they had been just empty shells, filled with pure evil. The impaled oblot, hanging on the tree, was dripping blood into a pool mixed with Atakos' blood, which was still seeping from his arm.

"Atakos." Cristaden ran over to him with her friends and the two fairies following close behind. He was lying on his side, his head resting on his arm. His usual caramel-toned skin was unnaturally pale. His fingers and feet were twitching sporadically and, upon turning him onto his back, Cristaden saw that his eyes were open. She sucked in her breath as her heart leapt in her chest. "Atakos? Can you hear me?"

The only response she received was the heavy breathing escaping his slightly parted lips. She placed her hand on his forehead. He was cold.

"What's wrong with him?" Zadeia asked.

"He used all the energy his body had left to kill the oblot," Kapimia said, kneeling down next to him.

Cristaden examined the wounds that extended from his shoulder to his elbow. She placed both hands on them and the blood stopped flowing as they closed. Yet Atakos was still unresponsive.

"What do I do now?" Cristaden asked Kapimia.

"He needs energy," Kapimia said. "Place your hand on his head and concentrate on giving him some of yours."

Cristaden did as she was told and brought forth her energy like she did when she was healing, but instead she focused on making it go throughout his entire body. After a few seconds, Cristaden felt the energy draining from her. It was too much to handle all at once. Feeling suddenly light-headed, she forced herself to release him and sat back, trying to catch her breath. There was still no change in Atakos. He was breathing just as heavily as before.

"I can't do it," Cristaden said, panting. "He requires too much energy. More than I can handle."

"Then we will help you," Kapimia said. "Keirak, sit on his left side and I will take his right. Cristaden, you will sit by his head. We must do this quickly."

The three girls sat around Atakos and placed their hands on his chest. With their fair skin and light eyes, they resembled three sisters to their observers. Even down to their similar powers. They closed their eyes and instantly began to go to work. Blue light immediately traveled down their arms and into Atakos' body, illuminating him completely. This light was much different from the white healing light as it descended from the tip of his head down to his toes.

Suddenly, the three healers were pushed back a few feet as a tremendous burst of energy exploded out of Atakos. The group watched as his body stood straight up and lifted into the air. His arms came out as if he was accepting a gift from the sky and he hovered for a moment. With blue light swirling around him, his floating body slowly descended until his feet rested on the ground. Bringing his arms down to his side, Atakos turned around slowly, looking down at his hands.

"Wow, I feel so much power coursing through my body." He suddenly shivered and the blue light dissipated until it was gone. He then noticed his torn, bloody shirt and the recent events all came back to him like a tidal wave. Quickly, he looked around. Expecting to see blood and carnage everywhere, he was shocked by what he did see. Only the oblots, shrinking into almost nothing, were dead and everyone else was okay. He blinked once and then twice at Zimi and Zadeia. "You're okay," he said. "How did this happen? Am I hallucinating right now? All of you. You're really okay? Are we dead?"

"No," Zimi said, laughing. "We're not dead."

Atakos looked at Zimi's leg, which had been torn apart by the oblot, and took a step toward him, unbelieving of what he saw. "But, Zimi ..."

"I healed them, Atakos," Cristaden said, beaming.

"But how did you ...?"

"And I healed you, too." She gestured to the fairies. "Kapimia and Keirak helped me give you your energy back."

Atakos recalled the blue light which made him feel so powerful. It was their energy, coursing through his body. He looked down at his arm and torn shirt. Through the sheer adrenaline he felt while he was attempting to save his friends, he had not realized how hurt he was until he saw his blood-soaked shirt and pants. He looked at Cristaden and tried to smile through his shock. "That's incredible," he said. Her new power was better than all of their powers combined.

"It was nothing really," Cristaden said sheepishly. She was taken aback when her friends suddenly came in for a group hug but she understood why. Their first real fight had gone horribly wrong. Without the fairies there and Cristaden's help, they would have died. They knew they had a lot to learn but it was comforting to know that they were still alive. They *survived*.

Kapimia looked at Keirak and nodded, knowing that her sister was feeling the same way. There might be hope for their future after all. She cleared her throat and turned small again, flying around them with urgency. "We must get you out of the forest as soon as possible. There's bound to be more of Brulok's minions lurking about."

Keirak changed back to fairy size as well. "Hurry," she said.

The teens broke up their embrace and quickly grabbed their backpacks. After changing their blood soaked, torn uniforms into the only other pair of clothing they had, they followed the fairies out of the clearing and back through forest. At a steady pace, they marched quickly in one line, this time making sure no one got left behind. Listening for foreign noises and watching for any movement around them, they did not dare speak, praying that Brulok's minions would not hear them. The forest was hot as the mid-day sun rose directly above them. Exhausted and parched, they realized they had not eaten or drunk anything since the night before.

After some time, the fairies stopped and turned to them. "This is as far as we go, children," Kapimia said. "The end of this forest is near so if you keep going straight, you will be out of here in no time."

Cristaden bowed. "Thank you so much for everything."

"Yes, we owe you our lives," Atakos said.

Kapimia and Keirak increased to human size and embraced each one of them. "We only did what we could to help," Kapimia said with tears in her eyes. "I only wish we could have done more."

As she approached Atakos, Keirak gave him a kiss on his cheek, causing him to blush. "You saved their lives, Atakos. You should be proud."

Cristaden felt a pang of jealousy at the sight of the beautiful fairy kissing Atakos. Keirak then looked at Cristaden and smiled at her, giving the same hug and kiss to her. "In another lifetime, we could have been sisters," she said and squeezed her hand.

"I would have liked that," Cristaden said, suddenly feeling ridiculous.

The two fairies returned to their normal size and, with a final farewell, they quickly flew back to Queen Lhainna's protected forest. They went so fast that, to the five members of Omordion's Hope, it seemed as if they had vanished.

They were on their own.

CHAPTER 23

"It can't be that bad," Atakos said after they had a moment of silence glancing at each other worriedly. "We fought and killed those oblots. If we had to, I'm sure we could do it again."

"But we almost *died*," Zadeia said, pointing out the obvious.

"We didn't. That's the most important thing. We can survive."

"I don't know about you guys, but my energy is spent," Cristaden said. "I don't think I can heal an enormous wound right now without some rest."

"She's right, Atakos," Zimi said. "We don't have the energy to fight."

"Let's just stick together and watch our backs," Fajha said. "Standing here discussing this is the last thing we should do."

"Okay." Atakos looked around them. "But stay close. We won't march in a single line anymore. Now that the forest is not as dense, we will walk with two people in front and three in the back."

Not wanting to be in the back anymore, Cristaden stepped up to stand next to Atakos while Fajha and Zimi made sure Zadeia walked in between them. They began their trek through the remainder of the forest, attempting to hurry but trying to keep quiet at the same time. The terrain was becoming increasingly rocky the further they got to the edge and plant life became practically nonexistent. The few trees they saw were tall and thin, the leaves on them turning a bright shade of orange, a drastic change from the trees in Sheidem Forest. The teens came upon a large rock formation, which they had to climb, feeling like easy targets along the way. They were afraid to use any of their powers, fearing that Brulok's minions might be able to sense their energy.

"This forest seems like it will never end," Atakos said as they reached the top. All he saw was more trees stretching out in front of them.

"By the change in terrain, it seems like we are almost to Osmatu," Fajha said, "but I don't see an end to this as far as my eye could see."

Cristaden stopped suddenly, prompting the rest of her friends to stop as well. There was a change in the air that did not seem normal. It was an eerie feeling. She started to make a comment but Zimi tapped her on her shoulder, interrupting her thoughts.

"Did you hear that?" he said, whispering.

Atakos, having not heard what Zimi heard, saw something at the corner of his eyes. Puzzled, he looked towards the object flittering past them. The sun reflected brilliantly off its tiny wings of yellow, green, and red. Its long tail dragged behind it in an enticing way. It took Atakos a moment to realize he was staring at a Harpelily butterfly once again. Fear rose in his throat. "They found us," he said. "Run."

Exhausted from the last fight and using every last bit of energy they had left, the frightened teenagers leapt off the rocks and ran. As they were running past a large group of butterflies, oblots, who appeared to have come straight out of the ground beneath the rocks, took off after them. With angry red eyes, they seemed to be much bigger than the last ones they fought. The ground shook as they pursued them, growling ferociously with hunger. No matter how heavy their backpacks were on their sore shoulders, the friends kept running.

Zadeia stole a glance behind her and shrieked. "There has to be about six of them!" She started to cry.

"Don't look back," Atakos said.

Looking straight ahead, they realized they were heading towards a cliff. It was a definite sheer drop on the other side because they saw nothing but blue skies beyond it, no forest and no mountains.

"What do we do?" Cristaden said.

Atakos thought of a quick plan and hoped it would work. "We have to separate. When we reached the edge, you and Fajha will quickly veer left and go over the cliff. Grab onto anything you can find to keep from falling. Zimi, Zadeia, and I will go to the right. This is our only chance. Does everyone agree?"

"Yes!" they said altogether even though the impending cliff looked terrifying the closer they got to it.

"When I say 'go' we will separate, got it?"

"Got it."

Zadeia could feel one of the beast's hot breath on the backs of her legs. "They're getting closer…" Tears were rolling down her face.

"Don't go until I give the okay." Atakos' heart was beating fast. What if his plan didn't work? They had no energy to fight and would surely die. If not by the monsters behind them, but by the sheer drop once they go over the edge.

"Now, Atakos?" Zadeia's trembling voice came loud and clear over the thunderous sound of the oblots' feet pounding the ground and the ghastly growling sound coming from deep in their throats.

"Not yet. Wait for it."

The cliff got closer and closer.

"I'm scared, Atakos …"

"Wait for it."

The cliff was almost upon them. In moments, they would go over the edge.

"Wait for it."

"Atakos!" Cristaden shouted. She was almost too scared to look.

"Now!"

Cristaden and Fajha dove to the left while Atakos careened to the right with Zimi and Zadeia. They were so close to the edge that they went over it, grabbing onto whatever they could find in order to prevent falling to the bottom. The oblots did not see the approaching cliff and, when the friends separated, it was too late for them to react. They did what Atakos had hoped and went flying over the edge. Their piercing screams could be heard as they plummeted to the bottom of the cliff until they were silenced when they hit the ground, killed on impact.

There was not much to grab onto at the edge of the cliff except for tree roots which were not strong enough to hold them. Cristaden and Fajha were quickly losing their grip. Atakos was also slipping and the twins had no choice but to conjure up the wind and carry him all the way to the bottom, while being careful not to land on the putrid smelling bodies of the dead oblots.

They were slightly elated when they didn't see either Cristaden or Fajha fall.

"They must still be up there," Zimi said.

When the three looked up, they found it difficult to see the top of the cliff from the ground. Their view was also blocked by protruding rocks.

"What do we do?" Zadeia said, beginning to panic. "Zimi, we should have split up. Why didn't we think—?"

"Zadeia," Atakos said, turning to his friend. "We have to stay calm. Can you help Zimi get up there?"

Zadeia huffed, wiping a tear from her eye. "I'll try but it's hard to pinpoint exactly where they are. I can't see them."

"Neither can I," Zimi said.

"Maybe if I move some rocks out of the way …," Atakos thought out loud.

"Not a good idea. If you move one rock, you could disturb the rock formation, which could result in an avalanche." Zimi chuckled a little, realizing he sounded a lot like Fajha. "We'll try our best to use the wind to guide me up there. It isn't anything like flying. We've never tried this before, you know. Hopefully it works."

"Just do something." Atakos stared up at the daunting cliff. "Please be okay," he said.

Cristaden grabbed onto a sturdier tree root, which held her weight well enough to allow her to climb it but she was worried about Fajha, who was on the verge of slipping. "Fajha, hold on," she said, trying to reassure him. The top of the cliff was only a few feet away. If she could climb to the top, then she could reach over and help him up. The others were nowhere to be seen but she had a sense they were still alive. Her main focus at that point was Fajha, who was beginning to lose his grip. He was too far from the tree root she was holding onto.

"Help me," Fajha said.

Cristaden climbed the root and pulled herself up. She saw no sign of the others. Looking over the side of the cliff, she had not realized how deep the gorge was. It was so deep that the objects at the bottom seemed as small as ants to her. Getting on her stomach, she held her hand out for Fajha to grab. "Give me your hand," she said.

Fajha looked frightened and gripped the root tighter. "I can't do it."

"Yes, you can, Fajha. Just give me your hand."

"If I let one hand go, I'll fall."

"No, you won't. I won't let you fall." Cristaden looked over the edge again and her heart began to beat faster. If Fajha fell, there was no bringing him back to life with her healing power. If the rocks protruding from the side of the cliff didn't kill him, he would die instantly upon hitting the ground.

"I'm scared, Cristaden." Tears sprung up in his eyes.

"It's okay. Just give me your hand."

Fajha released one hand and reached out for hers. They were still too far from each other so they both stretched their arms out as far as they could. When their fingertips touched, Cristaden felt a little bit of relief. Suddenly, Fajha dropped a foot away from her when part of the root he was holding gave way.

"Fajha!" Cristaden screamed. Her desperation could be heard echoing throughout the gorge below them. She tried to reach out further but now he was too far for her to grab his hand without falling over.

Cristaden felt the ground trembling beneath her and froze. Fearfully, she turned around and saw five oblots barreling towards her through the trees about a half a mile away. Her heart dropped to her stomach and the hairs at the back of her neck stood on end. She started crying, tears welling up in her eyes. "Fajha," she whispered.

"What's that sound Cristaden?" Fajha said, his almond shaped eyes looking terrified behind his glasses.

"Fajha," she said again, trying to reach further out for his hand. When that didn't work and the thunderous roar beneath her grew louder, she began to will for him to come to her.

"Cristaden, there's more of them coming, isn't there?" Fajha was horrified. By the sheer determination on Cristaden's face, he knew he was right. He suddenly saw his life flash before his eyes.

"Please, come up, Fajha, please." Tears were rolling down her cheeks as she tried to pull him up with her mind.

"Cristaden don't worry about me. Just get out of here."

"No, I'm not leaving here without you."

"You have to!"

Cristaden felt completely useless. She began to cry even more when she came to the realization that they were both going to die.

"You have to come up Fajha. We have to run away from here."

Fajha whimpered. "I'm slipping. I'm too weak to hold on."

"No. I won't let you." Cristaden tried harder to will him up and, to her astonishment, Fajha's body began to inch closer to her.

Fajha's mouth dropped as he started to move. "Whatever you're doing, don't stop!"

Within seconds, their hands met and she was able to pull him up. Standing up, they turned around. It was too late. They had no time to run.

The oblots, with their dripping, slimy mouths and their dark brown, matted fur, ran at full speed towards them. They were ready to tear them apart, knowing that the two could not possibly escape them.

Abruptly, a pair of strong arms grabbed Fajha and Cristaden from behind and pulled them back until they were floating over the gorge. They both let out bloodcurdling screams.

"Hold on tight, guys," Zimi said. Then with a swirl of cold air, they descended to the bottom of the cliff just as the oblots reached the edge, barking and growling at their departing meal.

When they finally reached the ground, Cristaden and Fajha collapsed. They were lucky to be alive.

"I thought we were done for," Cristaden said, taking deep breaths and wiping her eyes. "Thank you so much, Zimi."

Fajha thanked him also and then looked at Cristaden. "Cristaden saved my life. She tried reaching for me but I was too far for her to grab my hand. Then she pulled me up, right?"

"I think I did."

"What do you mean?" Atakos asked, noticing from Fajha's expression that it was more than just simply 'pulling him up'.

"I pulled Fajha up without touching him," Cristaden said. "I think."

"Are you serious?" Zimi said. The rest of the group looked at her in amazement.

"Yes. It took a lot out of me but it wasn't really a big deal. It was only two feet. It wasn't as if he flew up."

"But it was still incredible," Fajha said.

"Wow, Cristaden, you discovered two new powers in one day." Zadeia grinned. "That's amazing."

"Guys, I think we have a lot of potential," Cristaden said, standing up and helping Fajha to his feet. "Just like Zimi discovered he could freeze things and Atakos discovered his incredible strength,

I think we have so many hidden abilities that even Hamilda was not aware of."

The group grew silent at the mention of Hamilda's name.

After a long pause, Zadeia spoke up. "She's right. Before we began this journey we had limited powers. We have to find a way to tap into everything we are capable of doing if we have to fight any more of Brulok's monsters."

"Yes," Cristaden said. "I think those oblots heard me scream. If we stayed up there, we would have been torn to shreds by now."

"There must be hundreds of them in that forest," Atakos said. The friends solemnly looked up at the tall trees at the top of the cliff. "Just waiting for the fairies to make one false move."

"Well then," Fajha said. "It's up to us to save them right?"

"After we save Hamilda, we have another mission."

"We would have to find Brulok first," Zimi said.

"If the oblots are still going strong," Zadeia said, looking around, "he must still be out there somewhere."

The rest of the group finally took a moment to look around them too. They were so focused on escaping the oblots they had not taken in their surroundings. They were in a gorge with the cliff on one side and a small hill of orange rocks on the other side. The friends carefully climbed the rocks that barred their view of the entire area. Standing at the top of the small hill, they looked around. Orange and red rocks and boulders surrounded them with some boulders as big as houses, with absolutely no tree in sight. The sun was slowly descending, casting an orange glow on the entire terrain. There did not seem to be any end to it.

"What is this place?" Zadeia breathed.

Fajha stepped forward and adjusted his glasses. The pages of his Geography book had not prepared him for what he was witnessing firsthand. It was beautiful.

"This. Is Osmatu."

PART THREE
OSMATU

CHAPTER 24

When Aillios heard the news of his father's departure, he was anxious to discover the reason behind it. As the sun set, King Tholenod rode off with a team of twenty men on horseback along with his assistant Menyilh. The guards would only tell him that he was headed for Effit but would not tell him why he left so abruptly. Aillios was disturbed by it and considered following him but decided against it. He was so heavily guarded that his father would immediately be alerted if he were to suddenly disappear. No, it was best he stayed where he was.

Sighing heavily, Aillios sunk into the armchair next to the tall windows in his room and stared out into the fields. He was startled when he suddenly heard a loud knock at his door. "Who's there?" he said suspiciously, hoping it wasn't a guard, ordered to sit in his room until his father returned.

"It's Frolemin, dear. I've come with your hot bath water."

Aillios heaved a sigh of relief. "You may enter." Frolemin was his father's maid and she had been with the royal family for over thirty years. Although she was in her early forties, the years of hard labor had taken a toll on her and she appeared to be in her late fifties, with graying hair and wrinkles around her eyes. She entered his room with two young boys following her, carrying an enormous pail of steaming hot water.

"You may set it in there," Frolemin said to the servants, pointing to the bathroom, adjacent to Aillios' bedroom. The servants looked to be no more than ten. They carefully walked to the bathroom, trying not to spill a drop of water along the way. After setting the pail down, they then went up to Aillios and bowed before him.

"Thank you," he said. "You may take your leave." The two boys bowed again and left the room, trying hard not to glance back at the prince they rarely got to see.

"Why have you been assigned to me, Frolemin?" Aillios said. "Where is Trisalan?"

"She has taken ill, sir." Frolemin lowered her eyes. "She just learned that her mother has suffered and died some two months ago in the fields."

Aillios felt the rage boiling up inside him. Being so young when his mother died, he barely remembered her or even remembered mourning her passing. He could not imagine what it must be like to find out you lost a mother two months ago to brutality and her body is rotting somewhere in the marshlands with no gravestone. He stood up and pounded his fist on the windowsill. "Frolemin, I have to put an end to this," he said.

"I know, sir, but what is there to do?" She looked back up at him with tears in her eyes. "We are all doomed."

"Don't say that. There has to be a way." Aillios' blue eyes searched the fields, as if he were trying to find a way out for his people. Then a thought dawned on him. He immediately turned to the aging woman and walked right up to her. "Did my father say why he was leaving?"

"I don't know, I–I–" Frolemin struggled with whether or not she should tell him. She had sworn to the king that she would never repeat anything she heard and she had yet to break that promise.

"Frolemin, if you care about your people, you must tell me." His eyes were desperately searching hers, knowing that she knew the truth but would not say.

"Sir, you know he would have my head if I told you—"

Without thinking, Aillios lost his temper. "Your people are dying and he does not care. How could you stand there and worry about your head when children are out there parentless and losing their lives every day?" He then turned away from her, realizing what he just said. Her life would be in danger if she told him. How could he stand there and expect her to put herself in harm's way if he had just been sitting by his window, unable to do the same thing?

Aillios then heard Frolemin walk away. Her voice came out in a barely audible whisper as the door to his chamber closed. "I heard him mention something to Menyilh."

Aillios' head snapped around to look at her, shocked that she wanted to open up to him despite the dangers. "Yes?"

"About Effit."

"Did he say anything else?"

"They spoke of a wizard who has immense power. They are out to seek him in Effit."

"But that's ridiculous. A wizard?"

"That is all I heard. You must believe me."

Aillios considered what Frolemin said for a moment. What could his father want with a wizard? It wasn't like him to believe in outlandish tales and travel far to chase them. There had to be more to it that Frolemin did not know. Whatever is was, it couldn't be good. "I must go after him."

Frolemin stepped forward. "You do realize your father will kill you if he sees you."

"I have no choice. I must find a way to stop him before he does something irrational." Aillios went to his armoire and started pulling out clothes.

"No, wait," Frolemin said, putting her hands up to stop him. "I will be right back." She ran out of the room and, several minutes later, came back in holding a pile of worn peasant clothes and a sack that smelled of freshly baked bread. "You cannot track them wearing your princely clothes. They are bound to notice you." She handed him the pile of clothes. "I got these from the stable boy who's just about your size. He says he has a horse for you to ride."

"Thank you, Frolemin."

She smiled at him. "You don't have to thank me. Just find a way to put an end to this madness."

"I'll try. But it will not be easy." Aillios pulled out some dark clothes from the pile and started changing quickly, uncaring that the maid was still there.

"I must be going," Frolemin said quickly. "When you are finished, meet the boy at the stables. Oh, and I almost forgot." She handed him the sack of food after he removed his shirt. "I will tell the guards you are sick and I am tending to you. Please take care." She smiled at him again and raced out of the room. She had been waiting for him to take action. They all have.

A strange thought occurred to Aillios that, whichever road he took from that moment on could very well be the last time he was ever going to see Frolemin or his kingdom again. He may not even return alive. Nevertheless, he quickly changed his clothes and threw on a pair of brown boots and the stable boy's brown cloak, pulling the hood over his wavy, black hair. Tying the sack of food to his belt, he raced out of his room, making sure his footsteps were light so as not to be heard.

Aillios slowly crept down the stairs, keeping close to the shadows against the wall. At the landing, he peered around the corner and spotted a guard pacing the length of the hallway back and forth. Needing to go straight into the adjacent hall, he could not cross without the guard seeing him. He waited until the guard came close and then turned to pace away from him. Taking a deep breath, he knelt down and, checking once more to see that the guard had his back turned, did a roll to the other side and crouched against the wall. The guard heard the sound and turned quickly to see what it was as a little mouse raced up the hallway from where Aillios was hiding.

"Stupid mice," the guard said and continued pacing.

Without a moment's hesitation, Aillios ran down the hall away from the guard and descended down a short flight of stairs into the kitchen. Two kitchen servants were there along with the head chef. He bolted past them without so much as a glance and exited the castle through the back entrance, running right into another guard.

"What's the hurry lad?" the guard said.

Aillios' heart pounded like thunder in his chest. He brought his voice down low so the guard would not recognize it. "I have some food for the stable boy," he said, patting his sack and keeping his eyes down, hoping the guard would let him carry on.

"Food, hunh?" The guard peered closely at him. "I've never seen you here before. Where are you from?"

Aillios knew that the castle needed a gardener and that his father was having difficulty obtaining a good one. "I am the new gardener, sir," he said.

"Is that so?" The guard leaned in a little further to get a good look at him. "You look oddly familiar. Have we met?"

"I don't recall—"

"Ha! My cousin's nephew. You resemble him."

"Isn't that something?"

"Yes, he's about your age now, fighting in the battles against the west. A fine boy he is." When Aillios didn't say anything, the guard cleared his throat. "You may go."

"Thank you, sir." Aillios kept his eyes on the ground and walked away from him.

The two minutes it took to walk down the narrow path to the stable were the worse two minutes of Aillios' life. The hairs on the back of his neck were standing on end with anxiety as he tried not to look back at the guard watching him walk down the path. He felt that, at any moment, the guard was going to call out his name and come after him. Although he knew he would win the fight against him, he did not want to risk his father finding out about his attempted escape.

The door to the stable was closed so Aillios pushed it with his shoulder and quickly entered, shutting it behind him.

"Your majesty," he heard a voice say. Peering into the dimly lit stable, he spotted the stable boy at the far end. He was tending to a beautiful brown steed, giving him vegetables to eat from a wooden bucket. The boy couldn't have been more than seventeen years old and he was very dirty, with hair that appeared to have once been a darker shade of blonde but was now matted brown with dirt. He seemed terrified but willing to help.

"I thank you my good boy," Aillios said, advancing towards him. "What is your name?"

"It's Omlit, sir," he said, lifting his eyes to the horse. "And this is Thashmar." The horse neighed in response and stepped back as if he were ready to run from the approaching stranger. "He's the best horse we have. You will find him very agile and quick as lightning. Speak to him softly and he will listen."

Aillios smiled at him. "Thank you, Omlit." Having never been in the stable, he looked around. "Is there another exit?"

"Yes sir, at the back. Once you leave, you have to go through the horse pen and into the forest—" Omlit suddenly gasped, rushing to finish strapping Thashmar's saddle.

"What is it?" Aillios said.

"You must hurry."

"What about the guards?"

"Don't worry about them, go quickly." Omlit made sure the straps on Thashmar's saddle were tight one last time and helped the prince get on the horse. Aillios rode to the double doors at the end of the stable and, as they opened, a pile of hay an acre away from him burst into flame. All of the guards instinctively ran towards it.

"Go!" Omlit said, slapping the horse's backside.

In the blanket of night, with the guards rushing towards the flames, Aillios was able to slip past them without being seen. He heard the captain of the guard barking orders to the men, telling a few to douse the fire and ordering the rest to return to their posts and not allow anyone to escape. By then, it was already too late. Aillios had glided into the forest without detection and escaped the clutches of the dark castle. He feared for whoever risked his or her life to set the fire. If they were caught, it would be death. He shuddered at the thought, knowing the servants of the castle risked their lives for him. He knew he had to keep going and risk his life for them, too.

To begin with, Aillios had to find his father. Through many battles he had fought with him, Tholenod always set out near sunset and rested in the same area before beginning his actual journey. If he was still following his tradition, he would be at the cliffs overlooking the Stream of Asmis. The following morning, he would follow the stream to the Nikul River, which separated Mituwa, Feim, and Effit.

Aillios lit the oil lamp Omlit had attached to Thashmar and followed his good sense of direction, quickly making his way through the forest, away from the carnage and the devastation. The cliffs were about two hours away and he drove his horse fast through the trees, trying to shorten that length of time. He was hoping to get some rest before getting up at the break of dawn to follow his father and his team of men. Thashmar was just as agile as Omlit described him to be and gave Aillios no trouble while he galloped swiftly through the forest.

It was not long before Aillios heard the trickle of water from the Stream of Asmis. Once he approached it, he knew it would be only a half of an hour before he reached Tholenod's resting place. As he rode alongside the stream, he noticed how brilliantly it shown in the moonlight, as if beckoning him to come in for a swim. He prayed that one day, when his country was freed, he would build a home near the stream and settle down. It was a far thought, and a seemingly impossible one, but he always liked to dream.

Within no time, Aillios steadily approached the cliffs and he could see a small fire burning at the top. *Good,* he thought, *he did exactly what I thought he would.* He reached the hill that led up to the cliffs and decided to rest at the bottom of it, still far enough so he would not be heard. Although he was an excellent tracker, he wanted to awake before his father's team rose and follow them when they set off on their journey. He knew his father would not be aware that he was being followed. Tholenod was a cautious but arrogant man. He did not think anyone in his country would have the audacity to follow him, knowing what would happen if they were caught.

Aillios cut the light of his lantern and dismounted Thashmar. The horse whinnied slightly, shaking his mane. He talked calmly to the horse to keep him quiet and brought him to the moonlit stream so he could have a drink. An owl called out in a distant tree, the only sound he heard besides the wind rustling the leaves in the forest surrounding him and the trickle of water from the stream. He loosened the straps of Thashmar's saddle and removed it, taking the blanket out from underneath it and placing it on the ground. Only having a few hours before daybreak, he rested on the blanket and closed his eyes, allowing the sounds of the forest and the stream to lull him to sleep. The night air felt warm and, when sleepiness overtook him, he wished that he could stay in the forest forever.

In a panic, Prince Aillios suddenly stood up to the sounds of horses galloping towards him. It was mid-day and the sun was blazing hot on his back. How long has it been since the sun rose? His father must have set off hours ago! Panic stricken, he tried to find Thashmar. The horse was gone, including the forest and the stream. Looking around, he saw that he was in the middle of a familiar battlefield. A battle fought four years prior against the henchmen of Ojmodri, the leader of the rebellion, who set out to kill King Tholenod. It was an easy battle and Tholenod's army won quickly with Aillios as their general. Their slaves received harsher treatment after the battle as punishment for the uprising.

Aillios lamented over fighting them and never forgave himself.

Now he was back there, where it all began, experiencing the battle all over again as an army of two thousand men thundered towards him with

Ojmodri in the lead, wearing his war mask and waving his sword in the air. Having only homemade weapons to fight with, they had no armor because they could not afford to make them. Many of them were on foot. They came at him as if in slow motion and he saw their desperate faces. Running towards their deaths, knowing they had a slim chance of succeeding.

Suddenly fearful for his life, Aillios quickly tried to draw his sword as they came closer but realized he was still wearing the peasant clothes that Omlit had given to Ptolemin. He had no sword and no army. His heart began to beat fast in his chest. He admitted to himself that, although he was a good fighter in hand-to-hand combat, with an army of weapon wielding destroyers coming at him, he was going to die. He turned to run, almost tripping over his own feet. After trying his best to run faster, he suddenly realized he was going nowhere. The army was steadily approaching him and he could hear the cries and shouts of the men. They were screaming "Kill the monster!", "Murder the murderer!", and "Don't let him live!" He wanted to tell them it was not his fault, explain to them how his father convinced him it was best to fight, that it was the only way to save the monarchy and prevent the royal family from being hung from the nearest gallows. He wanted to explain to them how his father had convinced him that they were responsible for his mother's death. Only after the battle did he realize that his father had been wrong. Innocent people, sons of mothers, and fathers of sons had died by his hands.

It was too late to convince the army of his naivety.

They were upon him.

Ojmodri stopped only several feet away from him. He dismounted his horse and strode over to Aillios. Shaking, Aillios could see that he was not alive. He was dead. His arms were gray and patches of his bones shown where wounds once were and insects had disintegrated his flesh. Aillios' heart practically leapt from his chest when he realized that the entire army was just like Ojmodri.

Decaying.

"You have sent my people to their doom, Prince Aillios," Ojmodri said behind his hand carved, wooden mask. "For that I will not spare you."

He means to drag me to the underworld, Aillios thought, panicking. He tried to find the words to speak, to defend himself and his cause, but no sounds came out. It was as if he was under water, struggling to yell for help and not being able to breathe. Ojmodri stared at him through his mask with fire in his eyes. He lifted his sword and brought it over his head. Aillios tried to defend himself but became frozen, unable to move his extremities. He tried to scream but, again, no sound came out.

Aillios.

He was as good as dead. Today. He was going to die today.

Aillios.

He heard the voice the second time. It called out to him from somewhere in the crowd. His eyes searched the army desperately, trying to find the source.

Aillios.

It was a woman's soft voice, singing his name in a whisper. Suddenly, Ojmodri dropped his arm and took a step back as if in a trance. All of his men did the same, stepping back as well. . They then stood very still, as if they were statues on exhibit.

Aillios, the voice repeated. It was then that Aillios saw movement in the still crowd. At first he saw just the top of her light brown hair and then she came out from behind a tall, grotesquely decaying man.

Aillios, she said again, her voice sounding like it was in his head this time. She was the most beautiful woman he had ever seen. She appeared to be moving as if she were in water, walking slowly towards him with her long, brown hair floating around her pale face. She wore a long, pale-blue dress that only hugged her waist. Her brown eyes sparkled before the sun suddenly went behind a cloud and the world around him turned a dull gray. Aillios was enchanted by her and looked on as if he was under a deep spell. Stopping right in front of him, she made eye contact and he became lost in her eyes. Without moving her lips, she spoke to him:

> *Although we live in a world of despair, our actions may not define who we are. You should not have to take blame for someone else's faults. What matters most is what is in your heart. You know who and what you are. What you are is good. Do not dwell in the past. It cannot be avenged. Look ahead to a better beginning. Fight for what is right. But I must warn you, you may be defeated. Do not despair. I will offer you a kiss. A kiss of Asmis. A reflection not yours you shall have. Fear and confusion you shall not.*

With that she leaned over, kissed him on his lips, and pulled back with a smile. Never in his life had he ever felt something so warm and soft. The army behind her had disappeared and he was swooning, feeling like his body was floating in air, longing for another comforting kiss. The beautiful woman appeared to be floating also but her sweet smile had slowly faded. As he watched, her face turned very angry, almost frightening, and she raised her arms and suddenly pushed him, sending electric sparks igniting all over his body.

Then all he felt was pain.

Aillios opened his eyes. He was lying on the forest floor once again and he looked up at the sky, which was turning a deep shade of purple with the rising sun. Looking around, he saw Thashmar, several feet away, staring at him as if he was wondering what was wrong. He tried to get up and grimaced at a pain he felt in his chest. *It was a dream, was it not?* he thought. Yet, if it was a dream, why was he still feeling pain from where the woman had pushed him? Those sparks could not have been real. He looked around him to see where the pain could have come from but saw no other source.

As Aillios painfully stood up, he thought of what the woman had said. *'A kiss of Asmis … a reflection not yours …'* He looked at the stream. Could it have been Asmis who was in his dream? He recalled the legend of the woman the stream was named after. It was a tall tale, told to him by his servants when he was a young boy. They told him of a beautiful witch who once lived by the stream hundreds of years ago. She was a good witch but was persecuted by the people of Mituwa for practicing magic, which was banned in all the lands. She died a miserable death, being thrown alive into a deep part of the stream with weights tied to her hands and feet to prevent her from doing magic and escaping. It was a sad story but, before she was thrown in, she had vowed to have her revenge against the people of Mituwa. As a joke, they named the stream after her to mock her final words.

If it was Asmis than why would she come to me, a descendant of her persecutors? And what was the meaning of her last statement? Aillios took a few deep breaths in and realized that the pain in his chest was steadily going away. Suddenly, he heard a noise and cocked his head towards it, trying to listen closely. It was the sound of Tholenod's camp moving out. He almost missed them. He would have to move quickly to pursue them.

"Looks like I woke up just in time, boy," Aillios said to Thashmar. He threw the blanket on the horse's back and adjusted the saddle, buckling the straps together. He then mounted him and slowly climbed the hill to the top of the cliff where the camp once stood. The soldiers had already left and were making their way to Effit by following the stream. It would be a full day's journey to the banks of the Nikul River and, from then on, he would have to find a way to stay closely behind his father without being seen.

As Aillios followed the tracks left by Tholenod and his men, the message from the woman in his dream became a distant thought.

CHAPTER 25

Atakos opened his eyes and raised them to the rising sun. The air was cool and damp as if rain had fallen but he knew it was not so. They were dry, sleeping close together on their broken tent, having kept each other warm throughout the cold night. For two days, they climbed over hills of rocks until they found flat slabs big enough to allow the five of them to rest. They were mentally exhausted, physically drained, and hungry. Knowing they consumed the last of their provisions the day before, Atakos' stomach grumbled as he looked around. All he could see were rocks and more rocks. No water and no animals to catch. Even if they did catch an animal, they did not have the necessary tools to build a fire and cook it.

Atakos moved his arm to push himself up and felt the pain in his overworked muscles and stomach. How could they go on? They did not know if Hamilda would even be there when they reached Paimonu. The only thing they were riding on was the fact that Fajha's visions seemed to be steadily coming true.

"Wake up, everyone," Atakos said, carefully rising to his feet, trying hard to ignore the pain. "We have to get moving."

The usual moans and groans erupted as his friends began waking up.

"Do we have to?" Fajha said. "Just five more minutes."

"We have no choice. We have to find food and continue on."

Zimi laughed. "Find food. You say it as if it were possible."

Zadeia stood up and stretched her aching muscles. "Something has to give," she said, wondering what rock tasted like. Allowing her eyes to roam over the hilltops, she gasped as something caught her eye.

"What is it?" Fajha said, standing up so quickly, he almost fell over. He grabbed his glasses and shoved them on his face. Cristaden and Zimi followed suite and stood next to the others, looking for anything out of the ordinary.

"That has to be an illusion," Atakos said. He had not noticed it before. About a mile away, he saw a thin sliver of smoke rising from behind a tall hill. "Smoke!"

"Where there's smoke, there's fire," Zadeia said, smiling.

Zimi saw it now too. "And where there's fire, there's …"

"People," Cristaden said.

"Food," Fajha said.

"And water," Atakos finished, saliva gathering in his mouth.

Without hesitation, the teens gathered their belongings, descended down the small hill, and hiked in the direction of the smoke. Like his friends, Atakos was hoping there was food where they were headed but he was also cautious. They were five teenagers traveling with little provisions and confusion as to where they were headed. Strangers would pick up that something was not right immediately. It was risky but he was prepared to fight for his friends, food or no food.

Cristaden had been staring at Atakos and noticed his worrisome expression. He was frightened at what they would find and she did not have to read his mind to figure it out. There was something unsettling about where they were headed but she couldn't figure out what about it unnerved her. She decided not to say anything to alarm the others. They were excited and moving fast toward their target, unbeknownst to the concern of their two friends.

Osmatu's terrain was difficult to maneuver as they had to climb up and down small hills of rocks and boulders one right after another. The climb was tiring to their already weakened limbs but they kept moving. Finally, they reached the hill they saw the smoke rising behind. Stopping to listen for any noises, they heard nothing. When they reached the top of the hill, they saw that it was completely flat as if a giant had chopped it with a giant axe. The teenagers could see the smoke clearly now but they also noticed other lines of smoke rising from the same area.

"Here goes nothing," Cristaden said.

Crouching low, the teens went to the edge and peered over it. It was not just a few people they saw, it was an entire village, centered in an enormous clearing, surrounded by hills of rocks and boulders. They saw large tents and homes made of cement. The first smoke they saw from a distance was coming from a large bonfire the residents had made in the middle of the village and the other smoke was rising from their chimneys. It seemed as if they were preparing to celebrate something that day. The whole village was rushing around, decorating the outside of their homes with colorful flags and fake flowers.

"They don't *look* threatening," Cristaden said, her initial apprehension slowly melting away.

"How can you tell?" Zimi said.

"Well, the fact that they're hanging flowers and pretty flags might mean *something*," Zadeia said.

"That means nothing," Fajha said bluntly. "They could be happy people on their day off and mass murderers the other three hundred and sixty-four days of the year."

"They don't look like mass murderers to me," Cristaden said, watching as a few small children chased each other around the bonfire.

"Yeah right, those kids could be lunch," Fajha said. "Look at how close they are to that fire."

"Way to be optimistic, Fajha," Atakos said, rolling his eyes. "We have to decide what we're going to do."

"We could have one person sneak into the village and grab some food," Zimi said.

"Or we can just waltz right up to them and say hello," Zadeia said.

"And risk being blown up?" Fajha said. "I choose the latter."

Atakos thought for a moment. "I'm going with Zadeia on this one."

Zimi scoffed at the idea. "What do we do? Just walk up to them and say 'Hi, we're a bunch of fifteen-years-olds out in the middle of nowhere with nothing to eat. We all look like we come from different countries—which is strange, but just ignore that fact. Can you give us some food and water to drink and we'll just be on our way?'"

"Exactly," Atakos said. Bewildered, Fajha and Zimi whipped their heads around to look him. "Honestly, we can't risk having someone sneak in because they might take that person for a thief. And if that does not happen, how is that person going to be able to take enough food for all five of us that will last us for a long time?"

"I'm all for splitting a piece of bread five ways," Zimi said. "At least we'll have something to hold us for a bit."

Atakos shook his head. "I say we go up to them and be just what you said. Five fifteen-year-olds who got separated from their caravan when we went exploring. We are trying to get back home to Paimonu but have no food to help us get there. If they ask us why we look so different, we'll say our families settled there long ago from different countries. We're friends *because* we're different. Simple."

Cristaden sighed, knowing they had no choice but to agree with him. "If I sense something's wrong, we will quietly take our leave before they even notice we're gone. All in favor of taking a chance, raise your hand."

Cristaden, Zadeia, and Atakos raised their hands while Fajha and Zimi clasped theirs behind their backs.

"It's agreed then," Atakos said. "Three against two. Let's go."

"Don't say I didn't warn you," Zimi said.

The teens turned their shirts inside out so that the Lochenby emblem would not be visible and did a full inspection of each other just to be sure. Looking over the edge again, they noticed a path to the bottom that appeared to have been carved into the hillside.

Fajha shook his head when he remembered his studies of Osmatu. There was no mention of an entire village of people in his books. Something was wrong. He was sure of it. "Be on your guard," he warned.

"Remember our story and stick to it," Atakos said to his friends as a woman, who was stringing up flowers on the first house, noticed them walking towards the village. She was plump with hands that appeared rough with many years of hard labor. They could see that the sun had bleached parts of her brown hair blonde and leathered her skin years ago. When she saw the approaching teens, she alerted the people around her and came towards them, stopping several feet away, taking her time to size them up.

"*Hosmi mit-tan?*" the woman said, eyeing them up and down.

The teens stopped and frowned at each other.

"*Hosmi mit-tan?*" she said impatiently.

"Goodness, they speak another language." Cristaden turned to look at Atakos disappointedly.

"We are just trying to get to—," Atakos said but was interrupted.

"*Kesta?*" Bewildered, the woman looked back at the crowd gathering behind her and she spoke to them rapidly in her language. Cristaden tried to pick up the general vibe of the gathering crowd but, for some reason, she could not.

"What are we going to do now, genius?" Zimi asked Atakos.

"Hand gestures?" Atakos said and then shrugged. "I don't know."

Fajha stepped forward. He appeared to be listening closely to what the old woman was saying. "I know this language," he said.

"What? Are you sure?"

"Yes. It is Tuckeni, derived from Thackenbui, a very tiny island west of Sheidem, in the middle of the Saimino Ocean. It's so tiny, it's not mentioned on any maps. A few of them settled in parts of Northern Saiyut." He listened a little longer. "I think she is telling them that we do not speak their language, therefore we cannot be trusted."

"Of course we don't speak their language," Zimi said, frustrated. "They're not *from* Sheidem. We are."

"Like I said, I don't know everything she's saying, I'm only picking up some things. Seems like they're trying to figure out what they're going to do with us."

Cristaden's heart leapt in her chest. It seemed like the situation just turned from bad to worse. "Can you speak this language, Fajha?"

"I think I remember some of it."

"Then what are you just standing here for?" Cristaden grabbed his arm, her blocked ability making her extremely nervous. "Tell them why we're here before they kill us."

"Oh, now you're scared?"

"Just do it," Atakos said softly.

Fajha sighed. "Alright, but I don't think we should be talking to her. I will ask to speak to their leader." He stepped towards the crowd, pushing his glasses up his nose, and cleared his throat. "*Ti... tan... bamul... ni?*" he said.

The woman turned to him suddenly. "*Tan prali osa traeng?*"

"*Wah. Ti tan bamul ni?*"

The woman turned to a young girl standing next to her. "*Samila, allo et osa bamul.*" The girl, named Samila, ran off into the village and disappeared as she took a sharp turn after the second house.

The gathering crowd stared back at them dumbfounded.

"What did you ask her?" Atakos asked Fajha.

"I asked her if her leader was here."

"What did she say to the little girl?" Cristaden whispered.

"She told her to go get their *bamul*, which is their leader."

The air around them was tense as they waited. A couple of girls their age looked at Atakos and, after whispering something to each other, broke out into spouts of giggles. The woman who spoke to them glanced back at the girls and they immediately stopped giggling.

Atakos couldn't help but feel slightly embarrassed by their reaction to him. They appeared to be making fun of him but he could not tell. He never had any sort of attention from girls. It made him feel awkward and uncomfortable. He shifted his eyes back to the woman who had silenced them. Her eyes were dark and angry. Her heated stare forced Atakos and his friends to foolishly look down at the ground.

"*Avieni!*" A deep, hoarse voice boomed from the crowd. The crowd stepped aside immediately and a man came out from behind them. He was chubby with a round face and a shiny bald spot on top of his head that gleamed in the sunlight. His skin was tanned from the sun and his brown hair was graying at the sides.

"He's welcoming us," Fajha whispered to the others. "This is their leader."

The teens bowed simultaneously to the approaching man to show their respect.

"*Han anmu ti Maldaha.*" Their leader glanced back at the woman they had been talking to. "*Han anmu ateera ti Piedara. Osa mit etterateins warr de Tackein Provom arle norg an ni.*"

Fajha smiled at him and looked at the others. "He says that his name is Maldaha and his wife is Piedara. They are explorers from Thakenbur Island located west of here."

"*Hosmi mit-tan?*" Maldaha asked him who they were.

Fajha cleared his throat and, with great difficulty, gave him the excuse they had previously concocted. "*Osa…mit etterateins-vo…Osa allat desata…warr de…eten voni raspeel blat de. Osa mit-san…flachi allet hom te Paimonu.*"

Maldaha peered at him strangely. "*Mit-tan gree tan osa warr Paimonu?*"

Heat rose at the back of Fajha's neck. What was wrong with saying that they came from Paimonu? Why was he asking if they were sure they had come from there? He straightened his shoulders, ready to stand firm to their lie. "*Wah.*"

Maldaha's smile grew. *"Abai da. Tan mit avieni rete ni. Tan mit agni osa. Allo viet-han!"* He grabbed Fajha's arm and pulled him towards him to put his arm around his shoulder.

"What did he say?" Cristaden whispered in his ear.

"He says we are welcomed to stay here and that we are his guests. He wants us to go with him."

"Well, that's a relief," Zadeia said, sighing. "At least we're not going to be eaten today."

Something still doesn't feel right, Cristaden thought. *Why can't I use my sensing ability here?* She decided not to mention it and worry her friends. It could have something to do with the geography, although she did not know how.

Maldaha took hold of Piedara's hand, who seemed much more relaxed. She stopped giving them angry stares, but instead turned to smile at them.

"Ah, Colnaha," Maldaha said and then shouted to a boy, who seemed to be about their age, standing a ways behind the crowd of about forty curious people. The boy seemed apprehensive and shy, as if he was not sure whether to greet them or run away. *"Li ti han agrai,* Colnaha."

"He says that this is his son, Free-Spirited," Fajha whispered.

The boy's brown eyebrows raised and he suddenly looked amused.

Maldaha clasped his chubby hand on the boy's shoulder, releasing Fajha and Piedara from his grip. *"Han agrai prali tan traeng."*

"He does?" Fajha said excitedly. He turned to his friends. "Maldaha says his son speaks our language."

"Yes, I do," Colnaha said to him, his deeply accented voice hardly matching his small exterior. "And my name means 'free-spirited' but please do not call me that," he said matter-of-factly, his course, brownish-red hair flapping in the breeze as he spoke. "It's Colnaha."

Maldaha mumbled something to Colnaha and, when the boy nodded, he took his wife's hand, and walked away from them. He then demanded everyone to stop staring and to go back to their business.

"Oh thank goodness!" Zadeia threw her hands up after Maldaha walked away. "Finally, someone who speaks our language. We're saved!" She approached Colnaha and stuck her hand out. "My name is Zadeia. And this is my brother, Zimi, and my friends, Fajha, Cristaden and Atakos," she said, pointing to each of them.

Colnaha took her hand and quickly kissed it. "It is nice to meet you." He looked up and smiled when he saw her bewildered face.

Zadeia snatched her hand back and frowned, her cheeks suddenly flushed with warmth. Zimi cleared his throat after glaring at his sister and her strange forwardness and then looked back at Colnaha. "We are in need of assistance," he said. "Can you help us?"

Colnaha pulled his eyes away from Zadeia's face. "Of course. I overheard that you are from Paimonu."

"We are," Atakos said.

"How interesting."

"Why is that so interesting?"

"Well. I have heard stories of Paimonu and I can't imagine people with your … your …"

"Our what?"

"How do you say …?" Colnaha thought for a moment. "Your … *personality*."

"What about our personality?"

"Well, it's hard to imagine people with your personality living in a place like *that*."

"What do you mean?" Cristaden said.

"I heard it's a really rough place to live."

"Well, it's not rough for us, we like it there," Fajha said, sticking to the plan.

"Yes, I see." Colnaha rubbed his chin. He then shrugged his shoulders and brought his hand down. "So what brings you to our village?"

Cristaden took a few steps towards him. "We got separated from our caravan and we are just trying to get back home. Our journey has been long and we've been without food for a couple of days. We would be very gracious to you if you can spare us some food to help us with our journey home."

"We plan to leave right away," Atakos said.

"Oh no, please do not leave right away. You must dine with me first. My father has also asked me to show you around and, besides, you came at a great time. We have our annual Srickarst Festival tonight and you wouldn't want to miss that."

"Sikas?" Zadeia said. "What's that?"

"*Srick-arst.*" Colnaha corrected with a smile, accentuating each syllable. "It is a grand festival, celebrating life and our spirit. Along with a huge bonfire, there will be an enormous feast, dancers, and musicians. It is truly spectacular."

Atakos wrapped his arm around his growling stomach at the mention of food. He suddenly felt ill with hunger.

"We also have rooms at my home that can be set up for you to sleep tonight. If you wish."

Zadeia's eyes widened at the mention of a bed to sleep in. She looked at Atakos, who appeared skeptical. "Please, can we?"

Atakos noticed the others were staring at him also, awaiting his response. He thought for a moment before speaking to Colnaha. "Okay, we will stay for the festival but we must leave in the morning."

"That's wonderful!" Zadeia said.

"Good, it is settled then," Colnaha said. "Let me take you around our village."

Disappointed that they were not going to eat right away, the five friends began their tour of the Osmatuan village with the boy who seemed more and more like a prince to the people living there. They found out that he was in fact older than them, about to turn seventeen in mere months and that his parents had him at a late age. As they walked, the inhabitants of the village turned to wave at him and some even bowed. The cement houses they saw when they were standing on top of the hill were actually larger than they seemed, each one being carefully crafted to some form of elegance that suited each family. The architecture was amazing, ranging from homes that opened up to glorious courtyards and others that had perfectly sculpted stairs, winding up to houses built on small hills. There were statues of their gods situated in the middle of their few roads, being decorated for the festival. The six teens then came to the large bonfire they had seen.

"Why is it lit now when the festival is tonight?" Cristaden asked.

"It is part of a seven-day ritual," Colnaha said. "The fire has been lit for seven days and will be extinguished during the celebration. It is to honor our seven courageous gods that watch over us every day. A tradition we carried with us from Thackenbur."

"Why did you leave Thackenbur?" Fajha said.

"I was just a baby when we left and my father never speaks of it. All I know is that we will never go back."

"But your father said you were explorers."

"In a way, we are. We explore everything from our land to our thoughts. We often have lectures on the mind and how it functions."

Really? Atakos thought. *What a strange village. In the middle of nowhere, having lectures on the human mind? I wonder what they do for fun besides this celebration.*

"Who lives in that house up the hill?" Zimi said. Nestled on top of a hill behind the bonfire was a beautiful, blue mansion, overlooking the entire village.

"Oh, I saved the best for last," Colnaha said, beaming. "That is my home."

"Beautiful," Cristaden said, smiling.

"Thank you. My father and the village architects worked hard to build it. Let us go there now. I am sure a delicious meal has been prepared for you."

Zadeia grinned. "Good, because we're starving," she said.

"That *was* a delicious meal, Colnaha, thank you so much," Zadeia said, gleefully smiling from ear to ear. Although she did not know why, she could not take her eyes off him. He wasn't the best looking boy she had ever met, yet she blushed every time he made eye contact with her. The graceful way he moved, his thick accent, and his boyish grin mesmerized her.

"Thank you," the others politely said.

"You are very welcome," Colnaha said. "These special dishes were cooked in honor of your stay here as our guests."

"That wasn't necessary," Atakos said, feeling weird about how nice they were being treated. "I think we would have eaten anything in the condition we were in."

"It was no trouble at all."

"This house is gorgeous," Cristaden said, satisfied with her full belly. "I am absolutely in love with it."

They looked around at the beautifully decorated dining room with brightly colored flower designs carved into the wall. The sun shining through the big windows provided enough light to brighten the whole house. Even the two large rooms that were set up for them were intricately designed, with balconies coming off of each one.

"Where did you learn to speak the language of Sheidem, Colnaha?" Fajha said.

"My parents sent me to a boarding school there for my education," Colnaha said.

"Really?" Atakos' ears perked up. "Which one?"

"Oh, some dingy old school. What was the name? Oh yes. *Lochenby*." He said the word with so much disgust, one would think he was referring to pile of rotting garbage.

The teens suddenly got his full attention.

Fajha dropped his fork.

Zadeia's mouth spread into a toothy grin. "Really?! That's where—" Interrupted by her brother's swift kick under the table, she tried hard not to show how hurt she was, managed to force a smile on her face, and looked back down.

"That's where what?" Colnaha said curiously.

"That is where a classmate of ours went to school all the way from *Paimonu*," Zimi said, glaring at her.

"Is that so? What was his name?"

Zimi thought for a moment and shrugged. "You know, I don't recall his name. It's been so long since he left. I heard he only stayed for a month and disliked it so much, he moved to another city."

"What a way to go. All the way from Paimonu. It's too bad he did not stay."

Atakos and the others let out a quiet sigh of relief. That was close, almost too close. He definitely would have figured them out if they told him that they all went to school at Lochenby. He would start to wonder why they would all be sent from a place with no 'personality' to a prestigious school like Lochenby.

"Why did you leave the school?" Cristaden said, trying to put the attention back on Colnaha. He seemed deep in thought and his eyebrows were drawn together. He was so deep in thought that he missed the question. Cristaden had to repeat herself.

Colnaha smiled suddenly and then responded. "Lochenby was not for me. I missed my home too much. I only had to tell my parents I did not like it and they pulled me out." He leaned forward. "Where did you learn to speak this language of Sheidem?"

"A missionary," Fajha said quickly. "She taught all the people of our village to speak it."

"So the dialect of Paimonu is Sheidem because of this missionary?"

"Yes," the friends said in unison.

Colnaha rubbed his chin. "That's interesting. Where is she now?"

"She died." It was Cristaden's turn to quickly throw in an addition to the lie. "Of a massive heart attack." She almost smiled, having never realized how fun it was making up stories.

"That's too bad."

"Do you mind if we go exploring on our own?" Atakos said, desperate to get away from the random questions. If Colnaha were to dive deeper, he would start to realize their lies did not make any sense. He was hoping he wouldn't ask Fajha where he learned to speak Tackeni also. How many missionaries would have gone to Paimonu?

Colnaha smiled. "By all means do what you wish. I have some preparations to attend to for tonight's festival anyways. Feel free to go where you please. Just don't get lost."

The five friends quickly excused themselves from the table and made their way down the hall to the front door.

Once they were safely outside, Zadeia had a breakdown. "I'm so sorry. I don't know what came over me." She began to cry.

"It's okay Zadeia," Atakos said, reassuring her. "I don't think he suspects anything."

"I'm sorry I kicked you," Zimi said.

Zadeia managed to accept his apology between sobs.

Atakos thought it would be good to get away from the eyes of the villagers. "Let's get out of the village for a few hours," he said.

"What are we going to do?" Cristaden said.

"Well. Since we realized we can increase our strength and develop more abilities, let's work on that. We'll be here for the rest of the day so we might as well take advantage of this time to practice."

"Sounds like a great idea," Fajha said. "Let's do it."

The rest of them agreed and they descended the long staircase to the bottom of the hill. Taking one last look at the glorious, blue mansion behind them, they proceeded to leave the village.

Colnaha stood by the dining room window, watching the teens leave the village. "Senru!" he called to his servant. "Get me my orange suit. The one that is the color of the rocks."

Senru, an older gentleman with graying hair wearing a white uniform, put down the dishes he was clearing from the table and approached Colnaha. "Any particular reason, sir?" he said.

"I'm going hunting."

CHAPTER 26

"This looks like the perfect spot," Atakos said as they entered a clearing in the middle of a few small hills. "I think we are far enough from the village so they won't hear us."

"Speaking of being away from the village," Cristaden said, "when we first walked in, my sensory ability seemed blocked. I couldn't sense anything. As if there was no life around me. I could not even sense all of you. Since we left the village, it has returned."

"Really?" Atakos looked at her curiously.

"Can you sense the village itself right now?" Zimi said.

Cristaden looked towards the general direction of the village. "No. I can't."

"Neither can I," Fajha said. "I can't locate anyone we've met."

"That's strange," Atakos said. "I wonder if any of our powers work in the village."

"Well they work out here," Zimi said. His friends turned to see him moving around some loose rocks with his wind power.

"So what could possibly make the village virtually undetectable?" Zadeia said.

"Remember how Colnaha said that they left Thakenbur long ago and he does not know why?" Atakos said. "Maybe they are out here in the middle of nowhere so they would not be found."

"Even so, we would still be able to detect them," Fajha said.

"That's true," Cristaden said. "Living way out in the middle of nowhere should not block them from our powers."

After a moment of silence, Cristaden sighed. "I wish we can leave right now," she said in a small voice.

Atakos shook his head. "We can't. We need provisions and who knows how long it will take us to get through the Suthack Desert. We are only putting ourselves at risk of certain death if we leave hastily."

"So what do you suggest we do?" Zimi said, turning to Atakos, prompting the others to do the same.

Atakos wasn't deterred by the fact that everyone was looking at him to be the leader again. "We do exactly what I always say we do. We are the hope of this world. If we run from every situation we will never learn how to be real fighters. I say we be on our guard, get to know these people while we're here, and defend ourselves if need be. We should use the few hours we have before the festival to practice our new abilities in case we need to use them."

"I agree," Fajha said with a smile. "Besides I am interested to learn how you got so strong and work on Cristaden's new power."

Zadeia nodded. "We have a lot of catching up to do from all those years of slacking off."

"Hey, speak for yourself," Atakos said. "I never slacked off."

"We all did at one point or another," Cristaden said, playfully punching his arm. "Let's make up for that."

"It's best to concentrate on one person at a time," Fajha said. "The twins being one unit since the both of you usually work together."

"That's not right," Zadeia said, protesting. "Zimi discovered a new power and I'm stuck with the same old 'wind thing'."

"Okay, okay. We'll test the both of you separately."

"We don't have much time," Atakos said. "Let's start with Cristaden."

Cristaden sighed. "When I was on that cliff I felt the energy flowing into my fingertips pulling Fajha's hand towards mine. I'm sorry to say. I've tried it since then and it hasn't worked."

Atakos recalled a lesson Hamilda taught them years ago. "Sometimes it takes a great deal of emotion to realize a power. Until you master it you have to gain control over your emotions. I'm pretty sure when you saw the beasts running towards you, you were full of fear, right?"

Cristaden brushed a strand of blonde hair away from her face, taking a moment to think. "I suppose you're right. When I learned to heal I was so sad and devastated that the healing ability came naturally to me. I thought I was going to lose all of you."

"Do you think it only happens with negative emotions?" Fajha said.

"I don't think so," Zadeia said. "The day I learned to control wind, I was really happy because I got an excellent score on a test that I was certain I failed. I went outside and started dancing, not realizing I was making the wind dance with me too."

"See, you just have to tap into any emotion and make it grow," Atakos said.

"Okay, I'll give it a try." Cristaden stepped back and brought her attention to a tiny pebble on the ground. The first thing that came to mind was her life in Laspitu, so sad and lonely. When she felt the sadness welling up inside her, she tried to move the rock. It did not work. Used to living a lonely life in Laspitu during school vacations for fifteen years, the emotion she felt was not strong enough. Cristaden instead turned her focus to their mission. She thought of how Jogesh died and how Hamilda, the teacher they love so much, was kidnapped. The mere fact that they could very well find nothing at the end of their journey brought tears to her eyes. What's worse, Hamilda could already be *dead*. The tiny pebble suddenly flew towards a boulder, barely missing Zimi's head, and shattered to pieces.

"Whoa," Atakos said.

"That was awesome!" Zadeia said.

"She really can do it," Zimi said.

"Did you doubt her?" Fajha said. "I told you she can do it."

Panting, Cristaden sunk to her knees, burying her face in her hands. It was enough to make her burst out crying when she realized that Hamilda was not there to see it happen. "I miss her so much."

"I know," Zadeia said, taking a step towards her. "I do too."

"Wait." Atakos held his arm out to stop Zadeia. "Leave her alone, she'll get over it," he said in an angry voice.

Cristaden snapped her head up. "Why you …" She picked up a large rock with her mind and threw it at him.

Atakos put his hands up and stopped it in its tracks only a foot from his head and threw it back her way.

Seeing the rock coming at her, Cristaden let out an angry scream, directed all her energy towards it, and watched as it *exploded*.

After instinctively shielding their faces, her friends brought their arms down and looked at the small pieces of rock at Cristaden's feet.

"How did you do that?" Fajha said.

Cristaden's eyes were wide with astonishment. "I don't … know."

Atakos stood in shock, unable to comprehend what just happened. "Even I can't do that," he said.

"I don't know. I felt so angry and I just … wished it to break into pieces."

"And it did," Zadeia said. "Wow."

Zimi stared with his mouth hanging open.

"Incredible," Atakos said. "Now that you know what it took to make that happen, do you think you can do it again?"

"Yes, I think so." Before Cristaden had a chance to prepare herself, a rock sailed through the air headed straight for her. She immediately brought her hands up, causing it to explode without hesitation.

"Wow," Atakos managed to choke out. "Fajha, do you think we can try that too?"

"I hope we can," Fajha said. "That was so amazing." He pushed his glasses up his nose, picked up a large rock with his mind, and hurled it at Atakos. Atakos brought forward the energy he used to rip the oblot apart and wished the rock to explode. Before it reached him, it cracked in half and fell to the ground.

"Not bad," Fajha said. "Throw one my way."

Atakos did just that but Fajha could not break it in time. He had to duck as it flew towards his head.

"Remember what Hamilda always tells us, Fajha," Zimi said, matter-of-factly. "You have to have more confidence."

Fajha straightened his shoulders and adjusted his glasses again. "Alright, try it again, Atakos." Another rock flew at him and, this time, it broke in half.

"Woohoo." Fajha started to do a silly dance while chanting, "I did it, I did it, I did it."

Atakos rolled his eyes. "We broke the rocks in *half*," he said. "That's it. Our goal is to make it explode." He nodded at Cristaden to let her know that the three of them will practice together.

Cristaden was beaming, overcome with joy because she could finally join the group in their practices. Her happiness helped her to continuously lift rocks with the two boys and blow them up one by one. Fajha and Atakos became better and better at it. They went from breaking rocks in half to breaking them into several pieces. Cristaden continued to explode the rocks into thousands of tiny pieces, which made the boys furious. They had been moving objects for years. Cristaden learned to naturally blow up rocks on her second try. With their added anger, the rocks became easier to blow up. Within an hour, the three were exploding rocks one right after another. They kept at it for a half an hour more. Exhausted, they ended their practice and fell to the ground, breathing heavily. They definitely needed more stamina.

"Zimi–Zadeia," Atakos said, barely able to get the words out. Panting heavily he waved and pointed at them, indicating it was their turn.

"What could I learn?" Zadeia said, turning to her brother. "All I know how to do is move wind." Suddenly working alone did not sound appealing anymore.

Zimi thought for a moment. "Maybe we could use that gift. We could always move the wind around and use it to help us glide and lift up but, for goodness sakes, we are the Element Twins. Let's see if we can make a tornado. A small one, so as not to be seen."

"I honestly doubt it. But I want so much to believe we can pull it off."

"I think we can."

The twins stood across from each other and conjured up the winds. Their friends backed up far enough not to get carried away with it. Zimi moved the air in a semicircle towards Zadeia and she pushed it back towards him, completing the circle. They went on like that for several minutes, pushing the air around while increasing their speed. The small circle of wind was something new but it was not impressive. Thinking that moving wind would be her only gift, Zadeia began to get frustrated, desperately trying not to break the cycle. Zimi seemed like he was having an easier time with it, which made her even more upset. As her arms began to feel tired, Zadeia wanted so much to give up but she pushed herself to move the wind harder and faster.

It wasn't long before Zimi realized Zadeia was going so fast, he was finding it difficult to keep up with her.

The twins were so deeply involved with keeping their small circle of wind going that they did not realize a shadow forming overhead that covered the glare of the sun. Atakos, Fajha, and Cristaden looked up. The sky was going dark all of a sudden with threatening clouds. Just a few moments before, the sky was completely blue. They looked back down at the struggling twins and it dawned on them that they were the cause of it.

"We have to stop them," Cristaden said, getting nervous.

The sky rumbled and the feeling of electricity rose in the air. Something was about to happen but they weren't sure what it was. The three friends shouted for the twins to stop but, with the sound of the strong winds between them, they did not hear them. As drops of rain fell on their heads, Atakos made a split second decision to push them to the ground with his mind. As they hit the ground, a bolt of lightning struck where they had been standing followed by a severe clap of thunder.

"What—?!" Zimi cried out as Zadeia screamed. Instantly the strong circle of wind disappeared and the clouds cleared up, revealing the bright sky once again.

For a few moments, the friends were speechless.

Atakos shook his head as he, Cristaden, and Fajha walked back to the twins. He wasn't happy. "This has to be the worst possible place—"

"How did you guys do that?" Cristaden said, interrupting him.

Zimi looked at the ground where the lightning struck and then back at Zadeia. "It wasn't me. It was *her.*"

"I couldn't have done it without you, Zimi," Zadeia said, breathing heavily.

"That was out of this *world*," Fajha said. He glanced towards the direction of the village. "I hope the villagers don't think we had something to do with it. It's very strange for this area."

"Thank you for realizing how much trouble we're in," Atakos said. "As incredible as it was, they're going to know we had something to do with it."

"How?" Cristaden said. "Let's just act like we were surprised by it too. How could we possibly cause a thunderstorm?"

"Wait—" A thought occurred to Fajha. "I remember reading in my geography class that this region doesn't have rain."

"Yeah that's obvious, it's like a drought went through here," Atakos said.

"I mean the entire region, including parts of Sheidem Forest."

"What are you trying to say?" Cristaden said.

"Zadeia, how were you feeling when we were walking through the forest on that third day?"

Zadeia frowned at him. "Do you mean to tell me that I caused it to rain?"

"I'm just saying to consider the possibility."

Zadeia considered how she was feeling on the day of the big rain. Her thoughts were on Hamilda the whole time and she was really sad. She was also very scared. Terrified of the unknown. "It couldn't have been me."

Atakos shifted his weight and crossed his arms. Fajha had a point. "When we were ready to sleep, the rain stopped," he said.

"That's right, it did," Zimi said.

Zadeia's eyes opened wide.

Atakos walked over to her. "Can you wish it to rain right now?" They were already in as much trouble as they were going to be in.

Zadeia thought of life with Hamilda for a few minutes, allowing herself to fall into her sadness as she so often did. As tears started to fill her eyes, she looked up to the sky. Clouds were starting to form again.

"Stop," Atakos said, placing his hand on her arm.

Zadeia stopped crying. The sky instantly cleared up.

"Wow," Cristaden said. "I guess you always had another power besides wind!"

"I guess so," Zadeia said, eyebrows raised. She remembered how the rain was never ending at the beginning of each school year when she really missed home. The poor students of Lochenby, maybe as far as the people of Sheidem City, had to endure the results of her depression every year.

"The villagers are probably already wondering what happened, we can't give them more weirdness. We'll save that practice for another time, when we are far away from here."

Zadeia could not believe she had this gift all this time. She wondered when it began. It would be impossible to tell. It rained all the time in Sheidem City and in Udnaruk.

Or did it?

Cristaden approached her. "Wow, Zadeia. If you can make it rain and Zimi can freeze things, I wonder what else the two of you can do."

"It will be interesting to find out," Zimi said. "But we should be getting back before they start thinking we ran away."

"Before we go, let's get a little extra practice in," Atakos said.

"Like the ones Hamilda made us do?" Fajha asked.

"Exactly. We need one person to throw the rocks and the remaining four will fight them off."

"I'll throw the rocks," Cristaden said.

"No, you haven't had the practice that we have. I'll do it." Atakos backed up from the group and waited until they formed a circle with their backs facing each other. "Remember to have confidence. It's the only way we can win a battle on our own. Ready?"

Before they had a chance to respond, the first rock flew at the teens. It was then followed by many more, all soaring towards them at top speed. The twins pushed the rocks away with the wind, while Zimi sometimes froze them, turning them into blocks of ice that fell to the ground before reaching him. Fajha and Cristaden blew up the rocks that came at them and a huge rock pile of shattered pieces began to form at their feet. At times, Zadeia pushed some rocks toward Cristaden so she could blow them up to avoid hitting anyone else. Atakos made rocks fly behind them to see how keen they were. A couple of rocks hit Fajha on the back of his head and he got furious. Fajha irately exploded another rock but missed the one that hit him on his leg.

"Don't lose your concentration, Fajha," Atakos said, seeing the look of desperation on his friend's face. For a moment, he appeared to have been hovering over the ground, trying to avoid the one that hit his leg. When Atakos spoke to him, his feet were back on the ground. Atakos rubbed his eyes. *That was weird*, he thought. *I must be tired.*

When the rocks stopped coming, the four friends turned to Atakos. He appeared dazed and confused.

"Is everything all right?" Cristaden asked.

"Yes," Atakos said. "I-I think so."

"Why did you stop?" Fajha asked.

"I feel a little lightheaded. I think I need to lie down."

Zadeia nodded. "I think we all could use a little rest, don't you?"

"Definitely."

"Good," Cristaden said. "Let's go before they send out a search party and find out about our little 'secret'."

As the friends made their way back to the village, they did not realize that their secret had already been discovered.

CHAPTER 27

The rumble of drums penetrated the cool, night air as dancers leapt around the giant circle surrounding the bonfire. Dressed in all black, they were performing a form of classical Tackeni dance that only one village elder could teach. Their movements started off slow and sensual and, as the drums got faster, they became more alive and free. A few of the villagers began to chant a sweet song along with the beat of the drums. Colnaha steadily translated what they were saying to his new friends. Soon the entire village joined in, fluidly singing a melody about a lady who fell in love with a prince but got her heart broken at the end when he was forced to marry someone else. Towards the finale of the song, the mood became sad and the drums slowed again. Cristaden and Zadeia shed some tears as the dance ended, which led to some snickers from the boys.

The crowd cheered as the music died down and musicians immediately took the place of the dancers, doing their own choreographed dance while playing their instruments. The melody was not sad like before but more upbeat and lively. Several villagers stood up to dance, clapping their hands as they twisted and turned.

"How are you enjoying our festival?" asked Colnaha.

"Oh, I'm loving it!" Zadeia said, putting on her sweetest smile. When Colnaha smiled back, she turned away quickly so he would not see her blush. He was, by far, the most charming boy she had ever met. The way he tended to them when they came back to the village tired and drained was very kindhearted, as if he truly cared about them even if he only knew them for a few short hours. The way he smiled at her, as if she were the only one in the room, gave her butterflies. She could feel his eyes on her all night but she tried to focus on the show most of the time so their eyes wouldn't meet.

"This is really spectacular," Fajha said, trying to talk over the loud music. He always enjoyed the festivals back in Saiyut but was never allowed to stay and watch as one of the commoners because of his royal status. Being in a village that was not aware of his background was like being on vacation.

Atakos looked on at the dancing musicians in amazement. He had never seen such an extravaganza either. In Pontotoma, there were hardly any musicians like the ones from Thackenbur. Most of them played slow, dreary music, sounding more like they were only made for funerals. It was hard to imagine that these dancers and musicians lived in the same quiet village they walked into mere hours beforehand.

While the musicians were finishing up their spectacular performance, four villagers, carrying a platform on their shoulders, broke through the crowd. Seated on the platform was a magnificent statue of their seven gods. On the far left was a male with a horned helmet and a spear pointing high in the air. Next to him, in the middle back was a female with her arms raised high, holding up a sun. On the right was a round male with a snarling tiger by his side. On the bottom left, there were two lovers growing a small tree between them, a lady sat cross-legged in the middle with a serpent around her neck and a male was bent over her, praying with his hands clasped together. The villagers put the grand statue down close to the bonfire, right in front of an old man sitting on the other side of the circle. The teens had not noticed him before. He had long, grayish-white hair and his beard practically touched the ground. The pupils of his eyes were white and the white robe he wore suggested that he was a priest of some sort. He was chanting prayers that were lost in the loudness of the beating drums.

"Who is that?" Atakos asked Colnaha. It was funny how his features really stood out but the whole time they were sitting there, they had not noticed him.

"That is Olshem," Colnaha said. "He is our seer. He sees the future and he is also an experienced medium. At times, he has been able to make successful contact with our dead ancestors. He's amazing."

"Is he blind?" Cristaden said.

"It might appear so, but I do not think he is. He can get around very easily with little or no help. He claims he has the gift of 'sight', which allows him to see without eyes."

Gift of sight? Cristaden thought. She glanced at the others. They appeared thoughtful but Atakos was frowning at Colnaha.

"Does anyone else you know have this 'gift of sight'?" Fajha asked him after a short pause.

"They say it happens once every third or fourth generation. His great-great-grandfather was said to be a clairvoyant as well, although he did not use his gift very often."

"Is that so?" Zimi said and looked back at the aging seer. He was still chanting an inaudible prayer to their gods, bringing his arms up over his head and back down again repeatedly.

The five friends exchanged glances at the notion that this was the first human they had come across with an actual 'power'. They also wondered if it had anything to do with the village being undetectable.

Colnaha noticed their astonishment and moved to quickly change the topic. "This is the finale of the show. Afterwards, I can introduce you to him. He may be able to tell your fortunes." He chuckled softly.

"That should be interesting," Atakos said. Although he was doubtful any human had the ability to see the future, he remembered the sudden change of the fairy queen, Lhainna, when she attempted to 'read' him. He wondered if Olshem would react the same way.

Their attention was drawn back to the festivities when a blue mist suddenly appeared. It formed into the shape of a large serpent, which circled the fire until it exploded into the air like fireworks. As the drums and Olshem's chanting grew louder, the outsiders stared in awe as the mist came back down and changed shape into the seven gods.

"How are they doing that?" Fajha asked Colnaha but did not get a response back.

The mist gods were the exact replicas of the statue. They began to dance and interact with each other. The goddess with the snake around her neck, released it and watched as it circled the bonfire until the fire turned a bright blue. A blue tiger jumped over the fire and ran around the circle until it disappeared into a cloud of smoke. The dance of the gods became more crazy and random until they simultaneously jumped into the bonfire and extinguished it. The drums stopped and Olshem became quiet, bowing his head, prompting the villagers to follow his lead.

"Please tell me that was a trick of the eye," Atakos whispered to Colnaha.

"It is what you want to believe it was," Colnaha whispered back. "Was it an illusion? Or much more than that?" He chuckled when he looked at their awed faces in the light of the moon. They obviously had not noticed the projectors set high above the crowd. Colnaha then closed his eyes and bowed his head.

After a few minutes, the villagers stood up and cheered. The show was over and now it was time to sit, eat, and be merry. Tiny fires were lit all around to provide light to the festivities since the bonfire was no longer lit. A couple of women came to them with plates of food. Out of respect, they gave Colnaha his food first and then gave the rest to his new friends.

During their meal, Colnaha explained to the others about the holograms to clear up their suspicions of magic. He watched them as they laughed at each other and then he cleared his throat. "So are you going to tell me where you are really from?" he said.

Zadeia choked on her food and the others stopped chewing.

After swallowing the food in his mouth, Atakos slowly gave his response. "We told you. We are trying to get home to Paimonu." He knew it was a lost battle. Colnaha obviously did not believe them.

"Oh, come off it," Colnaha quickly said, lowering his voice, as if the villagers knew their language. "I knew from the moment you stepped into this village that you are not from Paimonu. Just admit it."

The friends looked at each other but did not know what to say. The silence among them was thick and impenetrable.

"I mean just look at all of you," Colnaha said, growing impatient. "It's obvious you come from different countries. The people of Paimonu do not even closely resemble any of you and they do not speak this language. So I'll ask you one more time. Where are you really from?"

Again the group was quiet. Cristaden looked at Atakos, searching his eyes, trying to find an answer to fix their newest problem.

Atakos frowned as a thought occurred to him. "Do your father and mother suspect that we are not from Paimonu?" he said.

"Atakos," Fajha said, throwing his arms up. It was his idea to stick to the plan but now he was giving them away.

Before Atakos had a chance to defend himself, Colnaha answered his question. "They were suspicious at first but I have convinced them that the idea of you being from Paimonu was possible. Of course I have a better education than they do so they have no choice but to believe what I say." He glanced up at his father who was sitting not too far from them, having a conversation with some village elders. He noticed his son's eyes on him and glared at him for a moment before returning to his conversation. Colnaha quickly looked back at his peers, hoping they did not notice the angry look his father had given him.

"Ok, we will tell you why we are here if you promise to keep it a secret," Atakos said.

"I can't believe this," Fajha mumbled under his breath.

The girls were quiet. Zimi said nothing, refusing to gloat about what they were facing. He figured 'I told you so' was inappropriate at that very moment and kept his mouth shut.

"We are from Lochenby," Atakos said.

"Ah. My school." Colnaha smiled but then his smile quickly faded. "How come I've never seen you before? I would have run into all of you at one point or another. I believe we are only one year apart."

"Well, it's such a large school, with so many levels."

"I guess that is true. But what brings you all the way out here? Hasn't the semester already begun?"

"Yes, it has. One of our teachers was kidnapped and we are on a journey to find her. We have reason to believe she is in Paimonu but even that we are unsure of."

"So you are risking your life traveling out here in the middle of nowhere to find a teacher? That must be some teacher." Colnaha whistled.

"Yeah, well, we aren't giving up until she is found."

"But what are you going to do when you find her? What if she was kidnapped by a bunch of sword-wielding ruffians?"

"We'll just have to figure that out when we find her." Atakos was upset that he had to tell Colnaha the truth but there was nothing else he could have said. He would not have believed them if they came up with another lame excuse or if they even stuck with the same story.

Fajha looked away from Atakos, disappointment written all over his face. Zimi began to think that sneaking into the village would have been their best option. That way, they would have avoided all the unnecessary questions.

"That's interesting," Colnaha said. He looked at each of them carefully as if he were thinking about what he was going to say next. He then lowered his voice to a whisper until it was barely audible. "I followed you this afternoon. Out by the hills. I know what you can do."

CHAPTER 28

The five teens stared at Colnaha in disbelief.

Shocked, Atakos reached over and tried to grab him. "You *followed* us? Why you—"

"Atakos, no!" Cristaden said. Fajha and Zimi pulled him back. Most of the villagers took notice and looked over at them.

Colnaha put his hands up and told the villagers that everything was okay in his language. He explained to them that they were just playing a silly Paimonu game. He then looked back at the shocked group and talked between his teeth. "Do you want them to find you out? I suggest you keep *quiet*."

"You spied on us?" Zadeia whispered when they settled down. She was really upset that he would do that, but then again they had only known him for less than a day. Why did she think he could be trusted?

"I didn't!" Colnaha glanced at their angry faces. "Ok. I did. But I only did it to be sure."

"Sure of what?" Atakos said. His hands were balled up into fists. If the villagers were not there, he would have grabbed Colnaha by his shirt and shook the truth out of him. How dare he spy on them? Worse yet, their Dokami secret was compromised.

"I will explain myself to you but I will not do it here," Colnaha said, glancing at his father once again.

"Why not? No one understands our language."

"I will not do it here," Colnaha reiterated to him firmly. He then stood up, encouraging the others to follow him.

Cristaden turned to Atakos and whispered in his ear. "I wish I can get a read on him but I can't."

"It's alright. Just be prepared for anything. He knows too much already." Atakos looked at the rest of his friends and they nodded. *We should have been more careful,* he thought. *We should never have practiced anywhere near here.* He felt that he was the one to blame for their mishap and wanted to apologize to them. But it was too late. If Colnaha told anyone what he saw, the whole Dokami nation could be discovered. For a moment Atakos considered getting rid of him and running away. Unfortunately, they were never raised to be violent towards innocent people. He sighed regrettably.

Colnaha took the teens down a side alley to the back of a building marked 'DECHTO', which was the Tackeni word for 'doctor'. The teens were half expecting to see a gang of people waiting there to capture them but it was just a small, vacant lot.

"So what is this all about?" Atakos said threateningly. He was prepared to fight.

Colnaha looked them over. He had a worried expression on his face, as if he were about to say something he did not want to say. "Well, it's like this …" He pointed to a flag, hung over the back door of the doctor's office. On it was an emblem, a twisted symbol of vines thick with thorns and words around it written in an old dialect. The flag shifted slightly and jerked forward, flying down to Colnaha's extended hand.

The teens stared at Colnaha, shocked beyond belief.

"You have …?" Zadeia was at a loss for words.

"Yes, I do," Colnaha said, rolling the flag between his fingers. "My ancestors are of Dokami blood."

"You mean to tell me that you—you're Dokami?" Atakos said.

"This is incredible," Cristaden said. She gave a nervous laugh.

"Do not be surprised," Colnaha said. "There are hundreds of thousands, perhaps a million Dokami all around Western Omordion."

"Of course there is," Fajha said. "Is the entire village Dokami descendants?"

"Not everyone here is of our race. My family is of Dokami descent along with a couple of other families but the rest are just normal humans who moved here with us."

"How interesting," Zimi said, "We were told there were some rebel clans who sought their own way of …" As he was saying it, it began to dawn on him.

"We are such rebels," Colnaha said.

"I thought you said you don't remember why you left Thackenbur," Atakos said.

"I lied. Well, technically I was too young to remember when it happened, but my father tells me stories about it all the time. There was a strong Dokami presence on Thackenbur but each and every person was taught to restrain their powers except my family. Olshem, the seer, is my father's father."

"Your grandfather," Zadeia said.

"Yes. You see, Olshem was a Wise Man of the entire Dokami clan. He had amazing abilities. He could call upon spirits, see the future, and control fire. Since he is one hundred and thirteen years old, and he never had to use his abilities much, his powers of divination have decreased considerably. Forty years ago he gave up his position for the next Dokami Wise Man. As you should know that is done every fifty years. My father, of course, thought he would be next in line. Olshem taught him everything he knew. He was prepared to be our leader. But it is not inheritance that chooses the Wise Man. It's the Dokami Council. They looked passed my father and chose Bontihm Fhakaemeli instead."

"Bontihm?" Fajha said.

"Yes, Bontihm. You've heard of him, I assume?"

"We've met him," Zadeia carelessly said. Zimi shot her a disapproving look and Fajha rolled his eyes.

"Have you?" Colnaha looked at her surprisingly. Then he blinked and continued. "My father was upset about the decision but he was too young, being only sixteen at the time. No one would have ever chosen him to be a Wise Man at that age. So he decided to show the Council all he was made of to prove his worth. He practiced really hard until it almost killed him. The Council ignored him. Twenty-five years ago, it was rumored that Bontihm had taken on an apprentice. This apprentice was to become the next Wise Man. And on top of that, she was a *woman*. HA! Can you believe that?"

The five members of Omordion's Hope stared back at him. They knew of whom he was referring to. That 'woman' was Hamilda. They kept quiet and let him finish his story.

"This angered my father. He wished that she was not good enough, that by the time Bontihm gave up his right to be Wise Man, the Council would have figured it out and gave the honors to him. But he soon learned that was not the case. About ten years ago, this *apprentice* of Bontihm's took on a special mission with the Western Army. A mission that was so top secret, even my father could not find out what it was. Even the most talkative members of the Council refused to talk. That made my father furious. He decided to leave the watchful eye of the Dokami Council for good. And that's why he took all of us, including his friends and their families, and came here to start a new life. His dream of being the next Wise Man was shattered." Colnaha seemed really upset. He had said the word 'apprentice' with such malice and contempt that they knew they should not tell him who their teacher was.

"So he hasn't been back to Thackenbur since?" Fajha said.

"Not once," Colnaha said. Then he frowned and rubbed his chin. "How did you ever get to meet Bontihm? The Wise Man never mixes with just any Dokami."

Atakos gritted his teeth. Colnaha was prying deeper into their lives and he did not trust him at all. Especially now that he just revealed to them that his father was an enemy of both Bontihm and Hamilda.

"You must trust me," Colnaha said, as if reading his mind. "I would never tell a soul. When I saw you out there today, I knew what you were. What puzzles me is how you ever got so strong. At your age, all of you can't possibly be self-taught runaways."

"We told you, we are in search of a teacher of ours who was kidnapped," Fajha said. "That is all. Yes, we are of Dokami blood but that is just it. We met each other by chance and we taught ourselves how to maximize our powers without any supervision."

"Really?" Colnaha stared at him for a moment. "Do you realize that if you use your power and exert excessive energy, there are members of the Council who can sense you and know in what general area you are in? The Council would never have permitted that. You would have been stopped a long time ago."

The teens looked at each other. Hamilda never mentioned such a thing. They weren't sure if he was telling the truth or lying to get them to admit the truth.

"So obviously, if you used your powers all these years, they must know of you and allow you to get away with it." Colnaha began to get very frustrated with them as they continued to stare back at him, not saying anything. "Why?"

Cristaden realized she could use her powers again when she sensed his anger. If she concentrated hard enough, she might be able to discover whether or not he was telling the truth or just making up stories. In her search of his mind she kept getting several words thrown at her from a slew of muffled sounds. She heard the words 'truth' … 'trust' … 'help' … 'friend' … and 'companionship'. She searched deeper and, to her disbelieve, started to make out actual sentences:

'Please trust me. Tell me the truth. I just want to be your friend. I am lonely here with no companionship. No one understands me. Maybe you will if you just trust me. I can help you … orb.'

Orb? Cristaden thought. *Where did that come from?* Colnaha was about to speak when she interrupted him. "What is this orb?"

"I did not say any—did you just read my mind?"

Atakos turned to her. "What orb, Cristaden?"

"He keeps referring to an orb in his thoughts."

"You *did* just read my mind. Amazing." Colnaha grinned but his smile faded when he saw the angry faces looking back at him.

"Just answer the question," Atakos snapped.

Colnaha huffed arrogantly. "You all were so much nicer this morning. I'm only trying to help you."

Atakos took a step towards him, slowly losing his patience.

Colnaha raised his hands in defense. "Okay. Okay. I'll tell you." He shifted his weight onto his right foot. "The orb is a device my father had acquired from Olshem long ago. It's made up of some type of … um … crystal that was developed by Dokami chemists centuries ago. These orbs hold tremendous power but when they lie dormant, they have the power to keep Dokamis hidden from the watchful eye of the Council. The major downside to having these orbs around is that, in whatever area they are in, Dokami power becomes utterly useless."

"Why would our Dokami ancestors develop such a thing?" Zadeia said.

"They did it to keep the Dokami of their time from using their fully developed powers. They were meant to be destroyed when those members of the Dokami clan died and the generations to come knew nothing of their powers. Each area that the Dokami lived in had one but they were all destroyed except for a few, kept in case a need for them was to arise again. Olshem acquired one, I do not know how, and he gave it to my father when he erected this village. My father put it somewhere here so the Council would not find us and also so the Dokami of this village would not be tempted to use their power and get caught. I do not know where it's hidden."

"I now understand why I wasn't able to detect this village," Cristaden said. "And use my power to sense things. But why are we able to use our powers here?"

Colnaha looked around him. "There is a glitch in the orb. It does not reflect its power in this small area. I discovered it when I was a little boy. Oftentimes I come here to test out my abilities. But I make sure to never use more energy than I should. If I did, the Council would come down on us for the use of our powers. We would be in big trouble. I'm hoping that, when you used your powers earlier today, they would not tie it to us. That is why it is very important for me to know why they allow you to use your powers."

Atakos and the others looked at Cristaden. "He's telling the truth," she said, sighing. She did not want to mention that he was very lonely and wanted their companionship. She felt that it was too private to share. In a way, she began to pity him.

"I think you will be safe here," Fajha said. "I'm pretty sure Bontihm found out we had run away by now and had alerted the Council to which direction we were headed. They must know we are in this area. They won't be coming after us."

"So you have their permission," Colnaha said. He looked at them curiously. "May I ask why?"

"We honestly cannot tell you," Cristaden said. "But trust me when I say we are in search of our teacher to bring her back to Lochenby and that is all you need to know. If we tell you everything, any old mind reader could pick it up from your head before you even say hello to them. And we can't risk that."

"You know very well that being a Dokami requires you to be able to hold secrets," Atakos said. "That's our life. It has been this way since the day we opened our eyes. Surely you must understand our position."

Colnaha raised his eyebrows and thought about what they had told him for a few moments. He began to accept that he would never know exactly who they were. Although he believed, from what they had let slip, that they may have something to do with the top secret mission involving Bontihm's apprentice, he did not know where they tied into all of it. Nevertheless, he did not want to force them to talk and destroy their lives. They were his friends, even if it was only for one day. He did not want to jeopardize that. "I see. Okay. That's fine with me. I will not ask you anything else. You've already told me more than you should have and vice-versa." He could feel the tension in the air begin to lift as the others released the breaths they were holding. "It would be better if we forget we even had this conversation. Is that alright?"

"Yes," Zadeia said as her friends mumbled their agreement to his statement.

The six teenagers were quiet for a few moments, having nothing to say to each other, until Colnaha broke the ice. "So. How would you like to have your fortunes read like I had mentioned earlier?" he said randomly. He was trying to come up with something to talk about. It was the first thing that came to his mind.

"Oh, I would love that," Cristaden said, smiling.

"Me too," Zadeia said.

Atakos, Fajha, and Zimi did not want to go but they couldn't leave the girls alone with He-Who-Knows-Everything.

As they walked through the village, on their way back to the once lit bonfire, Colnaha mentioned to them that Olshem used to be a very powerful fortune teller, but because of the orb and the limited use of his power, he lost a lot of his abilities. It still would come through even with the presence of the orb which showed how much strength he had. Some non-Dokami villagers amused themselves with his fortune telling because sometimes he would say something so indirect that supposedly it would have nothing to do with them. Others felt his gift came from dead loved ones, coming through him to speak. Whatever the case may be, the villagers never suspected that he was anything other than human.

When they reached the center of the village, not much had changed. People were still sitting around talking and laughing, having finished their meals. Colnaha brought the group to where Olshem was still seated, still as a statue, his eyes closed in deep meditation.

"*Attrai-han,*" Colnaha whispered to his grandfather. "There are some people here who would like their fortunes read." Wise Men were required to know all the languages of the Dokami people so he knew their language very well.

Olshem smiled and reached out with his right hand, beckoning for the first person to come. "Come here my child," he said to Atakos. He was not staring at anything directly and he appeared to be very blind.

Atakos reluctantly approached him and sat down. Olshem placed his hand on his head and smiled. "My son, you have good fortune coming your way within a period of six weeks." Atakos waited for him to keep going but he did not. He only stared off in space without blinking. Colnaha hustled Atakos off the ground and gestured for Cristaden to come.

"That's it?" Cristaden whispered as she passed Atakos.

"Yeah, I guess the sun will finally shine in six weeks," Atakos said, frowning. The others looked puzzled. They had assumed they would be getting a reading on a grand scale. What the seer had said seemed more like something a trained 'psychic' would say.

Olshem placed his hand on Cristaden's head and smiled once again. In a raspy voice he said, "You have a very strong and vibrant lineage."

Cristaden blinked at him as he released his hand from her head. She slowly got up and walked back to her friends. "Oh well, so much for psychic intervention." She smiled while the others began to chuckle.

"Go for it Fajha," Zimi said. "You have a strong lineage. I wonder if he will pick that up."

Fajha cleared his throat and pressed his lips together to keep from smiling. He sat down and, as the old man began to bring his hand to his head, he burst out laughing.

Olshem did not say anything or show any emotion but Colnaha was embarrassed. *Today is just not Olshem's day for seeing the future clearly,* he thought.

Fajha cleared his throat again and tried to keep a straight face.

"You are very intelligent and will get rewarded for being so," Olshem said and then released his hand. Fajha nodded and then stood up so the next person would sit down.

"I'm smart," he whispered to Zimi.

"Amazing," Zimi said. "How did he manage to figure that out?"

"Oh, stop it," Zadeia said. "You guys are being so rude. I feel bad for him." She walked over to the seer and sat down.

Upon placing his hand on her head, Olshem's eyes lit up for the first time. "My daughter, you are very strong and full of wisdom." Zadeia smiled at that and stood up to walk back to the group with her head held high. The boys could not hold their laughter inside and it came out in short gasps.

"For one who is always crying and asking dumb questions, you're very wise," her brother chuckled.

"Not funny, Zimi."

"That was not very nice to say," Cristaden said, agreeing with Zadeia.

"Why? It's the truth and you know it." Zimi walked over to Olshem and sat down.

Olshem placed his hand on Zimi's head and frowned. "My boy … you seem … stressed. Try to relax." The seer released his hand from his head.

"Ha, ha, ha," Zadeia said sarcastically as he walked back to them. "Someone needs to cool off."

"Whatever," Zimi mumbled.

Colnaha looked around for his father who had been there before they sat down. He finally spotted him and his mother walking back towards their house, seeming to be in a rather heated argument.

"Do you mind if we call it a night?" Atakos said.

"Sure," Colnaha said quickly.

"Yeah, we have a long way to go before we reach the shores of Paimonu," Fajha said with a huge yawn.

As they turned to leave, they heard the old seer choke on some words. They turned to look at him. The color had drained from his face and he repeated what he had previously said but louder so they could hear. "Do not go to Paimonu, children." He reached out for them with one shaking hand and he seemed very frightened. "Beware of the being with the many faces!" he cried out.

The five friends were shocked at first but, like a chain reaction, Zimi cracked up and the rest followed in laughter.

Colnaha was mad that they found it funny. He knew they were just trying to make light of the situation they were in but where were their manners? He thought of the spoiled rich of Lochenby who had little or no parental upbringing and little respect for elders. They had seemed so different. He brushed aside his annoyance with them and hurried them along. He wanted to speak to his father about some things that were concerning him.

When the group entered his house, Colnaha begged their pardon and excused himself. "I'm sure you remember how to get to your rooms. Good night all of you. I will be happy to see you off tomorrow morning."

"Goodnight," the five teens said in unison. They watched him hurry down the hall and run down a back stairwell. Even though the halls were empty, they kept quiet until they reached the girls' room. Once inside, they shut the door behind them and dropped their voices to a whisper.

"Can you believe that Dokami live here?" Fajha said excitedly.

"Not just any Dokami, but the descendants of the last Wise Man," Atakos said.

"And the old Wise Man himself," Cristaden said.

"What does not make any sense to me is if Maldaha was that strong, why didn't the Council want to choose him?" Zimi said.

"Instead, they allowed Bontihm to take on an inexperienced young girl as an apprentice to be the next Wise Man," Zadeia said.

"And why would someone as powerful as Maldaha want to allow his abilities to be blocked so he would never be able to use it again?" Fajha asked.

"Well, it's like Colnaha said, he simply did not want the Council to find him," Cristaden said.

"Why not?" Atakos said. "Why would the Council care where he is and what would they do to him if he is found?"

"You know …," Fajha thought for a moment before continuing. "Did we ever think there could be someone out there with a motive for kidnapping Hamilda? Other than to get to us?"

That last question made them stop and think. They never did think Hamilda could have any enemies. It never crossed their minds. Hamilda was such a good, kind-loving soul. No one could possibly hate her. But by the way Colnaha spat when he said the word 'apprentice', it allowed them to see that one does not necessarily have to do anything wrong for people to feel resentful.

"You think Maldaha may have something to do with her kidnapping?" Cristaden whispered with fear in her eyes.

"I don't know what to believe anymore," Atakos said.

"What about Olshem's last message about going to Paimonu?" Zadeia said.

"Yeah, what was that about?" Zimi said.

"He said to 'beware of the being with the many faces'," Fajha said, frowning.

"I wonder what that's supposed to mean," Cristaden said.

"I don't know," Atakos said. "We just have to keep our eyes and ears open and try not to be careless when we meet anyone anymore."

"Speak for yourself," Zimi said. "I was praying the whole time you guys would just keep your mouths shut."

"Yeah, we're lucky Colnaha even likes us," Fajha said.

"He may not like us after the way we laughed at his grandfather," Zadeia said.

"Well, we had to," Cristaden said. "In case he said something that would reveal our past to Colnaha. But it's okay, Atakos." She was sensing how he felt about revealing too much. "I read him. Colnaha's okay. He just wants to get to know us. That's all. You did the right thing."

"I'm not so sure about that," Atakos said. He looked at his friends. They seem to rely on him so much for direction but he could not understand why. He seemed to be always making the wrong decisions. "I think I'm going to sleep right now. I suggest you all do the same. We have to leave at the break of dawn. It's already getting late."

"Alright," Cristaden said.

They bid each other goodnight and the boys went to their room. For the rest of the night, the team prayed that what they would find in Paimonu was not a waste of their time or a complete catastrophe.

Colnaha descended down the back stairway to his father's office. From behind the door, he heard him talking to a man with a deep voice on his communicator. He leaned in closer to listen. The man's voice was rough and he sounded very upset. When he heard what they were discussing, he threw the door open and ran to his father.

"*Appi*, no. Don't do it *appi*, they are my friends," he said.

There were two other men there. They were the heads of the other Dokami families that lived in their village. They jumped up when Colnaha barged in and grabbed him, trying to hold him back so he would not stop his father from finishing his conversation.

"Don't do it." Tears began to flow from Colnaha's eyes. "They're on a mission, *appi*. Please don't do this to them."

Angrily, Maldaha gestured for his friends to keep Colnaha quiet. How dare he barge in like that and embarrass him in front of his friends? "Is that the fastest you can come?" he said to the man on the communicator. "They'll be in the desert by then, sir … Okay then … bye." He pushed the 'Off' button and angrily turned towards his crying son. "Take him somewhere where he can't be seen or heard. He will remain there until they are far away from here." He did not dare look at the pain in his son's eyes but left the room instead.

As his father's friends dragged him out of the office and down the hall, Colnaha tried to run but could not break free. He struggled as hard as he could but they still managed to throw him in the back closet. They then slammed the door, locking it behind them.

"NOOOOOO!" Colnaha cried, pounding on the door.

"There's no use shouting," one man said. "They can't hear you from here. I suggest you save your energy. It's going to be a long night."

Colnaha cursed himself for not being smarter. He could have pretended he sided with his father. He could have been able to warn his new friends. Now it was too late. He sat down in the corner of the closet and curled up in a ball, crying silently. They would never even know he was locked away.

Their fate was sealed.

General Komuh switched off his communicator and slowly turned to face Bontihm, who was white as a ghost. The old man had witnessed the entire conversation between the general and Maldaha. He was shocked to learn that Maldaha was indeed still alive and living in Osmatu. He was upset that the man would give away the teenagers' position without a care in his heart. Maldaha was apparently still out for revenge.

"You thought you could protect them and send me all the way here on a false mission to Hortu, didn't you?" Komuh shouted at him. He raised his hand to slap the old man but Bontihm began breathing heavily and clutching his chest. His knees grew weak and he fell to the ground. A soldier tried to reach out to help him but Komuh put his hand out to stop him.

Bontihm's face had turned a scarlet red and he looked like he was having trouble breathing. He tried reaching out for a helping hand but received none in return. The darkness began to close in on him when he realized he was having a major heart attack. He began wheezing loudly for a few seconds until his breathing stopped and his eyes rolled back into his head. It was the name 'Hamilda' that escaped his lips with his last breath and a tear fell from his eye.

"Check him," General Komuh said to the soldier who had attempted to help him. The soldier reached down and felt for a pulse.

"He's dead sir."

"Good riddance. Give his body back to his people. We did not need him after all."

A group of soldiers came to take the body away and General Komuh rushed outside to call for his team of men. "We have to quickly deploy to the Suthack Desert, *now*," he yelled to them. "It will take us a couple of nights to get there by air but that's where they're headed. Move out!" Komuh wanted to stay one step ahead of them but right now he was too far away thanks to Bontihm. Nothing was going to stop him from getting them back.

CHAPTER 29

As the sun began to peek over the horizon, the shores of the Nikul River came into full view. There were merchants and traders crossing the river from Effit to bring goods to the overseers of Mituwa. There were hundreds of slaves there as well, all tied to chains, and soldiers ordering them about. Prince Aillios peered from behind some closely knit trees, watching the swarm of morning activities. King Tholenod and his men were awaiting the all-clear signal to mount the most prevalent ship tied to the dock. The king was yelling at a messenger who was sent ahead to prepare the ship but had managed, to some degree, to get there too late.

"This ship should have been ready hours ago," Aillios heard his father yelling.

"Yes, your m-majesty," the messenger stammered. "I'm sorry, your majesty ... Yes ... so very sorry, forgive me, your majesty ..." The boy was young, possibly eighteen, and he was frightened and shaking, looking like he was ready to wet himself at any moment. How shameful it was for a boy like that, just at the brink of manhood, to be brought down to a level that was lesser than dirt. The boy would never fully realize his capabilities for the remainder of his meager existence. Aillios flinched when Tholenod unhooked a whip from his horse's saddle and lashed out at the boy's face, which bled on impact. Surely there would be a permanent scar there to remind him of his wrongdoing every day until his overworked body was thrown in the marshes. Aillios averted his tearstained eyes from the heartbreaking scene.

After taking a few deep breaths, Aillios tried to refocus on how to board the ship unnoticed. Surveying the dock, he could not see any way to avoid being seen. The area was very open and his father, being one who never let his guard down, was eyeing everyone there. "Well, Thashmar," he said to the horse lying next to him, "It seems as if my mission has been in vain." The horse whinnied and shook his head as if to tell him that all hope was not lost. Aillios looked back at the activity going on at the shore for the next couple of hours, seeking for an opportunity.

And then it came.

Like a gift from the heavens, a soldier wandered away from the melee of troops, slaves, and traders and snuck off into the woods near Aillios, all the while looking behind him to make sure no one took notice. He removed his helmet as he entered the woods. The oblivious soldier did not realize he was being watched. He was too busy humming a happy tune while carefully removing his lower armor to relieve himself. Out of courtesy, Aillios waited for him to finish. He then crept up behind him, brought his arm around his neck to restrain him, and covered his mouth with his other hand to prevent him from screaming for help. The soldier tried to break free but Aillios was too strong for him.

"Do not fight me if you do not want to get hurt," Aillios whispered in his ear. The soldier became angry and tried to fight back. Aillios released the soldier's mouth and, before he had a chance to utter a sound, hit him at the side of his head with his fist. The soldier became instantly limp in his arms.

"I told you not to struggle." Aillios brought his arms under the soldier's armpits and dragged him to the base of a tree. He had no time to waste. He stripped the man of his armor, leaving the soldier with only his undergarments. Hurriedly, he struggled with the chain mail and the chest plate. After putting on the arm and leg shields, he called Thashmar over to him.

"Here goes nothing." Aillios put the helmet over his head and slowly made his way to the shoreline with his heart beating so loudly, he thought everyone could hear it. As he approached the chaotic crowd, the king's general took notice of him.

"YOU THERE!" the general shouted. Aillios' heart almost leapt out of his chest. Sweat began to trickle down his face beneath the heat of the helmet. He knew he was in trouble.

"What are you doing out of ranks? Get back over there." The general pointed to the soldiers standing in two lines on the stairs leading up to the entrance of the ship. They were nineteen of Tholenod's finest, waiting for the order to board.

Aillios handed Thashmar's reigns to a young slave girl who was collecting the horses and bringing them on the ship through a side entrance. He then marched up to the lines and found the empty spot where he was supposed to stand. The sleeping soldier in the woods came to mind then. Wearing his underwear, he would wake up in a few hours to a different life. No one would believe he was ever a soldier of the king. They would consider him senile and most likely turn him into a slave. If he were smart, he would run away and never look back.

A man at the entrance of the ship gave the all-clear signal to the general. The general then barked orders for the soldiers to face each other and take one step back to allow the king to pass through. He then ordered all the soldiers to remove their helmets to show their respect. Aillios knew that if he refused to take off his helmet, he would draw attention to himself, so he had no choice but to take it off. He had a sinking feeling in his stomach when he realized that all was lost. Everything he had planned, all the time he spent tracking his father was about to come to a frightful end. When his father sees him, he would have him punished for disobeying him or executed. His hopes of freeing his people will be eliminated. He bowed his head as his father began walking up the flight of stairs. He knew he was inspecting all the soldiers as he normally did. Trying to think of a liable excuse was his only option.

King Tholenod proudly walked up the stairs, with his assistant Menyilh tagging behind him like a lost puppy, and looked over every soldier. He came across Aillios then, who had his head bowed, and paused. Aillios decided that he was just going to take what was coming to him. He slowly lifted up his head and made eye contact.

Tholenod appeared shocked. His face formed into a scowl and he turned to glare at the general. "Unbelievable," he said.

"How dare you look the king in the eyes?" Menyilh sneered at Aillios. "Look straight ahead."

Aillios averted his eyes and did what he was told.

"It would do you some good to teach your soldiers some respect, general," Tholenod said.

"Yes, sir," the general barked back, anger written all over his face.

King Tholenod then turned back to Aillios. He grunted angrily and then proceeded to finish his inspection up the stairs. Menyilh felt the need to sneer at him again, then hurriedly climbed the stairs after his master.

Aillios frowned. How could he not recognize his own son? He did not think his father had taken any form of hallucinogenic on his journey there, although he wasn't so sure. At any rate, he would recognize his own son, hallucinogenic or not.

The soldiers were ordered to march up the stairs after the king and take their place on the deck of the ship. As Aillios crossed the threshold of the ship, he caught his reflection on a piece of reflective glass tied to the ship's mast.

He froze in mid-step.

Staring back at him was a face that was not his own. This face was surrounded by reddish-brown hair and had very pale skin with dark green eyes. He looked just like the soldier he knocked out in the woods! But how could this be? He was so shocked beyond understanding. Then the words of Asmis came back to him:

'A reflection not yours you shall have
Fear and confusion you shall not.'

His dream had not been just a dream at all. Asmis, the witch, had come to him to give him another face to elude his father. She must have known the soldier would go into the woods. Although the possibility of getting someone else's face seemed ridiculous, there he was, staring at a reflection that was not his own.

Aillios tried hard to hide his contentment. He wished he could share his joy with everyone. By just trying, just risking everything, he had become a soldier of the king and was on his way to wherever his father was headed. Right under his nose. It was more than he could bear. Standing next to the other soldiers, he began to relax. He was no longer afraid.

CHAPTER 30

"Are you guys ready to go?" Cristaden said as she opened the boys' door.

"Just about," Atakos said. He checked the room to make sure nothing was left behind. Then he stepped out into the hallway with Fajha and Zimi.

Zadeia was standing outside their door waiting for them with arms crossed and eyebrows drawn together in deep thought. "Do you hear that?" she asked.

Her friends stopped to listen. Somewhere in the house they could hear a muffled pounding sound. It was a small but repetitive noise. As if someone was banging on a door.

"They must be fixing something in the basement," Zimi said.

Fajha was puzzled. "At this hour?"

Atakos looked out of the nearest window and, even though the sun was just beginning to rise, he saw people walking around. "I guess so."

Ignoring the sound, the five teens walked out of the house. Maldaha and Piedara were standing at the bottom of the stairs, chatting with other villagers. Colnaha was nowhere to be seen.

Maldaha excused himself when he saw them approach. "*Cuuzmosem,*" he said happily.

"Cuuzmosem," Fajha said. "Maldaha said 'good morning'," he told the others.

"Cuuz-mo-sem," his friends said as best as they could.

"*Goro mit-tan?*" Maldaha asked them how they were doing.

"*Osa mit-cuuz*," Fajha responded to let him know they were doing well. "*Vuumo ti* Colnaha?"

Maldaha went on to say that Colnaha was not feeling well. He had asked him to tell them that he was very sorry and to wish them a safe trip. Fajha translated this to his friends.

"That's odd," Cristaden said. "From what I picked up from him, he wanted to be our friend. Why would he just let us leave without personally saying goodbye? Even if he was sick?"

Zadeia lowered her head. "I guess we really made him angry," she said with watery eyes.

"Oh, Zadeia, stop crying," Zimi urged his sister, glancing up at the sky. "We can't expect everyone to like us."

Maldaha grunted and looked away. He then signaled a short, thin man standing close by to bring something and the man quickly walked away. When he returned, the five friends were amazed to see three brown horses with him.

"*Han hozmi*," Maldaha said proudly. "*De hozmi pra-tan de deseer Shuchak me son allo naih pas ush ot virei si.*"

Fajha turned to his friends. "He said that these are his horses. They will take us to the border of the Suthack Desert but will return here once they reach there. They will not enter the desert."

"Are they trained to do so?" Atakos said. "Or are they afraid?"

"I don't know. And I don't think I want to find out."

Piedara gave each of them hugs. "*Pangvithe*," she said, telling them to be careful. She was so different from the angry woman they met upon arrival the day before.

The man with the horses affixed several canteens of water to the horses' saddles. A young, pretty woman handed a small bag of food to Zimi and, after putting it in his backpack, he hoisted himself on one of the horses. Zadeia was brought up behind him. The woman then handed Fajha a wrapped tent and a small blanket. He thanked her and put them in his backpack, then mounted the second horse. Lastly, she handed Atakos a bag with a metal gadget used to create and sustain a fire for long periods of time, which he gladly took from her while mounting the third horse with Cristaden.

They were ready.

Without a moment's hesitation, Atakos led his friends out of the village, waving goodbye to Colnaha's parents and the other villagers along their way, thinking how nice and hospitable all of them were. When they were a safe distance from the village, the teenagers dismounted the horses to eat and drink. They did not plan on stopping until the day was over.

"Fajha," Atakos said. "Do you think you can locate Colnaha?"

"I'll give it a try," Fajha said. He closed his eyes for a moment. "I can't. The orb is too strong. I can't even detect the village."

"Well, I hope he's okay." Even after the spying, Atakos felt bad for Colnaha. It must be really lonely for him, being one of few Dokami in a village located far from civilization. But even so, the boy had a chance of freedom while being educated in Lochenby but he chose instead to return to that desolate village. Why would he? "There's nothing we can do now, we have to move out. Let's go."

Zadeia took one final glance behind them, hoping to see Colnaha running after them, realizing his mistake for letting them go without saying goodbye. All she saw were hills of rock with no signs of life. She sadly turned back around, wondering if they would ever see him again. She knew there was a very small chance they would ever be returning to Osmatu again.

Colnaha stopped banging on the closet door.

It was too late.

By now his new friends would be out of earshot and not coming to his rescue. He tried to adjust his eyes to the dark closet around him. During the night, he took some clothes off the hangers to sleep on. The closet itself was not very big so he had to sleep with his legs curled up in a fetal position so his back would not suffer. He was not at all claustrophobic. It was not the first time he was locked in that closet. He was pretty sure it would not be the last.

Colnaha's thoughts went back to his Dokami friends. He feared that the general his father was communicating with would harm them, or worse, kill them. Most of all, he feared that when the general caught up to them, they would blame him for giving them away. He did not mean for that to happen. When his father asked him to spy on them and discover their secrets, he did not know their lives were at stake. He regretted telling his father what he saw. He thought his father would welcome them, for they were runaway Dokami, like himself. Instead, Maldaha wanted to get back at the people who hurt him by offering their whereabouts to the general of the Western Army, knowing the

Council would be against them being caught. It was completely selfish and uncaring but his father had refused to listen to him. Even his mother tried to talk him out of it. Against her will, she was forced to go along with the plan. Maldaha's hatred for the Dokami Council was taken too far when he put the lives of five teenagers in harm's way.

There were footsteps coming down the stairs.

Frightened, Colnaha sucked in a lung full of air and held it. He recalled the time he had taken clothes down and not hung them back up when his father opened the closet door to let him out. His father was furious and slammed the door shut again and locked it for a few more hours. He dashed around, trying to hang the clothes up but realized it was too dark to be fast and efficient. The footsteps came closer as his heart began to pound faster. Then the footsteps sounded like they were walking away from the door until they disappeared altogether. Colnaha let out the breath he was holding. It must have been one of the servants using the basement door to enter the garden. Quickly he grabbed some empty hangers and began hanging each item of clothing as neatly as possible. He then felt around the floor for more clothes and was relieved to find nothing more.

Except for one thing.

Underneath the carpet was a small, hard object. Lifting up the carpet, Colnaha confirmed that it was a short chain attached to the floor. Having been in the closet several times before, he had never noticed it and could not understand why it was there. He yanked it but nothing happened. Pulling as hard as he could, the chain moved and, much to his surprise, a small trapdoor opened. Colnaha could not believe what he was seeing. A soft, green light poured out from a hidden room beneath the closet. Before he decided to go down the small staircase to enter the room, he knew what he would find.

It was the orb. The orb that kept them hidden from the Council for so many years. The orb that kept all their powers dormant and their village virtually undetectable by members of the Dokami clan.

Climbing down the narrow staircase, Colnaha finally laid eyes on it. Being the only thing in the small chamber, the black orb was resting on a cushioned pedestal with glowing, bright-green waves undulating inside it. It was magnificent to behold. Captivated by the rippling movements of the green waves, he recalled what his father had told him about it. If the orb was covered, it would turn completely black and its powers would be sedated but it could not be easily destroyed. It would take a tremendous amount of energy to accomplish such a feat.

Not wanting to be caught in the room, Colnaha bolted back up the staircase and slammed the trapdoor shut, putting the rug back as neatly as possible over it. He was breathing so heavily, he could not hear himself think. When he started to relax, the sheer magnitude of what he discovered hit him. But what could he do with this knowledge? If he took the orb, the Council would find their village and life, as they know it, would change dramatically. He did not know the exact consequences of taking the orb but he did not care. His father would have to pay for what he was doing and the hatred he had for so many people, especially the Dokami clan. It was a major decision to make but he had to decide quickly. To pull it off, it was going to take more than brains, he would need plenty of courage. Unfortunately, courage was what he severely lacked.

Just then, Colnaha heard noises in the hallway coming towards the closet door. His heart was hammering in his chest as the lock clicked. It was Maldaha, looking angrier than he ever had.

"Appi." Colnaha bent down on one knee, kissing his father's hand. "I was so wrong to go against you. You were right. What you did was right. I was just being foolish as always."

His father sighed and pulled his hand away. "One day you will see this world for what it really is. An unfair and desolate place. Only I can show you what is right and what is wrong."

Knowing that his father was very wrong, Colnaha only nodded. "Yes, appi."

"You are free to go. Your friends have left hours ago. I would not seek them if I were you." With that Maldaha walked briskly away from him with a scowl on his face.

Colnaha only smiled.

The ship reached the other side of the Nikul River, which was wider than Aillios had expected. He had never been to Effit before and wished he could see the country under different circumstances. There were forests of trees but he could see the snowy peaks of mountains in the distance. *Beautiful but tragic*, he thought, looking around. *The people of these lands could never enjoy its beauty until they are freed.*

The soldiers were told to line up and exit the ship. Before they got off the ship, however, a handful of Effit soldiers stopped them.

"By whose order do you have to enter this country?" the captain demanded.

"By *my* order," a voice rang out from the ship. King Tholenod pushed past his soldiers and leaned over the ship's railing, glaring down at the captain below.

"King–Thole–King Tholenod!" he stammered. "I did not know it was you. King Gomu did not inform us—"

"Your king does not know I have come. I could care less if he did. My being here does not concern him or you so if you would kindly let us exit this ship so we can go about our business, I will spare you a beheading."

"Yes–yes sir." The captain was visibly horrified and ordered his men to back up and let them pass.

The soldiers of Mituwa marched off the ship. King Tholenod glared at the Effit soldiers as he passed them. One day they would be under his command but he only wished that day would come sooner. It was an annoyance to deal with the other Kings of the Alliance and he tired of it long ago.

On horseback, Tholenod led his soldiers through the trees. When they were far from the shore, he turned his horse around. His expression was one his men were not familiar with. It was the look of apprehension.

"Men, we are headed to a dangerous place. This place has no name. The forest that surrounds it is dead for reasons I cannot explain. No creature or human being has dared to venture in this forest so I must warn you to be on your guard when we get there." He turned to his assistant, Menyilh, who was by his side. "How long would you say it would take us to reach there?"

Menyilh seemed ecstatic, gleefully grinning, showing off his brownish, slimy teeth. "It is said to be a three day journey from here, sire."

"Good." Tholenod turned back to his soldiers. "We will be there in three days. I suggest you prepare yourself. It will be something you have never seen before." With that he turned around and continued his trek through the trees, prompting the soldiers to do the same.

Aillios looked at the faces of the men behind him. They looked frightened. He knew they would be more frightened of Tholenod's wrath if they ran away. He, in turn, was curious. What was so important about the mountain within a dead forest? Why did his father, the great King

Tholenod, for the first time in his life appear uneasy? Whatever it was, in three days, he was going to find out, whether he liked it or not.

"We have been riding for hours," Zimi said while looking around at the mountains of rocks. "It doesn't seem like we are anywhere near a desert."

"We should reach it soon," Fajha said although he was unsure himself.

"You said that an hour ago."

"Yeah, but I'm pretty sure we're going to fall upon it really soon. It makes no sense though. My coordinates tell me that we should have reached there by now."

They went around a large boulder standing in front of them and all they saw were more hills of rocks ahead. A cool wind began to blow, giving them goose bumps. They got off the horses to throw their cloaks on to keep warm.

Just as Cristaden pulled her hood over her head, she pointed to the ground. "Sand," she said.

"We're getting real close," Fajha said, kicking a large rock to reveal more sand underneath. "It should be less than a mile away."

"Let's go then!" Atakos climbed back on his horse, pulling Cristaden up to sit behind him. The others followed his lead. They brought their horses to a gallop and urged them to go faster until they were at full racing speed.

Making the horses go faster was a big mistake.

Once they rounded a corner and the desert came into full view, the horses raised their front legs and dropped the teens hard on their backs. They then practically pivoted around and sprinted back towards Osmatu.

"The *canteens!*" Fajha shouted after the horses. "They ran off with our water!"

The five friends watched as the horses galloped farther and farther away until they disappeared behind a rocky hill.

The teens sighed helplessly.

"If we need water all we have to do is make Zadeia cry," Atakos said after some time.

"Sure," Fajha said, ignoring the unfriendly look he got from Zadeia. "But it never rains in this desert region. If there are inhabitants here they will know something is amiss."

"They probably won't think we had anything to do with it," Zimi said. "We can act like it's a miracle."

Cristaden laughed. "We can't allow ourselves to be discovered like we so carelessly did in Osmatu. We have to pass through here undetected. Who knows what kind of people could be living out here?"

"Guys," Zadeia said. "I don't think we have to worry about that."

Four pairs of eyes turned to see what she was observing.

At first all they could see were rolling hills of sand. Then they saw it in the distance. A very large bird was standing on the sand, pecking at something by its feet. Looking closely, they could see that it was a human skeleton, picked clean of its flesh but broken, as if a large animal had torn through it.

"That's a Valdeec bird," Fajha said, swallowing hard. "They are like vultures but much, much larger. And meaner. They seek out victims of the desert and start eating them even before they are dead. I was unaware they could be found in *this* part of the desert. They dwell further south from here. We're going to have to stay strong and not let this desert beat us or we'll be lunch."

Atakos took a deep breath. "Well, we can't turn back now. Let's go."

"Atakos, I'm scared," Cristaden whispered.

"Don't be frightened," he reassured her, putting his arm around her shoulders. "We have each other. That is five times better than being alone. We'll make it." As she nodded, he could not help thinking how much he did not believe what he was saying as the words rolled off his tongue.

"On to the Suthack Desert!" Fajha cried.

The Valdeec bird heard his cry and slowly flew away, eyeing its next potential meal.

PART FOUR
SUTHACK DESERT

CHAPTER 31

Walking on the rolling desert sand proved to be no easy task. With each determined step, the five members of Omordion's Hope felt like they were sinking, as if the sand was pulling them down. Before long, their legs felt so heavy it became increasingly difficult to lift them. Furthermore, the sun was burning brightly when they started their trek through the desert. As it began to set, a terrible coldness replaced its warmth.

"The cold air must be coming from the sea," Zimi said, shivering.

"Don't you think it's a little *too* cold to be coming from the sea?" Atakos said.

Fajha sighed. "Must I remind you that in this desert, the temperature changes frequently? It could be extremely hot during the day but freezing when the sun goes down."

"Is that so?" Zadeia said sarcastically.

"Fajha," Zimi said, "if you knew so much about this desert, why weren't we reminded before we left Lochenby, so we could prepare for this?"

"Well, when you're running away from an entire army, one doesn't think too clearly on everything we need to pack, don't you think?" Pushing his glasses up his nose, Fajha glared at Zimi. "Besides, it's not my fault if you forgot what I said."

Zimi put his hands up in defense. "Hey, I was just asking."

A steady breeze began to blow, making Cristaden's hairs stand on end. She wrapped her cloak around her tighter and shivered. Seeing that she was cold, Atakos took off his cloak and offered it to her. She smiled at him, appreciating the gesture. "I'll be fine, Atakos. Thanks."

"Maybe if we huddle together, we may be able to stay warm," Fajha said.

"We could do that but it would be even more difficult to walk," Atakos said, pulling a cramped leg out of the sand while putting his cloak back on. He felt that if he stood still at all, he would be buried in sand rather quickly.

Hearing a dull thud behind him, Atakos turned to see Zimi face down in the sand. He couldn't help but crack a smile to see his friend, who was usually so coy and confident, with a mouth full of sand.

"Oh my!" Cristaden said. "Are you okay?" She rushed to his side and, along with Zadeia, helped him stand. They brushed sand off his clothes and face as he spat it out of his mouth.

Fajha shot Atakos an approving grin, which he returned.

"I see you laughing," Zimi said, spitting out the remaining sand from his mouth.

The boys could not restrain themselves and burst out laughing.

"I'm glad you think it's so funny. When you fall, I'll be sure to laugh *extra* loud."

"Oh, are you okay?" Fajha said in a singsong voice, mocking the girls' concern.

Zimi flashed him an ungrateful look, causing Fajha to double over in laughter. Not realizing that the wind had buried his feet in the sand up to his ankles, Fajha took a step forward and he too was met with a face full of sand.

For the next hour or so, they could not get Zimi to stop laughing.

"Let's make camp here," Atakos said when they reached the bottom of a small sand hill. The sun was threatening to take all of the remaining light with it as it slowly sank in the horizon. "Once the sun sets, we won't be able to see anything." It was also helpful that the wind died down. Otherwise they would be buried in sand as they slept.

Setting down their backpacks, they got to work. As the sun disappeared, their tent was completely pitched, the food was ready, and a nice, warm fire was burning. They sat around the campfire and ate in silence, thinking about the rest of the journey ahead.

"I sure wish we had some water right about now," Zadeia said.

"I know," Atakos said and then sighed. "I didn't believe Maldaha when he said the horses wouldn't go in the desert. Who knew they were *really* going to run away like that? I wasn't even *thinking* about the water. Hopefully, we can reach the Hejdian Sea by tomorrow."

"Very unlikely," Fajha said. "At our pace, I don't think we've even made it halfway through the desert yet."

There was a unanimous sigh of frustration among the group. Fajha was being brutally honest but they could not blame him for being so. It was just that they were so thirsty and *exhausted*.

By now it was pitch black in the desert and they could see nothing beyond five feet of their fire. All they heard were sounds of insects and, at times, the distant squawk of a Valdeec bird. The moon seemed so far away that it provided no illumination whatsoever of the rolling hills of sand around them. Even the stars were tiny specks of dust in the black sky.

"This is so spooky," Zadeia said, trying to peer in the darkness.

"The faster we get to sleep, the faster morning will come," Cristaden quickly said. She got up and entered the tent, followed by Zadeia and Zimi.

Before Fajha went in, he saw Atakos about to douse the fire with sand.

"Hey, let's … wait. Until it dies on its own, hunh?" Fajha said, frightfully looking around at the darkness surrounding them.

"Alright." Atakos dropped the sand and irritatingly wiped his hand on his cloak. He was so tired of seeing sand everywhere, on his clothes, in his socks, in his hair, in his eyes, and even in his mouth. It was enough to make him crazy.

Atakos followed Fajha into the tent, which was really meant for three people, and squeezed in next to him, who lay next to Zimi, and then Zadeia, and then Cristaden. Despite the uncomfortable situation, the good thing about having a small tent was that their body heat kept them warm as they fell into a well needed slumber.

Fajha opened his eyes abruptly. It took him a moment to realize he was standing on a treeless, slippery wet, black mountain. At the base of the mountain was a valley of lush green vegetation and an expansive forest. Beyond the trees, in the distance, was a black cave. Everything seemed so peaceful and serene that he closed his eyes and took a deep breath in, slowly releasing it as his body began to relax.

A clamor made Fajha open his eyes again. Magnificently large birds suddenly flew up, out of the trees, and into the bright sky. At first he was amazed, even delighted by them, but when they started flying straight towards him, the fear he suddenly felt propelled him to turn and run. The ground beneath Fajha was so slippery that he tripped and fell, hitting his head on a sharp rock. Painfully lifting his head, he felt blood dripping down the side of his face. As he tried to stand up, he suddenly realized that his legs were frozen in place. The squawking of the birds grew louder and louder until they were on top of him. Arms flailing, trying to protect his face, Fajha tried to escape but couldn't. He knew he was meeting death head-on.

"Fajha," someone whispered, shaking him.

When he opened his eyes, Fajha thought he was still dreaming. The sound of birds squawking was still as deafening to his ears as they were in his dream.

"Don't move," Atakos whispered.

Fajha could see that everyone else was awake. They were staring wide-eyed at the tent around them. In the light of the still burning fire, they saw the shadows. The Valdeec birds had their tent surrounded. A few had landed on top of the tent, threatening to collapse it. A few more were even trying to chew through the tent, squawking in their frustration.

"This can't be happening," Fajha said.

"There must be so little to eat out here that they've become *desperate*," Zadeia said.

A scary, ripping sound came from Cristaden's side of the tent. She shrieked and practically climbed over Zadeia. The birds heard the noise and their pecking and squawking became more persistent.

"We have to *do* something," Cristaden said, crying. She was shaking violently.

"What do you suppose we do?" Zimi said. "There could be hundreds, if not thousands, out there ready to eat us alive."

"Well," Fajha said. "Fighting sounds much better than waiting for them to tear through this tent and have a midnight snack served on a platter, doesn't it?" He turned to Atakos. The other three did the same as if their fate were lying in his hands.

"Ok guys," Atakos said, seeing no other options. "I say we fight. We killed *oblots* for goodness sakes. These are just *birds*." His terrified friends nodded and looked up simultaneously when another tear was made on the roof of the tent. A Valdeec bird poked its gnarled face in and angrily squawked at them, while trying to pull its entire body through the small hole.

Their cue had come to get out and meet their predators face to face.

Atakos unzipped the tent and ran out first, kicking the first bird he saw charging at him. A huge flock of them came at him and he pushed all of them away with his power. They were much larger than he had anticipated, about the size of a small child with a wingspan of six feet. And very strong. After being pushed back a few feet, they flew back at him but this time Fajha came out and helped him throw them back even further.

Just as Zimi, Zadeia, and Cristaden came out, a couple of birds, which were on top of the tent, immediately attacked Cristaden, yanking at her hair and scratching her face.

"Help me!" she said, screaming. Her arms were flailing around in desperation, unable to use her power to blow them up.

Atakos turned quickly and forced both birds away from her. They then exploded into several large chunks of flesh and feathers, leaving Cristaden covered in gross entrails.

"Eeeew, this is disgusting," Cristaden said, wiping the gunk off her face.

"Heads up," Zimi said.

Several birds came from above and swooped down to attack them. Atakos and Fajha pushed some away while Zimi froze one. The frozen bird toppled to the ground and died at his feet. Cristaden blew one up and watched as the entrails rained down on them in a million pieces.

"This is so *gross*," Cristaden said, shielding her face.

"Maybe there's a better way," Zadeia said. She quickly used her wind power to pick up a flame from the small fire, concentrating hard as she placed it on her hand so it would not die out. When it didn't, she used the wind to blow it at an approaching bird. The flame shot out and set the bird on fire. The bird flew away, shrieking loudly into the night. As it flew away, it illuminated the sky.

Zimi was right. There were hundreds of birds. Just waiting for their chance to get at their next meal.

All of a sudden, their campfire went out with the flapping of a bird's wings and everything went dark. For reasons the teens could not understand, the squawking ceased and an eerie silence filled the camp.

"Oh no," Cristaden whispered. "We're going to die."

"Shhh, maybe they can't see us," Atakos whispered.

As if to prove him wrong, a bird swooped down and grabbed him by the shoulders.

"Aauuh! Help me!"

Fajha quickly reached out and grabbed Atakos' feet to keep the bird from flying away with him.

Atakos lost his cool for the first time. "Don't let go! Don't let it take me! Please don't let it take me!" he shrieked, his voice cracking as if he was on the brink of tears. The talons of the hungry bird were digging into his flesh, causing him extreme pain.

"Help me," Fajha said to the others. They felt around for him and tried to help pull Atakos down.

"Aah!" Atakos cried out again, desperately fighting off other birds that began to take advantage of his situation.

Just then, another bird pushed Zimi to the ground. It grabbed a hold of his hair, attempting to drag him away.

"NO!" Zimi cried out.

"Zimi, where are you?" Zadeia shouted. It was too dark to see anything. "I can't *see*! I can't see you!"

"I'm on the ground. I can't fight him off. Aah, oh no, it's *biting* me!"

"We have to do something!" Cristaden said and then screamed as she felt a Valdeec bird's wings brush by her hair. There was no communicating with the birds. Their only thought was to kill.

Zadeia tried to think fast. She could not see Atakos or Zimi. If only she had a light. If only she knew how to make fire. She became desperate. A warm, tingling sensation started to form in the palms of her hands. Curious, she closed her hands and squeezed them together, making a fist. Imagining fire coming out of them, Zadeia felt her hands getting hotter and hotter. As hot as her hands became, they did not hurt. The world went quiet around her as she channeled all her energy into her hands, and then, when she felt like they were ready, she opened them.

A tiny fireball burned brightly in each hand.

Zadeia could not believe her eyes.

Steadily the flames grew, illuminating everything around them. Cristaden and Fajha, who were still hanging on to Atakos, glanced back at her when they saw the light. Confusion swept over their faces.

Zadeia was dazed momentarily. Refocusing, she saw the Valdeec bird that was attempting to drag Zimi away by his hair. Making sure to take perfect aim, she threw one of the fireballs at the bird and it burst into flames, releasing her brother. The other fireball was aimed directly at the bird trying to fly away with Atakos. It burst into flame as well, releasing Atakos from its clutches. As Atakos fell, Cristaden and Fajha tried to catch him but they ended up in the sand, barely breaking his fall.

The Valdeec birds grew furious from the sight of the fire and suddenly decided to attack them all at once.

Without hesitation, Zadeia closed her hands again and opened them to reveal more fireballs. With the light emanating from her hands, the teenagers could see hundreds of birds coming at them.

Atakos, Fajha and Cristaden used their powers to push them away, giving them enough time to regroup. The five friends gathered in a circle, with their backs facing each other, taking on wave after wave of ravenous birds. For a brief moment, they were reminded of the practices they had with Hamilda and how she would make them stand just like they were and throw rocks at them. The only difference was that the rocks were three-foot, hungry, flesh-eating birds with sharp claws and beaks that were out to risk their own lives in order to get a bite to eat. There was no way the teens were going to allow a bunch of birds to beat them. They started this mission in order to save Hamilda. They were not about to let her down.

Cristaden, Fajha, and Atakos blew up several birds at the same time, while Zimi froze some and Zadeia set some on fire.

Every time they killed a few, several more came at them from behind the ones that were destroyed. Birds were being blown up, torched, and frozen left and right. But there was still so many of them. At times, Atakos and Fajha had to push them back because they kept getting too close for comfort, threatening to override their defenses.

A large Valdeec bird got close enough to take a swipe at Zadeia's face, creating a deep gash on her forehead. She immediately set that bird on fire but, while it burst into flames, it landed right on top of her. She pushed it off, fearing that her hair might catch on fire. When she realized she was not burnt, she looked up to see three birds coming straight at her. She didn't have enough time to create more fireballs. Screaming, she braced herself for the incoming attack. Suddenly the birds exploded into thousands of pieces. Zadeia turned to see Cristaden looking her way with her arms extended. She nodded to thank her but saw more birds coming. She quickly made two fireballs and set them on fire.

As the sun began to rise, the strenuous battle with the birds went on and on. There seemed to be no end to it. The smell of burning and rotting flesh began to fill their nostrils as piles and piles of dead carcasses surrounded them.

The teens began to lose energy. They were exhausted.

The remaining two dozen or so birds lunged at them, but when Atakos, Fajha and Cristaden tried to push them away, they failed, only pushing the birds back a mere two feet. Zimi lost his ability to freeze, only being able to slap some wind on the birds, which they fought against with their wings.

The Valdeec birds saw their opportunity and lunged at them, pulling at their hair and biting them repeatedly. The teens tried fighting them off but found it difficult. The birds were too strong and they were very weak.

Feeling like they were probably going to lose the fight after everything they've been through, Zadeia summoned up all her remaining energy and gave everything she had into her hands, turning them into torches. As she screamed for her friends to get down, she raised her arms and pushed her energy out through the fire, torching all the birds at once. Wriggling in pain, they screeched, trying to flap their wings to fly away. Some died instantly and would have burnt the teens if they didn't dive out of the way to avoid getting torched as well.

Relieved that all the birds were finally dead, Zadeia fell to her knees. Her eyes rolled back into her head as she collapsed face first into the sand.

CHAPTER 32

"Zadeia!" Cristaden cried, crawling to her friend's side. The boys helped her roll Zadeia onto her back. Unresponsive, her eyes were opened slightly and her breathing was labored. There was a large gash on her forehead where blood slowly dripped from, making its way down the side of her face and mixing with the sand in her black hair. Cristaden immediately tried to heal her but had to quit, making the gash on Zadeia's forehead only stop bleeding. Her energy was drained. "Oh, no," she said, panicking. "What am I going to do?"

"Don't worry," Atakos said. "She may regain some energy with sleep. Maybe we should let her rest."

"But look at you—look at us."

The boys had scratches all over their faces, arms, and hands. Puncture wounds were on Atakos' shoulders from the time the Valdeec bird tried to fly away with him. Zimi had small puncture wounds and bites on his head and Fajha had small bites on his head and shoulders. There was blood everywhere.

Then they looked at Cristaden.

Except for some entrails and blood from the birds, she seemed to have escaped unscathed. There was not a scratch on her.

"Are you ... hurt, Cristaden?" Fajha asked.

"Well, yes, I was scratched and–well, no I–I'm fine," Cristaden said, feeling her head and looking at her once scratched up arms and hands.

"Cristaden, do you realize your body healed itself?" Atakos said.

"Well, yes—I mean I do *now*. But what about you?" Tears escaped her worried eyes.

"We'll be okay for now," Zimi said. "We'll just rip up a shirt and bandage ourselves until you gain your energy back. Then you can heal us."

"Yeah," Fajha said. "We don't have any broken limbs or exposed bones. We'll be fine."

Cristaden wiped her eyes. "Ok."

Atakos stood up and went into the tent, coming back out with his other white shirt, previously torn from the oblot attack. He then ripped it apart while Cristaden tried her best to wrap their exposed wounds with the pieces.

Zimi and Fajha grimaced in pain as they stood up but they bravely ignored it, knowing they needed to get as far away from the overpowering scent of decomposing birds as possible. The sun was just starting to peek over the horizon, allowing them to see firsthand how many birds they fought and killed that night. Covering the sand as far as they could see, there must have been a thousand of them. Some burning birds had tried to fly away but ended up dying a quarter of a mile away.

"This is horrendous," Zimi said, making his way to the tent with his three friends. "Why did they all come here?"

Fajha grunted. "Do you see anything else to eat in this forsaken place?"

Zimi shook his head as they pushed a couple of frozen birds off the tent.

The tent was ripped in several places but was not in bad shape. The four friends removed their bags from inside and threw them on. They then made the tent into a hammock. Carefully lifting Zadeia, they hoisted her onto the tarp. For an hour they carried her, trying to find an area where they could rest. When they finally saw no more birds, they stopped and laid down on the tarp next to Zadeia.

They slept for two hours. Scenes of attacking birds plagued their dreams as they tossed and turned under the onslaught of heat from the sun. Their cuts and bruises ached and prickled but, because they were so exhausted, they managed to sleep through it for the most part. Atakos would jolt himself awake and look around every half an hour or so just to be sure Valdeec birds were not in sight.

There was still no sound or movement from Zadeia. It appeared as though she was sleeping soundly. The strip of shirt that was wrapped around her head had now turned a deep maroon from the blood seeping from her reopened wound. It was not significant enough to kill her but it was enough to need a small blood transfusion to bring her back to consciousness without Cristaden's help.

Cristaden was the only one who slept comfortably, having no visible trauma to her body from the attack. Her dreams were not comfortable though, with visions of dying friends and wounds that could not be healed.

Zimi had dreams of his military father, telling him that he wasn't competent enough to fight a battle and taunting him, trying to make him feel inferior. He tried to tell his father about how he had saved his sister from the deadly tree attack and his successes with the Valdeec birds, but his father would not hear any of it. Instead he left him to rot in a hot, desolate desert and told him never to seek out his family again.

Fajha's dream was even more horrific. He entered his grandfather's mansion in Northern Saiyut and noticed that it was unusually empty and unkempt. A thick layer of dust had settled over everything and dead leaves blew in from broken windows. Calling for his family, he received no response. Suddenly he heard a squawk coming from a room at the end of the giant front hall. After slowly making his way to the room, he peered through the crack of the open door. Seeing nothing unusual, he opened it slightly and poked his head through. It was the sitting room, furnished with comfortable armchairs and a grand piano in the middle of the floor. Two Valdeec birds were pecking at something at the foot of the piano. Fajha slowly entered the room to get a better view of the round object. Coming closer, he gasped when he saw that it was a human head. The eyes had been pecked out and part of its jaw was missing. It dawned on him that he was staring back at his grandfather's decapitated head.

"OH NO. HELP ME. HELP ME. PLEASE, HELP ME," Fajha said, screaming while flailing his arms.

"Fajha, calm down," Atakos said and grabbed his friend's shoulder. "It was just a dream. Take a deep breath and try to relax."

Fajha struggled a bit with Atakos and then allowed his friend's voice to bring him out of his torment. Shaking tremendously, it took him a moment to realize where he was. He still felt woozy from the blood loss and his body ached. Their two hours of sleep was not enough to gain back everything they had lost. He looked over and saw that Zimi and Cristaden were bent over a rather pale looking Zadeia. Bringing Zadeia's head onto her lap, Cristaden closed her eyes and placed her hand on her forehead. She began to hum softly as the palm of her hand started to glow. Color came back to Zadeia's face and the deep gash on her forehead healed, yet she was still unresponsive.

"Zadeia?" Cristaden gently called her, hoping she would open her eyes.

"Zadeia." Zimi shook her. "Zadeia, wake up."

Nothing.

Cristaden shrugged. "I don't know what to do, she's completely healed but she won't wake up."

"Do you think she requires an energy transfer like Atakos did in the forest?" Fajha said.

"She has all the energy she needs."

Frantic, Zimi looked up at Fajha and Atakos. Tears welled up in his eyes. "What are we going to do? We are nowhere near a hospital. It would take us two days to go back to the village. What are we going to do?" All he could think of was the dream about his father. He was so disappointed that he allowed anything bad to happen to his sister. How was he going to explain this to his parents?

After some thought, Fajha cleared his throat. "I think I have an idea of what's going on."

"What's that?"

"I just tried to locate her. It didn't work."

"What do mean it didn't work?" Atakos was puzzled. "She's right here. You're *looking* at her."

"Yeah, what do you mean by that?" Zimi grew scared.

"I mean … oh, how do I explain it?"

"I know what he means," Cristaden said. She brushed some sand off of Zadeia's face. "She's with us physically but mentally … she's far away."

Zimi started to freak out. "What are you saying? She's in a *coma*?"

"Not exactly," Fajha said. "I think I know how to bring her back."

"What?" Atakos raised his eyebrows. "Are you serious?"

Fajha thought of his recent dream and all the other dreams he had ever experienced. The dream world was a terrifying place to be in. "I've never done this before but I think if I bring myself to deep meditation, I can reroute my energy and focus on finding Zadeia. I may be able to enter her dream and try to locate her there." It was a huge risk but he was willing to take it to save his friend.

"How are you so sure you can do it?" Zimi said. He was skeptical but willing to try anything that could bring his sister back. He gripped her hand and felt tears stinging his eyes once again.

Fajha put his hand on his shoulder. "I'll try."

"So what if you do manage to enter her dreams?" Cristaden said. "And then you can't get back to your body? What if you get stuck in an astral plane or something and we lose *both* of you?"

Fajha took a deep breath and smiled. "I won't get stuck. I promise I'll bring us back together."

With that, Zimi crawled away from his sister, giving Fajha space to lie down next to her. Cristaden lifted Zadeia's head off her lap and placed it gently down on the tarp, backing away from them as well.

"Be careful," Cristaden said.

"I will."

Fajha closed his eyes and grabbed Zadeia's hand. Once again, as he always did during his meditations, he imagined himself to be in the vast garden located at his grandfather's summer home. This time he was searching for someone. He entered the maze of twists and turns and tried to focus all his energy on locating Zadeia. As he dreamt, he began to fall deeper and deeper into a trance. In his dream, he was just about to exit the maze when he noticed a sandy path leading into a … desert.

This is it, Fajha thought. Suddenly, as if a cloud lifted from his mind, he knew where Zadeia was. She was in the middle of the desert, sitting cross-legged in their pitched tent. Quickly, he ran to the sandy path and entered the desert. Looking back, he saw that the vast garden was gone and there was desert all around him. He turned around and around, trying to find the tent, but did not see anything but hills of sand.

"Zadeia!" Fajha called out. He received no response. He was just about to use his location ability again, when he spotted something in the distance. Standing on top of a hill of sand was a boy. There was something oddly familiar about him but before he could figure it out, the boy had vanished. Fajha took off running towards that direction. The sand weighed down his legs but he kept willing himself to keep moving. When he reached the top of the hill, he looked down at the valley below him.

And saw the tent.

"I'm coming, Zadeia," Fajha said. He ran to the tent and quickly unzipped it.

Zadeia was sitting cross-legged inside, expressionless, staring straight ahead. Her reddish-brown skin seemed paler than usual and the whites of her large, brown eyes were tinted red, as if she had been crying.

"Zadeia." Fajha grabbed her shoulders. "Zadeia, wake up. We have to go now."

For a moment, it appeared as if Zadeia would not snap out of her dream state but she slowly shifted her eyes to look at him. Fajha assumed she recognized him. If he could only get her to stand up.

Then Zadeia started screaming. Her eyes filled with tears as she tried to crawl to the back of the tent, clawing for a way to get out.

"Zadeia, it's okay," Fajha said, trying to reassure her. "It's me. It's okay. It's Fajha."

Zadeia continued to scream and began kicking her legs as if she wanted to kick him away. Crying, she shot her arm out and pointed to something behind him, then started screaming again.

Fajha quickly turned around. It was Colnaha. He was standing right outside the tent, threatening to come in. His hair was disheveled and he was very muddy, caked with sand and dirt. His skin was extremely pale but it was his eyes that terrified Fajha the most. They were blood red and cat-like, almost as if he were a zombie, coming back from his grave. As if to prove Fajha's theory right, he opened his mouth slightly and a slimy insect with long legs crawled out of it.

Then he attacked.

"Aaaaah!" Fajha cried out. With his quick thinking, he kicked Colnaha hard, sending him tumbling backwards. He then pushed him out of the tent with his mind. The whole time he was reminding himself that it was just a dream. If he allowed himself to believe what he was seeing was real, he felt that he would become a permanent fixture in Zadeia's nightmare. They would both be lost forever.

Colnaha came at them again and Fajha attempted to blow him up but only managed to break off a few of his fingers, which made Colnaha even more upset. As he charged towards the tent, Fajha pushed him away even further, which allowed him enough time to grab Zadeia's arm. "We have to go. Now."

"I can't," Zadeia said, crying. "I can't go out there. I want to stay *here*. Zip up the tent, Fajha. Let's just stay here."

"No, we have to get out." Fajha threw her over his shoulder and raced out of the tent while she kicked and screamed for him to put her down. He looked around for Colnaha. He was nowhere to be seen.

"Zadeia—," Fajha said but was interrupted by her screams. Turning around, he stood face to face with the dead Colnaha. Immediately, he pushed him back about thirty feet. Colnaha fell to the ground, only to get back up with incredible speed.

"Crap," Fajha said. He put Zadeia down on her feet and grabbed her by the chin, making direct eye contact with her. "Zadeia, *listen to me*," he said. He forced her to look at Colnaha. "This is just a dream, he is not *real*."

"No, no, no," Zadeia said and started crying again.

"Yes, it is. Zadeia, listen to me. Only *you* can control your dream."

Colnaha came at them again and Fajha pushed him away once more. "You have to realize that this is just a *nightmare*, Zadeia. You can make him disappear. This is *your* dream."

Zadeia's heart was beating violently against her chest. This was by far the worst thing she had ever encountered. Fajha was telling her something strange, something she could not understand. Where were the rest of her friends? Why had they abandoned them? Maybe it was because of the way she felt about Colnaha. They had sensed it, she was sure of it. And now, he had come back to haunt her. Her friends had left her. Only Fajha remained. Fajha was always so nice. She tried not to look at Colnaha. She *could not* look at him. He was an absolute nightmare that would never stop until she was dead— nightmare? It was what Fajha was trying to tell her after all, wasn't it? That this was just a nightmare. Zadeia stopped crying as an expression of recognition came across her face. "A dream?" she said in a small voice.

"That's it, Zadeia," Fajha said, trying to be careful with his words.

Zadeia placed both hands at the sides of her head and squeezed her eyes shut. "No, how is that even possible?" She grimaced when she heard Fajha push Colnaha away again. Then she heard Colnaha let out a horrifying scream. It took her a moment to realize that the scream had come from her mouth and she was suddenly clutching Fajha's shirt. "I'm so confused," she whispered.

"Zadeia, you have to believe me or we're going to be *stuck* here," Fajha said, pleading with her. "We're losing time."

Zadeia looked up at Colnaha. He growled ferociously at her and his body tensed as if he was ready to kill the first thing that came within reach. She decided to test out Fajha's theory. Steadying her gaze, she focused her attention on Colnaha and tried to move him, just slightly to the right. When his body moved a little to the right, she gasped.

"You got it, Zadeia. Do not hesitate. Make him go away." Fajha saw Colnaha charging at them again, looking as though he was about to enjoy a much-anticipated meal. "Do it. Do it *now!*"

"Go away," Zadeia said. In a flash, Colnaha was gone. Shocked, she fell to the sand and broke down in tears.

Fajha let her cry out her torment for a moment. He then reached down and brushed his hand along her black hair. "You did it, Zadeia."

"It seemed so real. Colnaha. He was—"

"It was just a nightmare. He's not really dead."

"How do you know?"

"I just do. Trust me."

Zadeia smiled and looked up at him. "Thanks for helping me." She wiped her tears and allowed Fajha to pull her up into a tight embrace.

When they opened their eyes, they were back in the desert with their friends looking on. For a moment they did not realize they were suspended in air until they hit the ground and Zadeia screamed.

"Boy am I glad to hear your voice," Zimi said.

"We thought we lost you, Zadeia," Cristaden said, tears glistening in her eyes.

"We thought we lost both of you," Atakos said.

"Were we just levitating?" Fajha said.

"Yes. As soon as you fell into your trance, your bodies floated up a few feet. We couldn't even hold you down." A thought occurred to Atakos. "You know, when we were practicing in Osmatu, I thought I saw you levitate off the ground. Now I know it wasn't my imagination."

"Wow. Levitation." Fajha smiled. "I would like to work on *that*. Maybe I can fly."

Atakos laughed. "Not right now," he said, looking around. "We've lost a lot of travel time." He offered his hands to Fajha and Zadeia and helped them up.

Fajha studied his friends for a moment. They were all healed, even him. There were no more cuts and bruises and they all appeared well rested. Cristaden must have healed them while he was in Zadeia's dream.

He smiled to himself and sighed, trying to put Zadeia's nightmare out of his mind. Their journey was turning out to be the most horrifying ride of his life but at least they had each other. It was the only thing that kept them going. As they gathered their belongings and began to walk again, he could not help wondering what other terrifying danger they would encounter along their way.

CHAPTER 33

The hot desert sun blazed overhead, burning their skin as the treacherous wind blew sand in their eyes and against their parched lips. The soft sand threatened to take them down with each excruciating step and, at times, the friends leaned on each other for support when they felt like giving up. It was, by far, the most uncomfortable part of their journey and, with the threat of dehydration, the most dangerous. They did not know when they were going to reach the Hejdian Sea.

Fajha tried to make sense of it. "I have to calculate the speed we are going times the length of time we have been walking. The desert itself is said to be about twenty-five miles long. The rate we are going is one mile per hour."

"That's it?" Atakos began to panic. "We have to go faster. We'll never get out of here!"

"Yes we will. So far, we traveled six miles today and ten miles yesterday. If we keep at this pace or increase it just a little bit, by this time tomorrow, we will reach the sea, even allowing ourselves time to get a full night's sleep."

"Sleep?" Atakos sighed. "Who can sleep with killer birds attacking us? We might as well keep walking throughout the night and reach the sea before morning."

"As much as I would love to say that's a great idea, we can't possibly make it out here in complete darkness. Even if we had Zadeia's fireballs to light the way, it's just too dangerous. We are better off staying in one spot and just trying to survive the night."

Atakos sighed again as he brushed sand particles off his eyelashes. "It was just a thought," he said and then another thought occurred to him. "It's hard to imagine Hamilda's captors took her this way." And then he bit his tongue.

There was a momentary pause when everyone started considering what they were avoiding thinking since they entered the Suthack Desert. That Hamilda may not even be where they thought she was.

"Hey, look at it this way," Atakos said, trying to change the subject. "At least we're not getting attacked right now."

Cristaden stopped walking and looked around. "What was that?"

Zimi shook his head and looked up at the sky as everyone stopped walking. "Can't we go *one* minute without something *bad* happening?" he said.

"What was what, Cristaden?" Atakos said, ignoring him.

"Did you hear that?"

"Hear what?" Zadeia said, quickly glancing around in fear.

There was no sound other than the wind.

"I don't hear anything," Fajha said.

"Maybe it's the desert," Zimi said. "Maybe it's finally getting to you, Cristaden."

"I'm not crazy, I heard someth—"

Then they heard it too. It was a very low, but unmistakable, animal screech that was on their right and then on their left in an instant. Then it was gone.

"What *was* that?" Zadeia said, backing into her brother.

"Look," Atakos said, pointing at the sand.

Three-toed footprints. All around them. The wind was already covering them up with sand. The teens were horrified. They heard the animal but they did not see anything run by them. The footprints were so *close*.

"Maybe they're not footprints," Fajha said. "Maybe they're animals that live under the sand. Like Montapu lizards."

"They sure look like footprints to me," Cristaden said. She nervously looked around and saw nothing out of the ordinary. The footprints were just about covered, resembling small holes in the sand. She suddenly felt as if something was standing directly behind her. Yelping, she turned around quickly to see what it was. There was nothing there.

"What?" Atakos said. "What is it?"

"I swear there was something standing behind—oh!" Cristaden pointed at the sand and jumped back in fear. Sure enough there were footprints directly behind her. They seemed to have walked right up to her and then walked away.

The frightened friends came closer together. They were definitely not Montapu lizards they were dealing with. The footprints were too big.

"What could it be?" Zimi asked Fajha.

"How am I supposed to know?" Fajha said shrieking.

"You're the animal expert. Don't you know what everything is?"

"Yeah, everything that has been *discovered*. For all I know, this could be some unknown species. I can't even *see* it for goodness sakes."

Atakos put his hands up to stop the bickering between his two friends. "This is no time to panic. Be on your guard. We don't know what this is or what harm it could do to us."

The animal sound came again. The teens looked left and then turned right but saw nothing. The same footprints were in the hot sand again, this time on their right side.

"Do you think there's only one of them?" Zadeia said.

"It's hard to tell," Atakos said. "It sounds like there's only one."

"I think we should get out of here," Cristaden whispered, her voice quivering.

"But what if that's what it wants us to do?" Fajha said. "What if it wants us to turn our backs?"

Zimi turned to look at him. "Are you suggesting that this creature may have some intelligence? It can just attack us while we're just standing here."

"Then why doesn't it?" Atakos said.

"Maybe it's … friendly?" Zadeia said. "Or maybe it's just a mirage, you know, like those tales of seeing hallucinations in the desert?" While the words were pouring out of her mouth, she knew they were not true. This was definitely not a mirage.

The friends looked around the desert, hoping to see anything that did not resemble sand. Concluding there was nothing there, they were startled when a creature suddenly appeared. Very close to them.

"What—" Cristaden's body became rigid and tense.

Atakos' heart went up to his throat. "What *is* that thing?"

"I've never studied anything *like* it," Fajha whispered. He couldn't take his eyes off the creature. Standing on two, chubby legs, it was as tall as a grown man with scaly flesh and short arms. Its head seemed too big for its upper body and it had a long tail. Complete with sharp teeth and red eyes, it looked like an oversized, oddly shaped lizard. It was staring at them intently and a low growl escaped its throat.

"Um, I don't think it's friendly," Zadeia said with a shaky voice. She instinctively took a step back in fear.

Zimi was going to say something sarcastic to his sister about 'friendly' predators but then it was gone. It seemed to disappear into thin air. If they were not sweating from the hot sun, they were definitely perspiring from the fear of not knowing what they were up against.

"What are we going to do?" Zimi said.

"I don't know," Atakos said. "But we can't just stand here and wait for it to attack us."

"What do you suggest?" Fajha whispered. "To keep *moving?*"

"No, no, no...Fajha, you don't recognize this creature *at all?* Not even a species that could be a member of the same family?"

"No, I have never seen anything that looks like it." Fajha saw the expression on Atakos' face. "What is it? What do you think it might be?"

"Remember what the fairy queen, Lhainna, told us? How Brulok's minions were everywhere on this planet but humans can't see them?"

"Yeah. I remember."

"Yes," Zadeia said. "She said they lurk in places just waiting for magical creatures to wander away from the safety of her forest."

"Precisely." Atakos' frown deepened. Although he thought he might have come to a conclusion, it just did not make any sense to him.

"But we are not magical creatures," Zimi said, picking up on what was troubling him. "We are descendants from another planet with special abilities. We are no different from the average native of this planet."

"That's why it doesn't make any sense to me. Fajha has studied every animal on this planet and he doesn't recognize this creature at all. It's as if it's not *from* this planet. It just has to be ..." Atakos allowed his voice to trail off. He did not want to think of the possibilities of coming up against another Brulok minion. His friends fell silent and glanced around quickly. The creature had not come near them since they had a glimpse of it. They feared it was plotting an attack.

"Well, I don't get it," Cristaden said, frustrated. "If this is one of Brulok's minions, why would it reveal itself, knowing we are just humans? And if it was out to get us, how come it hasn't attacked us y—" Just then, the creature came out of nowhere, jumped in front of Cristaden, pushing her down to the sand. It tried to bite her face but she pushed against it with her arms, trying to keep its mouth from touching her. With its front claws, it scratched her while growling venomously.

Zadeia started screaming while the boys stood their ground, too stunned to move.

"Kill it!" Cristaden managed to cry out, tears escaping her desperate blue eyes. "Kill it! Kill it! Kill it!"

The others snapped out of their shock and sent attacks on the creature all at once. It erupted into little pieces, creating an icy and burning pile of flesh.

"What was *wrong* with you guys?!" Cristaden screamed, pushing foul smelling pieces of the monstrous beast off of her. "I could have *died* while you just stood there and watched." She stood up slowly, feeling so disgusted by the entrails oozing off her clothes. As if she wasn't dirty *enough*.

"I'm sorry, Cristaden," Atakos said, watching the wounds on her arms slowly heal. "I don't know what came over me. I guess I was in shock."

"Well, at least we killed it," Zimi said, trying to reassure her.

Fajha was wide eyed, looking at the fresh pile of flesh and bones. He felt sick to his stomach. "Yeah, that's a relief," he said.

Atakos frowned. "Cristaden, if that thing was one of Brulok's minions, why do they keep attacking *you?*"

"I don't know," Cristaden said. "Maybe it's because of my power to heal. Like the fairies."

"But how can they sense what kind of power you have?" Zadeia said. She never considered Dokami descendants could be classified as magical creatures. Even if they were in that category, it still did not explain why Cristaden was always the first one to get attacked. "You haven't healed us since this morning."

"Whatever it was, let's get out of here," Fajha said. "I'm sure it can't be the only—" He was interrupted by choking gasps coming from Atakos. They all turned to see that his left arm was oozing with blood. Panic settled on the group instantaneously.

"What *happened?!*" Cristaden cried.

Atakos tried to speak but his words came out in short gasps due to the intensity of the pain in his arm. "I … don't … know … aah … it bit me … argh … I didn't … even see when … it happened. It … hurts … too much." He groaned and tried to raise his arm to see the damage but the pain was too great. Cristaden reached out and placed her hand on his arm to heal him.

"There's *more* of them?" Zimi said.

Screeching sounds suddenly erupted all around them.

"How many *are* there?" Zadeia cried, desperately looking around.

Atakos felt some relief as his wound began to heal under Cristaden's touch. "They're fast–that's what they are. They are so fast, we can't see them." He looked down at the sand again and saw footprints everywhere.

"How are we going to fight an unseen enemy?" Cristaden said, finishing up with his wound and glancing around her quickly.

Zimi felt the hairs on the back of his neck stand up and he turned around just in time to see another creature turning to whip him with its tail. Before he had a chance to open his mouth and warn the others, the creature knocked him over and disappeared. The impact he received from the strike was so intense, he felt like the bones in his ribcage were shattered. Eyes watering with the excruciating pain, he belched out a horrifying scream.

"Zimi, what happened?" Zadeia said. She thought he might have tripped and fallen over.

Zimi groaned, trying to stand up. "One of them hit me with its tail."

Cristaden immediately bent down and examined his ribs. He was bruised but his bones were not broken. She healed him quickly and helped him to his feet.

The teens turned their backs to each other and looked around them. They had to be on high alert.

Atakos came to a conclusion. "They are trying to outsmart us."

"What do you mean?" Cristaden said.

"The first one we saw was waiting for reinforcements. It made the mistake of attacking us without their help. They must have seen what we could do. So now they are trying to get at us quickly before we have a chance to attack. They will probably keep doing this until we are all dead."

Cristaden slowly nodded. "Maybe that's why they always attack me first. Maybe they don't want me to be able to heal all of you."

"I'm not sure if that's the reason. You are pretty invincible."

"But I don't know to what extent. If they bit my head off, I don't think I could grow another one."

"Nevertheless, our abilities seem to be useless with these creatures right now."

"Then what do you suggest we do?" Zimi impatiently asked.

"We've all been trained in all aspects of combat, am I correct?"

"Yes," Zadeia slowly said. "But how do we fight an enemy we can't see?"

"Hamilda has taught us how to 'feel' out the enemy with a blindfold on, hasn't she?"

Fajha shook his head. "Why did I not think of this myself? In this fight, we basically have the blindfolds on because we can't see our enemies."

"But we can still hear them," Zimi said.

Atakos quickly thought it through. It was their only chance to survive. It just had to work. "Everyone. Close your eyes and listen."

The friends did as they were told. Before long they heard the creatures loud and clear. They were running back and forth, coming together, and then separating. It was strange how, with their eyes open, they were not able to hear what was going on right under their noses. With the right focus, they could hear every step, every breath taken. They did not realize how many noises were blocked out when they were concentrating on seeing something with their eyes.

"Oh...," Cristaden said. Her stomach flip-flopped when she realized the extent of their dire situation.

"Now," Atakos said. "How many are we dealing with?"

"I think there is ... four."

"I agree," Fajha said. "Four."

"Four," Zimi said.

"Yes, four of them," Zadeia said.

"That's what I'm guessing too," Atakos said. He gulped hard, trying to remember what Hamilda taught them. "Now comes the hard part. We have to separate."

CHAPTER 34

"You want us to do *what?*" Cristaden said through her teeth. She whipped her head around to look at Atakos. "Are you *insane?*"

"We have to separate so they will attack us," Atakos said. "They would think we are more vulnerable that way. The faster we do this, the faster we can get out of here and keep moving. If we don't entice them to attack, we could be here all day."

"I'm afraid to admit it, but I think he's right," Zimi said. "They're waiting for an opportunity to get us when we least expect it. They may possibly be waiting for us to give up and leave."

"That does sound like the best way, Atakos," Zadeia said. She could not believe that she was actually agreeing with his crazy idea.

Cristaden was apprehensive. Those creatures seemed to be after her more than the others. The first one that attacked her was aiming to kill her right then and there. Not nip at her like the others were doing. It was definitely trying to kill her quick. "But I'm so *scared,*" she said. Her hands were shaking uncontrollably.

"Cristaden, would you like me to stay with you?" Zadeia said. "There are only four of them so we can afford to have two people stay together." She turned to Atakos. "Am I right?"

"I think it would be okay," Atakos said.

"That would be great, Zadeia," Cristaden said. "Thank you."

"Not a problem," Zadeia said quickly, which was responded by a snicker from her brother. She turned her head to glare at him and caught him shaking his head. He knew all too well she was staying with Cristaden because she was deathly afraid to be by herself.

"Okay, is everyone ready?" Atakos said.

There was no other way. It had to be done. "Ready," they said in unison.

"Okay." Atakos gulped. His hands were shaking and he almost regretted what he was going to say even before it came out. "Keep your eyes closed and take ten giant steps forward. Count off. One … two … three … four …"

By the time they reached number six, they were already far apart. If they weren't frightened before, they were now. Cristaden and Zadeia held on to each other tightly until they reached the tenth step and then pulled apart. Listening to the sounds around them, they were able to pinpoint exactly where the creatures were. The few moments before the attack were unbelievably excruciating.

Zimi was the first to be attacked. He heard one of the creatures coming at him from behind. It was going so fast it only gave him a split second to react. As the hairs on the back of his neck stood on end, he bent down really low and avoided a blow to his head from the beast. Bringing all his force to his foot, he kicked his right leg straight out behind him. The creature let out a horrifying screech as Zimi's foot made contact with its mid-section. Then he quickly spun around and brought forth his energy to freeze it. "One down," he said as the dead, frozen beast fell to the soft sand.

Another creature ran towards Atakos. When it was close enough, he bent down, putting his weight on his left leg. Bringing his right arm up under it, he sent it flying over his shoulder. When the creature hit the sand, Atakos immediately blew it up, creating a powerful explosion. "Make that two," he called out. He then closed his eyes to listen in case another one decided to attack him.

Cristaden and Zadeia, much to their unfortunate surprise, were attacked at the same time by two of the creatures. Cristaden heard one of the creatures running towards her. She tried to react but was too slow. It pushed her down to the sand in an instant and she fell on her back. It then got on top of her. Before any harm could be done, Cristaden grabbed the creature with her thighs and brought her legs up, doing a back roll with it. The beast was so heavy that she was sure it would crush her before she landed but she was stronger than she had anticipated and managed to switch their position. Now she was on top and she had the struggling beast pinned beneath her.

Zadeia's biggest fears were realized when she heard a creature coming at her from behind. She ducked. It went sailing over her head but, before it even touched the sand, it came back at her fast. Automatically, she put her hands up to shield herself from the blow, unintentionally setting the beast on fire. The creature was so strong, it fought to do damage even while it was burning. Zadeia sent two powerful fireballs its way, causing it to explode.

Cristaden's attacker was scratching her arms and face as she struggled to gain control of the situation. Taking the chance of getting badly hurt, she released the creature for a moment to summon up her explosion ability. The beast reached up and scratched her face with its sharp claws, cutting deep into her forehead. She tried hard not to break her concentration and blew up its head.

"That's four," Cristaden called out, pressing her hand against the large gash on her forehead as it healed.

The five teens breathed a sigh of relief. Fajha especially felt relieved because he did not have to fight any creatures. Turning around to face each other, the friends realized that their nightmare was not over. Standing in the middle of their circle was what must have been the mother of all the creatures. It was taller and wider than the others. It seemed to have come right out of the sand.

"Crap," Fajha swore under his breath.

A low growl escaped the throat of the beast as it turned to look at Fajha. "That is not what we are called," it said in a raspy feminine voice.

The friends held their breath and took a step back.

"You—you can talk," Fajha said.

"How is that even possible?" Atakos asked.

It spoke again. "We are desert *karsas*. We were sent by Brulok, a long time ago, to kill the magical creatures of Omordion."

"But we are *not* magical creatures," Zimi said. "What do you want with *us*?"

The karsas turned and looked at Cristaden. "Give us the girl and you are free to go."

"Never," Atakos said, taking two steps forward. "We're not leaving here without her."

"Then I will be forced to kill all of you."

"Give us your best shot."

With a loud growl, the mother karsas charged at him. He tried to blow her up but barely managed to break through her tough shell. Only a few scales flew off.

"What the—?" Atakos said. She was too strong for him. She wasn't as fast as the others but Atakos had to sidestep her to avoid being hit. Once she passed him, she came back around, her short arms flailing and her mouth drooling with anticipation. She grabbed Atakos and brought him to the sand where she pinned him down, trying to bite him. A burst of fire engulfed her face causing her to release her grip on Atakos. He backed away from her, stood up and ran to his friends, who had come together again.

The karsas rubbed her eyes but Zadeia's fire seemed to have done no damage to her face.

"What are we going to do now?" Zadeia said, tears erupting in her eyes.

"What do they want with me?" Cristaden asked her friends.

"I don't know," Atakos said. "It all just doesn't make any sense."

"Well we need some answers," Fajha said.

"Something tells me we're not going to get anything from *her*," Zimi said as the mother karsas let out a horrendous screech and came toward them at an accelerated rate.

"Scatter!" Atakos said without thinking through what he was saying. The group did just that, scattering in different directions, which confused the karsas for a moment. It turned into a bad idea as she quickly turned towards Cristaden, who was left standing alone.

"Cristaden, no!" Atakos cried. He had made the wrong choice. They were helpless against the mother karsas alone but if they had remained together, they would have had a better shot at defeating her. "Regroup! REGROUP!"

Before the karsas reached Cristaden, she was met with a series of blows coming from all directions. Some scales came off her back and arms, leaving behind exposed pink flesh. She screeched as the fire from Zadeia burned the exposed flesh but she still managed to keep moving towards Cristaden. All Cristaden saw was a monster coming towards her with the speed of a vehicle, her mouth opened wide, ready to devour her. Suddenly someone came at the beast from the side and tackled her down to the scorching sand. It was Atakos, who had unintentionally increased his speed so he could reach the karsas before she reached his friend.

The teens finally managed to regroup and they stood side-by-side, ready to finish the fight. Atakos let go of the monster and backed up to join his friends. "Give her all you've got," he said.

They attacked her. Every time she tried to stand up, she was met with all of their powers. Her scales were stripped away to reveal more and more pink flesh, which was being scorched and frozen repeatedly by the twins. Blood started to ooze out of her wounds as she screeched and shouted obscene things at them. With each strike, her language began to change and sound inaudible, almost like the sounds the other creatures were making, as if whatever magic spell that was cast on her was being stripped away. Cristaden saw an opportunity to kill her when all the scales had been stripped away from her face and she took it. Her head exploded into a million pieces.

The fight was over.

Zadeia threw herself to the sand. "I can't take much more of this," she said. "I'm going crazy. Please tell me we can get out of here quicker. I don't want to stay in the desert any longer."

The others could not console her because they felt the same way. The desert *was* making all of them go crazy. It was very hot and they had no water. Furthermore, they kept getting attacked by every living thing there. And then, to top it all off, to find out that wherever they went, if Brulok's minions were in the area, they would try to kill Cristaden. It was too much for them to take in all at once.

"Come on," Atakos said, trying to be strong for all of them. "I know we are all exhausted but if we don't keep going, we'll never make it out of here alive." Although he told them to move, he could not will himself to take a step forward. He was too depressed.

Cristaden silently went to each one of them to heal their scratches and bruises. All of her wounds had already healed and she felt okay except for the twisting knot in her stomach. She began to cry because she could not understand why she was under attack. First the oblots and then the karsas. There was no explanation for it.

Fajha removed his glasses to clean the sand off of them. Unbeknownst to the others, he had tears in his eyes. He was afraid. He was terrified that they would never see the Hejdian Sea.

"ATTEN–TION!" Zimi yelled. He stood firm, keeping his arms pinned to his sides. In a voice that sounded much like his army father, he shouted at his friends. "We are in a war people. We cannot give up now." He lowered his voice after getting their attention. "So what if those monsters are after us? Don't you realize how far we have come? Before this journey, we could barely dodge *rocks*. But now look at us. Just look at us. We are *strong*. Stronger than we could have ever imagined. We fought and killed oblots, killed a thousand killer Valdeec birds, and now we have destroyed desert karsas. And their *mom*. Remember when we could not even defend ourselves against a bunch of *trees*? We have learned to become a team. A fighting machine! Nothing can stop us now. I say let them come. Let them come and try to stop us. By the time we reach Hamilda, we would only need to stare at her captors and they would either die from our glance or head for the hills."

His friends smiled at the thought of crazy men with weapons of all sorts running at the sight of them. Zadeia picked herself up and brushed the sand off her clothes. Her tears were drying and she felt more confident.

"A lot of things have changed," Fajha said, feeling proud. Then he turned to Atakos. "Did you realize you ran really fast back there?"

"Yeah, you ran so fast, you were like a blur," Zadeia said.

"I don't know how I did it," Atakos said. "I only wished that I could get to the karsas before she reached Cristaden and … I did."

Cristaden smiled at him. Looking around, she felt so proud to have friends like the ones she had. They would never let anything bad happen to her. She was sure that if she was captured, like Hamilda, they would not rest until she was found. The thought brought tears to her eyes but, this time, they were tears of joy. Her eyes fell on Atakos again and she quickly looked away in embarrassment when she realized he had been staring at her. "Come on guys, let's keep moving," she quickly said.

The teens reluctantly turned away from the sun and walked for two more hours, the whole time dreaming of food and water as they trudged through the soft sand. As the sun began to set, they had to put their cloaks back on to keep warm. They were very exhausted but refused to stop walking until the setting sun did not allow them to go any further. The fear of Valdeec birds and whatever else was in the desert came back as soon as they decided to stop and make camp.

Fajha calculated that, because of the fight with the desert karsas, they were far behind schedule and would not reach the shores of the Hejdian Sea until sunset the next day.

The distraught teens tried to make the best of their situation with old childhood rhymes and jokes they had heard growing up. All was quiet when they fell asleep in their ripped tent.

Until the ground beneath them began to quake.

CHAPTER 35

Startled, the five teenagers woke up to find their whole tent shaking.

"An earthquake?" Atakos asked Fajha.

"I highly doubt it," Fajha said. "Not in this region." He tried to get on his knees but the rocking of the tent prevented him from doing so. "I'm afraid to know what it *really* is."

Before they could attempt to leave the tent, it began to roll as if it were rolling off a hill. The teenagers were thrown into each other and they started screaming, not knowing when the tent would come to a stop.

When the tent did stop rolling, the rumbling ceased and everything went quiet.

Trying to catch their breaths, the teens considered the possibilities of what might have happened. When they couldn't come up with one, Zadeia volunteered to go outside and use a fireball to see what was going on. She slowly left the tent and lit up the area around them.

"Guys, you have to see this," she said.

The others joined her outside and, one by one, steadily took in what they saw. Before them was a large, pointy hill of sand their tent had fallen from.

"Where did *this* come from?" Atakos asked.

"You do realize we were on top of this thing, right?" Zadeia said.

"What could have caused it?" Cristaden asked.

"If anything, now I know it wasn't an earthquake because they do not *create* hills," Fajha said, matter-of-factly. "They destroy them."

"No kidding genius," Zimi said. His snickering was returned with a punch to the arm.

Zadeia's fireball burnt out and she had to create another one. "What happened to the Valdeec birds? Did we kill them all?"

"I don't think so," Fajha said, looking around. "We're in a different part of the desert now. There may be some lurking about."

"I'm so tired," Cristaden said. "I just want to go back to sleep."

"We all do," Atakos said. "But not until we find out what caused this hill."

The teens shivered with the onset of a cold breeze.

"Anyone want to go … check it out?" Atakos said.

"Are you crazy?" Zadeia asked.

"It's not going to be me," Fajha said.

"Is there such thing as de-volunteering?" Zimi said. "Because I am."

Cristaden managed to only grunt.

"Oh come on," Atakos said. "We are the hope of this planet and we can't even check out a small hill?"

"If you're so brave, why don't *you* go?" Zadeia said.

Atakos gulped. He was scared just like the rest of them. His thoughts went back to the karsas. Only an animal or animals could have caused such a hill. He did not want to find out what it was but he knew he could not rest until he did.

Fajha took a deep breath. "I'll go," he said. Taking a couple of steps towards the hill, he thought he saw movement but could not see exactly what it was. "Zadeia, could you bring your light over here?"

Reluctantly, Zadeia slowly walked up to stand next to Fajha, lighting up another ball of flame in her hand. They both took a few more steps towards the hill until they were only inches away from it. The sand on the hill was rugged, not smooth, and it seemed to be *vibrating*.

Fajha peered closer to get a good view of what exactly he was looking at. Suddenly a small pair of eyes opened and stared back at him. He sucked in his breath. They were not staring at a hill of sand. They were looking at a nest. A nest of Montapu lizards.

"R–run–run!" Fajha managed to say. Grabbing Zadeia's arm, he turned to run and warn the others.

"What is it?" Atakos asked, turning to run also, not know what he was running away from.

"It's a nest of Montapu lizards!"

"The *poisonous* kind?" Cristaden said.

"There's only *one* kind."

They stopped when they reached the tent and hid behind it, knowing that it would not make much of a difference at all. As soon as Zadeia's light was not on them anymore, the lizards broke up their tall hill and came running towards them at full speed.

"If they bite you, you'll be paralyzed and then die," Fajha said.

"We have to prevent them from getting close to us," Zadeia said. She stood up and threw fireball after fireball at them. Some were caught in the fire while others avoided it completely. There were hundreds of them.

"Why do all the predators we fight come in large numbers?" Zimi said. "I prefer to fight the minions."

"Don't just stand there, help her," Atakos told his friends.

They stepped away from the tent and began blowing up the lizards groups at a time. Some lizards managed to get close to them and Cristaden annihilated those. The stench rising from the burning lizards was so overpowering that they wished they could hold their noses.

"Ugh, I can't take this anymore," Zadeia said. "They're so disgusting."

"Cristaden, didn't you say you dissected them before?" Fajha said.

"Yeah, but they were washed, dried and washed again," Cristaden said, killing a lizard by her foot. "By the time we got a hold of them, they smelled like roses."

"Watch out, there's one behind you," Zimi said to his sister.

Zadeia screamed and tried to burn the lizard behind her but almost burned her own shoes. She managed to kick it away and then set it on fire immediately afterward. Because she turned around, a few lizards were able to get close to her. Zimi froze them before they touched her. "Thanks, Zimi," she said, continuing her arduous task of throwing fire at the incoming lizards.

By now, the lizards had the group surrounded. For some reason, they kept up their relentless attacks as if they hadn't eaten in months or years. It seemed almost as if they were *possessed*.

"They're getting too close!" Fajha shouted. "Why are they doing this? They usually avoid conflict."

"What do we do?" Zadeia asked.

"Just keep going," Atakos said. "Eventually, we'll kill them all."

"Aah!" Cristaden cried out when one tried to bite her foot. She started kicking at them to get away from her.

Suddenly, from overhead, they heard a rustle of wings and some squawking.

"Please nooo …," Atakos whined, his caramel skin paling.

Zadeia threw a fireball up and it illuminated the sky. The Valdeec birds were back.

"Not now, *not now,*" Fajha shouted at them.

A few birds swooped down and grabbed some lizards, alive and dead. Others went in for the attack on the teens.

"Get away from us!" Zadeia shouted and set a couple of them on fire.

"We need to strategize," Atakos shouted over the noises around him. He blew up some lizards that were too close for comfort. Blood and guts oozed on his shoes. "We need to designate someone to take care of the birds while the rest will take care of these lizards!"

"I'll take care of the birds!" Fajha said. "Just keep an eye on my feet." Turning his attention to the incoming birds, he started blowing them up but the lizards around his feet were keeping him from concentrating. His friends kept missing a few because there were so many of them so he had to kick them away. He had to think of something else. When a lizard touched his foot, he willed himself to lift off the sand. Immediately, before he had a chance to think that he wasn't thinking straight, his feet lifted off the sand and he began to levitate. "Whoa," he said. He tried to find his balance but lost control and fell back on the sand, landing on a couple of lizards. He quickly stood up before they could bite him and then blew them up.

"I knew you could do it, Fajha," Atakos shouted.

"What did he do?" Cristaden asked.

Before Atakos could answer, Fajha willed himself to levitate again but this time, he regained his balance. He felt like he was on a tightrope but he just had to find his center of gravity to stay upright.

"That's so cool, Fajha," Zadeia said, setting a group of lizards on fire.

Fajha turned his concentration to the birds and continued to blow them up. There were so many of them. How many, he could not tell because the sky was so dark.

The five friends continued to fight but it began to feel like a losing battle. Fajha couldn't handle all of the incoming birds and the rest of them were losing control of the situation with the lizards.

"I have an idea," Atakos said. "These birds are just looking for something to eat, right? If we run, they might stay behind and just feast off the lizards."

"How are we going to run?" Cristaden said, blowing up a lizard and then a bird. "All our stuff is in the tent. We would have to pick up the tent and run with it. That's kind of hard to do when we can't run on the sand and these lizards are everywhere."

"Maybe we can just leave our stuff."

"Are you mad?" Zadeia cried.

"Why not?" Zimi said. "I think it's a great idea. I wish we had thought of it sooner."

"Right," Atakos said. "We have our cloaks on, so why do we need to take the rest of our things and our backpacks?"

"Atakos, I hope you know what you're saying," Fajha shouted from above.

"But it's dark out there," Zadeia said. "I can't make fireballs all night long, I'll get burnt out!" She set some lizards on fire that were attempting to bite her feet.

"That's where the tent will come in handy," Atakos said. "Cover me." His friends came in closer to him and tried to kill any lizards or birds that got too close.

Atakos bent down and ripped the tent into small pieces. The wooden sticks that held the tent up were separated into five pieces.

"I hope we won't need that tent anymore," Zadeia said.

"Don't worry," Atakos said. "We've slept without a tent. We could definitely do it again."

"Hurry," Cristaden said.

"Just about done." Atakos tied pieces of the tent around the sticks and handed them to Zadeia. She lit each one and handed them to each person. Fajha came down from his levitation and took his torch.

"Let's go!" Atakos said. They jumped over the remnants of the tent and leapt over approaching Montapu lizards. The sand was too soft and was pulling them down as they tried to avoid the creatures that were attacking them. Zimi and Zadeia froze and burned Valdeec birds that were in hot pursuit of them. Atakos, Fajha, and Cristaden blew up the Montapu lizards in their path.

The Valdeec birds did not do as Atakos had anticipated. Instead of feasting on the dead carcasses of the Montapu lizards, they preferred to chase moving targets and would stop at nothing to get what they wanted. Birds dove at them from above, scratching the tops of their heads with their sharp claws. The lizards ran fast to keep up with them.

"I'm beginning to think this was a bad idea," Cristaden said, steadily losing her stamina.

"Would you rather have stayed in the same spot, cornered with nowhere to go?" Atakos asked her while dodging a lizard with its mouth wide open.

"But what happens if we can't run anymore? We should have stayed to fight!"

"No, that would have been the *worst* idea!" Fajha said. "Those things are nocturnal. They would be after us all night long. And who knows how many are in this area. If we stayed there and lost energy fighting, then we would have been trapped and cornered. This way we have a chance of losing them, even if it's a small chance."

"And not to mention, it brings us closer to the sea then we were back there!" Zimi said.

Atakos almost fell into the sand after he kicked a lizard out of his way. "We need to do something, anything, to get them off our backs!" he said.

"I could summon up a storm …," Zadeia suggested.

"Whoa, I don't think that's a good idea," Fajha said.

"But it's a start," Atakos said. "We have to start thinking *outside* the box."

"But we don't know what serious repercussions it may cause. There are no rainstorms out here in the desert. We could seriously mess up the ecosystem!"

"Who here is against messing up the ecosystem?"

"Couldn't care less at this point," Cristaden said.

"Not me," Zadeia said.

"Ditto," Zimi said.

"Alright," Fajha said, blowing up a Valdeec bird that was trying to bite his head. "Don't say I didn't warn you."

Zadeia tried to redirect her energy towards the skies but, between the attacking animals and running for her life, it proved to be very difficult. "I can't do it," she said. "I think I have to stop."

"We can't stop," Atakos said. "Try again. I'm sure you can do it. Just ignore the lizards. We'll handle them."

"Okay." Zadeia kept running, trying to redirect her focus from the hundreds of lizards still running after them. *Think rain, think rain*, she thought over and over to herself. It was almost impossible to focus her attention but little by little she began to be unaware of her surroundings. Her legs were still moving but she felt like she was running on puffs of clouds. All became silent around her and the desert disappeared. It was replaced by the halls of Lochenby.

Zadeia.

She heard a voice call her name.

Zadeia, please–help me!

"Hamilda?" she stopped running. A bird brushed by her head, bringing her back to the desert.

"We have to keep *moving*," Zimi cried, looking back at his sister. He and the others had to stop running in order to protect her from the swarms of killer animals.

"I heard her voice … she was … calling me," Zadeia said with tears in her eyes. "She needs our help."

"RUN!" Atakos said, snapping her out of her daze.

"You heard Hamilda?" Cristaden asked Zadeia when they began to run again.

"Yes. I mean–I think it was her." Zadeia tried to recollect her vision but could not focus. She suddenly felt the sadness overtaking her like a wave, hitting her with a force so strong, she barely had time to refocus on something else to stop it from happening.

"We're getting closer to her with each step we take," Fajha said. "We just need to get to those caves." He looked up at the sky when he felt a drop of rain on his forehead. "Did you feel that?"

His friends felt it too. It was beginning to drizzle. The wind picked up as well, blowing sand at them. As their fires burnt out, they stopped running and threw the wooden torches to the ground, giving them an extra hand to fight. A flash of lightning blazed through the night sky, illuminating the entire desert around them. The lizards were seen digging their way into the ground to escape the incoming storm. The Valdeec birds were annoyed but barely faltering, still trying to attack them.

With another flash of lightning, Zimi had an idea. He used the same concept Zadeia had when she picked up fire and threw it. If he could only catch a lightning strike before it disappeared, it could work.

But it was easier said than done. With each lightning strike, he kept missing the opportunity by a mere tenth of a second. He tried counting the seconds between each lightning strike and noticed that they were getting closer and closer together. If he could only time it right, he could get it.

"On my word, everyone has to duck, okay?" Zimi shouted over the raging wind.

"What are you going to do?" Fajha asked.

"You'll see. Just get down as fast as you can when I say 'now'." Zimi looked up at the sky again and reached his hands towards it. A lightning struck. He pulled the energy of it towards him and caught it. For a moment the bolt seemed like it was frozen in time. "Okay, NOW!" he shouted. He then pulled the bolt of lightning down towards the wet birds and threw himself down to the sand with his friends. The whole desert sky lit up as lightning struck one bird and was transferred to the rest when they threw themselves against each other, trying to escape. Electrocuted birds fell from the sky one by one and then the lightning went out like a light when the last one fell. The rain and the wind continued to come down on the teens but their predators were either dead or gone.

CHAPTER 36

Breathing hard, the five friends stood up. Pitch black again, they could only see around them when the sky lit up with lightning.

"Zimi, that was incredible," Cristaden shouted over the rain.

"I didn't know if it could be done but I just decided to try it," Zimi said, smiling. "And it worked!"

"Yeah," Atakos said, smiling. "Truly fantastic." Having been in the desert for two days without a bathtub and water, he was thankful for the downpour to wash away the dirt, blood, and entrails from their fights.

The teens scrubbed their hands clean and used them to collect water to drink as well. Another flash of lightning illuminated the desert once more and the mood in the group soured. They were all thinking the same thing.

"I wish Hamilda could see us now," Atakos said.

"Do you think there's a chance we may never see her again?" Cristaden asked, while going from person to person to heal their minor scratches.

"There's a possibility for anything."

"I sure miss her, though," Fajha said. "I hope she's okay."

"Oh come on, guys," Zimi said. "We've come this far, don't lose faith now. We're getting closer to her, I can feel it—we can all feel it. We just have to keep moving." He looked at his sister and shivered. "I think you can stop the rain now, Zadeia."

Zadeia looked up at him with tears in her eyes. "I can't. I've already tried."

"This is not good," Fajha said.

Atakos thought for a moment. "Since being sad brings on the rain, try to think of a happy thought."

"I can't. Every happy memory I have involves Hamilda."

"What about that time we sat down with Colnaha's grandfather, Olshem?" Zimi said. "Remember how he said you were the wisest of us all and very brave? That sure cracked *me* up!" Then he burst out laughing.

"Oh Colnaha," Zadeia said. She started crying harder, causing the rain to come down stronger than before.

"Nice going," Fajha said.

Zimi just shrugged his shoulders and sighed.

Cristaden wrapped her arms around Zadeia. "I wish I can heal sadness," she said. "Don't worry, Zadeia. We are going to find Hamilda and bring her back. We just have to cheer up and keep going. We're almost there. Just a couple more days and she'll be with us again."

"I hope so," Zadeia said, sniffling.

Fajha placed a hand on her back. "With our talents, we are going to *thrash* whoever took her. Bam, bam bam!"

Zadeia looked up at him and smiled. With her smile, the rain suddenly stopped falling and her friends looked up in time to see the clouds fade away, revealing a large, bright orange moon. After squeezing the water out of their cloaks, they took full advantage of the hardened sand and continued their walk towards the sea. The five friends felt chilled to the bone as the wind blew mercilessly and Zadeia struggled to keep her fireballs lit. They were hungry and, worse of all, they were all tired. Their bodies felt like they were ready to give in. But they did not stop. They pressed on, knowing that if they stopped to rest, they could be attacked again, and even if they were not attacked, the biting wind and their wet clothes would keep them awake.

After a few hours, the wind did not falter. In fact, it felt like it was getting worse.

"Zimi and Zadeia, can't you guys do anything about this?" Atakos asked.

"It's beyond our control," Zimi said.

"Hmmm, perhaps this is happening because we interrupted the balance of nature here?" Fajha said. "Not that I'm *blaming* anyone but I'm not going to say I told you so."

NANDE ORCEL

"We did what we had to do," Cristaden said. "Otherwise, we would have been poisoned or dragged to some Valdeec bird nest and fed to some starving Valdeec babies."

"Wind, I can deal with," Zimi said. "It's those flesh-eating monsters I would rather not have to fight if I had a choice."

Fajha looked down at his frost bitten fingers. Fighting sounded better than freezing to death. He thought of his family's warm palace back in Saiyut. They had so many servants that he did not even have to lift a finger. There was one who cleaned his room. There was one to get him anything he wanted from the kitchen. There was even one that bathed him and put his clothes on for him if he permitted. Walking through the cold desert was a far cry from his rich and spoiled life in Saiyut. But ultimately it was worth it. He had bonded even closer to his best friends and learned a thing or two about what he was capable of doing as a Dokami and as a person. For those reasons, he was truly grateful to be where he was.

"Wow, how beautiful," Cristaden said. The sky was turning a deep shade of purple with the onset of the rising sun. The colors the horizon took on were amazing to watch. It was as if it were a portrait being painted by an artist very slowly but perfected better than anything anyone had ever created.

As the sun rose, so did the temperature, helping the teens feel warmer by the minute. It was a welcomed feeling but an annoying one also for the sand under their feet began to dry and get soft again. What was worse, the wind did not die down. Instead it picked up the dry sand and, while the sun rose even higher, created a blinding sandstorm.

"Oh great, just what we need," Atakos said. "More sand in our face."

"Take your cloaks and drape it over your faces," Zadeia shouted over the wind. "We will be able to breathe better and the sand won't get into our lungs."

"Also, we should link arms so we don't lose each other," Fajha shouted. "I can't see two feet in front of me."

The five friends covered their mouths and noses with their cloaks and linked arms. The wind was blowing so hard that they had trouble standing upright. The blowing sand grew thicker and thicker until it blotted out the sun and then the entire sky. With no visibility whatsoever, they walked on, determined to reach the sea and leave the heartless desert behind.

An hour later, the sandstorm was still not letting up. The teens began to feel lightheaded with heat exhaustion and the soft sand under their feet slowed them down until they were almost crawling. They gradually began to lose their momentum and their minds started to wander.

"I can't go much further," Cristaden said.

"We have to keep going," Zimi said. "But it will feel so good if we could just … lay down for a while."

"The sand," Fajha said. "It feels like a nice cushiony bed. All I can think of is…sleep." He yawned loudly underneath his cloak.

"Sleep?" Zadeia said, yawning herself. "Sleep sounds so … good right now. My muscles can't go on anymore."

Atakos' eyes began to droop and he had to struggle to stay awake. With the little rest they received the past few days, sleep sounded like the best option.

The sandstorm was dragging them under, making them forget what was best for them. One by one they collapsed into the sand, falling into a deep slumber of dreams.

Atakos was dreaming of the beach near his home in Pontotoma. He was running along the sand, kicking at random rocks and seashells. He ran up to the water and threw himself into it, washing the sand from his face and body. After going for a nice swim, he emerged from the water, ready to play his favorite childhood games. His father was there. And his mother. She looked very healthy and full of life as if she had never been sick.

"Atakos," she called out to him. "Come home for dinner."

"In a minute, Ma." Atakos ran the other direction, laughing as he jogged along the sand. Picking up a stick, he turned around and was about to throw it to his father when he saw something rise out of the sand. It was the mother karsas. She looked at him for a moment as if she were mocking him and then turned towards his mother. His mother, not noticing the creature, was still smiling and waving at him.

"Ma!" Atakos shouted. Looking at the karsas and looking back at his mother, he realized that the creature would reach her even before he put his foot forward to run. But he had to try. Using all his might, he ran fast and charged at the monster. In a split second, he was directly behind it and blew it up before it could attack his mother. His parents began screaming when they saw the monster Atakos killed.

How could I have run that fast? Atakos thought to himself. *Run fast … run fast … I did run fast that time … when … Cristaden … my friends were … we're in trouble!*

An alarm went off in his head and it woke him up out of the storm-induced sleep. There they were, lying on the ground, being buried with the suffocating sand by the storm. If Atakos did not think fast, they would be buried alive.

"Wake up, guys," he shouted, shaking his friends and turning them onto their backs. "Come one, WAKE UP." No one budged. It almost seemed like they were not breathing. *I have to run. I have to run and get them out of this storm. I have to try.* Removing the string from his hood, Atakos tied Cristaden's wrist to Fajha's and then he removed the string from Fajha's hood and tied Zimi and Zadeia's wrists together. He then grabbed a hold of Fajha and Zadeia's hands and mentally prepared himself.

"I'm sorry if you feel any pain my friends but this is all I can do."

Using the energy he had left, Atakos charged through the storm, gaining momentum with every step while dragging his friends behind him.

"Must get out of the desert, must get out of the desert," Atakos repeated over and over again to keep himself from losing hope. It became increasingly hard to do. The desert seemed like it would never end and the sandstorm seemed to be getting worse.

Just when he was about to lose hope, Atakos broke free of the sandstorm. It was as if a light was switched on. He went from darkness to light in a split second. There was no trace of the sandstorm before him but when he looked back, there it was, a wall of sand, raging like a tornado behind him. It remained in one area, taunting him with its sheer intensity. He concluded that it only went as far as Zadeia's rainstorm did.

Remembering his friends, he bent down to see if they were alright. Brushing sand off their faces, he tried to wake them again. Fearful that they won't wake up, he gave them mouth-to-mouth resuscitation while pumping air back into their lungs. One by one, they revived, coughing sand out of their lungs.

"How did we ever make it out of there?" Zimi asked, looking back at the wall of sand behind them.

"The last thing I remember was running," Fajha said. "I don't remember much after that."

"I sort of … dragged you guys out of there," Atakos said.

"That would explain why our wrists are tied together," Cristaden said and smiled at her attached partner, Fajha.

"Thank you," Zadeia said while she freed her wrist from her brother.

"We owe you one," Fajha said.

"Oh, it was nothing," Atakos said, thinking of how hard it was to drag four bodies behind him. If he had to do it again though, he would.

"How far do you think we are from the sea?" Cristaden asked Fajha.

Fajha looked around. "Oh, I don't think it's much further."

The friends turned and saw something they never thought they would see.

In the distance was the Hejdian Sea.

CHAPTER 37

"Could it be a mirage?" Zadeia asked. But she knew it was not a hallucination. The Hejdian Sea lay about a half a mile away from them. They were very close to leaving the hot and sandy desert yet it all seemed like a dream.

"Someone pinch me," Fajha said jokingly. Zimi reached over and pinched him really hard. "Yeow! I wasn't being *serious*."

"I think we are all pretty much awake," Atakos said.

"It looks so beautiful from here," Cristaden said, taking it all in. Under the bright blue sky, it was a deep shade of blue with no end in sight. It seemed very majestic as if it held secrets, waiting to be explored.

"What are we waiting for?" Fajha said, with a giant smile. "Why are we standing here like a bunch of idiots? Let's go!"

The five friends took off running towards the sea. Despite their stiff legs they ran, resistant to ever looking back at the fierce desert behind them. Giggling, they practically skipped over the rolls of sand, laughing as the sand, once again, tried its best to bring them crashing down. They knew that, within the hour, they would be that much closer to Paimonu and the Ardomion Caves.

Hearing a noise behind them, the teens stopped and turned around. All they could see was the raging sandstorm and nothing else.

"What was that?" Cristaden said.

"I don't know," Atakos said.

They waited for a little while but, when they didn't hear the noise again, they turned towards the sea again, determined to avoid any new fights with dangerous creatures.

Then the teens heard it again. It was a low rumbling sound but it was not coming from the ground. This time it sounded like it was coming from the air. They were forced to stop again so they could listen more closely. There was definitely something out there but they couldn't see anything through the wall of sand that blocked their view.

"Don't tell me it's another creature," Atakos said.

"I wouldn't say that," Fajha said. "It seems much…bigger."

Then the noise faded away.

"I wonder what that was," Zadeia said.

"Well, let's not stand here and find out," Zimi said.

Once again, they turned their backs to the sandstorm and headed towards the sea. This time, they kept a sharp ear out for whatever might have been behind them. A few minutes passed and they heard the noise again. It started off as a distant rumble. Then it steadily increased as if it were moving closer and closer to them.

Atakos frowned as they stopped walking again. Little by little, the noise began to sound less and less like any type of animal. It sounded more like a machine. A distant memory came back to him about a project he did in his mechanics class. For hours, he worked on making propellers for objects such as boats and airships that had the same sound. He was hoping it was not what he was thinking it was. "It sounds like … propellers," he said.

"Like on an airship?" Zimi said.

"Are you sure?" Cristaden said.

"I'm almost positive."

They searched the sandstorm, hoping to get a glimpse of what was coming towards them but the noise just kept getting louder and louder without any visualization.

And then they saw it.

The five friends sucked their breath in simultaneously as they regarded a large airship attempting to break free of the raging winds but not having much success. They never expected to run into any human beings in the desert at all. Especially people who owned a magnificent machine such as the one they saw before them. The airship was green and brown in color, and it was massive, probably bigger than a small building.

For a moment the teens said nothing. They just stared at the struggling airship, trying to comprehend why it was there. They considered running away but then a thought occurred to them. The airship could be their ticket to getting to Paimonu, and Hamilda, faster.

"Do you think we could convince them to take us to Paimonu?" Zadeia asked.

"If we could, it would take us only a half an hour to get there!" Fajha said.

"Sounds tempting, but guys, I don't know …," Atakos said.

"Consider this, Atakos," Cristaden said. "If we convinced the people of Osmatu to believe we were separated from our caravan, we can definitely do it again."

"I know, I know. But how many people need to know our whereabouts? What if the army posts pictures of us everywhere and these people tell them where they dropped us off?"

"They won't put pictures of us up because they don't want the Eastern Army to know we exist," Zimi said. "It would be too much of a risk for them."

"Yeah, we're just teenagers," Zadeia said. "People would begin to wonder why the Western Army is looking for a bunch of teens. They would look closely at the situation and I'm sure the army is too smart to let that happen."

Atakos sighed. "It would be nice to stop walking for a while and get to Paimonu now." Watching the airship rock back and forth by the wind, he came to a decision. "Zimi and Zadeia, do you think you can use the wind to help them out of the sandstorm?"

"We can try," Zimi said. The twins outstretched their arms and pulled the wind toward them to try and free the airship but all they did was pull the sandstorm closer.

Zadeia shook her head. "It's no use," she said. "Maybe we can try pushing the storm back and the rest of you can pull the ship forward?"

With the efforts of the twins, Fajha, Atakos, and Cristaden pulled on the ship as hard as they could. The ship only budged a little so they tried to shimmy it back and forth to get it out. The airship swayed from side to side but they lost control of it, causing it to turn over to its side. Nothing could have prepared them for what they saw. The words 'WESTERN ARMY' was clearly written for all to see.

It did not take long to realize who was aboard the airship.

A terrifying air of panic rose among the five teens. General Komuh was there, in the desert and, for all they knew, he could see them from where they stood. They could not allow him to bring them back to Sheidem City. They had come too far to let that happen.

"What are we going to do?" Zadeia said, taking a step back.

"Didn't Queen Lhainna tell us they were in Hortu, on the other side of Sheidem City?" Fajha said.

"Yeah," Cristaden said. "How did they know to come this far to look for us?"

"Colnaha," Zimi said accusingly.

Zadeia turned to her brother and frowned. "You don't know that."

"How else would you explain them getting here only three days after telling him our secret?"

Zadeia looked down and the others did not say anything. They were all thinking the same thing. Someone would have had to tell Komuh, who was in Hortu less than a week ago, where they were headed in order for him to get to the desert as fast as he did. He would have never considered a bunch of teenagers would risk their lives to cross a dangerous desert on their own. He would have checked north or even south before even considering going to the desert. Someone must have tipped him off.

And now they were in trouble.

"We have to run," Fajha said, ready to turn towards the sea again.

Atakos threw his hands up to stop his friends. "Wait," he said. "Give me a moment to think." He observed the ship, knowing the situation did not look good. "We can't outrun them. Once they break through the storm, they'll catch us."

Fajha looked back at the ship. Atakos was right. Running would be a very bad idea. "We have to try and disable the ship," he said.

"Exactly."

"How are we going to do that?" Cristaden asked.

Atakos turned to the twins. "Do you think you can do it?" he asked them.

Zimi considered it for a moment. "We can create a tornado out of the sandstorm in order to bring the ship crashing down."

Cristaden shook her head. "We could kill them."

"Or they could capture us," Atakos said. "We've come too far to be taken prisoner again and held captive until they find a need for us. Hamilda will die if she hasn't died already. And we will be...," He shook his head. "No, I can't see any other way."

Cristaden tried to think of an alternative but couldn't find one. It was possible that the members of the Dokami Council were not aware of what Komuh was planning to do with them. They had no choice but to fight for their own lives. "Ok," she said.

Without hesitation, the twins went to work, attempting to make the sandstorm into a tornado of sand. It took a couple of minutes but it began to work. The sand started moving like a cyclone making the airship spin around and around. In a matter of seconds, a tornado formed in front of them, threatening to take them with it as well. They watched as the aircraft spun out of control until it finally careened towards the sand and hit it, creating shockwaves through it. The five teens dove for the sand and covered their heads as the aircraft burst into flames, sending debris and flying embers their way. Raising their heads, they saw the once magnificent aircraft transformed into an enormous vessel of fire. Creating a huge crater, it was much bigger than they had assumed it to be earlier.

After standing up, it took them a moment to realize the sheer magnitude of what they had done. Not only was the ship destroyed, they may have killed many soldiers in the process.

"I can't believe we just took down an army aircraft," Zadeia said, feeling sick to her stomach. "How many do you think was on board?"

"Does it matter?" Zimi asked. "You heard the fairy queen. The army wants to use us for their own benefits. If they got a hold of us, we may never even see the light of day."

"Out of all the victories we've had," Atakos said. "This has to be our greatest."

"Oh, I don't know about that," Fajha said, smiling. "Let me think. Hmm. No. This was the best."

The boys doubled over in laughter while Zadeia only giggled, brushing her black hair out of her eyes. She was hoping the general was there by some odd coincidence and that it had nothing to do with Colnaha.

Cristaden did not find it funny. Although she despised General Komuh and the Western Army, she did not like the idea of taking the lives of soldiers who were just following orders. No matter how much trouble they would be in if they were caught.

"Guys, let's go," Atakos said, after breathing a sigh of relief.

With one final look at the destroyed ship, they moved on, making their way towards the majestic Hejdian Sea once again. Cristaden kept looking back at the massive burning structure, wondering if there was any life left inside that she could save. When she looked back for the fifth time, she saw tiny sparks shooting off the side of the aircraft.

"Hey …," she said, stopping to look more closely.

The others stopped walking and looked back at her.

"I saw sparks."

The friends peered closely at the burning ship.

"Are you sure?" Zimi asked.

"Definitely."

Then they saw it too. Sparks flew out of the side of the aircraft once again. Then a part of the ship fell away, creating a bridge to the sand. The teens watched in horror as General Komuh and perhaps fifty of his men exited the ship in technologically advanced sand trackers and headed straight for them.

"RUN!" Atakos screamed. Without hesitation, and almost tripping over their own feet, they turned and ran towards the sea, determined to reach it before they were captured.

"We have a visual on them again, sir," Lieutenant Gaojh informed General Komuh, who was seated in the back of the first sand tracker.

General Komuh lifted himself off his seat to look over the soldier's head. "That's right," he sneered. "We'll catch up to them soon enough."

"What will we do when we catch them? Should we dispose of them?"

"No!" Komuh shouted. "We need them alive. Those bothersome kids are our ticket to taking over the Eastern Army. Without them, we won't have a clear shot at it."

"But what if they put up a fight? They've made it this far without the help of weapons. They must be strong."

They *were* strong. Komuh could not believe what they did to his ship. Luckily, he and his soldiers were already strapped in because of the sandstorm and, because of the fireproof interior, they only suffered small injuries and no casualties. He patted the tranquilizer resting on his lap. "No, we won't allow them to get that far. We have to take them out before the other soldiers see what they're capable of doing."

"But what if they reach the sea before we do?"

Komuh gave a hearty laugh. "And then what? There are no boats where they're headed. They have no way to get across. They're trapped. Now stop asking me dumb questions, you're making me lose my concentration."

Lt. Gaojh did not respond. He glanced at Lt. Hodlin, sitting next to him, who only shrugged his shoulders.

General Komuh peered over the top of Lt. Gaojh's head once again. *Yes, run children,* he thought. *When I catch you, we have a nice little facility in the middle of nowhere that will hold all of you until we are ready to use you.* He snickered as he glided his hand across his tranquilizer. Hamilda Shing was a thing of the past. Whether she was dead or alive did not matter to him anymore. All he could focus on was getting the teens back so he could use them to take over Omordion, unbeknownst to his colleagues. He silently thanked the deceased Bontihm for making the biggest mistake of his life. Laughing at how the old man so graciously told the Western Army about his people, General Komuh took aim.

"They're catching up to us," Zadeia said, her voice quivering, looking back at the approaching vehicles.

"We're almost there," Atakos said as the texture of the sand changed beneath his feet. It seemed as if the tide was high earlier that day but the water was already receding.

"Did we ever think of how we are going to cross this thing?" Cristaden asked.

"The thought had occurred to me."

"Really?" Fajha said. "When?"

"Oh, a few times in the past...three minutes."

"Wonderful," Zadeia said.

"I could levitate across," Fajha said.

"That's great genius," Zimi said. "What about the rest of us? And what if you lose your balance? Are you a good swimmer?"

"I took swim lessons one summer—when I was nine. I'm sure I could—"

"Never mind that," Atakos said, glancing back at the approaching vehicles. "We all can't levitate so the rest of us would be stuck here. No, we have to think of something else and fast."

The friends began to pick up speed when the sand beneath their feet became wet and hard. They suddenly heard a loud popping sound and a tranquilizer dart whizzed past their heads, barely missing them.

"They're trying to *tranquilize* us," Cristaden said, tears springing up in her eyes. "Oh, no. We need to *do* something!"

"Does everyone know how to ice skate?" Zimi asked right before their feet touched the water. They did not have time to respond as the water before them was turned into a six-foot wide block of ice. As he skated forward, Zimi made a trail of ice for them to glide on.

"Brilliant," Cristaden said.

Atakos had to stop for a moment to find his center of gravity. He was not the best skater. "What if they use this ice trail to cross?" he asked.

"I'll take care of that," Zadeia said. She took on the challenge of sliding backwards and melting the ice behind them. When she was sure there was enough space between the icy patch they were on and the shore, she stopped and looked up. Komuh and his crew had reached the shore and were now dismounting their vehicles. Many of them were stunned and could not do anything but stare at the five teens in awe.

"Ha!" Atakos said while glancing behind him. He slipped and fell forward, banging his knee against the ice. "OW!"

Cristaden bent down to help him up. "Are you alright?" she asked.

Atakos looked up at her and blushed with embarrassment. When it came to ice skating, he was by far the worse skater out of all of them. And to fall in front of Cristaden was worst of all.

The teens looked back at their enemies, still stuck at the shore. General Komuh could be heard shouting curses at the astonished soldiers, telling them to get to work.

"What are they going to do?" Zadeia said.

"They have nowhere to go," Fajha said.

They watched in horror as the general and several other soldiers removed a large box from the back of one of the sand trackers. Opening the box, they pulled out an orange tarp, which they laid out on the sand. The large tarp was then hooked up to the sand tracker and a low buzzing sound commenced as air started pouring into it.

"A boat," Cristaden said.

"What are we going to do?" Fajha said, panicking.

Zimi added to the block of ice. "We should keep moving," he said, inviting his friends to follow him.

"They'll never stop chasing us," Zadeia said, frantically. "They'll catch up to us eventually."

"Calm down, everyone," Atakos said. "There has to be a way out of this."

Without thinking, Zadeia made a fireball and, winding up, she threw it as hard as she could. The fireball soared through the sky, and, just when she thought it would make contact, it fell short just several feet away from a sand tracker. When the soldiers saw it sizzle and die on the sand, they snickered and broke out into laughter.

"They're trying to kill us," one soldier said.

"With puny firecrackers!" said another, pointing.

General Komuh only glared at them without any emotion.

Zadeia's eyes filled with water. "I can't reach them."

"What about lightning?" Atakos asked Zimi.

"Sounds tempting," Zimi said. "But being on water is not the best place to stand during a lightning storm."

Atakos balled up his fists and watched as the soldiers dragged the finished boat to the water and pulled out another one to inflate. He considered going back to the shore to fight for a boat but thought it would be impossible. Twenty soldiers ran into the water and jumped into the first boat, along with General Komuh who was glaring at the teens while holding his tranquilizer close.

"We have to go now," Atakos said.

"We can't keep running," Fajha said.

"We have nowhere to run," Zadeia sobbed.

"Then we fight," Zimi said.

"What do we do?" Cristaden asked. "Blow them up? Freeze them? Set them on fire?"

Zimi shook his head. "I don't know," he said. "But we have to try something." He reached out and tried pushing the boat with his wind power but it caused the water to move as well which rocked the ice they were standing on. He was forced to stop and bring his arms back down to his sides, feeling defeated.

Atakos patted Zimi on the shoulder for his effort. "We'll have to wait until they get close. Then we'll throw them off the boat and take it."

"How do we prevent the other boats from following us?" Zimi said, watching as a third boat was being unfolded.

"We'll just have to see what happens."

We can't be taken prisoner now, Cristaden thought. *We've come too far!* Suddenly something tugged at her senses. It was the feeling she got when someone of importance was about to enter a room. "What—?" But she didn't have to time to figure out why she felt that way. A dark shadow suddenly blotted out the sun and all eyes turned towards the sky.

With a piercing shrill and a rush of wind from its expansive multicolored wings, a very large, blue bird flew straight towards them. "They still exist," Cristaden whispered. She couldn't believe what she was seeing. She remembered what Queen Lhainna had said about the chlysems. The bird was just as magnificent as she described. As her friends dove to the melting block of ice, Cristaden stood her ground. She was not afraid. The chlysem flew so close to her head that she felt its wings graze her face. One brightly colored, blue feather landed on her nose. Grabbing a hold of it, she turned to see the chlysem fly towards the shore.

Screams erupted at the beach when the large bird began its deadly rain of fire on the entire platoon. Sand trackers exploded left and right while soldiers threw themselves to the sand to take cover. The boats were melting with scorching fire and the soldiers, including the general, jumped off of them to avoid getting burned. One of the soldiers, who laughed at Zadeia's meager attempt to throw a fireball, dove under water to douse his burning back. The whole beach was set ablaze. Being sure that everything was destroyed, the chlysem gave one final squawk and virtually disappeared. There was no sign of where it went or where it came from.

The teens slowly rose to stand next to Cristaden. They took a moment to process what they were seeing. Across the water was a troop of angry soldiers, running around trying to find ways to douse the raging fires around them, who did not have any means of transportation left. A very wet General Komuh was standing by the water, glaring defiantly at the group of five teens who began to cheer uncontrollably.

"That was incredible!" Zadeia said.

"Did you see what just happened?" Zimi said.

"Where was that bird when we needed help all this time?" Fajha said.

Atakos couldn't take his eyes off of the raging fires. "I wonder where it went," he said.

"Maybe it's still here," Cristaden said, searching the skies. "Maybe the sea is where they live, invisible to Brulok's minions."

"You can run," Komuh shouted from the shore. "I will catch up to you sooner or later!"

Atakos laughed and shouted back at the distressed general. "You may want to watch out for deadly Valdeec birds and poisonous Montapu lizards, Komuh! They come out at night!"

The angry scowl on the general's face caused the friends to erupt in even more laughter.

"Come on guys, let's go," Zimi said, continuing to make a trail of ice for them to glide on.

Cristaden almost forgot about the feather that had fallen off the chlysem. She opened her clenched fist to examine it. It wasn't there. *Impossible,* she thought. She was holding on to it very tightly the whole time. She searched the ice around her feet but couldn't find it. It was gone, just like the chlysem.

Vanished without a trace.

CHAPTER 38

The Hejdian Sea

Across the blue-green water, the teens glided, setting a comfortable pace to prevent any accidents. After a few hours, they began to wish they had a boat. The sliding was tiresome and strenuous. They had to stop a few times to allow Zimi to rest but the burning sun above and the warm water below threatened to melt the ice. He had to pull energy he didn't have into making thicker ice. They didn't know how much longer he would be able to continue.

"I didn't realize the Hejdian Sea was this big," Zimi said, trying to find any sign of land ahead of them but seeing nothing in the horizon.

"It is the sea, Zimi," Fajha said sarcastically. "Not a lake."

"I'm tired," Zadeia said.

"Don't worry, Zadeia," Atakos said. "We'll make it to Paimonu. And then we could rest." As he reassured her, he was not even sure of his own words. He was exhausted and saw no end to the sea in sight, which made him even more tired. He suddenly wished they could all fly like birds and reach there faster. Even though Fajha could levitate and the twins could use wind to glide, flying was something different altogether. They never heard of any Dokami who could fly. Nonetheless, they had to keep it moving.

Atakos brought his attention to the ice beneath their feet which would often collect all kinds of sea creatures. It was the most entertainment they experienced since they left Lochenby. Zadeia contemplated collecting some to eat when they got to Paimonu but she chose to wait until they were closer to shore so they would not spoil.

"It's really amazing to see the different species," Cristaden said, picking up on his thoughts. "We could never get this view if we were on a boat." As she skated forward, she saw a large fish, frozen in the ice, with a thousand razor sharp teeth in its long mouth. "Oh, I would not want to swim with that one." She shuttered. As she continued along she saw a very large mammal, whose fin was frozen in the ice. It was a baby whale, its spots fading but still visible under the water.

Cristaden stopped. "Oh, you poor thing," she said.

"What is it?" Atakos asked her, as him and the others glided back and surrounded her.

"I feel so bad for it." Cristaden peered closely at the whale. She could see that it was still breathing but it appeared to be stunned, as if it did not understand what was going on and didn't know how to react. Moments later, it tried to swish its tail from left to right in an attempt to free itself but its fin would not budge. It tried to pull the fin out but, the more it pulled, the more painful it became.

"We have to help him," Cristaden said.

Just then, the whale let out a piercing scream that resonated through the ice and into the air with so much intensity that it caused their knees to buckle. The teens simultaneously covered their ears with their hands. Letting out another bellow, the whale jolted to and fro, attempting to free itself from the frozen ice.

"Zadeia, can you melt the ice so we can free him?" Cristaden shouted.

"It might take some time," Zadeia said. "Zimi has made the ice so thick that it definitely will be harder for me to melt it." She got to work melting the ice but each passing minute seemed like an eternity. She was trying hard not to burn the baby whale.

"I'm so sorry about this," Zimi said. He was visibly upset over the trapped whale.

"It's ok," Zadeia said, trying to reassure him. "I'll get him out."

Suddenly, they heard a monstrous sound. It resembled the noise the baby whale made but it was deeper and much louder. The friends looked up in time to see a humungous tail rise out of the water in the distance and splash down, causing huge waves to roll towards them and splash over the ice.

"Oh my goodness, it's the mother," Cristaden cried. "Go faster, Zadeia!"

"No," Atakos said. "We have to get *out* of here."

"We can't just leave this poor creature here to suffer. If we can help it, maybe the mother won't attack."

Atakos looked at the slowly melting ice and back at the fast approaching mother and he knew there was no time. "We can't stay here." He panicked. "We have to go. *Now.*"

"No, we have to *free* him," Cristaden cried, tears beginning to gather in her eyes. "He needs our help." She pleaded to Zadeia. "Please help him."

Zadeia nodded and continued to melt the ice.

"She's coming …," Fajha impatiently said.

"I know," Zadeia said. "I'm trying to go as fast as I can."

Cristaden attempted to speak to the mother whale as she so often spoke to all her animals. *Mother whale, please calm your fury. We're trying to help your baby. Just give us a chance and we will free him.* The whale was filled with so much rage that her plea was left unheard. The mother sped towards them, more persistent than before. She lifted her tail and dropped it, sending waves of water rushing towards them again, this time going up to their ankles.

"Almost there," Zadeia said as she melted the last of the ice around the fin. "There!" she cried, triumphant when she saw the baby whale escape the clutches of the ice.

"He's free," Cristaden shouted. Her enthusiasm was short-lived when she realized the mother whale was still coming at them as determined as ever. Picking up on her thoughts, Cristaden understood that she still viewed them as a threat to her baby and would stop at nothing to eliminate them. It was too late to run. "I'm so sorry guys," she said in a small voice.

"Brace yourselves!" Zimi cried.

With one blow from her head, the mother whale broke the ice they were standing on and sent them toppling into the sea.

Fighting to get back to the surface for some air, they swam with all their might, which became increasingly difficult because of the turning water caused by the mother whale. The whale swam away from them, allowing them to make it to the surface to take in gulps of air. Before they could think of what to do next, she came back, sending them back down under the water.

The teens tried to dodge her attacks but she was simply too strong for them. Under water, their powers did not work and even the twins were not given enough time to react. After the third attack, their lungs began to fill with water. One by one, they sank, losing the fight and falling into the deep abyss of the sea.

As he began choking on water, Atakos thought of his family and how they would never see him again. Nobody would ever know what happened to him and his friends because their bodies would never be found. They would never know they died. All hope for rescuing Hamilda was now gone.

As his vision began to get fuzzy, he saw the most beautiful sight he had ever seen. It was a woman. She had long, flowing red hair, tinted green skin and green eyes. She was absolutely beautiful. She swam up to him and smiled the prettiest smile he had ever seen and then kissed him. Before he closed his eyes, he felt the most warming sensation coursing through his body. He was positive that he was experiencing what it must feel to die a beautiful death.

Atakos opened his eyes. He was lying on a beach of black sand. Waves crashed on the beach and grazed his feet. His friends were all lying next to him, waking up as well. Quickly sitting up, he looked out at the sea. "Am I dead? Are we ... all ... dead?"

"I don't think so," Fajha said. He sat up and looked around. His head felt so woozy that he almost went back down to the sand again.

"Then where are we?" Atakos asked him.

Fajha kept looking around him and he opened his eyes wide as a thought dawned on him. "Paimonu," he said with a smile.

"You're kidding me."

"See for yourself."

Atakos turned around. Indeed, he saw a black mountain in the distance and the tropical forest that surrounded it. It was a beautiful sight. He squeezed the black sand beneath his fingers and let out a scream. The others around him were sitting up to look around also, not believing what they were seeing.

"But how did we get here?" Zadeia said.

"We couldn't even *see* the island anywhere in the distance, and now … we're here?" Cristaden asked.

"How *did* we get here?" Zimi asked.

The group was silent as they suddenly remembered the mother whale and her relentless attacks. That was the last thing they remembered.

"We should be dead right now," Fajha said under his breath. He was thinking what they were all thinking. For them to go from near death to ending up on a beach was impossible.

"How could this happen?" Atakos asked. As the words were leaving his mouth, he suddenly remembered something. "It wasn't a dream."

"What wasn't?" Fajha asked.

"I dreamt that a woman swam up to me. She had the most beautiful bright green eyes I've ever seen. She wrapped her arms around me and then she—she kissed me."

"What?" Cristaden asked, feeling a sharp pang of jealousy.

"I don't know. At first I thought it was a dream, that I was dying, but now I don't think it was."

"What do you mean?" Zimi asked, very intrigued by the story.

Atakos sucked in his breath. "Queen Lhainna."

"What about her?" Fajha asked. "Do you think she saved us?"

"Everything we have encountered corresponded to what she told us. Brulok's minions, the chlysem, General Komuh …"

"Yes, yes, but what does this have to do with that woman?" Cristaden said.

Before he responded, Zadeia stole the words right out of his lips. "She was a ceanave," she said.

"Exactly."

The thought processed in their minds. That ceanaves had saved them made perfect sense. That would explain why they did not die. That would give an explanation as to how they got to Paimonu so fast.

"Lhainna did not know if they still existed anymore," Fajha said.

"Through our eyes, she will know now," Atakos said.

"Do you think she's watching us?" Zadeia asked.

"I think to some degree, she could 'see' what's happening. But I don't think there's much she could do to help us. We're pretty much on our own."

"Someone is looking out for us," Zadeia thought out loud, as she looked up to the sky. "We've come this far. Let's not fail them."

With that thought, they rose to their feet and brushed the sand off of them and smiled. Against all odds, they had made it to Paimonu in one piece. It was incredible. With one final look at the blue-green Hejdian Sea, they said goodbye to it and thanked the ceanaves that helped them. Then they proceeded to walk towards the tropical forest.

"I've never seen black sand before," Atakos said. "Fajha, do you know why it's like this?"

"Well, if I recall from my geography lesson, Paimonu rests on volcanic ash. Three hundred years ago, a Volcano erupted, creating this island and the black land around it." He pointed to the tall mountain in the distance. "That is Sremati Volcano. It has lain dormant for three hundred years and the inhabitants of this island do not fear it, they worship it, bringing sacrifices to it every year to keep it happy."

"What *kind* of sacrifices?" Cristaden asked but was afraid to hear his response.

"No one really knows but it has been rumored to be animals or even small children."

The teens cringed as the picture of animals and children being thrown into the pits of boiling lava came to mind.

"But it's only a rumor," Fajha quickly said, noting everyone's apprehension. "The inhabitants do not perform sacrifices when outsiders are around because they fear it might anger their god, Sremati. Fear of the unknown is how rumors like these are spread."

"So which way are we headed?" Atakos asked.

"There," Fajha said, pointing at Sremati Volcano. "That's where the inhabitants live."

The group froze.

"Come on. It's the only way we're going to find out how to get to the Ardomion Caves. I honestly do not know how to get there from here and which direction to go."

Groaning, the friends entered the forest of trees and exotic plants. They then came to a clearing with a small waterfall emptying out into a pool below it. It was a freshwater pool and they could see fish swimming around. Laughing, they removed their dirty uniforms except their underwear and jumped in for a swim. Taking their chances, they drank the unsalted water and caught some fish for Zadeia to cook. After washing the dirt off their clothes and cloaks, they hung them on the tree branches that surrounded them.

Sleepiness then gripped the teens after they ate and they decided to get some rest before venturing any further. Sensing no danger, they went to sleep, curled up next to each other on the soft, black dirt. The sun sank and they slept all night, not knowing what they would discover when the sun rose.

PART FIVE
PAIMONU

CHAPTER 39

The soldiers in the Effit forest were silent as they rode their horses through the trees. King Tholenod whispered something to Menyilh and the assistant's eyes looked shifty while he looked around. Aillios was only three soldiers behind his father but was not close enough to hear what he was saying. Tholenod then raised his arm to signal the soldiers to stop. Turning around, the look on his face was of sheer determination. He did not look the slightest bit frightened or intimidated but Aillios never knew him to be scared of anything his entire life. If he was frightened now, they would never know.

"Alright men," Tholenod said. "We are entering the dead forest. Be on your guard but do not be afraid. We do not want to show any fear."

For a few minutes, Aillios could feel the tension in the air. The other soldiers were stiff as they rode on but he could tell they were nervous. The trees they passed began to lose their color and the amount of leaves they held until they were completely surrounded by dead trees. Aillios could still make out the distant cry of a bird far behind them, in the more lively part of the forest, but there was no life ahead of them. He noted how strange it was that even the ground was bare and dried up, as if rain had not fallen there for many years. There was no grass or bushes, just really dried up, dead trees.

What a strange, mysterious place, Aillios thought. *Who could ever live here and survive?*

"We will have to leave our horses here and climb up the mountain," King Tholenod said when they stopped again. "I will need ten soldiers to enter the cave along with myself and Menyilh. The rest of you will stay here as lookouts. If there is any sign of danger, I must be notified immediately."

Mountain? Aillios thought. *What mountain?* He looked everywhere and there was none to be found. If there was a mountain, he would see it. All he saw were trees.

Just then his father moved his horse aside.

That was when he saw it.

Aillios could see the top of a mountain sticking out of an enormous crater in the earth. It was tall but, being mostly underground and covered by dead trees, it was easy to miss.

King Tholenod chose ten soldiers he wanted to take to the cave. Aillios was lucky to be one of the ten. "We will have to climb down the side of the cliff and then up the mountainside," he said.

This should be interesting, Aillios thought. He was anxious to see what they would find when they went into the cave dug into the side of the mountain, its gaping mouth so uninviting that several men were reluctant to dismount their horses. Could there be a real wizard living there? What could be waiting in the cave that even the brave soldiers of the king were frightened?

"Get moving," the captain shouted when he noticed the overall apprehension of the soldiers. He had an angry scowl on his face to show his disapproval. "No weapons."

Aillios glanced at the mountain and frowned. No weapons? What if there was something there they would have to fight? Luckily he was trained in hand-to-hand combat but he wasn't sure it would be enough against wild beasts.

Aillios was the first to dismount Thashmar and the rest followed suit. Steadily, the soldiers marched toward the edge of the cliff with the king and his creepy assistant. The cliff was not steep like Aillios assumed it would be. It had a drop of about four feet but then the rest of it stretched out to the foot of the mountain, which resembled more like a tower than an actual mountain. The group jumped down and slowly walked the rest of the way to the base, being careful not to slip and fall. When they reached the foot of the mountain, Aillios looked up and gasped. He had never seen anything like it. There really was no explanation for it. It was considerably darker than the earth around them, as if it wasn't meant to be there in the first place. The dead trees protruding from it reminded him of skeleton-like fingers, reaching out towards them whenever the wind blew. Shaking his head, he gathered his bearings and took a deep breath. The mouth of the cave was about two hundred feet up and he needed to focus on getting there in one piece.

Two by two they climbed, trying to keep a steady pace up the dark mountain. One soldier lost his footing and almost fell if Aillios had not grabbed his arm and helped him back up. They had to maneuver around the dead trees while they made their way to the mouth of the cave which proved to be very difficult. When they finally reached their destination, they could see a soft light coming from the end of a dark tunnel.

Who could live in this foul smelling, rotting cave? Aillios wondered. He looked around at the other soldiers who had beads of sweat rolling down their determined faces. Tholenod motioned for two soldiers to stand watch at the mouth of the cave, which they gladly did. The rest, including Aillios, followed him in. The walls of the cave were dusty and reeked of rotted flesh. It took Aillios everything in his power to keep from vomiting. The closer they got to the light, the stuffier the air became. At one point it seemed that the entire group was panting for air. Surprisingly enough, the air began to clear as they approached an archway into a very large, windowless hall. It resembled that of a great hall in a castle. Torches protruded out of either side of the walls, burning brightly. The hall was virtually colorless except for a once red but faded to almost gray carpet extending throughout the entire length of it. Cobwebs clung to everything the eye could see which meant that the dusty cave had not been cleaned for perhaps over fifty years.

Cautiously, the soldiers proceeded down the length of the hall. They kept their eyes opened to make sure they were not walking into an ambush. King Tholenod ignored the apprehension of his soldiers and followed Menyilh. At the end of the hall, they saw the one piece of furniture in the entire room. It was a golden throne.

And there was someone sitting on it.

The person was slumped over as if sleeping or dead, Aillios could not tell which. Judging by how many cobwebs covered the individual, he assumed they were staring at a dead person who had died a long time ago but had not yet decomposed. It was a horrifying sight to see.

King Tholenod put his hand up to stop his soldiers from going any further. He and Menyilh then approached the throne. Aillios could now see that the person on the chair was an old man with long gray hair and a long gray bread, practically touching his feet. The robe he wore was faded gray but, like the faded hall carpet, he could see that it was once a darker color, most likely black.

"Is he alive?" Aillios heard Tholenod whisper to Menyilh. His response came when the old man slowly opened his yellowed eyes.

CHAPTER 40

Colnaha put his ear against the door of his father's office. The enraged voice of General Komuh resonated from the communicator. "Yes. They have destroyed my ship and everything else. Our trackers and our boats. It took me several hours just to get this damn receiver to work. I've had it up to here with those kids. Now you better get out here *right now* and get us out of here." The general grunted some profane words after his tantrum.

Maldaha hesitated before he responded. "It was my duty to tell you where the teenagers were headed. In no way did you mention that I would have to leave my family and aid you—"

"You better choose your next words carefully, Maldaha. Are you saying that you choose *not* to help the leader of the army that serves and protects you and your family? That's a federal offense. Punishable by imprisonment for a very long, long time."

Colnaha knew General Komuh was threatening his father only because he was his fastest way out of the desert and to the teens but he was right when he said his father would go to jail for a long time for not obeying him. But would his father choose to move his people again to avoid imprisonment?

"Okay," Colnaha was disappointed to hear his father say. "On one condition."

"No conditions!"

Maldaha ignored Komuh's demand. "Seeing as though it is nighttime, I cannot possibly leave the village without arousing suspicion. My people will be inclined to know where I've gone. I will have to wait until morning and then tell them I need to visit a sick friend. You don't want the other villagers to know of your plan, do you?"

The general did not respond. There was a lot of commotion in the background. Men were shouting. Some were screaming.

"General, we need your help!" a soldier shouted.

Komuh swore under his breath. "Do what you can!" he yelled at Maldaha. Before disconnecting, he swore again. "Damn birds…"

As his father put down the receiver, Colnaha ran down the hallway and up the stairs. He stopped for a moment to catch his breath and hoped that his father had not heard his light footsteps. When he did not hear anything, he breathed a sigh of relief and continued to walk through the first floor hallway. He was just about to climb the stairs when his father stepped in front of him, most likely coming from the secret staircase that led up from the basement.

"Son," Maldaha said, seemingly very surprised. "What are you doing up at this late hour?"

Colnaha had to think fast. He could not say he was having trouble sleeping because his father would know something was bothering him. "Uh, I have some pain in my stomach. It was so fierce, it woke me up. Must have been that meat I had for dinner." Colnaha bit his tongue when he realized his mistake. His whole family had eaten the same meat. If there were something wrong with it, they would all be sick.

Maldaha glared at him. "You didn't happen to be in the basement just now, were you?"

Colnaha's hands felt moist and clammy as he tried to come up with another excuse. "No. I was walking up and down the hall here to ease the pain." He then gave his father the same look. "Is everything alright, appi?"

Maldaha's face softened. Colnaha could not help noticing how much he had aged over the course of four days. The lines on his face seemed deeper than they had before. Dark, puffy circles had formed under his eyes. He wondered why his father chose to suffer in the way that he did. "Sometimes, in your lifetime, opportunities may come and go," his father said. "But don't let your mistakes and wrong choices set you back, son. Learn from them. That is when you will achieve your goals in life." He then ruffled his hair and climbed the stairs to go to sleep.

Colnaha wondered what his father could have meant with his little speech. Perhaps he was trying to say he made a mistake when he told the general about his friends. Then again, his father would never admit his wrongdoings. He claimed so often that everything he did or said was right—no questions asked.

Colnaha thought back to what General Komuh demanded. They wanted to use his father and the village's only aircraft to search for his friends and capture them. He could not allow that to happen. His mind wandered back to the orb beneath the closet floor. For days he had considered taking it and escaping Osmatu but he couldn't bring himself to do it. Every time he saw an opportunity, he let it pass. He was too scared.

As Colnaha climbed the stairs, an odd feeling took over him. This was it. This was his only chance to leave Osmatu and begin a new life. If he remained there, what would his life be like when he was his father's age? Would it be fulfilling? Most likely the answer to that question was a solid 'no'. He loved his parents, he would surely miss them, but he had to act before morning.

With his mind made up, he slowly climbed the stairs and walked past his parents' bedroom. Entering his own room, he shut the door tightly behind him and went to work packing a bag with clothes and other provisions he would need. He wrote an apologetic note to his parents and laid it on his pillow.

Colnaha then turned off his light and waited in the dark for the entire village to go to sleep. He knew it would only be a matter of a couple of hours but each minute felt like an eternity. Beads of sweat dripped down his back with anticipation.

Finally, when all was quiet, he grabbed an unlit oil lamp and slowly crept out of his room. Trying not to make the floorboards creek, he tiptoed past his parents' bedroom door where he heard the usual soft snore from his father. He then quietly crept down the stairs and casually walked down to the basement. Checking to make sure no one was in the office, he grabbed the key for his father's aircraft, went to the very familiar closet, and opened the trapdoor. The soft green light of the orb poured out of the tiny room. He felt a sudden chill go down his spine but he ignored it, slowly creeping down the stairs, being careful not to make any noise.

The orb was standing on the pedestal as it had a few nights before and for, perhaps, many years before that. In all his life, Colnaha never believed the moment would come. The moment when he would touch the orb, take hold of it, put it in his bag, and leave the shelter of Osmatu with it. It burned so brightly as if the inside of it held a raging, green fireball, rolling around in waves. Quickly, he touched it with the tip of his index finger and jerked back, expecting to feel pain. But the orb was cool to the touch. With no time to lose, he yanked it off the pedestal, took a gray cloth from his bag, and wrapped it tightly. As soon as he wrapped it, he felt years of dormant Dokami strength returning to his body. It felt amazing to be free from the constraints of the orb that he almost wanted to destroy it right then and there. But he knew he could not demolish it even if he tried. It would take an amazing amount of strength and power to obliterate it. He placed it carefully in his bag and closed it tightly. By morning the Dokami clan of Osmatu would be fully aware of what he did.

Creeping out of the closet, Colnaha headed for the servants door and left the place he knew as home. He continued walking through the garden and out the back gate. Lighting the oil lamp, he made his way up a winding, unpaved road away from the village. For twenty minutes he walked among the rocky hills to the camouflaged entryway of an underground shelter where his father kept their aircraft. Descending down a flight of stairs, he opened a black door marked 'FORBIDDEN', flipped on the light, and entered the shelter. His father had built it in case the village was under attack and they needed a place to hide and make their escape without detection. There were sacks of dried food and barrels of water to sustain a whole village of people for two weeks if necessary. Rows of cots lined up against the right wall and several lavatories were attached to the left wall. At the end of the long room loomed the aircraft. Designed to hold two hundred people if necessary, it was still a shiny gray color after all those years.

Immediately, Colnaha made his way to the aircraft. Once inside, he dropped his bag and blew out the oil lamp. He flipped on all the switches on the control panel to power up the engine. After leaving the aircraft to grab food and water from the shelter, he made sure he had enough fuel and went back in. Sitting in the captain's chair, he found the switch for the ceiling panel and watched as it opened, revealing a clear, starry night. His father had taught him how to fly the aircraft in case anything happened to the older members of the village. For that he was truly grateful.

"Here we go," Colnaha said while the wheels tucked into their compartments and the aircraft hovered over the ground. Grabbing the lever he thought was to bring the ship up, the aircraft suddenly dipped to its side. "Aah!" he screamed, bringing the ship back to its first position. Taking a deep breath, Colnaha located the right lever. The aircraft rose steadily out of the shelter and he turned it until he was facing the direction of Paimonu. Without further hesitation, he pushed the lever to go forward and was on his way. Colnaha was so proud of himself that he almost wished his father could see him and congratulate him. Putting his father out of his mind, he made his way towards the Suthack Desert to find his friends.

Maldaha woke just as the sun was beginning to peek over the horizon. He stretched and wearily climbed out of his bed. The threats of the previous night slowly came back to him and he groaned, knowing fully well what he had to do.

"What is it darling?" Piedara asked, rolling over to look at him.

"It's nothing, go back to sleep. I have to check on something." Maldaha decided to tell his wife about the phone call after he checked on the ship. If anything was wrong with it, he would have an excuse to give to the general and not upset his wife.

He put on his shoes and went down the two flights of stairs to his basement office. Reaching up to grab the aircraft key from its hook, it took him a moment to realize it was not there. He searched his desk and the entire office but came up empty-handed. Suddenly remembering Colnaha sneaking around the night before, he bolted up the stairs to the second floor and slowly opened the door to his son's room. His greatest fears were realized when he saw the made bed, empty except for a letter resting on the pillow.

"No, no, no ...," Maldaha said over and over again. He feared it would happen for some time but he had hoped his son would be smarter than that. Walking over to the bed, he picked up the letter, his heart sinking as he began to read it.

Appi,

I would like to apologize for what I have done but I am not sorry. You brought us here because of your own insecurities with the Council and have kept us hidden for years, living like prisoners in our own village. You have put the lives of five teenagers in danger and you continue to do so, collaborating with that insufferable General Komuh. For whatever reason you felt all this was necessary, I will never know. But what I do know is I am not like you. Being your only son, it is my duty to correct your mistakes and to help this world be free of people like you. I have taken the orb and the aircraft and will be far from here by the time you read this. Perhaps I may never see you again. I love you for you are my one and only father and I always will. Tell mother I love her as well and will miss her terribly.

Colnaha

Maldaha crumpled the letter in his hand and felt like screaming. It was worse than he thought. He could not believe his son had taken the one thing that kept the Council from finding their village. Colnaha was rebellious but he never thought he would do something so *horrific*. Clutching his chest, he did not have to go to the secret room under the closet to see if his son was telling the truth about taking the orb. Very easily, Colnaha's bed dragged across the floor until it slammed against the wall. His dresser, lamp, and shoes followed, along with anything else Maldaha could find to throw from where he stood. Amidst all the swirling and flying objects, Maldaha had to think of a way to explain to General Komuh why he would not be helping him out of the desert that day or any other day afterwards.

CHAPTER 41

Cristaden opened her eyes. The sun was just beginning to peak through the trees in the tropical rainforest that surrounded them. She sat up and looked down at her sleeping friends. They all slept hard that night. Perhaps it was the deepest slumber they had ever experienced in their lifetime. Besides the exotic birds and different types of insects, there were no monsters around that disturbed them and for that she was very grateful.

After stretching and yawning, Cristaden wondered how good it would feel to allow her friends to keep sleeping, to roll over and close her eyes once again, transporting herself back to the dream world she grew so accustomed to during the night. But she knew they already had overslept and should have continued their mission over an hour before then.

"Wake up, everyone," Cristaden said. "We have to get going."

Familiar groans erupted around her.

Fajha yawned. "I was having the most glorious dream," he said.

"What was it about?" Zadeia asked, sitting up and stretching.

"I was with this girl…I don't remember how she looked like but we were in love. We were running together, hand and hand, in the courtyard behind Lochenby. Just running towards the lake. Oh, it was wonderful." He reached for his glasses and sighed as he put them on.

Zimi smirked and then stood up. "Definitely a dream alright."

Fajha stood up and sighed again. He never did have any luck talking to girls back in Lochenby. The usual response he would get was a quick wave and some fast legs running down the hall and out of his sight.

The five friends pulled their clothes down from the trees and put them on. They were all dry and smelled of the rainforest. Frozen fish they had caught the night before were cooked and eaten very quickly.

"Alright guys." Atakos motioned for all of them to gather around him. "Fajha, how long do you think it will take us to reach the cave?"

"I'm not sure which direction it is but once we find out, we should be there before the end of today. This island is not that big."

Emotions ran high all around.

"Do we really have to go to Sremati?" Zadeia asked.

Fajha looked up at the volcano. "It's the only way. We have to ask the people of Paimonu which way to go. Otherwise, it could take days for us to search this entire island."

"He's right," Atakos said. "We have no choice."

"Alright then, what are we waiting for?" Zimi said. "Let's go."

Throwing his cloak over his shoulder, Fajha led the group out of the clearing and through the rainforest, towards the black volcano.

As the sun rose, the air began to feel sticky and hot, causing the teens to perspire profusely. The insect population increased so much the deeper they travelled, that they had to keep waving their arms and swatting them to keep them out of their faces.

For an hour they kept walking until they reached an enormous valley of crop fields, perhaps a mile long and several miles wide. The farmland was lush and green with vegetables of all kinds. Among the vegetation were huts with smoke rising out of their chimneys and people walking around, pulling out the ripe vegetables from the land. Sremati Volcano loomed in plain sight beyond the fields.

"I thought you said they live on the mountain," Zadeia said to Fajha.

"They do," Fajha said. "These must be their farmers."

"Anyone volunteer to ask one of these people for help?" Cristaden said.

"How about we all go together?" Atakos said.

"Sounds good to me," Zimi said, attempting to hide his apprehension.

They walked up to an elderly woman. She wore a long yellow dress and a large hat to protect her face from the sun. She was bent over, pulling vegetables out of the ground. They could see she had a basket full of them at her feet.

"Excuse me," Fajha said, trying to be polite. It appeared as if the old woman had not heard him for she neither lifted her head nor responded to him. "Excuse me," he said again but got nothing in response.

"She must be hard at hearing," Zimi said. He walked up to her until he was almost three feet away from her and obnoxiously raised his voice. "Hello. We are new here and we would like some help."

"Zimi …," Cristaden began, thinking that he was being very rude to her. She then realized that the old woman had not acknowledged him. She continued to pull out the vegetables from the ground as if she did not realize that Zimi was standing right in front of her.

"She must be deaf…and blind," Zadeia said.

"Come on Zimi, we'll ask someone else," Atakos said.

The teens backed away from her and continued down the path between the fields.

"That was strange," Atakos looked back at the old woman who was busy pulling out another vegetable. She yanked it out and threw it into the basket with perfect aim. He frowned. *She's not blind.*

The next person they came across was a middle-aged man. Wearing a straw hat and suspenders, he was planting new seeds to take the place of freshly picked vegetables very carefully and precisely.

"Excuse me sir," Zadeia said. Just like the old woman, he neither looked up nor responded. He continued planting his seeds.

"Oh this is ridiculous," Fajha said, throwing his hands up. "Hello!" he shouted, causing his voice to echo throughout the valley. No response. The man continued his planting.

"This is so strange," Cristaden said.

"I have an idea," Atakos said. "Maybe they are just ignoring us because we are in a group. Maybe if we separate and pretend we are alone, they may take pity on us."

""I'll try anything," Fajha said.

With that, the teens separated. They were on their guard and if anything were to go wrong, they would let out a scream and fight until the others found them. Within ten minutes, they regrouped.

"What's the status report?" Atakos asked.

"Nothing," Zadeia said. "I tried to speak to a little boy. He didn't even acknowledge my *existence*."

"Yeah," Fajha said. "I approached a young woman and she didn't even lift up her head."

"I approached a woman also," Cristaden said. "Same thing."

"I yelled right in a man's ear," Zimi said. "*Nothing.*"

"I tapped a man on his shoulder," Atakos said and his friends gasped. "He quickly turned around and looked *past* me with a terrified look on his face. Then he went back to pulling vegetables out of the ground."

Silence settled among the bewildered teenagers.

Zadeia hugged herself. "Maybe we *are* … dead," she said.

"No," Cristaden said. "We are very much alive. This is just too strange."

They tried hard to think of other reasons why they were being ignored but could not. Fajha mentioned that he heard the people of Paimonu did not take kindly to tourists on their island but he never heard of what they were experiencing. They looked up at Sremati Volcano and could see many finely built houses and huts around its base.

"Maybe we will have better luck there," Atakos said.

"I hope so," Fajha said, trying to hide his fear.

They were all a little bit frightened. Walking past the crop fields, the five friends did not dare speak to the villagers there, who did not look up even once to acknowledge their existence. It was almost as if they were invisible to them and the whole island was just a dream they could not wake up from. As the mountain came closer, they could see children running around and people chatting with each other. Laughter could be heard throughout the mountainside and music was playing. Despite being on a volcano, the village was covered in green grass and plants of all kinds except for the black road that passed through it. There were huts made of straw and even two story houses made of cement and painted various colors. Trees with pink and white flowers lined the road, letting all know that the villagers took pride in their homes, taking the time to plant many exotic trees and flowers. The teens could see a group of men digging a large hole for a young tree and their happy voices carried over the mountainside.

"They're bound to talk to us over there," Fajha smiled, listening to the cheerful music.

"I'm sure," Cristaden said sarcastically. "They might see us coming and run screaming." She chuckled a little bit and stopped when she realized that what she said might actually happen.

"Come on," Zadeia said. "We are not bad people. I don't see any reason for them to be worried about us."

"Yeah," Zimi said. "We're just trying to find Hamilda."

With the mention of Hamilda's name, the sense of urgency returned to the group. They picked up their pace and headed up the road that led to the village on the mountainside. The black volcano was menacing but the sound of music from the village was very enticing.

The closer they got to the village, the more their fears began to be realized as the laughter began to taper off. The boisterous music slowly died down. By the time they turned into the village it was like a ghost town. Their smiles faded as they looked around for anyone in sight. Smoke was still rising from the straw huts and cement houses but the crowds they saw from the fields were no more. There was no one outside.

"What the …?" Atakos started but could not finish his sentence. "Where did they go?"

"It seems as if they dropped everything and went into *hiding*," Zadeia said, looking at a wooden toy top that was still spinning as if a child had just pulled its string and ran away. The toy stopped spinning and rolled on the ground until it came to a dead halt.

"Look," Zimi said, pointing to the fields they had come from. The workers were gone.

"What happened to them?" Cristaden said. No one had an answer for her question.

The only sound they heard was the wind as they walked up the road. Their hearts were pounding like brass drums as they looked around, half expecting to be attacked at any moment by warriors. But nothing happened. Everything was dead quiet.

A noise behind them startled them. They looked back and saw a piece of cloth flapping in the breeze from the balcony of a wooden house. Letting out the breath they were holding, they turned back around.

A woman stood several feet away from them.

Surprised, they jumped back. Zadeia screamed.

"Don't be frightened children," the woman said in a thick accent. She was wearing a long brown dress and a straw hat, resembling the ones the farmers wore in the fields. Her wavy hair was brown and her skin was dark but they could not get a good look at her face because of her hat and the shadows caused by the sun behind her.

"At least someone's talking to us," Cristaden said. She stepped forward.

"Cristaden, no," Atakos said in a frantic whisper.

"Do we have any other choice?" she whispered back. She then bowed to the woman. "My name is Cristaden and these are my friends. We have come a long way to seek the Ardomion Caves but no one here wants to talk to us. In fact they act like we are not there and now they're in hiding."

"Ah, you seek the ancient caves," the woman said and then smiled. "You see, the word 'Ardomion' means 'ancient'. I apologize for the rudeness of the farmers. They do not take too kindly to strangers. They like to pretend they don't see them, hoping they would decide to leave this island. As for the villagers? You have just come at an inopportune time of prayer." She chuckled lightly. "They retreat to their homes and pray three times a day to their god Sremati."

"That explains it," Zadeia said and sighed. "I guess this is what Colnaha meant when he said we didn't match the personalities of the people here."

"Guess so," Zimi said.

"You say 'their' god," Atakos said. "Do you not worship him as well?"

"Oh no. I was once visiting this island, like you, and I decided to stay. I like it here. It is very peaceful being away from all the war and devastation." As the woman spoke, people began to filter out of their homes. Somewhere nearby music began to play again and children ran around to regroup with their friends.

"Can you tell us how to get to the ancient caves?" Fajha asked the woman, relieved that things began to appear normal once again. He was excited that she spoke their language.

The woman turned and pointed behind her. "If you continue up the road that winds around the mountain, you will see the caves once you are on the other side. You just have to figure out a way to get down there. It's very tricky."

"Thank you for your help," Cristaden said.

"You're very welcome."

"What is your name?" Zimi asked.

"It is Sanei."

"Sanei, have you noticed any strangers lurking about?"

"Besides the five of you? No."

"Thank you, Sanei."

"Good luck." She nodded and walked away from them.

"She was nice," Atakos said.

"See, you have to take risks," Cristaden said. "She was very sincere. I didn't even pick up anything evil about her."

As they continued to walk up the road, Zadeia shivered. "Something seemed oddly familiar about her though. I just could not put my finger on it."

"Zadeia," Zimi said. "You're always thinking something's wrong with everything."

"That isn't true! Oh, never mind."

As they walked up the winding road, the villagers nodded and smiled at them. They seemed very friendly and warm but they did not approach them to talk nor did they speak to them from afar. It was understandable if they just wanted to be left alone. The more outsiders that came, the more problems they would have.

The air among the group changed from complete apprehension to nervous anticipation. The thought still remained that perhaps Hamilda was not there at all and that Fajha's visions were incorrect. If she was not there they would not know where to begin looking for her and their entire mission would be in vain.

Atakos looked around him at the forlorn faces of his friends. "Come on guys. If she's not here we have a lot to be thankful for. Before we started this journey we lacked confidence and we could not come together as a team as hard as we tried. Our abilities were *elementary* compared to where we are now. Imagine if we did not have this experience? Three years from now, we would be required to lead an army with little knowledge of our capabilities. Our journey has not been in vain."

Cristaden smiled at him and shook her head. "My biggest concern is not so much if she is here. It's if she is still …" Her voice trailed off, not wanted to continue.

"You mean if she's still alive?" Zimi said, completing her thoughts. "Don't be afraid of saying it. If she's dead, we have to be prepared to handle that. I think about that all the time. What if we are just too late?"

Zadeia sobbed. "I miss her. I know we should consider the possibilities but I don't want to. She *has* to be alive." Tears slid down her face and her brother reached over and put his arms around her shoulders.

Fajha was scared. It was his visions that led them to Paimonu. There was a fifty percent chance that he was wrong and the group would blame him. Even if they did not, he would blame himself. Throughout the entire journey, he had tried to scan for Hamilda time and time again. He still could not locate her as hard as he tried. When they arrived on the island, he tried again but to no avail. He could not sense her anywhere on Paimonu. The closer they got to the caves, the more apprehensive he felt about trying to locate her again. It would be a great disappointment if he could not find her, as it would be for all of them.

"Oh don't worry about it, guys," Atakos said, trying to reassure them, "Everything will be alright. You'll see." He had trust in Fajha's visions. He had faith that Hamilda was where he said she would be. If she was alive, he wondered what she had been enduring for the past couple of weeks and if she would ever be able to recover from it. They all missed her. She was their teacher and, in a way, like their mother. It would be unbearable if anything horrible happened to her. But what if it *was* too late? What if she *was* already dead? Captives without a ransom are well known to keep their victims for only a short time and then get rid of them.

"Ransom," Atakos suddenly thought out loud. As his mind began to process what he was thinking, his chest tightened and he felt like he couldn't breathe. "I just thought of something. You know how Hamilda was captured but her captors did not ask the school or the army for any ransom?"

"Yeah?" Fajha said. "What about it?"

"What if we *are* the ransom?"

The teens stopped dead in their tracks. They couldn't believe it never occurred to them.

"Ransom?" Cristaden said.

Atakos turned to face his friends. "You know how our ancestors have fought hard to keep our race a secret because, in the past, people attempted to capture Dokamis to use them to take over planets? What if someone found out about us? What if they are waiting for us right now in those caves and we are headed into a trap?"

The air of anticipation among the group made a drastic change to fear.

Fajha frowned. "But what about my visions?"

"Your visions may have nothing to do with her captors," Cristaden said.

"But they could have made Hamilda send those visions to you so we would come here," Zimi said.

"No," Fajha said defiantly. "I don't believe it. My visions came to me when I was meditating. They weren't *sent* to me. And if they were, why wouldn't Hamilda tell me it's a trap? Her captors would not know what she was sending."

"You know we could just be getting all worked up for no reason," Cristaden said. "It's simple. Someone she may have encountered in her lifetime captured her because they were jealous or obsessed with her. It is very easy to find out she is a teacher at Lochenby. That's what I think happened."

"That's what you would *like* to think happened," Zimi said. "But something tells me that's not the case."

"Oh come on you guys!" Atakos said. "We can stand here and contemplate this until fish fly but the fact still remains. We have to rescue Hamilda regardless of the situation. If they know we are coming, we fight. If they don't know we are coming, we *fight*. What we have to do is prepare ourselves for *anything*."

Fajha agreed. "We have to fight regardless of any situation."

"Just prepare yourself for anything and stay close together. We will use our senses to the best of our ability to detect what is waiting for us and we'll give them a *tough* fight."

"Yeah!" Zimi cried and then looked around sheepishly at the villagers that stopped to stare at him.

The friends smiled, waved at the people around them, and continued walking.

"These people definitely think we're crazy," Fajha said, pushing his glasses back up his nose.

The petals from the flowering trees rained down on them each time the wind blew. Looking over the side of the volcano, the five friends could see the green valley below and the blue-green sea in the distance beyond the trees of the forest. They began to understand why Sanei wanted to stay after she visited. It was a beautiful tropical island and the population was equally charming.

Putting their arms across each other's shoulders, they braced themselves for what they were about to encounter. Walking around a bend in the road, they saw an amazing sight before them. The breathtaking view of the rest of the island was a vast green forest with orange and red flowers carpeting the canopy. At first they did not see the ancient caves but, upon further inspection, they spotted them not to far away from the base of the mountain. There were three openings on the top of a small hill with one of them being considerably larger than the rest.

"They look like the cave in my visions," Fajha said. "The only difference is that I never recalled seeing the other two, smaller openings."

Atakos shuddered at the thought of entering such a dark and foreboding place. "Fajha? Do you think you can scan for her again?"

Fajha's heart skipped a beat. It was the one thing that terrified him but he had to try again. This time, he took a few deep breaths to relax his muscles. Maybe if he wasn't so tense, his location ability might work better. Raising his feet off the ground, he gave himself the feeling of flying. He closed his eyes and imagined himself flying around the canopy of the rainforest, searching for Hamilda. In his mind's eye, he suddenly felt her presence. He opened his eyes and practically fell back to the ground with excitement.

"I felt her presence," he said, pointing to the caves. "She's in there!"

"That's great!" Zadeia cried.

"Did you sense anything else?" Atakos asked. "Like who she's with?"

"If I don't know who I'm looking for, I can't locate them. All I could focus on is the aura that surrounds her."

"Well?" Zimi said.

Fajha did a search again. A few minutes later, he finally spoke. "She's deep in the caves and…surrounded by *a lot* of evil."

CHAPTER 42

Most of King Tholenod's soldiers took a step back when the dusty, feeble, old man opened his eyes and sat up on his throne, casting a sinister look at all who joined him in his isolated cave. Aillios stood his ground which made the old man give him a hard stare before returning his focus on the man standing in front of him, King Tholenod.

"You have awoken me from a deep slumber," the old man said in a low raspy voice. "Why have you come here?" His knuckles turned white as he gripped the armrests of his golden throne in anger. "Speak quickly. I lack patience for dimwitted *fools*."

Menyilh nervously stepped forward to give a proper introduction for his king. "Before you stands King Thol—"

He was interrupted by a wave of a hand from the old man to silence him. "Yes, yes. You are the king of that retched land called Mituwa. I have known for some time you were eventually going to come here, I just did not know when. You see, my senses are not like they used to be for I have been laying here since long before you were even born. Before you ruled, I was king of all these lands. My soldiers would not have cowered in fright as yours do now. Times have changed greatly. This disgusting world has changed for the worse." The old man shifted annoyingly on his throne to get a better look at King Tholenod. "What brings you here?"

"It has come to my attention that you used to be a great wizard in these parts—"

"Used to be!" The old man's voice echoed in the great hall. "Do you have any idea who I AM?" he shouted, his face turning red.

"Well, yes, I—"

"You, who call yourself King of the *People*. You parade around like you have all the power in the world. What power do you have that you seek *my* help?"

"My lord," King Tholenod bowed down before the old man.

Aillios was shocked. Never in his life has his father ever bowed to anyone. He was always the one making everyone bow to *him*. Aillios thought he would never see the day.

"I have come to seek your guidance and ultimately your help. I plan to take over Omordion and, although I have a great army, it would take much more than my army to defeat those western ingrates. I need your help."

So that's what his father was up to. Aillios should have known. Why else would his father travel this far to come to a desolate place like this dead forest if not to convince some old wizard to help him? How many more alliances will his father form to finish what he started?

The old man rubbed his chin as dust particles drifted off into the air from his raised arm. "Is that so?"

King Tholenod bowed his head once more. "Yes."

The old man leaned forward. "I have sat on this throne for hundreds of years feeling nothing but hatred for this world and what it has become. I want nothing more than to rid this world of its inhabitants. But I have grown old. These years have taken its toll on me. For me to rise out of my throne now, it would only be for a really good reason."

Aillios frowned at the old man. He had to be senile for saying he had been on his throne for hundreds of years. He seemed very ancient indeed but he concluded that the old man was exaggerating and his mind was slipping drastically.

"I assure you, you will not regret it," his father said. "With your help, we could rule this planet and turn all the freemen into our slaves."

The old man peered at him. "There is much you don't know about this planet." The side of his mouth curled up in an awkward, evil grin.

"I will need your guidance."

The old man nodded at the king and gazed around the room at his terrified soldiers. "Yes, if this planet will be brought to its knees you will need my help." With layers of dust falling and swirling all around him, he stood up. The robe he wore was long and faded black with a rope tied around his middle. He descended from his throne and made his way to the wall on their left and pressed a button that made the wall lower, revealing a very large ancient map of Omordion. The map showed the outline of the continents that still existed but all of them had different names. In the very middle was the word *Oeua*. Surrounding that word were mountains, plains, rivers and pictures of various things that resembled demons.

Aillios' jaw tightened as he looked over the yellowed, evil map. Throughout all of his lessons growing up, he had never seen one like it before. It must have been hundreds of years old, maybe even over a thousand. He wondered how the old man could have acquired it.

"I am sure you are not aware of the many secrets this planet holds but how could you?" the old man said. "These are very well kept secrets that even the leaders of this planet are not aware of."

"What do you mean?" King Tholenod asked. "What kind of *secrets?*"

"In due time, you will come to know of them. Right now the most important thing is to eliminate obstacles in your way."

The old man pointed to the area on the map that was far northeast from where they stood, across a wide ocean. It was a tiny island with the name *Koelo Mok* written across it.

"Volcano Island," the old man said. "Known today as Paimonu. The island that sits directly in the middle of Eastern and Western Omordion."

"Yes, I've heard of it," Tholenod said, frowning. "I heard that the people on that island worship the volcano they call Sremati."

"The Sremati worshipers are not your concern. What should concern you are the new visitors to that island. Five teenagers. Descendants of a great race of people who came to this planet three hundred years ago."

"A great race of …?" Tholenod walked closer to the map to get a better look at it.

The wizard sighed deeply. "In Western Omordion lives a race of people who call themselves the Dokami. They have been on this planet for three hundred years. They have extraordinary powers but they restrain it so no one would come to know of them. They seem to think if evil people were to find out about their power, they would be taken captive and used to take over the world."

Dokami? Extraordinary powers? Aillios could not believe his father was buying into the old man's tales. How could such an extraordinary race of people live on Omordion for hundreds of years and remain undiscovered? It all sounded very ludicrous to him.

"I have never heard of such a thing," King Tholenod said.

"Of course not," the old man growled. "No one knew of them until about ten years ago when the Western Army got a hold of five of their children and began training them to fight *you*."

Tholenod stepped back from the force of the old man's words. He turned to look at Menyilh with sheer anger. It was his assistant's job to find out the plans of the Western Army but the information that was given to him did not include what the old man had just mentioned. He was furious.

Menyilh could only apologize and ensure the king that there was no way he could have discovered what those plans were.

Aillios did not know whether or not he should believe what the old man was saying but he could see that his father was taking in all the information given to him with careful consideration.

"What should I do?" King Tholenod asked. "Should I try and capture them and use them to take over the planet?"

"NO!" the old man shouted. He extended his hand and stepped forward, grabbing Tholenod by the shoulder, surprising everyone in the hall. "You should kill them. Kill them as soon as you get your *hands* on them. Kill them while they are not powerful enough to defeat your army."

King Tholenod smirked. "Five teenagers could defeat my army? I don't believe it."

"Believe it. Or you will meet your end."

"But how do I find these teenagers? How do I know who they are if I see them?"

The old man rubbed his chin. "I will aid you in your search."

Aillios looked at his father, then to the old man, and then back to his father again. He wanted to know why the old man was so interested in helping his father do such a heinous act. He seemed like he had nothing to gain by helping his father. Since he knew who Tholenod was and that he would eventually come to see him, he must obviously know what kind of person he was. Aillios' father did not take too kindly to alliances of any sort. He always had a dream to rule the entire planet solely and to his own accord. Partnering up with the old man meant that he would have to follow his direction, which is something Tholenod rarely did.

The old man must have something up his sleeve and he wanted to know what it was.

Aillios brought his gaze back to the old man and was taken aback by him staring at him rather fiercely. His temples drew into a frown and he blinked several times before returning his glare to the king.

"That is excellent," Tholenod said, rubbing his hands together. "With our alliance, we will surely overthrow all the rulers of this planet." He let out a hearty laugh that was cut short when he thought of what their next move was going to be. "When should we depart for Paimonu?"

"As soon as possible."

"Alright. I shall go prepare my soldiers for our new destination." Tholenod nodded at him and turned to walk away.

"Oh and by the way," the old man said, stopping the king in his tracks. "I have another important thing to tell you. One that has to be taken care of before our departure."

"What is it?" Tholenod turned around to face him.

"It is in regards to your *son*."

Aillios' heart beat hard in his chest. The blood drained from his face. *What could he possibly know about me?*

"My son?" Tholenod frowned.

The old man snickered. "Your own son has turned against you. He will one day ignite a series of events that will lead to your death."

What?! Aillios did not like the direction the old man was headed.

Tholenod was furious. "I know my son pities the slaves but I can never accept that he would kill me, indirectly or directly. I don't believe you."

Aillios began sweating profusely. His hands felt clammy and his legs began to shake. It took every ounce of control he had not to lash out at the old man.

"Why don't you ask him then?" The old man lifted his hand and pointed *right at Aillios*. "He's standing right there," he said with a smirk.

At first Tholenod looked around Aillios, appearing very confused.

Suddenly, Aillios began to feel a cooling sensation move throughout his body. It seemed as if the old man was causing it but he was not sure how. But then, little by little, his worst fears were realized as his pale complexion began to change, replaced by his familiar tanned skin. He knew without even looking at a mirror that his hair was black and curly again and his eyes had returned to a bright blue. The disguise given by Asmis was no more.

"Blasphemy," his father cried out. His face turned red with anger. "Traitor!"

The old man was a true wizard after all.

"Father, I—" Aillios took a few steps forward to explain himself but his father pointed at him in a fit of anger, stopping him dead in his tracks.

"Seize him!" Tholenod said.

The seven other soldiers in the hall charged at him immediately.

Aillios had little time to react. He kicked one soldier back and elbowed another in the face. He then swung his leg behind another soldier's knees, causing him to trip and fall flat on his back. Another soldier tried to punch him in the face but Aillios blocked it and then punched him instead. The soldier went reeling back with the shock of the blow and knocked into another soldier. He then grabbed one soldier and threw him into the last incoming soldier. While the soldiers took a moment to recover from their shock, Aillios ran towards the exit.

"After him," he heard his father shout. "Do not let him get away. Kill him if necessary!"

Aillios' heart dropped but then he became full of rage. His father was sick. The need for power had turned him into a demon. There was no saving him from his sickness. Perhaps the old man was right about Tholenod's imminent death. The world would be a much better place without a murderous and treacherous king.

As Aillios ran, he could hear the footfall of the seven soldiers behind him. He did not have to look back to know that they were all intent on killing him. Evil laughter could be heard from the old wizard and it brought chills down his back.

With his heart beating fast, Aillios ran through the dark tunnel that led to the entrance of the cave. He could not help thinking that he could possibly die before leaving the dead forest. He would not be able to help the slaves anymore. Even if he did not die, he could never go back. He made a quick vow to stay alive so he could bring down his father's reign.

After punching the two soldiers waiting at the entrance of the cave, temporarily confusing them, Aillios saw the other ten soldiers, including the captain, waiting at the edge of the crater. They were still unaware of the situation and were laughing with each other, barely 'looking out' as his father had commanded. The shouts of the soldiers behind him changed all that and they became on high alert.

Aillios had to think fast.

There was no other way to go. If he had to get out of the forest alive, he would need Thashmar. There was no place to hide in the dead forest because, without any leaves or bushes, the colors of his suit of armor and even his underclothes, could easily be seen. He made a last minute decision to climb down the mountain and face the ten soldiers waiting on the other side.

Aillios grabbed a dead tree branch and swung himself over to the side of the mountain. He then began to climb down carefully but with increasing speed as the soldiers behind him began to climb down as well. Upon reaching the bottom, he practically crawled up the crater, at times tripping over some loose rocks.

Climbing over the edge, Aillios was met by the other ten soldiers. They were surprised he was there but were ready to fight with their weapons drawn.

Aillios stepped forward and prepared himself to fight. But before he could do anything, the other nine soldiers climbed up behind him.

He was surrounded.

One of the soldiers from the cave stepped forward. "We have orders from the king. Do not let him leave the forest *alive*."

The captain growled. "Then we shall carry out his orders."

CHAPTER 43

The entrance to the black caves loomed in front of the five friends. It was uninviting and smelled of earth mingled with sulfur from the volcano. Rain had begun to fall all around them, enveloping them with a steady mist rising from the ground. The music on the volcano behind them had ceased as the townsfolk rushed back into their homes and found shelter from the rain.

"It looks so scary," Cristaden said, looking at entrance of the largest, foreboding cave. She had the hood of her green cloak pulled down over her head, almost covering her eyes. "Do we have to go in there?"

"We have no choice," Atakos said, taking off his hood to get a better look at the cave.

Zadeia blinked the rain out of her eyelashes. "Fajha, can you get a read on her?"

Fajha tried to wipe his glasses on his cloak but to no avail, considering the cloak was soaking wet. He then gave up and put his foggy glasses back on his face and brought down his hood to cover his head more efficiently. "I can still sense her physical being. She's here and she is very much alive."

"Can we press on?" Zimi asked. "If we don't get going, we are going to be swimming in this."

"Zadeia?" Atakos asked. "Will you do the honors?"

"My pleasure," she said. The cave entrance was then illuminated with a fireball in her hand. She moved forward, ahead of her friends, while everyone followed closely behind her, trying hard not to fall on the slippery, wet ground.

The group came to a halt when they were faced with two tunnels to choose from.

"Which way, Fajha?" Zadeia asked.

Fajha shut his eyes and tried to focus. Because his attention directed to the left tunnel, he suggested they take it, hoping he was right.

Zadeia's fireball burnt out and for a moment they were in complete darkness until she lit another one.

"Which way?" Zadeia asked Fajha when they were faced with two more tunnels.

Fajha closed his eyes and focused on trying to find Hamilda. He pointed to the right tunnel. "This way," he said.

Following closely behind Zadeia, they proceeded to follow the tunnel. Spider webs were everywhere and they had to break through them to get by.

"Are you sure she's down here?" Atakos said. "It seems like no one has been down this tunnel for years."

Fajha began to doubt himself once more. During the previous summer, he practiced finding his sister so much that, by the start of the school year, he felt like he was ready. When he went to Lochenby, he would often try to find random people and he was always accurate. This was the first time he had to locate someone from a great distance. He continued to doubt himself even though he had been one hundred percent correct the previous times.

"Maybe they went in one of the other entrances or something," Fajha suggested, trying to reassure the others but more so to reassure himself.

"Yeah … or something …," Zimi said sarcastically while brushing a cobweb off his reddish-brown face and black hair.

"She's in here. I can feel her presence and it is only getting stronger."

"We believe you, Fajha," Cristaden said. "Don't worry about it. We'll find her."

Fajha smiled weakly while trying to think positive. He decided that he lacked confidence in himself and he left it at that. He returned his focus to finding Hamilda when the tunnel they were following split into three tunnels.

"Which way?" Zadeia asked.

Trying to concentrate on all three tunnels created more of a challenge than he anticipated. With the tunnel splitting into two, he could easily tell which tunnel was the right one because one would feel empty and the other one strongly held Hamilda's presence. The way his ability worked was like an invisible line leading to the person. With the three tunnels, the left one was empty and the other two held Hamilda's presence.

Fajha pointed to the middle and right tunnels. "Either one," he said.

"What do you mean?" Atakos said. "How do we choose which one?"

"Both of them will lead us to her," Fajha said. "I can't explain it. I just know that at the end of both of these tunnels we'll find her."

"Well, let's take the middle one," Zadeia decided. Her fireball died and they were enveloped in darkness once again until she lit another one. They proceeded down the long tunnel, steadily gaining speed until they were practically running to reach the other side. Then the tunnel opened up into a chamber. Seeing as far as the fireball would permit, they could not tell how large it was. From what they could see, the dark chamber was empty. The other tunnel they could have taken opened up to the chamber also, which confirmed Fajha's calculations.

Fajha's stomach became queasy when he realized they were standing in the same room as Hamilda. "She's here," he said, suddenly feeling the need to vomit. He would be happy if she was there but, at the same time, it did not seem likely considering they were standing in an unlit and stuffy part of the cave that barely allowed much air to breathe.

"Are you sure?" Atakos asked.

"She's very close to us."

Cristaden couldn't imagine that their teacher could be held in a place like the one they were standing in. It made her sick to her stomach, too. She decided to try and read Hamilda's thoughts to see what kind of condition she was in before rushing to her in case they were walking into a trap. As she was concentrating, she realized she was trying too hard.

Hamilda was simply not there.

"I can't get a read on her," Cristaden said. "She's not here."

"What?" Zadeia said, turning to look at her.

"What do you mean?" Fajha put his hand on her shoulder. "What do you mean, she's not *here?*"

"I tried to read her thoughts but I can't get a read on her at all." Cristaden's eyes filled up with tears. "It's as if she is not here at all."

"Are you sure about this?" Zimi asked her.

"I'm sure."

Fajha's upset stomach turned over. Cristaden was beginning to be an expert at picking up people's thoughts. How could she not be able to pick up Hamilda's?

Atakos sensed Fajha's worries. "I'm sure there's a logical explanation for this. I mean she could be—"

"Dead?" Zadeia said.

"Well, no—I mean—that's not what I meant—"

"That would be the only explanation," Zimi said.

"Please don't say that," Cristaden said.

"We knew going into this journey that we may be faced with many different possibilities. This was one of them."

Sniffles were heard coming from Zadeia. They were all scared. Throughout their journey they attempted to think positively. They half expected to find Hamilda alive and well and like her old self again but that was not reality.

The empty cave was the reality. Anyone held for a long time there would be lucky to be alive.

"We have to find out, don't we?" Zimi said, trying to bring the group back to focus. "The faster we make the discovery, the faster we could get out of this prison." He was trying to be reassuring but, as they always did, his comments came out insensitive. He was scared, though he did not want anyone to know it. He could never bring himself to show his true feelings.

"Zimi, I wish you would just …" Cristaden tried to talk but she could not find the right words to say. In a way, they all knew Zimi was right. If Hamilda was dead, it was best not to prolong their anticipation.

The group huddled in close together and waited a moment for Zadeia to light another fireball. When she was done, they started to inch forward. They were still wary of walking into a trap but they forged ahead. The fireball helped them to look around at the cave, which was larger than they initially assumed. It stretched farther than they could see and the ceiling was about fifty feet high, dripping with water, possibly leaking from the fresh rain outside.

They moved further and further into the cave. At first they did not see anything. Before they could conclude there was no one there, they noticed a pair of bright red eyes staring back at them in the suffocating darkness. The glow from Zadeia's fireball enhanced the brightness of the eyes with the rest of the cave being so dark.

"What is that?" Zadeia asked, stopping short along with the rest of the group.

"Maybe it's a bat," Atakos suggested.

"The eyes are too big to be a bat," Cristaden said. She knew it could not be an animal because she was still unable to pick up the thoughts of anything in the cave, animal or human. "It's definitely not an animal."

"Then what could it be?" Fajha asked.

"Hello?" Zimi called out. "Who's there?"

"Zimi," Zadeia whispered with panic rising in her voice. "What are you doing?"

Zimi listened to see if he got any response. Nothing. Furthermore, the eyes were not blinking. "I don't think they *are* eyes."

"What could they be?" Cristaden asked. They sure *looked* like eyes.

"Well, let's check it out," Atakos said.

The teens inched forward, holding onto each other for support. They could not see what the eyes were attached to because it was too dark. The anxiety among the group was so intense, they felt it weighing down on them as they walked.

Moving closer still, they could see a dark figure attached to the red eyes staring back at them. It appeared to be shaped like a person but it was not moving or breathing in anyway.

"I'm scared," Zadeia said, whimpering. Because she was the one holding the light, she was the closest to whatever it was they were looking at.

"Well, since Cristaden says she doesn't pick up anything alive in this room, maybe it's a statue," Atakos whispered.

"Maybe it's not," Zimi said, whispering back.

"Way to be optimistic, Zimi," Fajha whispered.

"I think we should try to call out to it once more," Atakos whispered.

"Why?" Zadeia asked. "So it could attack us faster?"

"At least if it does, we'll stop wondering whether or not it's alive." Atakos cleared his throat. "If you are alive, say something," he shouted to the figure.

The friends came to a grinding halt. They heard nothing. The figure in the middle of the room neither moved nor responded. It stood very still, almost as if it *were* a statue.

"We have to try and get closer," Atakos said. "So we can see what it is."

"Why do I have to be the one with the light?" Zadeia whined.

"Keep moving, Zadeia. It'll be okay." Zimi tried to offer some words of encouragement to his sister but he knew she was not listening to him. She was frightened along with everyone else.

They inched forward again, looking around the area of the cave they were approaching to make sure there was nothing else in the room besides the frozen figure. Seeing nothing, they steadily took a few more steps. The closer they got, the more they can pick out something that appeared to be a face on the statue.

Upon further inspection, the face became clear.

Zadeia gasped when she saw it.

They all wanted to step back but fear gripped them, causing them to remain frozen.

What they saw was truly a face of evil, perhaps the scariest face they had ever seen. The eyes were red, the eyebrows were drawn together in anger, and the mouth was turned up in a sneer.

It was the face of a monster.

Unlike the monsters they fought along their journey, the pale skin on its face appeared humanlike. The five teens could see that it was female, with long black hair pulled together behind her head. She was wearing a long black robe that covered her slender body.

Nothing could have prepared them for what they saw.

It was definitely human.

It did not take them long to realize that the evil being they were staring at was Hamilda.

CHAPTER 44

Aillios looked around at the nineteen men, determined to carry out the king's orders to kill his only son. He could not help thinking of how he had once fought alongside those very same men in battle years before. Although he did not know them personally, he still considered them to be his comrades. By the way the soldiers glared at him, it made him wonder if they would enjoy killing him, if they had always hated him.

Nevertheless, Aillios was surrounded. If he did not think quickly, the dead forest would be the last thing he saw before his eyes closed forever. Deciding he was not going down without a fight, he dashed toward one soldier. Before the soldier could strike, he punched him hard in his abdomen and yanked the sword out of his hand. He then fiercely sliced the soldier across his chest while he ran by, breaking free of the intimidating circle of men. The soldier groaned in pain and fell to the ground.

Aillios ran straight into the forest of dead trees as eighteen angry soldiers followed him in hot pursuit. He did not realize how dense the dead forest was when they initially arrived but now, as he ran, the branches of the trees were like thorns, scratching his face and pulling at his clothes. To get by, he cut down branches in his path to avoid getting scratched or stuck, which slowed him down. Listening to the footfall of the soldiers behind him, he could tell they were having trouble because their fast pace slowed as well. Seizing an opportunity to lose them, he increased his speed, swiftly cutting branches with his sword. Looking over his shoulder, he saw that they were nowhere in sight but he could still hear the angry shouts of desperation to find him. He knew if he didn't do something quickly, he may be put in a position where he had to face all of them again. Turning back around, he spotted a wide tree a few feet away in a small clearing. Ripping off a small piece of the shirt under his armor, he hung it on one of the low branches of another tree and hid behind the big tree. He then heard twigs snapping and footsteps coming closer. He knew the soldiers would stop because they could no longer hear him running through the trees.

"He has to be around here somewhere," Aillios heard the captain say.

"Look!" one soldier cried. He noticed the piece of Aillios' shirt.

"He did come by here then," the captain said. "Alright, let's split up. You six go this way and the six of you go that way. The rest of us will search this area. When you find him, do not allow him to escape. It's kill or be killed so don't hesitate. Kill him fast and efficiently and then report back to me. Now go!"

Aillios' heart was beating in his chest as he waited for the twelve soldiers to get as far away as possible.

When they were gone, he peered around the side of the wide tree and saw the closest soldier to him, walking away from the tree, unaware that he was only a few feet away.

Seizing the opportunity, Aillios ran up behind the soldier and grabbed him, thrusting his sword through his back. As the soldier fell, the other five soldiers, including the captain, heard the noise and turned quickly, preparing themselves to defend and attack.

Aillios quickly stepped in between two soldiers, facing one and allowing the other to get behind him. The eager soldiers raised their swords and brought them down, intent on slashing him. With a quick motion, Aillios circled around the soldier he was facing and grabbed his jaw from behind, snapping his neck. The other soldier unintentionally slashed the soldier in front of him down the length of his body. He was bewildered for a second so Aillios took the opportunity to thrust his sword into the stunned soldier's abdomen. He fell to the ground, barely clinging on to life.

The remaining three soldiers ran up behind Aillios.

One soldier raised his sword to attack him. Upon hearing their approach, Aillios released the head of the soldier he was holding and stepped out with his right foot, bringing his left knee down to the forest floor. Taking his sword, he blocked the strike from above, pivoted on his right foot and, while getting up, cut off the soldier's right leg above the knee.

The soldier howled in pain and fell as the captain came from behind him, attempting to drive his sword into Aillios. Aillios took his right arm and blocked the attack, which proved to be the wrong move because he allowed to captain to punch him in the face with his other fist and kick him hard in the abdomen, causing him to drop his sword.

The captain laughed as he took a couple of steps toward Aillios and lifted his sword above his head with both hands. Aillios quickly recovered and grabbed the captain's forearm and stepped out with his right leg. Bending down, he pivoted his right hip, flipping the captain onto his back, twisting the captain's arm. Still holding on to the captain's forearm, he raised his right leg and stomped on his chest, grabbing the sword from his twisted hand. As the captain hollered in agonizing pain, the last soldier ran up to Aillios. He turned and thrust the sword into the soldier's lower abdomen and brought the sword up, slicing intestines and major organs along the way.

The soldier died instantly.

Aillios turned to the captain under his foot and scowled at him. "I will let you live but when you come around, you tell my *father* that I will not be killed. What the wizard said was wrong. I could never kill him because I am not *like* him."

The captain chuckled, exposing blood-coated teeth. "You cannot escape. Wherever you go, we'll find you. We will complete the task your father couldn't bring himself to do on the day you were born." He then spat blood onto Aillios' face.

Furious, Aillios' jaw tightened and he wiped the blood off his face with the back of his hand. "I change my mind," he said before plunging the sword into the captain's chest. The captain's eyes opened wide in surprise before blood poured out of his mouth.

Aillios heard shouts and footsteps running through the forest headed his way. He broke out into a run, going back the way he came, towards the wizard's mountain. Following the path of broken branches all the way back to the clearing, he knew he had to keep moving. They were catching up to him fast.

"There he is!" he heard a soldier cry out from behind him.

Running as fast as he could to the horses, he quickly untied Thashmar who whinnied and shook his head. Aillios took one glance at the grisly mountain and a shudder ran through his body as he thought of his hardhearted father. Turning back to see the soldiers break out of the trees one by one, he mounted his horse. "Ya!" he cried. Thashmar ran towards the approaching soldiers, allowing Aillios an advantage to cut down anyone that came too close. Two soldiers went down and the rest of them avoided his sword as he rode by.

"Get him!" one soldier shouted as they ran for their horses. "Before he gets away!"

Aillios guided Thashmar through the trees, not sure of which direction he was going. All he knew was that he had to get out of the lifeless forest and away from the murderous soldiers chasing him as fast as he could. Deep down, he knew what the captain said was true. He was in the heart of Effit, a country allied with the very man who wants his capture or death. All the countries that surrounded the dead forest were on his father's side. His father would need only to call him a traitor and every soldier in Mituwa, Feim, Effit and Srepas would be after him.

There was nowhere to go, nowhere to hide.

Without a disguise like the one given to him by Asmis, it would take him a *year* to get to the Western side, if he could get there at all without being caught. Knowing his father, his picture would be plastered on every building in every town. There would be a huge reward for his capture until he was found. The poor enslaved people would be happy to kill the king's son for a reward they would never receive. He did not know where to go. He could not even cross the river into Mituwa without being spotted.

Aillios broke through the line of lifeless trees into the more familiar plush and green forest. Veering off to the right, he was able to lose the ten soldiers behind him for a few moments until they picked up his trail once again. They were far behind him but catching up fast. He would have to find somewhere to hide in the forest until he was able to escape. His only worry now was how he was going to lose ten soldiers, knowing they would search the forest for days to find him.

Aillios heard rushing water and guided Thashmar towards the sound. What he found was a deep ravine. Thinking there was no other place to hide, he guided Thashmar down a steep, narrow path into the ravine, praying the whole time that the horse would not lose his footing and send them both crashing into the water below. Finding an area large enough to hold them both, he dismounted the horse and used his body to press him against the rocks. Thashmar whinnied in frustration but Aillios rubbed his head and comforted him until he was quiet.

The thundering sound of galloping horses headed straight for the ravine.

"Do you think he went down there?"

"It's too steep."

"You couldn't get a horse down there."

"Alright, let's split up then," a soldier said, taking charge of the situation. "The three of you find a way to get down there and the three of you should try to get to the other side. You two go right and we'll go left. We'll have this place surrounded and he will have no place to go." With that decision, they separated, carrying out their plan to trap the prince.

Knowing he could not stay where he was because he would eventually be seen, Aillios had to get out of the ravine. He mounted Thashmar and went further down until he came to a place that was wide enough to turn the horse. With Thashmar turned around, he made his way back up the narrow path to the top of the ravine. He then rode in the direction of the two soldiers sent to trap him. Following the ravine, he eventually saw them. They heard his approach and turned to face him.

"He's over—" one soldier tried to cry out as Aillios galloped towards them. He removed a small dagger from his belt and flung it at the soldier, getting him right between the eyes. The other soldier did not have time to react before Aillios cut him with his sword as he rode by. Before the two soldiers had a chance to fall off their horses, he was gone, making his way through the forest and away from the ravine. He encouraged Thashmar to go faster, refusing to stop, knowing that the remaining eight soldiers would follow his trail until he was found.

For hours, Aillios rode this way and that, tiring his poor horse until he finally felt like the other soldiers were too far away to catch up to him. The sun was beginning to set, making it harder for the soldiers to find him in the darkening forest. He decided to stop and dismounted Thashmar, patting the horse on his head.

"Good boy," Aillios said to the panting horse. "I'm so sorry you had to go through that." He pitied the animal and suddenly felt a connection with him. As it stood, Thashmar was the only friend he had left.

As he removed his armor and hid them at the base of a hollow tree, Aillios suddenly felt alone in the world. Thinking back to the twenty-three years he spent growing up in Mituwa, the thought occurred to him that he would never be able to return to the place he called home again. He could no longer help the tortured slaves he grew to care for so much. His eagerness to help rid Eastern Omordion of slavery had come to a close. Now he was useless. All of his hopes and dreams were no more.

A soft whinny from Thashmar brought Aillios back to reality. "What is it Thashmar?" On edge, he looked up into the darkening forest, putting his hand on his sword. He half-expected to see soldiers coming from behind the trees. Instead he saw a tiny, bright light heading straight towards him.

A firefly? As it got closer, Aillios could see that it was too big to be a firefly. "No, it can't be. What is that?" The light was about the size of his hand and burning too brightly to be a bug of any kind. It circled in front of him slowly, doing a hypnotizing dance that captivated him. It came close to his face and that was when he could make out a face, arms and legs.

"Whoa!" Aillios cried and fell backwards, trying to get away from the creature. He let out the breath he was holding in a series of coughs. *I'm going crazy*, he thought. But there was no mistaking the light in front of him, doing the weird dance. "A demon?" he asked himself out loud, not expecting to get a response back from the strange, bright light.

Instantly the light grew to human size and a beautiful girl with flowing red hair and bright purple eyes stood in front of him. She wore a long, shimmering white dress and she was engulfed in a white light, blinding him for a moment until it tapered off, leaving a steady glow around her. "Not exactly," she responded.

Aillios stood up slowly, then squeezed his eyes closed and shook his head. When he reopened his eyes, she was still there.

"I'm not a hallucination," the beautiful girl said. "And you're not dreaming." She smiled at him and reached her hand out to introduce herself. "My name is Kapimia."

Aillios took a step back, looking her up and down. He had never been afraid of anything in his entire lifetime. With all the strangeness he encountered since he left the castle, he was terrified.

Kapimia retracted her hand and shook her head. "Don't be afraid. I won't hurt you."

"What are you?"

Kapimia smiled once more. "I'm a fairy."

"Fairies don't *exist*."

"Oh but we do, Aillios."

"How do you know my name?"

"My mother told me I would find you here."

"Your mother?" Aillios asked and then a thought occurred to him. "Are you related to that dead witch Asmis?"

"*Asmis?*" Kapimia shook her head and laughed. "Oh gosh no. My mother is Queen Lhainna of Sheidem Forest. She has sent me here to rescue you and to inform you that we can aide you in your quest to free your people."

Aillios searched her face. "How?"

"I have to get you to Paimonu. Five teenagers are there who can—"

"Five teenagers?" Aillios frowned. "In Paimonu?" His jaw tightened. "The wizard sent you here, didn't he? I understand now. This is some kind of trick."

"Wizard?" Kapimia grimaced. "What wizard?"

"You can tell him I won't go down without a fight." He drew his sword with fury in his eyes.

"Whoa." Kapimia waved her arms. "Put the sword down. Please, Aillios, tell me. What wizard?"

"The old wizard in the mountain. He had an old map. He referred to Paimonu as Koelo Mok. He told my father to go there to kill five teenagers who are a threat to him."

"Koelo Mok?" Kapimia said. "He must be very old ..." She stared hard into Aillios' blue eyes and all the color slowly drained from her face and her bright glow faded to a dull gray. "Brulok," she said, her eyes widening with fear.

Upon seeing her reaction, Aillios knew she had nothing to do with the wizard. "Who's Brulok?" he asked her, putting his sword down.

Kapimia desperately searched his face. "Describe him to me," she pleaded, taking a few steps towards him.

Aillios tried remembering the details of the old man. "He had a long, gray beard, gray hair and gray eyes. He wore a faded black robe. Very dark man." Aillios began to feel concerned. For a magical creature to fear him, perhaps the old wizard in the mountain was as powerful as he claimed to be.

"He must have grown very old." Kapimia suddenly became frantic. "We must go. They are in terrible danger!"

"Where are we going?" Aillios asked her, his heart racing with anticipation.

"To Paimonu, of course."

"You must know that, pretty soon, this entire region will be looking for me. My father has formed an alliance with that wizard and has ordered my death. He fears that I will eventually kill him."

She placed her hand on his arm. "That's awful. I'm sorry to hear about your father. Brulok is an evil, evil man. I don't know why he's so evil but I know we are not safe here. We must go now before the spell my mother placed on me wears off and I am detected."

"But I already told you, I cannot leave this forest without being seen."

"Mount your horse," Kapimia said, ignoring him. "He's really worn out from the run you just gave him."

"Oh really? And how do you know that?"

"He told me, of course. And he also says you are a kind and gentle man."

Aillios frowned at her and mounted Thashmar. "You can talk to animals?"

Kapimia smiled while removing the rope that tied her white dress together. "Of course." She gave Aillios one end of the rope and brought the other end under the horse and to the other side. She then took the rope from him and tied it. For some reason, it seemed much longer than it initially did.

"Are you ready?" Kapimia asked Aillios.

"Ready for what?" he asked her, confused about what she was doing.

"Hold on to Thashmar's reigns and lean forward," Kapimia instructed him. When he did as he was told, she turned back into her original size and grabbed the rope, lifting the horse off the ground.

"Whoa!" Aillios cried out, gripping tighter to Thashmar's neck. It was hard to imagine a thin rope could hold a man and a horse as steady as it did.

"Hold on tight," Kapimia said in a tiny voice.

Thashmar was lifted higher until they were above the trees. Then they started to head away from the setting sun. Aillios never envisioned that he would ever escape his father's clutches, especially not with the help of a fairy. In fact, it was not until they saw the Srepan Ocean, which separated Eastern and Western Omordion, that he finally felt freed.

CHAPTER 45

"Hamilda!" Zadeia said, taking a step forward. Hamilda did not respond or move. She was frozen like a statue with hideous red eyes and a freakish grin.

Atakos grabbed Zadeia's arm and held her back. "No," he said.

"But it's Hamilda. We've come all this—"

"I still can't read her," Cristaden said, interrupting Zadeia. "The person standing there is *not* Hamilda."

"That's impossible. It looks just like her."

"Zadeia, get a hold of yourself," Zimi said. "She's standing here in a dark cave with no light. Look at her eyes! Don't you think there's something *wrong* with her?"

Zadeia took a moment to look around the cave and then brought her eyes back to Hamilda and gasped. How could she be so blind to what her friends clearly observed? She nodded and shied back, shrinking in with them once again. Illuminated by her fireball, Zadeia's eyes were glowing with terror.

"Do you think she's under some kind of spell?" Fajha said.

"Magic or not, this is scary," Atakos said. "I wonder if she could even hear what we're saying."

"If her soul is not in her body then it's possible she can't hear us."

"Wouldn't you be dead if your soul was not in your body?" Zadeia asked.

Fajha shook his head. "Her soul could be lost in a dream, like yours was back in the desert. In order for that to happen, you usually have to be lying down or sleeping. She wouldn't be just standing like that."

"Then what's wrong with her?" Zimi asked.

"There's only one way to find out," Atakos said. He bravely took a step forward to walk towards Hamilda. The others tried to stop him but he waved a hand at them to assure them that he will be okay. He then took several steps towards Hamilda and stopped about two feet away from her. Her eyes were expressionless, showing no signs of life. Her skin seemed hard and pale as if she was made out of wax. He wanted to touch her, to see if her body felt as cold as she looked, but he was too afraid to do so. Instead he called her name.

After receiving no response, Atakos waved his hand in front of her face.

No reaction.

"Hamilda," Atakos said again, hoping to get something, *anything*, but was disappointed once again. Concluding that Hamilda's body was just an empty shell, he was about to turn away when her eyes shifted and looked directly at him.

"Aah!" Atakos screamed. He backed up so fast, he crashed into Zadeia.

"What happened?" Fajha asked. He didn't have to wait for his reply because, much to the shock of the teens, Hamilda began to speak.

"Hamilda is gone," she said in an unrecognizable voice. It was deep and rough. Nothing compared to the soft, angelic voice of their teacher. She took a menacing step forward, forcing them to take a step back. The way she moved was unnatural, more mechanic-like than fluid.

Frightened, Atakos' voice quivered. "What do you mean 'she's gone'?"

Just then Zadeia's fireball went out and they were blanketed in complete darkness. The friends grew even more frightened as she struggled to make another one. Her nerves were so shocked, she could not get it right. Before Zadeia could manage to light another one, however, the room was filled with light as torches, strategically placed on the cave walls, lit up simultaneously.

Hamilda was suddenly standing *very* close to them.

The five friends backed up so fast, they almost crashed into the wall behind them. Hamilda cocked her head but did not change her horrid expression. It was obvious she lit the fires. "Hamilda is no longer here," she said. "Her spirit is no more."

"I don't understand," Zadeia said with tears in her eyes.

Cristaden spoke in a small voice. "What she's saying is true. Her spirit is not here. What we see here is not Hamilda."

"But how?"

With red eyes gleaming in the light of the torches, the evil woman scowled. "She wasn't allowed to carry on Jogesh's legacy before he died. She couldn't have children because of her duty to teach you. Her hatred toward you children and her will to end her life led her to me. I am her *hate*. Once a mere reflection in her mirror, she allowed me to take over, possessing her completely."

"That's impossible," Cristaden said. "Dokamis are gentle people who prefer to live in peace. You cannot be a part of her."

"Oh but now I am she. When Dokamis become filled with rage, their rage can become its own entity and engulf them completely if they allow it. Other times, they can internally destroy themselves before that even happens." Her wicked smile curled up even more. "She did not tell you that did she?"

"Well where is she now?" Zadeia asked.

"She's gone! She's no longer coming back. I am here to carry out her final wishes."

"And what would that be?" Fajha said, balling his hands into fists to keep calm.

"To kill you. To prevent you from stopping me. The people of Omordion will die for what they did to Hamilda."

Atakos' initial fear was realized. They *were* set up. A trap set by Hamilda herself, or something possessing her mind. She was never kidnapped in the first place.

"Hamilda would never request such a thing," Zadeia said, her voice rising until she was practically shouting. "You're lying!"

"I do not lie," Evil Hamilda simply said. "I only do what I am told."

"How did you know we would come here?" Atakos asked.

"It was too easy." She laughed crazily and pointed right at Fajha. "When he meditated in the stables, Hamilda saw his vision. She did not understand it then but when I possessed her, I knew it was a vision of the future. I knew he would have the vision again and know where the caves were because of his education. I just had to steer you in the right direction when you reached the volcano. The inhabitants of this forsaken place would not have led you here. So I grew impatient."

Cristaden suddenly remembered the woman who gave them directions while the townspeople went into their homes to pray. "You were … Sanei," she said.

Evil Hamilda only smiled.

"Olshem was right," Atakos said. "He told us to beware of the being with the many faces."

Evil Hamilda laughed again. "That old man still has some power I see. After all these years, hidden under a heavy cloak, he can still manage, hunh? He doesn't even remember his own name. How ironic. Osmatu will be first. They are all going to die."

"We won't allow this!" Zadeia screamed.

Evil Hamilda eerily smiled. "Your destiny has already been sealed. You cannot beat me. Hamilda told me how *weak* you are. You might as well give up and don't waste my time."

The five teens were hurt by her words. They recalled the last day they practiced with Hamilda and how their performance was lousy because of their lack of confidence.

This made them very upset.

"We will never surrender to you," Fajha firmly stated.

"Oh?" Evil Hamilda looked down at him. "And just how are you going to stop me?"

Although Atakos did not want to hurt Hamilda, he couldn't stand by and wait until she killed him and his friends. "If innocent lives on this planet are in danger, we will fight to protect them."

Evil Hamilda's smile turned into a mean scowl and her eyes flashed red with anger. "Let's not waste any more time then." With nostrils flaring, she balled her hands into fists. "I have a world to destroy."

Intent on just knocking Evil Hamilda down in hopes of capturing her, Atakos used the ability he had to blow things up against her, but on a smaller scale, only sending a powerful burst of energy her way. Before it could reach her, she deflected it. The energy returned to him, knocking him flat on his back.

Fajha attempted to do the same thing but ended up on his back also.

Standing up, the two friends, along with Cristaden, tried to hit her one right after the other, hoping she would not have the chance to deflect the second or third attack. Without so much as moving, the energy bursts deflected off of Evil Hamilda, who stood before them smiling.

The three friends ended up on their backs.

"This isn't working," Cristaden whispered to Atakos.

"Let's wait until she attacks," Atakos whispered back. He stood up, helped his friends to their feet, and turned to face the evil woman, who had begun pacing the floor back and forth.

Evil Hamilda suddenly stopped, realizing they were waiting for her to attack. To humor them, she went in for the attack but, before she could execute it, Atakos sent a burst of energy her way. She staggered slightly and then laughed. "Is that all you have?" she asked him.

"Zadeia," Atakos said, quickly turning to his friend.

Zadeia nodded and stepped forward. She then threw two fireballs at Evil Hamilda, who *absorbed* them and then retracted the fireballs back at her. "Aah!" Zadeia screamed. Smoke was rising from the top of her head but she was not burned. Before she could retaliate, she was met with a series of energy blows from Evil Hamilda and thrown hard on her back. Her head hit the ground with a sickening crack and her friends could see blood pouring from the back of her head onto the cave floor.

"Zadeia!" Cristaden screamed. With the boys stepping in front of them to block any attacks, she knelt down to immediately heal Zadeia before she died. She was shocked that Hamilda, possessed or not, would try to kill them.

"I cannot believe how weak you truly are," the evil woman taunted them. "This is going to be very easy." She sent a powerful burst of energy at the boys, sending them crashing into Cristaden and the almost healed Zadeia. Zimi rolled over Cristaden's bent back and landed on his head. Atakos landed on his elbow and hollered in pain as he heard and felt it break. When Fajha was hit with the blow from Hamilda, he levitated off the ground and slid back, only tripping over Zadeia's legs.

Cristaden hurriedly finished up with Zadeia and quickly healed Zimi. She was in the process of healing Atakos when she heard Evil Hamilda laugh again. She looked back at her, full of silent rage.

"How pathetic," Evil Hamilda said. "Look at what you have to rely on in order to fight me." Prepared to throw an attack Cristaden's way, she was met with an ice attack from Zimi. Her quick reflexes deflected the ice, which he blocked with an ice shield he quickly created.

Zimi was trying to buy time until his friends were healed. As Cristaden finished healing Atakos, he overheard him discussing a strategy with the others behind him and he backed up to listen.

"This is what we'll do," Atakos said. "We'll stand firm until she attacks. Then we'll scatter. She can't chase all of us so I'll run fast and attack her from behind." He grabbed Cristaden's hand, startling her in the process. "Cristaden. You *have* to stop healing. I know you are following your instincts but we need you to fight."

Cristaden looked at him with tears in her eyes. "I know, but—"

"We'll just have to be more careful not to get seriously injured." He winked at her and smiled. "We'll be okay."

Cristaden smiled back at Atakos as the five friends stood up.

Impatient with the progress of the fight, Evil Hamilda offered a new attack. With electricity building up in her hands, she sent lightning their way. The teens were so bewildered, for a moment they forgot their plan.

"Run!" Atakos yelled and started running. But it was too late. Evil Hamilda's target was found. Screaming, Cristaden fell to the ground in a heap of burning flesh from the lightning strike.

"Cristaden!" Fajha shouted and knelt down next to her, scared to touch her.

Atakos' heart dropped but he knew she would survive. "Fajha, she'll be okay. Stand up and fight!"

As Fajha stood up and hit Evil Hamilda with an energy blast, Atakos ran so fast, she did not see him get behind her as she deflected Fajha's attack. He wasted no time hitting her with powerful energy, pushing her to the ground. A little shaken, she angrily turned to hiss at him. With her mind, she grabbed a hold of him, brought him all the way up until he hit the fifty-foot ceiling of the cave, and then let him fall towards the hard ground. A sweep of wind from Zimi softened his fall but he still landed painfully on his back.

The lights went out suddenly, enveloping everyone in darkness once again.

CHAPTER 46

It was pitch black in the cave until a horrified Zadeia managed to light a fireball.

At first they did not see where Evil Hamilda was. She was not standing where she had been just moments before. Cristaden was curled up in a ball, moaning in agonizing pain. Atakos was attempting to ignore his pain and stand up. The others were afraid to move, afraid to know what her next move would be.

"Where did she—," Fajha began. Absolute horror prevented the rest of his words from coming out. He could not warn him, it was too late.

Evil Hamilda was standing behind Zimi. With a wicked smile, she placed her hands on his head and electrocuted him.

"Zimi!" Zadeia cried, watching her brother hit the floor. His body wriggled with seizures from the electricity. Filled with rage, Zadeia gave Evil Hamilda all she had from her fire ability, causing the fireballs to spray out like torches from her hands. She watched as the evil woman went up in flames and then quickly threw fireballs at the torches closest to her, giving them enough light to see.

For a moment, the five teens thought Evil Hamilda would perish, that the fight was over, that Hamilda's body would be no more, destroyed by Zadeia's very own hands. The raging fire turned from red-orange to green and then disappeared, leaving the evil woman unscathed. She smiled at Zadeia and sent the same torch-like fireballs back her way. Zadeia dove to the ground with an unnecessary fear of being burnt.

Almost healed, Cristaden pushed herself up from the ground, limped to Zimi's side, and dragged him to a corner. Barely alive, he was not breathing. She began the healing process as fast as she could despite what Atakos had told her. They needed Zimi's help as much as they needed hers.

Atakos tried hard to get off the ground, ignoring his injuries. He could not stand by and watch his friends go down one by one. Mustering all his strength, as bruised as he was, he got up and ran faster than lightning to Fajha's side. His friend had to take a step back because he did not see his approach.

"Whoa," Fajha said, clutching his chest. "You're lucky you didn't get blown up."

Atakos shrugged. "Sorry," he said.

Before Evil Hamilda could attack them again, a very powerful blow came from Atakos and Fajha and she flew back, landing hard on her back. Quickly rising to her feet, they could see their attack had an effect on her.

The side of her mouth was dripping with blood.

She angrily wiped it away and her eyes lit up like fire, blazing murderously at them. "I underestimated you. No matter. It *won't* happen again. You cannot defeat me."

The two boys hit her again simultaneously. This time she did not land on her back. She glided through the air and made a move to land on her feet. However, before she could touch the floor, a sheet of ice came her way from a fully healed Zimi and she slipped on it, falling hard on her back once again.

Zimi rushed forward and hit her with as much ice as he could while she was down and unguarded. Breathing heavily, he stopped only when she was wrapped in ice and frozen solid, her expression unchanging. It appeared that Zimi accomplished what he had hoped to do but the ice cracked and then shattered all across the floor of the cave.

Evil Hamilda got right back on her feet without hesitation.

Zimi quickly backed up until he reached his friends. "She's too strong for us," he said, his voice quivering like it never did before. He was petrified.

"We can't let her beat us," Atakos whispered. "We have to come up with a plan." Before he could think of one, they were hit with an explosion of fire. They fell to the ground with severe burns except Zadeia.

As Cristaden's body healed itself, she grabbed Fajha, who was badly burned, and began the healing process. Zimi was in the same condition as Fajha but Atakos only had burns on his arms, which he used to block his face during the attack. Even though he was in pain, he ran away from the group to distract Evil Hamilda while his friends were being healed.

Determined not to fall for his scheme of trying to get behind her again, Evil Hamilda hit Atakos with a series of energy attacks as he ran by. He was too fast and the energy bursts hit the walls instead, causing a downpour of large rocks, blocking both entrances to the chamber.

Atakos picked up a large rock across the room and threw it at Evil Hamilda. While she blocked the incoming rock, he ran up behind her and punched her, knocking her down. Before he could attack again, she picked him up with her mind and threw him against the wall. With the unhealed trauma he received earlier, he fell to ground, unconsciousness.

"Over here!" Zadeia shouted as she, Zimi, and Fajha hit Evil Hamilda with fire, ice, and energy.

Cristaden took the long way around the cave to reach Atakos to heal him. She was beginning to be physically worn out from all the healing but she could not stand and fight while someone lay unconscious. As she was healing Atakos, he opened his eyes. "You're going to be okay," she said, smiling.

Atakos gave her a warm smile and grabbed her hand to stop the rest of the healing process. Staring at each other for a moment, neither of them spoke. They knew there was a good chance they would not come out of the fight alive. It would only be a matter of time before they ran out of energy and Evil Hamilda would kill them.

Atakos sat up and put his arms around her.

Cristaden sucked in her breath and held it, suddenly feeling time stand still. Amid the chaos happening on the other side of the cave, it was comforting to feel his arms around her. She closed her eyes, let out the breath she was holding, and took a moment to breathe in his aroma. Her heart was thudding in her chest. She wondered if he felt the same nervousness, the same flutter in his stomach that she felt.

Suddenly, Atakos grabbed Cristaden by her shoulders and pushed her back to make eye contact.

"What is it?" she asked him, trying to regain consciousness.

"I know how we could beat her."

Cristaden frowned. Apparently he did not feel the same way. "How?"

"When Fajha and I hit her at the same time, it seemed to have a major effect on her. I say we give her all we got at the same time. No holding back."

Cristaden considered it for a moment. To give her all they got meant that they would have to use their ability to blow things up against her. Simultaneously. "But that will kill her."

"Precisely."

"But Hamilda—"

"Hamilda is gone. That is not *her*. You even said so yourself. You can't even feel Hamilda's presence within her. Can't you see we're losing energy? If we don't kill her now while we still have enough energy left to do so, she'll kill *us*."

Cristaden could not imagine killing the woman they viewed as a mother for so many years but she had to remind herself that she *was* gone. Hamilda was no more. What Atakos said was right. The evil woman would stop at nothing to kill them. "You're right," she reluctantly said. "Let's do it."

Atakos stood up. He then lifted Cristaden up off the ground and into his arms.

"What are you doing?" she asked him, bewildered.

"Trust me."

Before she knew what was happening, they were standing next to their friends. They had to quickly dive to the ground as Evil Hamilda deflected the attacks she had just received from the other three.

Atakos whispered his plan to the others and explained to them why they had no choice but to follow through. "On my word we attack all at once," Atakos whispered before they stood up again. "Give her all you got."

The group nodded as Zadeia fought imminent tears from clouding her vision. Although she was sad, she agreed with the rest of the team. They wanted to end the fight just as bad as Atakos did. She gritted her teeth and mentally prepared herself to give the evil woman everything she could.

When they were ready to stand up, the five friends stood with a purpose. That purpose was to destroy the evil woman that stood before them. Standing firmly side-by-side, they were ready to finish what they started. They could not allow anyone to destroy the planet. They were

Omordion's Hope, the only hope left alive for humanity. They *had* to survive.

Deep down in her heart, Cristaden couldn't shake the feeling that they were making a mistake. She was sure they all felt the same way. Looking at the woman who raised them, she could not help but feel sorry for her. Filled with so much pain and sorrow, she had lost her soul to pure hatred and did not have enough strength to fight against it. All she needed was someone to fight for her. Cristaden knew they were the only ones who could do that but did not know how. In a last ditch effort to save Hamilda, she did a search for her presence one last time.

Nothing.

Cristaden sighed and gave up all hope. There was no bringing Hamilda back.

"Now," Atakos whispered.

The five teenagers geared up to give Evil Hamilda their all. As they began to unleash their strongest attacks, Cristaden felt something that took her by surprise.

"Stop!" Cristaden cried out. "*Wait!!!*"

But it was too late.

As a blinking of Hamilda's presence broke through against Evil Hamilda's will, the group attacked.

"NOOOOOO!" Cristaden ran forward and threw herself in front of their teacher. A bright white light erupted from her, deflecting the attacks sent Hamilda's way. The others were thrown back by their own force. Within the light, Cristaden grew white wings and her clothes were replaced with a long white robe. She grabbed Evil Hamilda and flew up with her out of harm's way. Near the ceiling of the cave, she stopped and hugged her, pressing her head against her chest. Filled with hatred, the possessed woman tried desperately to push her away but Cristaden refused to let go, proving to be much stronger than she.

For the first time, Evil Hamilda looked frightened and actually began to quake with fear. "Release me," she said.

Suddenly knowing what she had to do, Cristaden whispered for her to be still. "Remember all there is to remember," she said before engulfing her with more blinding white light, causing her to shut her eyes.

When Evil Hamilda opened her eyes, she was standing in her living room at Lochenby. She saw her husband, Jogesh, tickling a younger

Hamilda on the couch. She was laughing hysterically and then broke out into angry shouts for him to stop.

"Why are we here?" Evil Hamilda was angered by the vision. It reminded her of the prison of Lochenby and all the agony she endured after Jogesh was killed.

Before she knew what was happening, Evil Hamilda was transported to the lake behind Lochenby. The sun was shining brightly that day and there was a cool breeze as the fall season began to settle in. The leaves of the forest surrounding the lake were turning orange and red, struggling to hold on to their branches as the steady wind pulled at them.

Evil Hamilda was standing over Jogesh and herself once again. The two lovers were sitting and laughing by the lake with their toes in the cool water. Jogesh whispered something sweet in her ear and she laughed before they gave each other an extraordinary kiss. Bending low to look into her eyes, Jogesh told Hamilda he loved her and that she was the best thing that ever happened to him.

"I don't want to see this," Evil Hamilda shouted, covering her ears, attempting to keep her eyes shut. Then she was transported even further back in time. When she opened her eyes, she saw the children when they were five years old, sitting in the grass at the ranch as she showed them small Dokami tricks they could attempt to master.

Before Evil Hamilda could comment on the scene, she was taken to another place. She saw herself hugging the children in her classroom, on a rainy day, as they cried for their families. Evil Hamilda heard the younger Hamilda telling them she would protect them and never let anything bad happen to them. Little Zadeia looked up at her and told her she was her best friend. Evil Hamilda suddenly tried to reach out for Zadeia but was transported further back in time.

She was seven years old.

Standing in front of Lochenby, Evil Hamilda looked on as her mother and father were saying goodbye to little Hamilda before leaving for their doomed late night stroll. They told her they loved her and would see her in the morning. Seven-year-old Hamilda told her parents not to go. She asked them to stay with her. They smiled at her, telling her not to upset the babysitter and to go right to sleep.

Evil Hamilda started screaming, "I don't want to see it. I *don't* want to see it!" She closed her tear-filled, red eyes but Cristaden told her to open them. When she opened her eyes again, she saw herself the next morning, crying on her bed over the deaths of her parents, with objects flying around her. All of a sudden, an angel sat down beside her. When little Hamilda looked up, all the objects immediately fell. She was staring up at Cristaden.

"Don't cry," Cristaden told her. "Your parents told me to tell you they love you very much and to not despair. They did not want to leave you but sometimes things happen in our lifetime that is out of our control. They want you to be happy and to know they are watching over you with every step you take."

Little Hamilda hugged Cristaden with her eyes squeezed tight. The tears that flowed became tears of joy. She got a final message from her parents.

Cristaden stood up from the bed and turned to Evil Hamilda, who was wide-eyed and astonished. "The angel. I remember. That was … *you?*" Her red eyes filled with tears she was trying to fight back. She then remembered why she thought Cristaden was so familiar to her when she met her as a little girl.

"Well, I wouldn't call myself an angel," Cristaden said. "Just someone from your future that came to you from this very moment. You did not know it then but now you know why I came to you."

"How are you doing this?"

Cristaden shrugged. "I'm not exactly sure. I wished that I could and it just … happened. Must be an ability I have." She frowned. Throughout the whole excursion into Hamilda's past, it hadn't occurred to her that she never heard of a Dokami having this ability. There must be so much about Dokamis they may never come to realize.

Evil Hamilda stared back at Cristaden. The children Hamilda raised had grown a lot stronger than she thought possible. All those years Hamilda spent training them was not in vain. They risked their very lives to save the teacher they loved.

A bright light then blinded Evil Hamilda once again. When she opened them, everything was white and she was standing on what seemed like clouds. To her astonishment, she saw her parents standing several feet away from her, holding hands and smiling at her. She sucked in her breath out of shock and then started crying. She wanted so much to run up to them and touch them but she stood firm, still very frightened about what was happening. This had to be the land of the afterlife. But how could Cristaden have the power to bring her there? Dokamis can't—

Another bright light shone and Evil Hamilda was forced to close her eyes again. When she opened them, before her stood Bontihm, the man who raised her like she was his own daughter. If she was in the land of the afterlife, why was he there?

As if he read her mind, Bontihm walked up to her and said five words she wasn't prepared to hear. "Hamilda, I have passed on."

Evil Hamilda shook her head and erupted in tears. "It can't be true." Everyone was leaving her. She felt so alone.

"Do not despair, my child. It was my time to go. I want you to be happy and no longer be enraged." Bontihm stepped forward and gave her a hug and she squeezed him tight, saying goodbye to her adoptive father for the last time.

Cristaden watched the scene before her with sadness in her eyes. Bontihm was dead. The one person she would have ever called grandfather besides her own was gone. Last they heard, he was with General Komuh and very much alive. She wondered if the general had anything to do with his death. Sadly, she watched as Bontihm said his final goodbyes and disappeared.

Evil Hamilda looked around frantically. Searching. And then she spotted him. There he was, looking just as wonderful as he did when Hamilda last set her eyes on him. Not at all like the nightmarish images she had grown accustomed to seeing in her dreams. Jogesh told her that he loved her and walked up to her, giving her an affectionate hug and a kiss that did not last long enough. He told her he would always be watching over her. He then told her something she was not expecting.

"You must come back, Hamilda," Jogesh said. "Please don't give up and let the hatred consume you. You have to live for the baby you carry. Our baby."

Shocked, Evil Hamilda placed her hand on her stomach. She did not have to doubt his statement. For the first time she allowed herself to sense it. She was pregnant. Fear came to her eyes when she realized the damage that may have been done to the baby during the fight. Her heart sunk when she recalled the moments she almost killed her beloved pupils too.

Jogesh grabbed her shoulders and pulled her close. "The children will be okay. They have already forgiven you. As for the baby? Don't worry about him. He's strong. Like his mother."

Hamilda nodded once and smiled, fighting back the tears that threatened to fall. "And his father," she said.

Cristaden's heart filled with joy and tears welled up in her eyes. She was about to wipe them away when a hand gently tapped her shoulder. Startled, she turned around sharply and stared right into the eyes of a man. A man who seemed familiar to her but not familiar at all. She looked back at Hamilda who was silently crying in Jogesh's arms. They did not seem to notice the man who gently pressed for her attention.

Turning back around, Cristaden peered at him. He resembled her people back home, in Laspitu. He had dark features, like her mother and father, and brown hair. He was very handsome and reminded her of … Allowing her brain to quickly process what she was seeing, she noticed parts of his face that reminded her of her *mother*. The way his eyes turned down a bit at the edges, the shape of his lips, even the dimple below his lower lip that became more defined as he smiled at her. An uncle, maybe? One she had never met before.

"Who are you?" Cristaden asked curiously. Whoever he was, she was sure he was deceased. Otherwise he would not be there.

"I was sure you would remember me," a voice, so deep, yet soft and gentle, escaped his moving lips.

An alarm rang out in Cristaden's head. *This voice*, she thought. *Why do I know this voice?*

"Don't be alarmed," the man spoke gently. "You may think you do not know me." He reached out and touched her temple. "But your memory of me is still here."

"Memory? But I've never seen you before."

The man grabbed her hands, which she allowed him to do with ease. She did not know him but somehow she trusted him more than she thought she should.

"Let me show you," he said.

Suddenly the cloud Cristaden was standing on disappeared and her eyes forcibly closed.

Everything went black.

CHAPTER 47

Cristaden opened her eyes and saw Lochenby before her. Turning around quickly, she did not see the strange man. Before she could question why she was there, the sudden laughter of students approaching her interrupted her thoughts and she dodged out of the way, barely making it behind a bush so as not to be seen. How could she explain her long, white dress and wings? Slowly lifting her head, she peered over the bush and saw a group of five boys walking past her. They were a couple of years older and their uniforms were slightly different than the ones she and her friends had grown accustomed to wearing for ten years. One boy looked in her direction and her heart almost stopped. Surely he had seen her. But he looked away, laughing at a joke another boy said.

They can't see me, Cristaden thought. *This* has *to be a memory.* Then she peered closely at the one who told the joke. It was a memory. *His* memory. She recognized the boy although he had to be around eighteen years old. The same downturn of his eyes, the same way his dimple flashed when he laughed. It was the man she had spoken to in the spirit realm. He was showing her a part of his life.

A student. From *Lochenby* of all places. She cringed when she saw one of the boys look her way again.

"Don't worry," said the strange man, who was suddenly standing behind her. "They cannot see us. This is my past. I want to show you what happened. I think it will be easier for you to understand this way."

"Understand what?" Cristaden asked. She was almost positive he had her confused for someone else. So what if he seemed familiar. She knew positively she had never met him before.

The man did not answer her question. Turning towards him, she noticed a film of wetness over his eyes as if he were about to cry. But spirits don't cry. Do they?

Cristaden turned back to look at her familiar boarding school but they were no longer standing outside. They were in a bedroom. The man's younger self was occupying one of the twin beds in the room, sleeping soundly. The walls, she noticed, was a rich brown color and made of cement instead of the wooden walls she was used to seeing at Lochenby. A steady stream of light came in through a small window near the bed, suggesting that it was midday. There was a small desk in the corner and a thick, rustic door that led out into a small kitchen. They were definitely not in Lochenby anymore. It seemed like they were in a cottage.

"Is this your room?" Cristaden asked the man. "I mean, was this where you lived?" She was silently hoping she would not be ignored this time.

"Yes," he said. "This was my home. After I graduated from Lochenby, I returned here and was prepared to work with my father." He suddenly frowned and sighed. "At least, that's what I thought I was going to do. Until the dreams started."

"Dreams?" Cristaden heard the man's younger self moan in his sleep. He smiled broadly and gripped his pillow tighter. He then rolled over and sighed deeply, chuckling a little bit while readjusting his position. "It doesn't seem like you were having a *bad* dream."

The man smiled. "No, not bad at all. They were the best dreams of my entire life. You see, I had a small talent. A talent for seeing the future through my dreams."

"Talent?" Cristaden frowned. She wouldn't necessarily call the ability to see the future a mere talent.

"Well more like a gift. That's what we used to call them when we were little. At the time, we did not know how strong the Dokami blood ran through our veins."

Cristaden's eyebrows rose. "You are ... of Dokami blood?" she asked with a shaky voice.

"Yes."

"What is … your … name?" Maybe she would remember having heard his name during Hamilda's history lessons of the Dokami clan.

"Kheiron."

"Oh," Cristaden said, disappointed. Never heard of him. There were hundreds of thousands of Dokami around Western Omordion. All of them had interesting stories to share about their life. Perhaps there was a spirit realm for only Dokami descendants and she fell upon it when she conjured up Hamilda's loved ones. It was apparent that this man, Kheiron, needed her help. Whatever it was, she would try her best. He seemed like a nice person.

As if to answer her thoughts, Kheiron placed his hand on her shoulder. "You haven't heard of me, of this I am sure. My name was not one to roll off even the loosest tongues after I passed. I came to you because I believe there are some things you need to know and to take back to your friends. Some things that will help you with the fight against the destructive nature of the East. You only need to listen and I promise you, when my story is finished, you will understand completely why I came to you."

Cristaden only nodded her head slowly. This was why he was there. To help *her*. She turned back to the younger Kheiron who rolled out of bed and then stretched. He seemed a little disappointed that his dream had come to an end. It seemed like a bright idea came to him all of a sudden because he quickly stood up and searched his room frantically until he found what he was looking for. A green travel bag. Taking the bag, he stuffed some clothes into it and other provisions. He was preparing himself for a rather long journey.

"Where were you going?" Cristaden asked Kheiron.

"I had seen a vision in my dreams. It was of a beautiful woman. I thought I knew where I could find her and I knew that I could not rest until she was found. So I packed a bag."

"Just like that? What if you couldn't find her?"

"It was a chance I was willing to take. I had never been so sure of anything my entire life."

Younger Kheiron went to his small desk and pulled out a piece of paper and a pen. He wrote vigorously for a few minutes and then stood up again, quickly grabbed his bag, and left his room.

"I left a letter for my family," Kheiron said. "I knew it would be a long time before I returned, maybe even years. I had to act quickly before they returned so they wouldn't stop me." He gestured for Cristaden to follow younger Kheiron through the kitchen and out the front door.

Stepping outside, Cristaden felt like she was having a wave of déjà vu. She remembered something about walking out into that fresh air but she could not put her finger on it. There were tall trees surrounding the cottage, some with pink flowers and others with orange and white flowers. Springtime. Flowers lined the path leading down to a rocky beach. The ocean lay just a hundred feet from the front door of the tiny cottage. There was a long sleek boat tied to the dock and Cristaden watched as the younger Kheiron boarded it and paddled away from shore. Then the boat seemed to turn slowly around and head back towards shore. Cristaden was confused at first, thinking he had changed his mind, then noticed the dock was missing and they were standing on a sandy beach. The cottage and the flower trees were gone, replaced by a dense forest. Young Kheiron had reached his destination.

Cristaden looked around them "Is this …?" She was afraid to ask.

Kheiron looked away from her, at the forest surrounding them, and nodded, confirming her suspicions. "Yes. It's the north end of Sheidem Forest."

"This is where you thought the beautiful woman from your dreams lived?"

He nodded again. "This was where she lived."

"I thought there were no human inhabitants in this forest." Cristaden frowned. For the first time since their journey through Kheiron's memories began, she was sure he had been insane in his past life.

Kheiron made direct eye contact with Cristaden. "There aren't any," he said. She could see that he was being serious, which confused her even more. She looked on as the young Kheiron, who left the boat tied to a tree, eagerly enter the forest.

The scene before them changed again and they were standing in a small clearing within the forest. Night had fallen and the stars twinkled while a steady fire burned near the sleeping Kheiron, who diligently set up camp there, intent on spending a long time in the forest until he found what he was looking for.

"Watch carefully," Kheiron said. "I want you to see this."

Cristaden looked on, afraid to blink in case she missed something of importance. And then she saw it. A soft light, making its way through the forest, growing brighter with each passing second.

Cristaden's heart beat faster in her chest.

She had seen this light before.

When the figure stepped out of the dense forest and into the clearing, Cristaden gasped. She hadn't changed much over the years, she looked exactly the same as she remembered her, only a little more enlightened and intrigued. Queen Lhainna, with her blonde hair cascading down her back, glided towards the sleeping Kheiron and whispered his name once with a smile on her face, trying her best not to wake him.

"The beautiful woman in your dreams ... was ...?" Cristaden never considered that he would be dreaming of a *fairy*.

"Lhai." Kheiron said her name with such affection and adoration in his voice that Cristaden thought he might have been close to tears. "She knew I was coming. She was waiting for me." He smiled. "She too had seen me in her dreams but she did not know what kind of person I was. So she came to me only when I was sleeping. Every night for over six months, just watching and waiting. By my dreams, I only knew where I had to wait for her to find me so every day I waited. Every day, for what seemed like centuries, just waiting."

As Kheiron spoke the vision in front of them changed to match his explanation. "One day, I decided to give up, to go back home. I was sure my family thought I had perished by then. Lhai got nervous when I began to pack up my things and, in her haste, she approached me. I thought a *goddess* came up to me—an *angel*. I could have sworn that my body gave up some unknown fight and I had died, that it was my destiny to die and meet this angel."

They watched as Queen Lhainna came out of the forest abruptly and approached the retreating Kheiron. She begged him not to go. All he could do was stare back at her, dumbfounded and unable to move. She explained to him that she had been watching him every night but was too scared to approach him when he was awake. When he heard what she said, he came to his senses and grabbed her hands. He did not want her to fear him. They stared into each other's eyes for what seemed like ages, while unspoken words passed between them. There was a reason they were brought together, a reason that was unclear to them. One thing for certain was the love they had for each other. More than anything they knew, they were absolutely sure their love could withstand any obstacles that they faced. All that became apparent when they looked into each other's eyes.

Kheiron made the visions before them pass by in a steady pace. Cristaden saw younger Kheiron interacting with the other fairies while dancing and singing. She even spotted Kapimia in the mix, looking as beautiful as ever with her long red hair flowing down her back. It was strange to see how Kapimia, Lhainna, and Kheiron looked to be about the same age even though Kapimia was Lhainna's daughter and Kheiron her lover. Cristaden also noticed she did not see Keirak, which puzzled her. She concluded that Keirak might not have relished in the fact that her mother was involved with a human. Regardless of anything, Lhainna and Kheiron continued to kiss each other passionately whenever the opportunity presented itself. The two of them, when alone at night, would gaze at the stars and make passionate love in the moonlight, Kheiron explained. Every moment they spent together was beautiful and memorable. If Cristaden did not know that Lhainna was a fairy, she would have thought the two of them were a match made in heaven. In a strange way, they were soul mates.

"For three years, we lived like this," Kheiron said. "Not having a care for the world around us, focused on each other and nothing else. We both knew she would outlive me, that eventually I would die, and we would be separated but I did not care. I needed her in my life. I vowed to remain in the forest with her until I died of old age."

Cristaden noticed the other Kheiron was now around the same age as the Kheiron standing next to her. Her stomach turned when she realized he would not live as long as he had anticipated. "What happened to you?" She was curious but, at the same time, unwilling to discover his tragic end. "How did you die?"

The vision changed. "One day, Lhai fell ill. There was nothing we could do to make her feel better no matter how hard we tried. Oddly enough, I thought I was the direct cause of her sickness, that my being with her was killing her. I contemplated leaving in order to save her life but she was adamant on my remaining with her. I was in agony and frustrated until, a few weeks later, I finally understood why she was sick. The other fairies informed me that Lhai was with child." He paused and took a short breath in as if the memories were too painful for him to bear.

Cristaden's eyes widened. "Queen Lhainna was pregnant?" Was it possible for humans to have children with fairies? She looked on at Kheiron's memories and saw Lhainna with her ever-expanding waistline and Kheiron, always protective over her, always holding her around her midsection, singing and talking to the growing baby regularly. Lhainna was glowing, finally feeling better, and they were happy once again. The other fairies did their best to prepare for the baby. Even Kapimia was ecstatic, running to and fro with her assigned duties of preparation. They did not know whether to expect a human baby, a fairy, or a half-ling. So they tried their best to prepare for anything.

Throughout the duration of her pregnancy, Lhainna had to remain in human form. She could not shape-shift as much as she tried which suggested that the baby was more human than fairy.

Standing next to Cristaden, Kheiron watched the unfolding mystery with a glimmer of sadness in his eyes. It was obvious that he missed Lhainna and longed to be reunited with her. He gradually brought Cristaden to the time of childbirth, taking his time, not to benefit her understanding but for his own delight. Each passing image was the closest he could get to his Lhai while reliving his past. He sucked in his breath when Kapimia shouted, "They're here. They've finally arrived!"

"They?" Cristaden asked. "You mean she had more than one?"

"Yes, twins." A broad smile replaced Kheiron's sadness and he boasted proudly just like a doting father would. "They were beautiful. Twin girls. I loved them so much." The next vision that came was of Lhainna holding one baby and Kheiron holding the other. The other fairies were swirling around them, trying to get a good look at the beautiful babies. They gave them gifts and swooned over them for days.

Cristaden did not like the way Kheiron using the word 'love' in past tense when he spoke of the babies. She feared that something bad had happened to them. "What did you name them?"

"I left that for Lhai to decide. She chose Kira and Keirak. Named after me, of course."

Cristaden's heart went up to her throat and she brought her hands to her mouth in shock. "You're Keirak's *father*." She said it as a statement rather than a question. "One of these babies is Keirak."

"Keirak is mine."

"But she's a fairy. She's not human at all." She tried to swallow the lump in her throat but could not when something suddenly dawned on her. Throughout their run-in with Queen Lhainna and the other fairies, she had never met nor seen Kira. She was sure that being Lhainna's daughter, she would have been there right alongside Kapimia and

Keirak. A tear came to her eye when she realized that Kira could very well have died with her father. But how?

"At the time we did not know if they were human or fairy, it was too early to tell." Sensing Cristaden's fear, Kheiron's face grew dark and his voice became deep with frustration. "Two years later, all that changed. Lhainna was meeting with the other fairies so I took the girls for a walk around the forest. Such smart girls they were, always learning new words and phrases to say every day and as independent as they could be at the age of two."

Cristaden looked on at the two girls walking with their father. Both had fair skin, whitish-blonde hair and blue eyes, much like their mother, but they did not look exactly alike. The way they danced while they walked reminded her of little sprites.

Kheiron shuddered and his words came out in quick bursts. "We walked through the forest. Lhai had not warned me. I mean there wasn't a need to because I, personally, was not in any danger. But the girls, my girls, were easy targets. It was my fault really. I brought them too far out. We saw the butterflies first—" He choked then and could not finish his sentence.

He did not have to. Cristaden knew all too well what was about to happen because she had lived through it herself. When the oblots attacked, the other Kheiron was not expecting it. One of the girls automatically changed into a fairy. She flew back to the safety of Lhainna's protected forest. The other could not. She stood there, mouth opened in shock as the oblot charged at her. Kheiron jumped on top of her, covering her with his body, and waited for imminent death. In an instant, he and the toddler were whipped up in the air by an unseen force and carried back to the safety of Lhainna's forest. The queen had heard Keirak's cry and flown as fast as she could to save them. She was almost too late but managed to reach them in time and used all her strength to carry them back to her forest.

Kheiron was devastated. He had put his children's lives in jeopardy. Lhainna tried to console him but he was inconsolable. He paced back and forth, wringing his shaky hands together in fear and wiping at fallen tears on his cheeks from time to time. Lhainna blamed herself. She knew she should have warned him, but she was living a dream, so much so that the thought of Brulok and his minions was a far thought, something she had not even considered in over four years. Being human, he was in no danger, but she never anticipated that he would leave the forest with the girls, not even for a moment.

Kheiron sniffled. "We knew the awful truth. Keirak was a fairy and Kira was, no doubt, human. When she grew older and started wandering around alone, she could easily overstep her boundaries and get in harm's way. Unable to defend herself or fly away fast, she would be killed instantly. How could we protect her? How could we trust that if we looked away for *one* moment, she would not be gone forever?

"Our love for each other was powerful but we both knew the safety of our children came first. Lhai had a cloaking spell. She knew that on fairies, it would last a long period of time but she did not know the affect it had on humans."

Cristaden reached out and grabbed Kheiron's arm for the first time. "What do you mean by cloaking spell?"

Startled, Kheiron looked down at her and his expression softened. "You see, I had to save my daughter's life no matter what it took. We decided that as soon as possible, that day even, Lhai and I would have to separate our daughters and separate from …" He suddenly looked away.

Cristaden knew what he was going to say before he said it. In her head the words 'no, no, no' were repeating over and over again. "Wasn't there any other way? Couldn't you have stayed and just kept Kira from leaving? Was it that hard to keep her in your sight??"

Kheiron looked hurt by her words. It seemed that, at one point, he might have regretted his actions but it was too late. "We reacted hastily in our fear. It was our worst mistake. We tried to tell ourselves that the only way Kira would be safe was for me to take her away and to return with her when she was old enough to understand her boundaries. We thought we would have had to keep her locked in a cage to protect her here in this forest but we wanted her to have a full life. A human life. We were foolish and irrational."

Cristaden, who had already grown attached to the lovely couple and their daughters, felt the pain that Kheiron did. "That's so sad," she said. Watching the other Kheiron pack up their things and then waiting patiently while the cloaking spell was administered, she sadly knew that he would never return to the forest after he left. She wasn't even sure he would make it past the awaiting oblots alive. She was scared to discover what happened to the beautiful toddler standing next to him that twisted her curly locks between her fingers, trying to put her hair in her mouth.

When it was time for Kheiron and Kira to leave, he put on a brave face and lovingly kissed Lhainna and Keirak. Lhainna had to hold Keirak back to prevent her from following her father and sister. The girls began to cry and reach out for each other. They were inseparable, this was the first time they were forced to be apart from one another. Soon their tears turned to screams as if they knew that was the last time they were ever going to see each other again. Kheiron and Lhainna were crying too, they couldn't bear to be apart, not even for one minute.

No matter how much Cristaden wiped at her eyes, the tears kept flowing. Hearing the cries of the little girls felt like pure devastation. It was agonizing to watch much less listen to the screaming. Poor Kira. Her life was cut too short.

Kheiron wiped his eyes and continued, changing the vision as he went along. "At first the cloaking spell worked. We made it all the way to my boat. I uncovered all the years of leaves and dust from it and placed Kira inside." His voice broke. "Before I could get the boat in the water, the spell had worn off."

Cristaden wanted to cover her eyes when she saw the oblots slowly coming out of the forest one by one but she knew she had to watch. She had to know for sure what happened next.

"They came at us. There were three of them. Kira was screaming. Pointing. She tried to climb out of the boat to help me push it to the water but I told her to stay. She was too little to help me. Just as I managed to get the boat into the water, I was attacked from behind. One of the oblots tore at me, biting a chunk off my shoulder. I was in so much pain but I did not give up. I had my daughter's life to save." Kheiron sighed. "I did not know how afraid the oblots were of water. There they stood, huffing and puffing at us from the shore, taking giant steps back when a wave rolled onto the sand. Even though I was in tremendous pain, I was triumphant. I had saved my daughter's life. She was safe."

Cristaden watched as the badly wounded Kheiron wrapped his shoulder tightly to stop the bleeding and paddled across the ocean using his good arm. Kira slept most of the time and only awoke to eat. At times she woke up crying and screaming and Kheiron had to console her. He was not doing so well either. His wounds were infected and if he did not get help, Cristaden knew they would kill him.

Finally, Kheiron reached the dock near his small cottage. A group of people from the other homes nearby ran out to meet him. They grabbed Kira and carried Kheiron to his room. By then he was delirious and suffering with a raging fever. Some of the neighbors fed his daughter while others tended to his wounds. Cristaden overheard someone say that it was too late, that he would die before sunset. Another person mentioned how they were trying to keep his family away so they wouldn't see him in the state he was in. When they were sure there was nothing that could be done to save him, they requested that his family come in to pay their last respects.

From the front door, Cristaden watched as four people entered the house. Her heart skipped a beat. She was confused by most of Kheiron's story but this had to be, by far, the most confusing. The four people, an aging man and woman, and a man and woman near Kheiron's age walked past Cristaden and surrounded Kheiron's bed.

"What is this?" Cristaden asked but received no response. She watched as the dying Kheiron spoke loving words to the aging couple, who were his parents. They gripped his hands and cried for him. He then turned toward his sister and her husband and spoke his final words. "Please take care of her. She's a sweet girl. She won't give you any trouble. Please do not mention my name to her and make my child your own. I do not want her to seek out her mother. She would be in terrible danger if she did." Tears fell from his eyes.

A neighbor walked in with Kira then and Cristaden watched as her very own grandparents and parents took the child into their arms. Her mother tried to ask Kheiron what his daughter's name was but it was too late. Death had already taken him away. They cried in agony over his death but then wiped their tears to focus their full attention on the present left for them.

Cristaden knew what words would be said next before they were even spoken. The woman she referred to all her life as mother looked down into Kira's pretty blue eyes. "We will call you … Cristaden."

CHAPTER 48

Cristaden's knees buckled and she fell to the floor, erupting into tears. All those years of trying to fit in, trying to be normal yet knowing she was different. Her brother's teasing words came back to her then. He always tried to convince her that she was adopted, that she did not belong to their family. Maybe the kid knew more than she thought he did. Everything she knew about her family was a lie. Her mother was her *aunt* and her father—her uncle by *marriage*. At least her grandparents were still who they were supposed to be but everything else she was brought up to believe was not true. Her name, her true birth parents—

Cristaden sucked in her breath. *Queen Lhainna is my mother? I just saw her not too long ago. Nothing about her actions gave away that she had been reunited with her long lost daughter. It just doesn't make any sense. And this man. This man standing next to me right now, is my father? This can't be real, I must be dreaming. That's it. It's all a dream.*

Rough hands grabbed her arms and pulled her up into a tight embrace. As much as she wanted to deny everything she had seen, deep down she always felt the disassociation with her family since she was very small. Some part of her, hidden for so many years, awoken and told her that everything he had shown her was true. Kheiron was her biological father, and she loved him. She finally found what she was looking for all her life. A sense of belonging.

"Thank you," Cristaden whispered. She did not know what else to say.

"I know," Kheiron said. "It's a lot to take in. Just remember I love you and I tried to do the best I could to keep you safe. I will always be with you." He kissed the top of her head and held her close.

When Cristaden opened her eyes and pulled back slightly, she found that it was not Kheiron she was hugging anymore, but Hamilda, staring down at her with bright green eyes. They were standing on the soft cloud again, blanketed by a thick fog. "Hamilda," she said. Evil Hamilda was gone. The Hamilda she grew up with had made a triumphant return.

"I'm sorry," Hamilda said, unable to stop crying. "I'm so sorry."

"It's okay. It wasn't your fault. You lost control of your demons. I can't imagine what it must have been like to lose the ones you love."

They wiped each other's tears. Cristaden opened her mouth to tell Hamilda all she encountered but did not know where to start.

"You don't have to explain. I saw everything."

"Okay." Cristaden looked down. A wave of sorrow overtook her when she thought of her father, who lost his life trying to save hers. She wished she had more time with him.

Hamilda picked up on what she was thinking. "Your father was very brave. He knew you were special. I knew you had tremendous power since the day I met you when you were four years old. Now I understand why. Those memories, both mine and your father's, were made possible by you. You helped us see into the past with your gift. You are truly an amazing individual."

Cristaden looked up at her mentor. It was true then. She was more powerful than she ever imagined. "I just wish things were different, that's all."

"They could be. Just reclaim your destined life, as I have. Everything happens for a reason. There is so much I have to make up for. But I'm not well. I haven't yet accepted the loss of my loved ones. I have to go somewhere to heal. I mean *really heal*. When you get a chance, you should do the same."

Cristaden smiled. It would be nice to reacquaint herself with her mother and twin sister. "I will."

Hamilda nodded and the two closed their eyes, wishing they were back in the cave again. When their nostrils filled with the familiar musty smell, Cristaden aided them back to the ground.

They were met with the shocked faces of Atakos, Fajha, Zimi, and Zadeia.

Hamilda.

Normal again.

Her eyes no longer red, her skin no longer stone-like. She looked just as they remembered her. Black, curly hair, bright-green eyes, and olive skin.

Cristaden with her white robe and *wings*.

It was unbelievable.

As Cristaden stepped aside, Hamilda broke the silence. "My children." Her voice cracked as her eyes filled with tears. Her students ran to her and wrapped their arms around her. For a moment it reminded her of how they used to hug her when they were five years old. "I'm so sorry I put you in danger." She sniffled, trying to fight back more tears. She looked at each of their faces. "I never meant to harm you. I could have *killed* you." She broke out into more tears when she realized how close she was to losing every last person that meant anything to her. And this time, it would have been by *her* hand.

"It wasn't your fault," Zadeia said.

"We're just glad to have you back," Fajha said, smiling.

Atakos looked back and forth at Cristaden and Hamilda. "We were so worried. We thought we would never see you—"

"You're not safe around me," Hamilda whispered.

"What are you talking about? It's okay now. You're back. Everything will be alright now."

She released them and backed away. "No. I must go away. You're in danger as long as you're with me."

"What?" Fajha said.

"That's not *true*," Zimi said.

"You don't have to go," Zadeia said, reaching out for her.

"I must," Hamilda whispered, fighting back more tears. "Cristaden, please explain to them ..." She let her voice trail off. It pained her to see them cry.

Cristaden knew Hamilda was already planning her escape. There was no convincing her otherwise.

"I love all of you. Remember that," she said before the lights suddenly went out.

"No!" Zadeia shouted, quickly creating two fireballs.

Hamilda was gone.

CHAPTER 49

"Look down there!" Kapimia shouted over the wind.

At first Aillios did not see anything but an expansive blue-green sea but, as their altitude began to drop, he noticed a tiny speck in the water. It grew until it was a beautiful tropical island surrounding a black volcano. After so many hours of flying over the ocean, they had finally reached their destination.

Paimonu.

"Wow," Aillios said. He had never seen anything like it. Being so used to the rolling green hills of grass and fogginess in Mituwa, the rainforest of Paimonu seemed like another world to him.

"Oh, just wait until you get down there," Kapimia shouted. "It's exquisite."

"Incredible," Aillios said as they got closer to the island. He could make out various waterfalls and a valley of vegetation below.

"We're coming in for a landing!"

Aillios braced himself as the fairy guided him and Thashmar through the canopy of trees and gently placed them down not far from the road that led up to a village on the side of the volcano.

Kapimia changed to human size and released the rope from around Aillios and Thashmar. Shrinking the rope back down to its regular size, she tied it around her white robe. "Well, I guess this is it," she said, her purple eyes sparkling. She gave Aillios her best smile and stuck her hand out. "Good luck."

"Thank you," Aillios said, bending down to shake her hand.

With that she turned back into fairy size. "I must go before the cloaking spell wears off."

"Wait. Where do I go?"

"Just follow the road. You'll see the caves on the other side of the volcano." And then Kapimia flew off, disappearing from sight.

"Thanks," Aillios said sarcastically. "Thashmar, if I ever wake from this dream, I give you permission to stomp on me and rip out my hair with your teeth. I'm going crazy." The horse only whinnied and shook his head, weary from the long journey.

Looking up the road ahead of him, Aillios sucked in air and slowly released it. "Let's go," he told Thashmar.

As they trotted up the road, Aillios could not help feeling a sense of relief and sadness. It felt so wonderful to finally be free of Eastern Omordion but he was still worried about the millions of slaves he left behind. Trying to put the unjust reality out of his head, Aillios rounded a bend in the road and came upon the village. The ground was still wet with rain although he did not see a cloud in the sky. He noted the pink flowering trees and the brightly colored houses lining the road but saw no sign of any inhabitants. There was no smoke rising from the chimneys, which suggested they might not be inside.

"Come on Thashmar," Aillios said. "Kapimia said something about some caves so let's try and find them." He rode his horse up the road that curved around the mountainside. He still kept his ears open for sounds of life but heard nothing. The air was so fresh that he took a moment to breathe it in and allowed his muscles to relax. "So peaceful," he said. Paimonu's beauty was enough to make him want to stay and forget all the bad things happening halfway around the world. He looked down at his hands and thought of how nice it would be to use them for picking vegetables instead of fighting. Sighing, he shook his head. His reality could never be that cheerful. He would always be the son of the evil king who started the world war and created the devastation of Eastern Omordion. Wherever he went, he could never forget that.

Rounding the curve around the volcano, Aillios finally found the inhabitants of Paimonu. An enormous crowd silently stood ahead of him. They appeared to be watching something very closely. When he approached them, some turned to look at him while others ignored him and continued to stare out over the mountainside. He dismounted Thashmar and tied him to a tree. Curious to see what the people were staring at, he pushed through the crowd and stopped when he reached the edge of the road. He saw a dense tropical forest and the caves that Kapimia spoke of. Suddenly the ground shook slightly as sounds of explosions came from within the caves. The villagers were muttering things to each other in their language. Growing up in the castle, Aillios was taught many languages of Omordion but was disappointed to learn that he could not speak the language of Paimonu.

Turning back to look at the caves, Aillios wondered if the teenagers he sought after were still inside. Looking around at the crowd, he did not see anyone that stood out. The inhabitants pretty much looked the same and wore the same type of clothing. The males were bare-chested and wore dark colored shorts and the females of all ages wore brightly colored cloths that wrapped around their bodies. His eyes drifted to a little boy, squatting by the side of the road not too far from where he stood, wearing only a pair of white shorts. He was playing with pieces of dark wood, connected by thin strings to form a dancing puppet man. It was encouraging to see a child so free to play without fear. He walked towards the little boy but then stopped abruptly. There was something about the boy's puppet that made him hold his breath.

The puppet had no strings. In fact the boy was not even touching it. It was moving on its own.

"How..."Aillios' voice trailed off when the little boy looked up at him with terrified blue eyes. The puppet fell to the ground, turning back into a pile of wood as the frightened boy ran away, disappearing into the large crowd. Bending down, Aillios inspected the pile of wood and found no mechanism that would have caused the wooden pieces to move on their own. But how had he made them move?

Before Aillios could think of a reasonable explanation, he heard the sound of propellers coming from directly overhead. Dropping the wood, he stood up and saw an aircraft flying towards them at a rapid pace. He then watched as it came in for a landing about a hundred feet from the crowd. Many people were drawn to it as others held back.

After cutting the engine, a teenage boy with reddish-brown hair and pale skin disembarked the aircraft and slowly made his way to the first group of people he saw. He was asking them a series of questions in a language Aillios did not recognize but was not getting any answers. He appeared very frustrated and desperate. Aillios edged closer to him and heard him asking someone questions in a different language. The Sheidem language. Now this was a language Aillios was familiar with.

"Excuse me," Aillios said as he approached the boy. "I heard you were inquiring about five teenagers."

The boy seemed taken aback by Aillios' attire and thick accent, so unlike the people of Paimonu. "Yes," he said slowly. "Do you know where I can find them?"

"Why do you ask?"

The boy looked apprehensive. "They are my friends. Have you seen them?"

"I was told they were in the caves just over the side of this mountain."

"Did the people here tell you that?" The boy looked around. "They won't even talk to me."

"I was told by...you wouldn't believe me if I told you."

"Try me."

Aillios hesitated but then decided to come out with it. The boy would never believe him anyways. "A fairy brought me here."

The boy thought for a moment. "You've lost it. Everyone here is mad."

"No, no. I know what you're thinking. I think it's crazy too but she told me they were in danger. That they needed *my* help."

The teenager stared hard at Aillios. "If it is true what you say, why would she choose *you* to help them?"

Aillios froze. For all he knew the boy could be a spy sent by his father intent on killing the five teenagers he sought. He shook his head. "Never mind." He then quickly walked away from him.

"Wait!" The boy shouted and ran after him. "My name is Colnaha," he said when he reached him, stopping the prince in his tracks. "I have come from Osmatu in search of some friends of mine that passed through there many days ago. If I have said something to offend you, I apologize. It's just that I'm determined to find them because I believe that they are in terrible danger too."

"That's what I was told. In danger from *whom*?"

"The Western Army."

Aillios stared hard at Colnaha. It didn't make any sense. "Why would they be in danger from the very army that is training them to destroy the Eastern Army?"

Colnaha frowned and turned away from the man as a wave of nausea overtook him. *So that's why the army was after them,* he thought. *That secret mission. The reason why the Dokami Council allowed them to increase their powers. They were being trained to defeat the Eastern Army. Bontihm's apprentice must have been their teacher. The one who was kidnapped. The next Dokami Wise Man!* He was hyperventilating inside but tried not to show it to the strange man. "They're corrupt," he simply said, turning back to face him.

"Corrupt?" Aillios couldn't believe it. It seemed like the only people he could trust were the five teenagers in the caves and perhaps Colnaha. He seemed genuine enough. "I'm going to tell you something. Please do not be alarmed. I mean all of you no harm." He took a deep breath. "I am Aillios, son of King Tholenod of Mituwa."

Colnaha took a step back with fear in his eyes.

"Don't worry," Aillios assured him. "I am against what my father stands for and that's why I was sent here. I have to find your friends and help them overthrow him. I will do whatever it takes to make sure that happens."

Colnaha could relate to Aillios' story because, in a way, he ran away for the same reasons. "So did your 'fairy' tell you where we can find them?"

Aillios chuckled at Colnaha's sarcasm. "Yes, she told me they were in the caves." He pointed to where the dissipating crowd once stood. "Just over the side of this mountain. I heard some explosions coming from there a little while ago."

"Sounds like a fight. We must go."

Colnaha took off running up the road with Aillios following close behind. They stopped right at the edge and looked over the side of the mountain at the caves. Just then, a woman, wearing a long black dress, ran out of one of the smaller openings. She stopped for a moment to look around, then looked up at the mountain, making eye contact with her two spectators. She had beautiful, curly black hair and striking green eyes. Caught off guard by her natural beauty, Aillios took a step back.

In the blink of an eye she was gone.

"Did you see that?" Aillios asked.

Colnaha searched the forest with his eyes. Was that Bontihm's apprentice? "Strange," he said. "I wonder who she was."

"You know, I have seen some strange things since I arrived on this island."

"Strange like how?" Colnaha asked, tearing his eyes away from the caves. "Besides the 'fairy', I mean."

"Oh, I don't know. The silent people who live here. A little boy playing with a puppet with no strings. A goddess leaving a cave and disappearing into thin air …"

"No strings, you say?"

"Yes. The boy was just sitting there and he wasn't touching the wooden pieces but they were dancing like a puppet without strings."

Colnaha peered around him. It sounded like a Dokami trait. He thought long and hard before he spoke again. "If you're going to be of any use to us, you're going to have to know a few things."

"Know what?" Aillios was confused.

"What we are." Colnaha looked regretful but he knew it was better to fill him in about their heritage so Aillios wouldn't go into a state of shock if they ran into trouble.

Aillios thought back to what the old wizard had said about Dokamis and he wondered if the little boy with the wooden pieces had anything to do with them. He wondered if Colnaha was one of them as well. "You mean … the Dokami?"

Colnaha squinted at him and frowned. "How did you hear of that name?" Was Aillios the only one who knew? Was their clan's secret existence completely compromised?

As if to answer Colnaha's thoughts, Aillios said the one thing the teen never wanted to hear. "Now is not the time to tell you how I know. The important thing is my father knows about the Dokami as well. Your friends are in greater danger than you realize."

"We must hurry!"

Aillios agreed and followed the boy down the mountainside and through the trees. Before they entered the caves, he could not help but wonder what this adventure had in store for him and if he would ever make it out alive.

CHAPTER 50

"We have to find her," Zadeia said.

"She used a secret passage out of here," Cristaden said. "There's no point in going after her. In a few minutes, she'll be off this island."

"She didn't *have* to go," Zimi said, looking away as his eyes glazed over with tears.

"She didn't even give us a chance to say goodbye," Fajha said.

"It's for the best," Cristaden said. "Hamilda's sick. She has a lot of healing to do."

Atakos nodded. "There's no way she would be completely normal after her ordeal. Maybe we'll see her again someday."

"Maybe," Zadeia said, wiping her eyes.

"Come on guys," Cristaden said, pulling everyone in for a group hug. With her newly discovered strength, she was easily able to heal everyone without placing her hand on each individual wound. A bright white light surrounded them and then dissipated. Cristaden had her Lochenby uniform back on and her wings had disappeared.

"Amazing," Fajha said, feeling better than he ever had in his entire life.

"You are incredibly talented Cristaden," Zadeia said.

"Cristaden, where did you get the wings?" Atakos asked. "Our clan can't grow wings. Right?"

Cristaden was very confused about it also. Kheiron told her she was human. The wings were long and white, not at all like fairy wings. She suddenly remembered the blue feather she received from the chlysem. Could it be possible that it didn't disappear? She frowned. "The chlysem must have given me my wings. I think he *fixed* me."

"Why would that 'fix' you?" Zimi said. "I don't get it."

Cristaden looked at each of her friends. "Well. It's like this ..." She began with what happened to Hamilda and then she told them about Kheiron. They stared at her, wide-eyed, unable to say anything, unable to breathe. Hamilda was having a baby, which was the greatest news they had ever heard. Bontihm passed away leaving the Dokami nation without a Wise Man. Cristaden is half-fairy. Queen Lhainna's *daughter* and Keirak's *twin sister.* They began their journey intent on finding Hamilda, not knowing what they would find along their way or even if she would be there when they reached their destination. They endured countless hours or days without food, desperate to risk their lives against all odds and fighting every obstacle that came their way. They never expected, never even dreamed that their friend who, at the beginning of their journey, had only a minor gift, would turn out to be more powerful than they ever imagined. They lowered their heads and bowed to her. Princess Kira. It had a nice ring to it.

"No, no, no," Cristaden cried, waving her hands at them. "For goodness sakes, don't do that. I'm no different than I was an hour ago people. I'm still the same person."

"Can we at least call you Kira?" Zadeia asked with a big smile. "Please?"

"No."

"Pleeeeaaaaase???"

Cristaden frowned. "NO."

Zadeia pouted and crossed her arms, receiving a few snickers care of Zimi.

Atakos approached Cristaden and took her hand. She looked up into his hazel eyes and froze, captivated by the way he was looking at her. "Princess. I could get used to that." His mouth turned up into the warmest smile he had ever given her. Snatching her hand back, she let out a nervous laugh and searched her brain for something, anything, to change the subject before anyone noticed her blushing.

"Well, where do we go from here?" Cristaden quickly said, trying to keep her voice steady.

"First of all, let's find a way out of this cave," Fajha said, looking around.

"I couldn't agree more," Zimi said.

EPILOGUE

Deep in the cave, the five teenagers were looking for a way out. The two entrances were blocked and, as hard as they tried, they did not see where or how Hamilda got out. They were about to give up when Fajha pointed at something on the ground at the base of the wall where he stood.

"Look!" he shouted.

The others ran to him and saw what appeared to be a hole in the ground. "It's just a hole, Fajha," Zimi said.

"It's more than a hole. Bend down."

As Zadeia lit a fireball to provide illumination, they squatted to have a better look. Sure enough, it was a small, diagonal tunnel that went under the wall.

"So that's how she did it," Zimi said.

"Let's not waste any more time," Atakos said. The air in the cave was becoming increasingly oppressive. "So, since you found the tunnel …" He smiled at Fajha. "After you."

"Oh, sure," Fajha said. "If I get stuck, I'm blaming you." Removing his glasses and putting them in his shirt pocket, he sat on the ground and slid his legs through the hole, which was larger than he thought. He shimmied through until his friends could not see him anymore. Then he started sliding.

"Aah!" They heard him cry out.

"Fajha!!!" Zadeia screamed.

"Fajha, are you alright?" Atakos called out to him.

"Yeah," he shouted through the hole. "There's just an unexpected drop down here. But it's safe to go through. Just be careful."

"Okay, we'll take your word for it."

One by one, they slid through the hole. Fajha was right. Just several feet in was a drop that opened up into a small chamber. Fajha put his glasses back on and helped guide each friend down until they were all safely through the hole. Zadeia lit a fireball and looked around. There were two tunnels in front of them. Again, they were faced with the dilemma of which one to choose.

"Well, I can't tell where to go this time," Fajha said. "My location ability can only give specific directions when the person I'm looking for is very close. Unfortunately, Hamilda's far away from here by now."

"That's okay, Fajha," Cristaden said.

Atakos sighed. "We'll just have to choose one and if it leads to a dead end, we'll retrace our steps and take the other one."

"But which one do we choose first?" Zadeia asked.

"On the count of three, we'll all point to a tunnel," Zimi said. "Whichever tunnel gets the most votes is the one we choose."

"Good idea, Zimi," Zadeia said. "I think that is the brightest idea you've come up with—ever."

Zimi grinned, so proud of himself.

"Okay," Atakos said. "Ready?" When he got the okay from everyone, he counted to three. Expecting the votes to be divided, they were surprised when they were all pointing to the right tunnel.

"Well, as strange as this may seem, the vote is unanimous." Atakos chuckled. "Right it is."

With Zadeia leading the group, they went down the chosen tunnel. Their hope to see the outside world diminished when they ran into a thick layer of dust and cobwebs once again.

"Oh, we're going the *wrong way*," Cristaden groaned.

"We should turn around," Fajha said.

"I say we keep going," Atakos said. "The deal was to find a dead end and *then* turn around. Just because Hamilda didn't use this tunnel, doesn't mean it does not lead to the outside. We saw *three* entrances to the cave, not two."

Everyone sighed when they realized he was right.

Being the one in front, Zadeia got stuck with the most cobwebs. "What a pain," she whined. Then the inevitable happened. She was met with a dead end. "What was that you were saying about three openings, Atakos?"

Her friends stopped and groaned.

"This is ridiculous." Zimi rolled his eyes. "Why did we all choose *this* tunnel? Now we have to turn around and start all over. We could have been *out* of here by now."

"Calm down, Zimi," Cristaden said. "Let's just go. We'll be outside in no time."

"Easy for you to say," he mumbled. "I'm. So. Hungry."

Fajha was going to say something about hunger when he noticed a symbol on the wall in front of them. "Zadeia, can I see your light?"

"What is it Fajha?" Zadeia asked, holding up her fireball to provide him with more illumination as the others gathered around them.

"There are some markings here." Fajha slid his hand along the wall so everyone could see what he was looking at. "It's an ancient language," he said, recognizing the different styles of symbols. There was one symbol he had seen before. "Open."

"Open what?" Atakos asked.

"This must be a door of some sort. I'm not positive but these symbols represent ones found on ancient space crafts. I learned about them in my scientific language class." Wiping as much of the writing as he could with his hand, he stopped when he uncovered a handle.

"You're right," Zadeia said, astonished. "It *is* a door. What is a door doing in the middle of a cave?"

"I'm not sure."

"Well, aren't you going to open it?" Zimi asked.

"Maybe we shouldn't," Atakos said. "What if there's something really bad behind this door?"

"Unless its booby trapped, this door hasn't been opened in a really long time," Zimi pointed out. "What's the worst that could happen?"

"Well there's only one way to find out," Cristaden said. "Open it, Fajha."

"Alright. Here goes." Fajha turned the handle down and pushed on the door, which glided open a little too easily. The teens braced themselves for alarms to sound or multiple devices to explode but nothing happened. They were met, instead, with a large room.

"It looks like the inside of a spacecraft," Zadeia said, stepping inside.

The friends could not believe what they were seeing. Massive control panels and machinery lined the walls around the room. They could see a door on the other side suggesting there may be more rooms.

"Never mind the door, what's a *spacecraft* doing in the middle of a cave?" Atakos said.

"I'm trying to figure that out," Fajha said. "From what I can see, it's as if the ship is welded into the cave. As if the cave was formed *around* it."

"Odd." Atakos touched the biggest button he could find on one of the control panels and lights lit up on all the machines around them.

"This doesn't appear to be the room used to control the ship, there are no windows or chairs," Zadeia observed, extinguishing her fireball. "I wonder what it's used for."

"I think I know," Cristaden said. "Come look at this." She was pointing at a yellow button on the control panel in front of her. There were twenty buttons just like it all in a row with different dates on each of them. When she pushed the button, a hologram opened up and they saw a planet exploding. The inscription at the bottom of the hologram simply said 'DOKAR'. The five friends watched in amazement as the planet exploded into nothingness and a male voice said, "We are free."

Zadeia grew excited. "Dokar. It's the planet our ancestors lived on. This must be the ship they used to land on this planet!"

"It *can't* be," Fajha said, frowning.

Atakos considered the possibility. "It could explain why it's lodged in this cave."

"The inhabitants of this island can very well be Dokami descendants," Zimi said, excitement rising in his voice.

"Incredible," Cristaden said, pressing the button that was before the one she pressed. It showed Dokar on land before it was destroyed. They saw the familiar tropical rainforests and the waterfalls. "They fashioned this island to resemble Dokar. They must have planted the trees and flowers. Even the homes are similar."

"Amazing," Zadeia said. "This must be their memory room. The whole history of our ancestors at our fingertips. Wow."

"Maybe we might learn something we don't know about them," Fajha said.

The feeling of elation was so high among the teens, they forgot about their need to get out of the cave. They went from button to button, relearning the important history lesson Hamilda had taught them. They saw how the Dokamis landed on Omordion and caused the Sremati Volcano to erupt, covering their ship, thus creating the cataclysmic event that changed the east side of Sheidem Island. When the lava cooled, they saw the Dokami clan digging tunnels to create the very cave they stood in. The large room they fought Hamilda in was used for the first council meetings held on Omordion. Rules of restraint were discussed and executed. Families who wished to move to another country were brought in and granted permission to leave as long as they stayed within the borders of Western Omordion.

There was so much information to take in that the friends considered leaving to find something to eat and returning to connect with the Dokamis of their past.

They were about to leave the ship when Atakos spotted a black button, apart from the rest, covered with layers of tape. He carefully removed the tape and considered pushing the button. Scared that his actions could inadvertently destroy the ship, he thought he should alert his friends. Then he noticed a date beneath the button, which only meant that it was indeed another memory, imprinted into the ship's database. But why was it taped over?

"Come see this," Atakos said, getting everyone's attention. They crowded around him, just as curious as he was to see why the button had been deliberately taped over. He pushed the button.

A large hologram appeared, much larger than the ones they had grown accustomed to seeing. It was dated three weeks before the destruction of Dokar. A man with dark features and a blue robe sat down and introduced himself as Tre-akelomin Gre-ashyu, leader of the Dokami clan.

As Aillios and Colnaha searched the caves for *Omordion's Hope*, Gre-ashyu told the recorder many secrets. Secrets that even Hamilda and the Dokami population of Omordion did not know. Secrets he did not want to reveal but he knew would be lost forever if his people were annihilated. He was very depressed and, at times, crying.

The hearts of the five friends pounded as they listened to him pour out his soul. That day they learned of something they did not think was possible.

The biggest secret of all.

To Be Continued In…
Book Two of the Omordion Trilogy:
RISE OF JMUGEA

GLOSSARY

Characters (by order of appearance):

King Tholenod ~ (Thaw-lin-odd) tyrant of Mituwa who forms an alliance with the other kings of Eastern Omordion to defeat the Western Army

Dokami Clan ~ (Do-KA-mee) secret race of people who blended in with the inhabitants of Western Omordion for three hundred years

Hamilda Shing ~ (Ha-mill-da) teacher of Omordion's Hope

Jogesh Shing ~ (Jo-GESH) Hamilda's husband

Bontihm Fhakaemeli ~ (Bon-tim Fa-KAI-me-lee) Wise Man of the Dokami clan, raised Hamilda as his apprentice when her parents died

R. K. Rohjees ~ (Row-jeez) principal at Lochenby

General Komuh ~ (Ko-mo) general of the Sheidem City branch of the Western Army, overseer of Omordion's Hope

Emperor Kolhi ~ (Cole-hee) emperor of the western country of Laspitu

Emperor Vermu ~ (Ver-moo) emperor of the western country of Saiyut and Fajha's grandfather

Emperor Mashie ~ (Mah-SHEE) emperor of the western country of Pontotoma

Emperor Trusu ~ (Troo-soo) emperor of the western country of Udnaruk

Keshi Bayaht ~ (KE-shee Bay-YAHT) Fajha's mother and Emperor Vermu's daughter

Fajha Bayaht ~ (Fa-ja Bay-YAHT) fifteen-year-old member of Omordion's Hope, born in Saiyut with the power to move objects; the 'brains' of the group, he is excellent with geography, knows several different languages, and learns how to 'locate' people from afar

Atakos Croit ~ (A-ta-kos Croyt) fifteen-year-old member of Omordion's Hope, born in Pontotoma with the power to lift heavy objects

Zimi Emyu ~ (Zim-ee Em-yoo) fifteen-year-old member of Omordion's Hope, born as a twin in Udnaruk with the power to manipulate wind, water, and fire

Zadeia Emyu ~ (Za-day-A Em-yoo) fifteen-year-old member of Omordion's Hope, born as a twin in Udnaruk with the power to manipulate wind, water, and fire

Cristaden Feriau ~ (Kris-STADE-en Fe-ree-ah-o) fourteen going on fifteen-year-old member of Omordion's Hope, born in Laspitu with the ability to 'fix' broken bones

Rhokh Grouseli ~ (Roke Graw-se-lee) Atakos' friend at Lochenby

Bho and Len ~ (Bo and Len) two popular boys at Lochenby

Menyilh ~ (Men-yeel) King Tholenod's straggly assistant

Captain Lughm ~ (Loo-gim) captain of the Southern Udnaruk branch of the Western Army who unknowingly led his comrades into an ambush in Rostihme Village

Lieutenant Emyu ~ (Em-yoo) lieutenant ordered by Captain Lughm to take Kireina back to the army base

Private Hodin ~ (Hoe-den) private ordered by Captain Lughm to take Kireina back to the army base

Kireina ~ (Kee-RAY-na) fourteen-year-old girl rescued from the destroyed Rostihme Village, lost her mother during the attack by Feim soldiers

Major Garunburj ~ (Gar-UN-Berj) major of the Southern Udnaruk branch of the Western Army

Tre-akelomin Gre-ashyu ~ (Tray-AH-ke-lo-men Gray-AASH-yoo), leader of the Dokami clan on Dokar

Maes Minat ~ (Mize Min-aht) the leader who developed the Dokami system of restraint when they landed on Omordion three hundred years ago

Lieutenant Gaojh ~ (Goj) one of General Komuh's lieutenants who was sent to deliver bad news to Hamilda. He was later ordered to keep an eye on the members of Omordion's Hope when Hamilda was kidnapped

Coach Mulhn ~ (Malln) Atakos' fencing teacher

Mrs. Noume ~ (Noom) Cristaden's Anatomy teacher

Ms. Leit ~ (Late) Zimi and Zadeia's Biology teacher

Lieutenant Hodlin ~ (Hod-lin) one of General Komuh's lieutenants who were ordered to keep an eye on the members of Omordion's Hope when Hamilda was kidnapped

Lieutenant Fohln ~ (Fole-n) one of General Komuh's lieutenants who were ordered to keep an eye on the members of Omordion's Hope when Hamilda was kidnapped

Queen Lhainna ~ (LIE-na) the fairy queen of Sheidem Forest

Princess Kapimia ~ (Ka-Pi-mee-a) Queen Lhainna's eldest daughter

Princess Keirak ~ (Kay-rack) Queen Lhainna's youngest daughter, Kira's twin sister

Saraimen and Lanchie ~ (Sa-RYE-men and Lan-chee) two fairies who had to carry Queen Lhainna back to their home after she became delirious

Prince Aillios ~ (I-lee-os) King Tholenod's son

Frolemin ~ (Fraw-li-min) King Tholenod's handmaid

Trisalan ~ (Tri-SA-len) Prince Aillios' handmaid

Omlit ~ (Ohm-lit) stable boy in Mituwa

Thashmar ~ (THASH-mar) Prince Aillios' horse given to him by Omlit

Ojmodri ~ (OHJ-mo-dree) general in Mituwa who started the war against King Tholenod and was killed along with his army

Asmis ~ (AZ-miss) a witch who was executed by drowning in Mituwa

King Haudmont ~ (Hod-mont) king of Srepas

King Gomu ~ (Go-moo) king of Effit

King Basanpanul ~ (Bah-SAN-pahn-ool) king of Feim

Brulok ~ (BROO-lock) evil man who attempted to destroy Omordion's magical creatures five hundred years ago but disappeared, leaving his minions to finish the job for him

Samila ~ (Sa-MEE-la) girl sent to find Maldaha

Maldaha ~ (Mall-DA-ha) leader of the Tackeni village in Osmatu

Piedara ~ (Pee-ay-DA-ra) Maldaha's wife

Colnaha ~ (COLE-na-ha) Maldaha's son

Senru ~ (Sin-roo) Colnaha's personal servant

Sanei ~ (Sa-NAY) woman in Paimonu who helped the teens find the caves

Kheiron ~ (Kay-ron) Queen Lhainna's lover, father to twins Keirak and Kira

Kira ~ (Kee-ra) Queen Lhainna's daughter, Keirak's twin sister

Tre-akelomin Gre-ashyu ~ (Tray-AH-ke-lo-men Gray-AASH-yoo) [second appearance] leader of the Dokami clan on Dokar

Places:

Omordion ~ (Oh-MOR-dee-an)

Hechi River ~ (Heh-chi) River that separates Mituwa from Srepas

Mituwa ~ (Mi-too-wa) a country in Eastern Omordion where King Tholenod rules

Srepas ~ (SHREE-pahs) northernmost country in Eastern Omordion

Lochenby ~ (Lock-en-bee) boarding school on Sheidem Island

Sheidem ~ (Shay-dim) an island south of Laspitu and north of Saiyut where Lochenby is located

Pontotoma ~ (Pon-toe-toe-ma) country south of Sheidem in Western Omordion where Atakos is from

Saiyut ~ (Say-yoot) country west of Pontotoma

Udnaruk ~ (OOD-na-rook) southernmost country of Western Omordion where Zimi and Zadeia are from

Laspitu ~ (Lahs-pee-too) northernmost country of Western Omordion where Cristaden is from

Hotel Ramoul ~ (Rah-mool) Hotel located in Sheidem City

Feim ~ (Fame) southernmost country of Eastern Omordion

Effit ~ (EFF-it) country below Mituwa and east of Feim

Osmatu ~ (Oz-MA-too) rocky terrain after Sheidem Forest and before the Suthack Desert

Hortu ~ (Hor-too) village west of Sheidem City where Bontihm resides

Thackenbur ~ (Ta-kin-ber) Island where Maldaha lived before he moved his family to Osmatu

Tackeni ~ (Ta-kin-ee) people and language derived from Thackenbur Island

Suthack Desert ~ (Soo-tahk) desert between Osmatu and the Hejdian Sea

Paimonu ~ (PI-mo-noo) island near Sheidem where the teens believed Hamilda was being held captive

Sremati Volcano ~ (Shri-MA-tee) volcano on Paimonu

Rostihme Village ~ (Rus-teem) village in Southern Udnaruk where Kireina is from that was attacked by Feim soldiers in the middle of the night, killing hundreds while taking some people captive

Chrulm Village ~ (Sh-rull-m) village in Udnaruk

Stream of Asmis ~ (Az-miss) beautiful stream Tholenod follows heading towards the Nikul River, named after the witch Asmis who was executed by drowning

Nikul River ~ (Ni-cool) river that separates Mituwa, Feim, and Effit from each other

Ardomion Caves ~ (AR-Doh-mee-on) caves near the Sremati Volcano where the teens believe Hamilda is being held captive

Oeua ~ (Oh-E-oo-a) Omordion's original and ancient name

Koelo Mok ~ (Ko-E-Lo Mock) ancient word for the island of Paimonu

Magical Creatures:

Flitnies ~ (flit-nees) small people who tended to the land and performed magic; lived on Omordion hundreds of years ago

Chlysems ~ (kli-zems) large blue birds with multicolored wings that breathed fire; lived on Omordion hundreds of years ago

Ceanaves ~ (See-An-naves) Very strong sea creatures who resembled humans but had tinted green skin and fins on scales, eyes the color of the sea, and pink, blue, green, or purple hair; lived on Omordion hundreds of years ago

Beasts of Prey:

Oblots ~ (OB-lots) minion of Brulok, bear-like large beasts with red beady eyes and razor sharp teeth and claws

Harpelily Butterflies ~ (Harp-e-lilee) beautiful butterflies with long tails that mesmerizes fairies and leads them to oblots

Valdeec Birds ~ (Vall-deek) large, vulture-like birds that live in the Suthack Desert

Desert Karsas ~ (Kar-sus) Brulok's minions who resemble an oversized, oddly shaped lizard; as tall as a grown man with scaly flesh, short arms and a long tail

Montapu Lizards ~ (Mon-ta-poo) poisonous, sandy-colored lizards that live in the Suthack Desert

Miscellaneous:

Radicirculatem on a GDFP 36 model automobile ~ a circular radio designed for a child automobile. In Chapter 7, Atakos asks Fajha, who seems to know everything, if he knew what it was but, of course, Fajha knows nothing about automobiles

Tackeni: The Language of Thackenbur Island

Abai ~ well

Agni ~ guest

Agrai ~ son

Allat, allet, Allo ~ got, get, to go

An ~ of

Anmu ~ name

Apeero ~ husband

Appee ~ child calls father

Arle ~ located

Ateera ~ wife

Attrai-ha ~ grandfather

Avieni ~ welcome

Bamul ~ leader

Blat ~ attacked

Cuuz ~ good

Cuuzshoden ~ goodnight

Cuuzvappa ~ goodbye

Cuuzmosem ~ good Morning

Da ~ then

De ~ the

Dechto ~ doctor

Desata ~ separated

Deseer Shuchak ~ Suthack Desert

Dozh ~ sleep

Eten ~ caravan

Etterateins ~ explorers

Flachi ~ trying

Goro ~ how

Gree ~ sure

Han ~ me & my

Hom ~ home

Hosmi ~ who

Hozmi ~ horses

Kesta ~ what

Me ~ but

Mit ~ are

Mosem ~ morning

Naih ~ no

Ni ~ here

Norg ~ north

Osa ~ we & our

Ot ~ they

Pangvithe ~ be careful.

Pas ~ further

Pra ~ take

Raspeel ~ ruffians

Rete ~ stay

San ~ just

Shoden ~ night

Si ~ there

Son ~ will

Tackein Provom ~ Thackenbur Island

Tan ~ you

Te ~ to

Ti ~ is

Ush ~ once

Van ~ why

Vappa ~ bye

Velmapa ~ hello

Viet ~ with

Virei ~ reach

Vo ~ also

Voni ~ when

Vuumo ~ where

Wah ~ yes

Warr ~ from

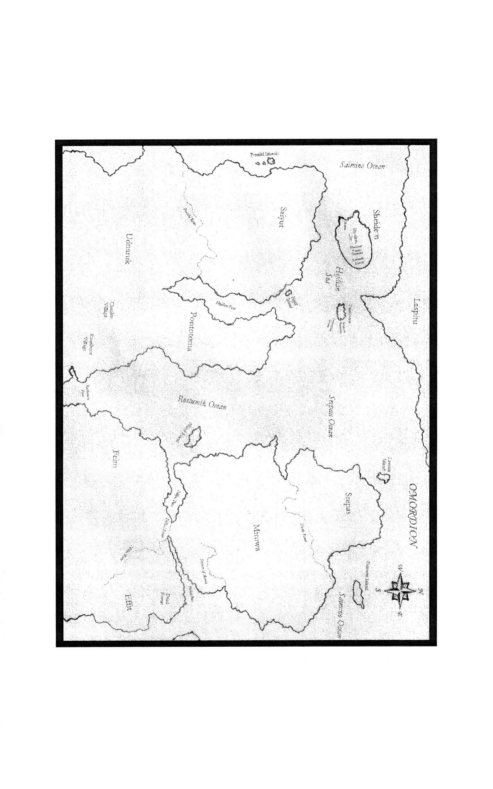

CPSIA information can be obtained at www.ICGtesting.com
Printed in the USA
BVOW08s1659160314

347697BV00001B/2/P